w35

# Curtain Call
## or
# The Distinguished
# Thing

ANTHONY QUINN

# Curtain Call

## or

# The Distinguished Thing

A Novel

VINTAGE

1 3 5 7 9 10 8 6 4 2

Vintage
20 Vauxhall Bridge Road,
London SW1V 2SA

Vintage is part of the Penguin Random House group of companies whose
addresses can be found at global.penguinrandomhouse.com.

Penguin
Random House
UK

First published in Vintage in 2015
First published in hardback by Jonathan Cape in 2015

www.vintage-books.co.uk

A CIP catalogue record for this book is
available from the British Library

ISBN 9780099593232

Penguin Random House is committed to a sustainable future for our
business, our readers and our planet. This book is made from
Forest Stewardship Council® certified paper.

Typeset in Palatino LT Std  by Palimpsest Book Production Limited,
Falkirk, Stirlingshire

Printed and bound by CPI Group (UK) Ltd,
Croydon, CR0 4YY

For Mike
and
for Pete

'So here it is at last, the distinguished thing!'

Henry James (attrib.)

# I

# The Second Arrangement

# I

Stephen squinted towards the cloudy sash windows. He knew he ought to have them cleaned, but he liked the way they lent the day outside a soft and mysterious murk. It didn't seem to matter that you couldn't really see out of them. He picked up another charcoal stick and turned back to the sketch, while Lady Trevelyan talked on.

'. . . though I really don't know how Tom puts up with the beastly things the newspapers say about him. It isn't as though any of the others have a better plan for running the country – Tom's only fault is that he sees what's wrong and jolly well says it! Of course at the root of it is jealousy. To have that sort of breeding and education and accomplishment, well, it's bound to raise the hackles of *little men*. And such a handsome fellow too! – I don't believe I'm the first to notice his resemblance to Douglas Fairbanks . . .'

Stephen wasn't sure how much more of this he could stand. He possessed an intensity of concentration that only a rare breed of irritant could disturb. Alas, it seemed that Lady Trevelyan, with her high, hectoring voice, belonged to that unhappy genus. His attention had wandered again from his drawing. He dipped his head behind the easel and yawned extravagantly.

'Hmm?' he said, hearing a sudden interrogative note from the other side.

'I said, do you not admire him?'

'Er, Douglas Fairbanks?'

'No, you silly man – I mean Tom – Sir Oswald Mosley!'

So *that's* who she was talking about. Why did he call himself Tom if his name was Oswald? 'To be honest, Lady Trevelyan, I've no opinion about him one way or the other.' He gave a little shrug. 'Though I don't greatly care for that moustache of his.'

'No opinion? But, Mr Wyley, you must read the papers . . .'

He sneaked a glance at the wristwatch he had been careful to fasten on the frame of his easel. 'Ah, yes, the papers – I always start to read them, and little by little I . . . fall behind. By the time I've caught up the news has changed, and then I think, why bother?'

Lady Trevelyan gave one of her dismissive laughs and pressed on with her encomium of 'dear Tom'. Stephen, eager to conclude the session, spent two minutes vigorously cross-hatching with a pencil before snatching the paper from its mount and presenting it for inspection.

'It's just a study, of course,' he explained. 'A little throat-clearing before we start on the canvas.'

He watched her expression twitch with delight as she contemplated his handiwork. The sketch, with its artful editing of the sitter's double chin and the softening of her snouty nose, was designed to please. He could have given a masterclass in portraiture as flattery. It was why so many of them came to him. Lady Trevelyan, like all the others, made no mention of Stephen's cosmetic dexterity: that was an unspoken part of the contract, as was his fee. Their brief acquaintance, however, had inclined him to wonder about the money. The ratio of guineas earned to hours confined in her company was already looking to be a poor deal.

'Lady Trevelyan, I do beg your pardon,' he said, interrupting her absorption in the sketch. 'I'm rather late for an

4

appointment across town. But we shall meet soon' – he gave the bell-rope a tug – 'to begin the serious work.'

Mrs Ronson, the housekeeper, was prompt in bringing his guest's coat, though neither she nor Stephen were able to do much about Lady Trevelyan's parting monologue, a disordered flurry of society gossip begun as she was almost, agonisingly, out of the door, and extended for several minutes on the landing. In the end Mrs Ronson practically had to strong-arm her down the staircase before Stephen could safely close the door. Consulting his watch again, he found that he actually was running late, with no time to change. Exasperating, really, after he had gone to the trouble of booking the hotel. Not very debonair to show up late *and* ungroomed.

Five minutes later he was taking the stairs two at a time, having squirted on a bit of cologne and straightened his tie's hurried knot in the hall mirror. He'd fix it on the way. Something else was bothering him as he descended to the pavement and broke into an awkward half-run: the shoes. They were pinching with a vehemence he could almost have taken personally. He had bought them the previous day in a new shop on the Brompton Road, failing to notice the tightness across the uppers. Damn. He should have gone to Lobb. The August day, the last of the month, was sultry but overcast, with that granular quality of light that seemed to anticipate rain. Turning into Royal Hospital Road, he flagged down a cab and, once inside, tried to compose himself. His reflection played hide-and-seek in the window. He was vain (he knew) of his toffee-coloured hair, brushed back from his forehead. His handsome, symmetrical face lacked only (which he didn't know) a small quirk of individuality that might have rendered it truly interesting. He fiddled with the knot against his collar and, having moulded it to his liking, speared a tiepin through the yielding silk.

5

Stephen Wyley had been lucky in most things, and had learned not to mind being resented for it. Born just late enough to have escaped the Great War – he turned eighteen the week before the Armistice – he was able to take a place at Oxford left unclaimed by one of those young men ahead of him in academic distinction, now stretched cold beneath a field in France or Belgium. He proved to be no scholar, preferring to refine his talent for drawing, and after graduating went to study at the Royal Academy. Around the same time he found himself the beneficiary of a small inheritance – or, as some called it, a small fortune. A friend on hearing the news remarked that Stephen could now supply his future biographer with a title: *The Life of Wyley*.

It enabled him to buy a flat in Chelsea which he furnished from the proceeds of the small oils he had begun to sell. His natural affinity was for landscapes, but that changed when a Scottish grandee of his acquaintance commissioned a large portrait of his three children. *The Daughters of Fitzroy Traquair*, shown at the RA in the summer of 1931, was the making of his name. The *Burlington Magazine* hailed him as 'the British Sargent', and the *Telegraph* sent a man to take his photograph. Before long Stephen was a sought-after guest at the houses of collectors, artistic patrons, titled worthies. The invitations began to pile up. Gratified at first by his social elevation, he soon came to distrust. He was clear-sighted about his technical skills, considering himself to be a distinctive painter of nature but merely an adequate portraitist. That estimate proved at odds with his rising acclaim. In his cups he would say that he only took commissions from people he despised, because they were too stupid to see what an inferior talent he was. His reluctance to turn them away hid a deeper insecurity: he hadn't enough money to stop pleasing others, and had far too much to feel pleased with himself. In retrospect he realised that being discovered was not entirely a blessing; he had never quite possessed himself since.

The cab had crawled to a halt amid shoaling, honking traffic at the top of Sloane Street. This was getting him nowhere. He paid the driver and stepped out, making a beeline for Knightsbridge Tube. His shoes felt ever tighter as he skittered down the escalator towards the platform, almost deserted in the mid-afternoon lull. He was thinking about her again as the train burst out of the tunnel, its updraught warm and frowsy against his face.

They had met nearly four weeks ago at a friend's private view in Bury Street. Stephen was stooging around when he spotted her gazing in rapt concentration at one of the still lifes. She was slim, on the short side, with brown, shoulder-length hair framing a strong, full-lipped face. Her dark eyebrows were plucked and shaped. He thought he had seen her somewhere before.

'If you stand there much longer your eyes are going to burn a hole through it.'

She looked round, unstartled, and gave him the once-over. 'I'm sure Henry will forgive me,' she said coolly. Her voice was low, with a pleasing hoarseness at the back of it.

'You like his work?'

She nodded. 'I bought one of his a few years ago – square, about so big, of a ceramic jug with primulas. And I'm pleased to see he's now on the way to being quite unaffordable.'

Stephen smiled. 'I remember that ceramic jug. Well . . . if I'd known Henry had such discerning clients I'd have brought along a few pictures of my own to hang here.'

'You paint?' she said, a thin note of scepticism in her voice.

'Stephen Wyley,' he said, extending his hand, which she took.

'Nina Land. Your name is . . . familiar to me.'

'That's odd, because your face is familiar to *me*. Have we met before?'

She shook her head decisively. 'I would have remembered. Perhaps . . . you've been to the theatre recently?'

He frowned, rummaging in his memory. 'Hmm. I saw a thing the other week called *The Second Arrangement*, at the Strand. Rather good.'

'Ah, glad you thought so – I was in it. Hester Bonteen . . .?'

He narrowed his eyes appraisingly, and then the clouds parted. '*Yes* – the lover!'

Nina held up her palms in a gesture of *c'est moi*. Stephen continued to stare at her. 'Well – may I say – I was impressed. Really. The scene where you read the letter from him . . . the lady sitting next to me was in tears.'

'But not yourself . . .'

'I thought I should be a man about it,' he replied. She gave a slow smile, and he read in her expression a quickening interest. Stephen held her gaze, before saying, 'I always wonder about acting – I mean, how you do it night after night, the same thing. Doesn't it become –'

'A bore?'

'Yes. Just so.'

'No – because it's a different crowd every night.' She paused. 'They don't know what you're going to give them. Before I go on, I think of someone out there in the dark, looking at me for the first time, not knowing what to expect. That's the challenge – the excitement. It doesn't matter that you've given the performance before – it's new to *him*. Or her. You're creating this very intimate connection with complete strangers. So you see' – she gave a little laugh – 'you can do certain things over and over without it ever becoming a bore.'

Stephen nodded. 'Like – having a cocktail, for instance.'

'Among other things,' she said, her eyes still on him. He sensed the moment there to be seized.

'Well, speaking as a complete stranger, what d'you say we sneak out of here?'

'What for?'

'A cocktail,' he said casually.

She screwed her mouth into a pout that implied he'd misread her: much too forward of him. He was about to back away in apology when she said, 'Why not?'

The cocktail led to dinner, which led to a nightcap at his club, and thence to a taxi to her lodgings off Baker Street. She didn't invite him in, but there was sufficient meaning in their kiss goodnight for them to know that this would not be the end of it. Two lunches together followed. The next week they had a late supper at the Ivy, right after she came offstage. The kiss afterwards lasted rather longer than the first one. That was when they decided upon this afternoon's assignation.

At the kiosk outside Russell Square Tube he bought a *Times*, his favoured shield of respectability. The Imperial's monstrous Gothic facade of egg-and-bacon terracotta peered down on him. As he went through the hotel's revolving doors he made a quick reflexive scan of the foyer, not feeling quite imperturbable. The desk manager asked for his name, and Stephen almost blundered into giving his own.

'Ah yes, Mr Melmotte,' the man said in echo. 'Your wife is already in residence. Do you have any luggage?'

Stephen shook his head, smiled, and went off to the lift. The busy anonymity of the clientele – travelling salesmen and pie-faced couples from the provinces – put him at ease. Ordinarily he would have preferred the Cadogan, or Claridge's, but there was a greater likelihood of running into someone he knew there.

He got out at the fourth floor and followed the rising numbers along the corridor. The door to the room – their room – was hung with a notice, DO NOT DISTURB. He hesitated, reading an ulterior meaning in the words. It wasn't too late to turn back. And yet the gravitational pull of desire mixed with curiosity was strong: he had to risk it, or else wonder till the end what might have been. He tapped so quietly on the door he felt sure she wouldn't have heard, but then from within came the soft pad of footsteps on carpet, and the door swung open.

'Hullo,' said Nina with a wry grin. 'That knock sounded like a small boy come to the headmaster's office for a thrashing.'

'Mm, it was a bit feeble,' he admitted. They kissed rather awkwardly on the threshold, and he walked in. He was pleased to see they had given them a suite and put flowers on the table, as he had requested. She had opened the windows, through which the faint drone of traffic from the street drifted up. He sauntered over and peered down at Russell Square, at the plane trees and the beetling pedestrians, all heedless. Behind him she rattled the ice in her glass.

'Thirsty?' she said brightly.

'Parched.'

She began tipping ice cubes into a tall glass like her own, then dousing them in Scotch. She brought it over to where he stood, still gazing out of the window. He handled it absently, then took a deep swallow. A dry little chuckle escaped her.

'Having second thoughts?'

He turned round, jolted by her intuitive stab. 'Why d'you say that?'

'You look rather distracted.'

'Actually, what's bothering me,' he said with a wince, 'are these *bloody shoes*. I think I'd better –' He went over to the bed and plumped down on the edge.

'Here, let me,' she said, kneeling down and tugging at his shoelaces. With brisk authority she plucked one foot then the other out of their leather vices. They came off with a sucking gasp.

'Phew! That's a relief.' He began to rub his tortured feet. 'I think this one's given me a blister . . .'

'They did seem rather tight,' she said, raising herself next to him on the edge of the bed. Then, turning her back, she pointed to the zip on her dress. 'Now. Perhaps you could help me get out of this.'

Afterwards, as they lay there, the sweat cooling on their skin, Nina propped herself up on an elbow. He sensed her watching him, so he kept his eyes on the ceiling. Presently, she picked up his wrist between her fingers, and after a few moments said, 'Well, pulse is normal. Respiration seems fine, too.' Then she gave his forehead a soft tap with her knuckle. 'Anything to worry about up here?'

'Nothing,' he replied with a nervous half-laugh.

'Nothing? Not even a little something?'

'Maybe . . . a little something.'

She nodded, content not to push it any further. She traced a meditative finger around his collarbone and shoulder, then said, 'By the way, why "Melmotte"?'

'Oh . . . from a novel I'm reading. *The Way We Live Now*. Melmotte's a city financier, with a shady past.'

'A scoundrel?'

'Of course.'

She leaned over to the bedside table and looked at her wristwatch. 'D'you have a cigarette?'

For answer he slipped out of bed and padded across to the sofa where his clothes were strewn. He checked inside his jacket, and then realised where they were: he could see the packet now, on top of his paraffin heater, back at Tite Street. 'Damn.'

He picked up the telephone and listened to it ring at reception. After a minute or so, he hung up. 'Hopeless. I'll have to go down to the bar.' She watched him bend down and pick up his shoes. 'Oh God,' he groaned.

'I'll go,' she said, throwing back the covers and springing out. 'Save you crippling yourself.'

He tossed the shoes away, and gave her a look of rueful adoration. 'Darling, you're a brick.'

'I know,' she said, wriggling into her camisole. 'Aren't you lucky?'

The impudent glance that accompanied this remark made him laugh. He folded himself onto the sofa, admiring the unselfconscious speed with which she dressed. The acting life, he supposed. When she had gone he picked up her thin mulberry-coloured cardigan, jumbled among his own apparel, and held it to his face. He inhaled a scent of Jicky, tobacco and indefinable notes of *her*. The thing inflamed him with a sudden tenderness towards its owner. Then a noise at the window diverted him: a pigeon was clock-working along the ledge. The window was still ajar, and Stephen went over to shoo it away: the last thing they wanted was a bird in the room. He leaned out for another look at Russell Square, subtly altered from earlier, the traffic thickening towards rush hour, the light becoming bluish-grey. The lamplighters would be out soon.

It was odd, he thought, how people changed when they were out of their clothes. Prior to this afternoon, Nina had revealed a character of Olympian self-possession. That first night, while he had been all charm, she had been cool to the point of unfriendliness, wrong-footing him with her conversational feints and jabs. If he hadn't felt such an overpowering physical compulsion he might have been inclined to shake hands and walk away. True, she had warmed up a little in the half-dozen times they had met since, but he still caught in her eyes a hawkish scrutiny that froze him in his tracks. Before today he wasn't absolutely sure that she even *liked* him. So it was a surprise that, this afternoon, in bed, she had been geniality itself. Whatever else you were in bed, you could not be ambiguous.

12

He'd known a few theatre people in his time, and had found them to be garrulous egomaniacs and needy bores. Nina seemed different; she wasn't fragile and she didn't go fishing for praise, however willingly he would have bestowed it. Perhaps she had become adept at concealing that mad streak that so afflicted her profession – she was an actress, after all –

The door opened, and the moment he saw her he knew something was wrong. The colour in her face had fled, and her eyes were glassy with shock. She took hesitant steps into the room, like a sleepwalker. Stephen came away from the window.

'My dear, what on earth is it?'

She looked at him, distracted. 'I've just seen something . . . quite upsetting –'

'What? What did you see?'

He walked her over to the sofa and they sat down, knee to knee. 'Light one for me, would you?' she said, handing him the cigarettes. '. . . I'd just got out of the lift and was coming up the corridor when I heard this awful frightened' – she shook her head – '*pleading*. A woman's voice. It was coming from one of the rooms, before you turn the corner. So I stopped, went back, and this time I heard it more clearly. She was saying, begging, *No, please*, and then a low muttered voice, a man's – I knew he must be hurting her. I mean, really hurting her.' He offered her the lit cigarette, and saw her hand tremble as she drew it to her lips. 'Well, I knocked at the door, and the noise just – stopped. I said something like, 'Is everything all right?' and put my ear close. Silence. Then I said, quite loudly, that I was going to call reception and ask them to come up. Seconds later I heard a scuffle inside, and hurrying footsteps. The door flew open and a young woman dashed out – face white as chalk, tears, hair all over the place – sobbing, simply terrified. Before I could do anything she was past me and haring down the corridor.'

'Good God,' Stephen murmured.

Nina stared straight ahead, concentrating. 'There was no use chasing after her, so I walked in, rather scared, and saw a man pulling open the curtains. He turned round as he heard me, with this furious scowl – he just shouted *Get out*, so I did.' She dragged long on her cigarette, then looked at him. 'It was horrible – the sound of him attacking her . . .'

'Obviously a maniac,' said Stephen, quickly getting dressed. 'Come on, you'd better take me there. We can't have his sort running round the place.' Within a minute he was ready, his shoes unlaced. They came out into the corridor, and with a little tilt of her head Nina indicated the direction. The hotel, an Edwardian relic notable for its scale rather than splendour, had corridors as long as runways. Nobody else was about as she led him onwards. They turned at a right angle, and he saw her counting off the rooms. At the one whose door was ajar, she stopped. Room 408.

'It's this one.'

'Sure?'

She nodded, but grabbed his hand as he made to enter, whispering, 'What are you going to do?'

He gave a considering look. 'Have a word.'

Stephen gave the door a perfunctory knock and felt himself squaring his shoulders as he walked in. It was a mirror image of their own suite, without the grace notes of flowers and the Scotch. One curtain had been left closed. The bed looked rumpled, though possibly not slept in. He cleared his throat. 'Hullo?' He heard Nina stepping close behind him. It occurred to him that the man, whoever he was, would take against strangers barging into his room. He opened the door to the sitting room, craned his neck within – also empty.

'Well, there's nobody here.'

She raked her gaze about the room, frowning at the

window. 'It was this room. He was standing right there. Honestly.'

'I'm sure he was. But he's scarpered.'

They stood there for a few moments, uncertain, then returned to their room. Stephen lit a cigarette and poured them each another tall Scotch. 'Down the hatch,' he said, putting the glass in her hand. Nina stared at it absently, then set it down untasted. He waited for her to speak.

'What d'you think we should do? Tell the desk manager?'

Stephen wrinkled his nose in demur. A doubt had wormed into his mind. 'Tell him what? I mean, all you saw was a woman bolting out of a room. It might just have been – I don't know – a lovers' tiff.'

She looked aghast at him. '*What?*'

He tried to sound a reasonable note. 'I'm only saying – you may have misinterpreted –'

'Why on earth would you doubt me? I'm not a hysteric. I know what I heard, and it was no lovers' tiff, as you call it.'

Stephen, alarmed at the sudden adversarial tone, held up his hands in a pacifying gesture. Averse to arguing in general, he was particularly keen not to cross someone whom he had spent an afternoon getting close to.

'I don't doubt you,' he said. 'I'm just thinking of our . . . situation. If we make a report, they'll ask for our names. And there'll be no pretending then. D'you see?'

Nina looked away, considering, then gave a reluctant nod. He was right. They weren't supposed to be at this hotel in the first place. Her gaze drifted, wistfully, to the disordered bed they had lately shared.

'If only I hadn't insisted on going down for cigarettes . . .'

Stephen shook his head. 'I should have gone myself. Then none of this would have . . .' He fell silent, not sure where that line of thought might be tending. If he had gone down to the bar instead, then presumably *he* would have overheard the disturbance on the way back. But would he have stopped, like her, and interrupted it? He could not altogether convince himself he would have done.

Nina checked her wristwatch. 'Nearly six. I ought to be on my way.'

'Surely we've time for another drink?'

She shook her head. 'I'm afraid not. Dolly can't stand 'avin' to rush me.' This last sentence she cockney-cawed in imitation of her dresser, the redoubtable Dolly. In an effort to rekindle the earlier mood he snaked an exploratory arm around her waist and lowered his face towards her. She smiled rather sadly, and detached herself from him.

'I'm sorry, darling. That business with the girl has shaken me up, I don't mind telling you.' Stephen must have looked slightly crestfallen, because she gave a comical wince of apology as she took his hands in hers. 'You must think me an awful ninny.'

He took her self-deprecation more seriously than was intended. 'I don't think that at all. Actually, I think you're smashing.'

She raised a cheek for him to kiss, laughing, which made him feel less sore about being fobbed off. Having swiped a brush through her hair and attended to her make-up in the mirror, she was ready to go. They were just crossing the foyer when a voice ambushed them.

'Wyley!'

Stephen looked round, his heart plunging, and took a moment to register the floridly handsome face, the blazing eyes and confident leading chin. What abject timing he had today, he thought.

'Gerald – hullo.'

'Fancy running into *you*,' the man drawled, his eyes already sliding away from him to Nina, bright with expectation. With a casualness he didn't feel, Stephen said, 'Nina Land – Gerald Carmody. Gerald and I have known one another for years,' he added.

'Ah, Miss Land,' said Carmody, 'I've been lucky enough to see you onstage. *The Dance of Death* – at the Lyceum? Remarkable!'

Nina gave a queenly tilt of her head at this suavity. Carmody was now shooting inquisitive looks between them, and Stephen realised he would have to be quick with an explanation.

'Nina has agreed to sit for a series of portraits I'm meant to be doing – of the leading lights of theatreland.' He looked to her for confirmation of this lie.

'He says I have a very sculptural head,' Nina explained, unblinking.

Carmody craned forward excitedly. 'Leading lights? Then you should do me! You know I'm trying to raise funds for the Marquess in Drury Lane?'

'Why's that?' said Nina.

'I'm the manager, for my sins. Our last run was a disaster, and with the rent at two hundred and fifty a week it's touch-and-go whether we can hold off the bank.' He gave Stephen a narrow-eyed speculative glance. 'As a matter of fact I'm organising a dinner for a month or so, a charitable thing to whip up some cash for the old place. We've already got Larry and a few others on board. I'm hoping to tap prosperous fellows like yourself.'

The prompt was too brazen to ignore. 'If I can help in some way . . .' said Stephen, aiming for vagueness.

Carmody's voice rose in enthusiasm. 'Well, that would be marvellous!' He was already taking a pen from his breast pocket. 'Are you still down at Chelsea?'

'Best way to reach me is through the gallery. Dallington's, on Bury Street.'

'Capital. I'll send you a note about it.'

Nina gave a polite cough and said that she had to dash, allowing Stephen an excuse to get away. They shook hands with Carmody and hurried out of the hotel into Southampton

Row. A cab picked them up almost immediately. Once settled Stephen gave vent to a groan.

'Hellfire. That was awkward.'

'How d'you know him?'

'I hope he didn't see us coming out of the lift . . . Hmm? Oh, we were at Oxford, though I didn't know him well. Still don't – we occasionally bump into one another. He's had quite a career.'

'Wasn't he an MP?'

Stephen nodded. 'One of the youngest ever to be elected. Was tipped for the Cabinet, I think, but made a lot of enemies. The party kicked him out.'

'He soon got his claws into you,' she smirked.

Stephen grimaced. 'Yes – worrying, that. Much as I'd like to help his theatre, I'd rather not get involved. Carmody's a dangerous sort.'

'Dangerous?'

'Well . . . the company he keeps. He was once – and still may be – very thick with Mosley. You know he runs the weekly magazine for the blackshirts?'

'Oh dear,' said Nina. 'He doesn't look the type.'

Stephen thought of asking her how she imagined the typical blackshirt would look, but instead turned a brooding face to the office buildings of Holborn as they slid by the cab window. He could pretend to himself that Carmody would forget all about it, that it was merely a part of his chancer's routine. But he suspected a streak of tenacity in him. Nina seemed to pick up on his troubled silence.

'Don't worry about him. He's probably just trying to make himself look grand – I'll bet he's never met *Larry* in his life!' The taxi had pulled up at the foot of the Aldwych's long curve. 'I'm going to hop out. But before I do, Mr Melmotte' – she leaned across him – 'give me a kiss and wish me luck.'

Stephen happily obliged, then watched as she sauntered up the pavement, straight-backed, hands in her coat pockets, all confidence. He could almost imagine her to be whistling. What a girl she was!

On arriving home at Elm Park Gardens he let himself in, and cautiously interrogated his reflection in the hall's gilt mirror for evidence of his afternoon. He was fussing with his tie again when the drawing-room door opened and Cora appeared, sheathed in an exquisite emerald-coloured gown. Her face was pale and creased in anxious concern.

'Darling – I thought you'd forgotten about dinner,' she said. 'You've got ten minutes to get ready.'

Stephen smiled at his wife. 'I hadn't forgotten. I'm just going to get out of these shoes.'

# 2

On the Wednesday Nina awoke to an unplaceable sense of foreboding. From downstairs she could hear Mrs Keeffe, the landlady, chatting away to one of her boarders. And that smell . . . honestly, who could think of eating kippers at this hour? She turned over in her bed, trying to get comfortable on the lumpy mattress. What was it? she wondered, picking through the previous night for clues to this lowering mood. Not the show – she had just *torn* into it onstage, they all said how marvellous she'd been, even Dolly. Then they'd gone to the Ivy for a late one, and she'd got tight, but not terribly so, not roaring like ten men. So was it the other business, the eventful afternoon at the Imperial? No, that wasn't it either, but now that she had it in mind she would indulge herself for a few moments thinking of his face, his lovely hands with their tapering fingers, and his sweetly earnest compliments. *I think you're smashing* . . . Fancy! as Dolly would say.

Too bad he was married. He hadn't tried to conceal it, or not for long anyway. And she had exercised her own small deception the night they had met at the gallery, pretending not to know him when she was quite familiar with his work as a society portraitist. Having truanted from the gathering and agreed to dinner, she had to wait until pudding for him to confess that the lady he'd told her about at the theatre

– the one who had blubbed at her performance in *The Second Arrangement* – was in fact his wife. Nina had muffled the stab of disappointment by asking questions about her, to which he replied in an even, perhaps rather neutral tone. She – Cora, was it? – had been a secretary at the Royal Academy when Stephen was there. Good family, stockbroker class, large house on Richmond Hill. They had two children, a girl and a boy, both at school; after that they had talked of other things. It was only when Stephen telephoned her the very next day to invite her to lunch that she felt the first vibrations of his seriousness.

The question of whether she ought to have resisted didn't really trouble her. She had fielded the attentions of married men before, without notable pain on either side, and this time seemed no different. Both of them knew what they were doing. Nina wasn't interested in Stephen's wife, and even if she had been, why on earth would they spend the small time they had together talking about her? He had charm – a charm born irresistibly of shyness – but he was plainly not to be trusted, in anything. His behaviour at the hotel, for instance, now that she thought about it, was far from exemplary – quite apart from dishonouring his marital vows. When she had suggested reporting the incident to the desk, his immediate instinct had been to protect himself. But didn't that girl need protecting too? It came back to her now, the whimpering ('please, *no*') she had heard in the hotel corridor, the door flung open and the girl's face in front of her, goggle-eyed with terror as she bolted past. Nina shook her head as though to empty it of the offending image. It was horrible, quite horrible . . .

And yet even *that* wasn't the thing, naggingly stuck there like a thread of meat behind a molar. She looked at her alarm clock, and thought she might as well get up: at this hour there would still be hot water for a bath. Wrapped in her dressing gown she darted across the landing and into the bathroom, locked the door and turned on the taps, listening to the pipes clank and whinny as the tub filled. Once satisfactorily immersed, she lit a cigarette and rested her head against the porcelain roll-top.

She had been at Mrs Keeffe's boarding house for nearly four years. It was an unlyrical Victorian red-brick on Chiltern Street, and she had hated the place the minute she walked in – hated the linoleum floors, the mournful furniture, the dingy microbial wallpaper, the bedraggled aspidistra in the window. But four years ago it was a rent she could afford, and the house was only a hop, skip and a jump away from the West End. She had never got to know any of the other guests, and even to Mrs Keeffe she spoke only when she had to – the occasional encounter on the stairs, or that afternoon her mother had visited –

That was it – the foreboding – it was lunch with her mother, today. Worse, lunch with her mother *on her birthday*. How old was she now? Nina calculated it at fifty-nine, though that was certainly not an age Mrs Land would admit to. Her company didn't count as an ordeal, exactly, though it did demand on Nina's part a careful management of irritations brewed over a lifetime's exposure to her mother's brittle vanity and pettish grievances. Having the example of such a mother had made her determined not to be remotely like her, and the vigilance it entailed was faintly exhausting. Whenever she explained this to friends she realised how undaughterly she must sound. Her mother's life had not been an easy one, both through her own failings of character and the operations of fate, and Nina knew she ought to feel sorry for her instead of harping on her tiresomeness. The result of these guilty ruminations would be a birthday gift whose extravagance her mother would unsuspectingly take as her due.

She crushed her cigarette on the saucer and climbed dripping out of the tub. The heat of the bathwater had steamed up the mirror, presenting an irresistible *tabula rasa*. With her finger she traced a dainty pair of initials, NL + SW, and encircled them with a heart. 'Silly,' she snickered after a moment, and wiped it clear. She stared at her reflection, warily amused by her towel-turbaned head: it reminded her of the genie she had played in panto at the Eastbourne Hippodrome. Below it her face glowed pink. She had turned thirty-two in April, supposedly in the prime of her acting life, yet she knew how precarious was the ground beneath her. A string of bad notices, an unsympathetic director or a stone-cold flop could disable you, to say nothing of that pack of younger, brighter, hungrier actresses snapping at your behind, taking your work. That was the trouble – you were always worrying about the one at your back.

She had just descended to the hall when a door behind her moaned on its hinges and Mrs Keeffe sidled into view. She was a mousy-haired widow of uncertain age whose slight stoop made it look as if she were trying to peer up her interlocutor's nose. Nina occasionally wondered what she wore under her never-changing floral-patterned house-coat, though felt it would be no hardship at all to remain ignorant on the subject. Her landlady treated Nina with a mixture of disapproval and respect, the former born of an older generation's understanding of the word 'actress', the latter encouraged by a vague perception of her lodger's glamorous life: Mrs Keeffe had once seen her being dropped off outside the house in a Rolls-Royce.

'Didn't hear you come in last night,' she said, addressing a point some distance over Nina's shoulder.

'Ah – we had a late one,' Nina replied.

Mrs Keeffe gave her head a little shake. 'Well, I hope someone brought you to the door. 'Snot safe for a lady' – she gave Nina a lightning once-over – 'out on her own in the West End.'

'Whatever d'you mean?'

'You don't read the paper?' Her mouth formed into a perfect 'O' of prim dismay. 'Been another murder – girl found outside a hotel.'

*Another* murder? Nina was not aware there had been a first. 'And the police think it's the same . . .?'

'Oh yes. Same man. Strangles 'em,' she added with a ghoulish twinkle.

'How awful,' said Nina. She had walked home alone last night. 'A friend dropped me off anyway – in his car.'

'You don't wanna know what he does to them . . .' continued her landlady.

'No, I'm sure I don't, Mrs Keeffe,' she said, opening the front door and turning to offer a little wave. 'If anyone calls, I'm out all day. Goodbye.'

By the time Nina reached the restaurant in Maiden Lane her mood was on another downswing of agitation. Her mistake had been the bookshop on the way. She had already bought her mother's birthday present on Regent Street – a vertiginously priced bottle of Patou's Joy – and, with a few minutes to spare, had popped into Foyle's for a browse. She had chosen a couple of books – Elizabeth Craig's *Bubble and Squeak* for her mother; *South Riding* by Winifred Holtby for herself – and was taking her little chit to the payment desk when she spotted it in the shop's selection of new books. It was a compendium of reviews by James Erskine, theatre critic of the *Chronicle*, and carried the ominously punning title *Withering Slights*. She plucked the top one from the little stack and, with a hollowing sensation in her chest, riffled through the index. And there she was, unarguably, *Land, Nina*, 91–2 – a reprinted review of her first-ever starring role, in a play called *Fire in the Hole*. Her eye sought out the paragraph she had read in the paper four years ago:

It is difficult to judge whether at this age Miss Land's horse-faced looks are going to turn to beauty, or else settle into something gaunt and hard. There is no doubt she can act, though she tends to be elusive in the emotional passages: does true feeling rage beneath that cold exterior or is she merely benumbed? She is glamorous but ungainly, does not know how to walk, and has not acquired enough sense to avoid showing her plain legs. Yet there is a quality – a disconcerting sultriness – that draws your eyes to this coltish creature and prevents you from noticing others. If I sound hesitant, it is only because I write this with my fingers crossed.

She could recall it, almost word for word, and the outrage that followed. Ungainly? Plain legs? *Horse-faced?* His words of praise offered no balm to his strictures, keen as paper cuts. Yet back then there was comfort at least in knowing that the review, however mortifying for a day, would be forgotten by the next, when Erskine would have someone else pinned beneath his critical microscope. Now the thing had been resurrected for all to read, ambered forever between hard covers. At the time she had written in furious complaint to the *Chronicle*, explaining to the editor that she *did* know how to walk, and what credentials did their 'esteemed critic' possess to judge whether etc., etc. Thank God common sense had prevailed: she had torn the letter into pieces. Admitting the hurt would be to hand victory to the swine. But it did hurt – it rankled.

Across the room she spotted her, ensconced at a banquette. Nobody ensconced herself quite so comfortably as her mother. She was talking to the maître d' in a simpering manner that Nina knew of old; it involved a good deal of giggling and tapping of the man's forearm. As she approached the table she felt herself to be interrupting something, though her mother greeted her with a small squeal of delight that seemed half genuine and half display for the diners nearest to them.

'Darling!' she cried, as Nina leaned through a cloud of Floris to kiss her powdered cheek. The maître d', with a courtier's air of ingratiation, bowed to her and stepped away.

'Hullo, Mother – happy birthday,' she said, amused by her mother's false surprise at her proffering gifts. *What – for me?* she seemed to say. Annabel Land carried the slightly tense demeanour of a one-time English rose who had not yet accepted the fade of her bloom, and probably never would. In fact (Nina had to admit) she looked good for her age, with a clear-eyed gaze, a hard, high bust and only the smallest wrinkles at her eyes and mouth. She maintained an astonishing confidence in her own attractiveness: that her twenty-odd years' seniority to the maître d' might be an obstacle to flirtation would never have occurred to her. She expected men to take her at her own estimation, which was high. She hardly glanced at the Elizabeth Craig cookbook, seeming to sense the richer prey awaiting in the Dickins & Jones box.

'Oh, you shouldn't have!' cooed Mrs Land, eagerly clawing at the sleek package and prising out the bottle of Joy. Having dabbed a little of the perfume on her wrist, she plunged into an ecstacy of inhalation. Nina, watching, raised her just-filled glass without comment. Her mother, not content with this silent toast, picked up her own glass. 'Happy birthday to me!'

Nina gave an involuntary laugh: the line was so very characteristic of her. Mrs Land, an only child born to doting parents, had been raised on an inviolable idea of her own deserts; producing children of her own had never encroached on that principle. As a girl Nina had not been encouraged in a similar indulgence of her will, though when she was five she had wanted to be an admiral in the British Navy. She had imagined that, as reward for her valour on the high seas, the King would set her up in one of the grand mansions on Piccadilly, or Park Lane – the sort they were knocking down nowadays.

Interpreting her daughter's laugh as simple affirmation, Mrs Land handed over the tasselled menu. 'I'm going to have the lobster mousse, then the grouse,' she declared brightly. 'They do game *so* nicely here.'

Nina sensed her mother's cheeriness might not be entirely due to the birthday fuss. 'How's Felicity?' she asked, wondering if her older sister was pregnant again.

'Fine, fine. John's doing awf'ly well at the Treasury.'

'And Bee?' Bee was her younger sister, and her mother's favourite. Mrs Land sighed.

'Still hasn't settled at the school, poor darling. The headmaster's a perfect brute, she says. Oh, she asked me whether you could get her a box at the play for a Saturday in October.'

'Quite probably – if she can pay for it.' Bee (her actual name was Elizabeth) was a teacher, like her mother, and had inherited from her, if not the application, then certainly the sense of entitlement.

'You can't get a box . . .?'

'Not for free,' said Nina crisply.

'Well, just two in the stalls, then.'

As lunch proceeded in its desultory way, she wondered how long it would take her mother to ask how she, Nina, was getting along. Whereas most civilised people she knew regarded conversation as a form of tennis – you put a few questions over the net, then your opponent would lob a few back – Mrs Land was strictly in the business of receiving rather than serving. By the time Nina had finished her fillet of plaice she was low on supplies of chat, and so decided on provocation instead.

'I'm thinking of going up to Liverpool,' she said. 'To visit Pa's grave.'

Mrs Land tucked in her chin sharply. 'Why on earth would you do that?'

'Because I've never seen it.'

'There's nothing to see. They put him in an unmarked grave.'

'Yes, I know. I thought it might be time to have a headstone made.'

From the disbelieving look on her mother's face Nina knew she had hit a nerve. Charles Land was for years unmentionable in the family. During a lonely and incompatible marriage to their mother he had worked, amid long absences, as a freelance journalist, a sheet-music salesman and a director of a short-lived railway company. Three years after the birth of his youngest daughter he chucked in everything and cleared off; he was last heard to be on his way to America. He got as far as Liverpool, where instead of taking ship he disappeared into a rackety life of drink and debt. Letters from him arrived intermittently at their home in Westbourne Park (the shabby-genteel side), then petered out, and they were left with only rumours of his whereabouts.

When, some years ago, Mrs Land received a letter from a vicar in Toxteth telling of her husband's death – he had been living in a home for vagrants – Nina was surprised by her own grief. She had been six or seven when he left, but she could remember a tall, rather strapping man with a ready laugh (he had been most amused by her naval ambitions) and had nursed a curiosity about him undaunted by her mother's pursed silences. At some point, maddened by an obscure impulse to see his resting place, Nina had written to the vicar, who had replied in a kindly, reserved manner that Charles Land was buried in a plot at St James's Cemetery, Toxteth. She had been undecided over what to do about it ever since.

Mrs Land's mouth tightened pointedly. 'I'd say it's a ridiculous waste of your time and money.' Seeing Nina's philosophical shrug, she added, 'What d'you think you owe to *him*?'

'Well, my existence, I suppose . . .'

Her mother's scowl looked about to set firm when the maître d' reappeared to clear their plates, and she reverted to flirtatious gaiety. After another perusal of the menu, and another consultation with the waiter, Mrs Land decided she would have the crème brûlée. Nina had a cigarette. By the time coffees were served the good mood had been restored, and the matter of the headstone forgotten. Talk had turned to her mother's recent dinner invitation from their friend and benefactor Mr Dorsch. He was a German-born businessman who, having settled with his family in Westbourne Park (the fashionable side), had more or less saved the Lands from destitution after their father had scarpered. He had sponsored Nina and her sisters through their time at St Paul's Girls, an education that would have been beyond their means even if Charles Land had stayed put. It was understood that Mr Dorsch's patronage sprang from the very high regard in which he and his wife held Mrs Land, whom they had employed as piano teacher-cum-governess to their own children. The wife, Monica, had died three years ago.

'But Mr Dorsch has asked you to dinner before,' said Nina warily.

'Not since Monica passed away. And Eric was very particular about it being a dinner *à deux*.'

'I see. And do you have reason to think he may . . .?'

Her mother's studied little laugh confirmed it: Mr Dorsch, or *Eric* as he had become known, was on the market again, and she had put herself at the front of the queue. Nina's immediate instinct would have been to advise caution – to Mr Dorsch. The thought of that kindly, urbane gentleman linked with her mother for life was a consummation devoutly to be avoided. But of course she betrayed no such misgiving.

'I suppose he's still doing his charitable works,' was all she did say.

'Oh yes. Eric is a great philanthropist,' replied Mrs Land, with a rather complacent nod. 'He's one of those people who only thinks of others.'

Nina found herself biting back a tart reply as Mrs Land scooped the last of the crème brûlée into her mouth. She lit another cigarette and watched as her mother rearranged her handbag to accommodate her birthday gifts. This involved taking out that day's *Daily Mail*, with a below-the-fold headline on which Nina's eye happened to fall. SECOND TIEPIN MURDER: GIRL FOUND OUTSIDE HOTEL. It was the one Mrs Keeffe had been telling her about this morning. She idly craned her head around to read:

> The body of a young woman was discovered yesterday morning near Russell Square, Holborn. She had been strangled and left in a service yard at the rear of the Imperial Hotel. The pathologist estimated that she had been dead for about six hours. According to a police spokesman, the victim's tongue had been pierced by a metal pin, a grisly signature that links it to the murder of another young woman in the Haymarket last month. *continues page 3.*

Nina felt a sudden panicky acceleration in her heartbeat. It was the reference to the Imperial which had done it. If the girl had been found yesterday morning that meant she had been murdered the same day she and Stephen had been there. And now she thought again of that unpleasant scene in room 408, and the scowling man she had interrupted. Could it possibly be the same? – a sudden clarified memory of the terror-struck girl flashed in her mind's eye. How had it not registered before?

'*Oh God,*' she said in a half-whisper.

Mrs Land looked up. 'What's the matter?'

'Nothing – I've just been reading that grisly story – the murdered girl . . .'

'Oh, isn't it dreadful?!' cried Mrs Land. 'They say he stabs a tiepin through their tongues.'

The note of relish in her mother's voice was very like her landlady's that morning. People loved to know ghastly details. And they loved even more to let others know.

'Mother, I'm sorry, I just have to make a telephone call,' said Nina, rising from the table. She hurried, unseeing, through the dining room and found the phone booth in a side corridor. The air within felt unpleasantly warmed from the chaotic emotions of recent usage. In her diary she found the number of Stephen's studio at Tite Street, and recited it to the operator. On the fifth ring he picked up, his drawled 'Hullo' echoing as though from a deep well.

'Stephen, it's me. Have you seen the paper today?'

'Um, no. I think the *Standard*'s lying around.'

'Have a look at it. Please – it's important.'

Hearing her troubled tone, Stephen leaned across his sofa and plucked the paper off the floor.

'What's on the front page?' she asked him.

He considered. 'Some story about a murder . . .'

'Read it out to me.'

He did so, his voice curious at first, then slowing into realisation as he read down the column: '. . . the Imperial Hotel, Russell Square. Hmm.' He fell silent; she could almost hear his mind working.

'You understand, don't you?' she said. 'Same day.' A tap on the glass behind made her jump. A man was outside, waiting to use the telephone. Blast. 'Stephen, there's something I need to tell you. May I come to the studio?'

'You mean now?'

'Yes, right now.'

He looked at his paint spattered hands. He had actually been blazing away, hard at it, but of course he assented, just before the line went dead.

Half an hour later a cab was depositing her at the foot of Tite Street. She had almost bundled her mother out of the restaurant in her haste (Mrs Land had looked rather put out), waving a distracted goodbye before half sprinting down to the Strand. In the cab she tried to compose herself, but only by degrees did the frantic flutter of her heart subside. She wanted to be able to talk to him about it coolly, rationally.

His housekeeper let her in with barely a glance. Nina had worried at first that it might look odd, a young woman turning up unannounced in the middle of the afternoon, but then she realised that Stephen would have models and all sorts trooping up and down the stairs here. She was just another in his regular cavalcade of guests.

His smile when he opened the door did something to reassure her: they would be in this together. He took her coat, and asked if she wanted a drink.

'Thanks, no. I had a couple at Rule's – to get me through lunch with my mother.'

'Ah, and how is the sainted Mrs Land?' asked Stephen, as though he knew her.

'Same as ever,' Nina said, 'only more so.'

As she stood at the window, irresolute, Stephen sidled up and reached out to pull her close. But she withdrew from him and instead went to pick up the *Standard*, with its unwelcome freight of significance. She sat down to read through the report again, then looked in anxious appeal to Stephen.

'It's him – the man I saw in the room. It *has* to be him.'

Stephen narrowed his eyes a little. 'You can't be certain. Look, there's a lot of men out there mistreating women, all the time. But very few of them are murderers. Hardly any! The man you saw – well, no doubt he's a brute, but it doesn't follow that he's –'

'Stephen, listen to me,' she cut in abruptly. She patted the sofa, inviting him to sit next to her, and took a deep breath. 'There's something I didn't tell you – something I'd forgotten myself, I was in such a state, you remember? The girl – the girl he was hurting – when she ran into me –'

'Yes?'

'I saw . . . marks.'

'What d'you mean, marks?'

'On her neck – bruises, the sort you would get from someone's hands trying to . . . throttle you.'

His frown had turned quizzical. 'You didn't say that at the time. I mean, how could you forget something like that –'

'I know, I know. But I did see them! It happened so quickly, I didn't take them in. Or, I don't know, probably I wanted to put them out of my mind. It just seems to me too great a coincidence that there would be *another* maniac lurking around the hotel ready to strangle a girl.'

He said nothing. He only stared at her, frowning slightly, as though he were making a decision about her. Then it dawned on her, with a chill.

'You think I'm making it up, don't you?' she said, trying to keep her voice steady.

He shook his head, and waited a beat before replying. 'No, I don't think that. On the contrary, you should probably go to the police. If you've seen the killer, they'll want to know about it.'

Nina bit her lip, pondering the implications. The responsibility of it had loomed in her vision, disconcerting her. After some hesitation she said, 'I'm not sure, really, how much help I can be . . .'

'But you *did* see him,' he said gravely.

'Yes – though only for a matter of seconds.'

'Would you be able to pick him out again?' asked Stephen, sounding to his own ears like an investigating officer.

'Yes. No. I don't know,' she said with a helpless shrug.

They held each other's gaze for a few moments. Then, with a decisive air, Stephen stood up and went over to his long work desk. He returned to the sofa carrying one of his larger sketch pads and a charcoal stick. He sat down at an angle to her, and, readying himself, brushed back a lock of hair from his forehead.

'What are you doing?' she said.

'You're going to describe his face to me. And I'm going to sketch it.'

'Really?' she said uncertainly.

'Why not? The police use artists all the time for this. They work with the eyewitness to make an approximate study of the suspect. Well, then – that's in my line, and I can't imagine I'd be any worse at it than they are.' He saw the doubt in her gaze. 'Just think of it as a "wanted" poster, like in the Wild West.'

He flourished his charcoal stick like a conductor with his baton, and she laughed. 'Right,' he said. 'Let's start with an outline of his face. Was it round, or long, or squarish?'

'Long, I suppose,' she said, and watched as his expression focused, his hand quick and assured as it moved the charcoal around the paper. In a coaxing tone he invited her to describe the features, and, not wanting to let him down, she found herself recalling the contours and creases of the face with greater precision than she had expected. Principally it was the man's eyes – narrow, with very dark irises – that came back to her, and as she directed Stephen's marks and shadings she began to feel a strange empowerment, as if she were a spy, furnishing the vital coordinates of a secret location. And she loved to watch Stephen work, his faraway look of concentration, the tip of his tongue absently hovering between his teeth – the everyday oddity of his left-handedness.

After ten minutes of this concerted effort Stephen, finishing with a few darting flurries, stood up and held the drawing a little distance from her.

'Well?'

Nina squinted at it for some moments, then gave a slow nod. 'That's really rather *good*.'

'Don't sound so surprised!' He laughed.

'Yes, but you usually draw from life, not from someone describing it.' She leaned forward to scrutinise his handiwork. 'I couldn't swear it, but there might have been something fleshier about the lips . . .'

He returned to the sketch and worked it over a little – erasing, adding, refining – before he handed it back to her. The mouth had been plumped, as required. It briefly amazed her that something in her mind's eye should take on this vivid material form.

'That's him,' she said. 'Or as close to him as I can remember.'

Stephen opened his cigarette case, from which she plucked one and lit it. They smoked for a meditative minute, the sketch lying on the coffee table between them. Nina felt an inward shudder as the stranger's eyes, sump-black, seemed to fix on her. She stood up, and wandered over to the mirror at the fireplace. She addressed Stephen's reflection in it.

'May I ask you something – does my face look "gaunt" or "hard" to you?' She couldn't even bear to mention 'horse-faced'.

Stephen blinked at the question. 'Er, no. Neither. Why do you ask?'

She hesitated, then said, 'Oh, just something a critic wrote about me when I was doing *Fire in the Hole*.'

'Tsss. What rot. Should like to aim some fire up *his* hole, the blighter.'

Nina laughed. 'Ah, my defender!'

He felt pleased at having said the right thing, and made

a mental note to avoid any reference to the words 'gaunt' and 'hard' in her presence. Nina had returned her attention to the drawing. 'So – when do we take it to the police?'

Stephen paused now, looking shifty. 'I've been thinking about that . . .'

'Oh?'

'I can't go to the police. They'll ask me why we had a room at the hotel . . . If that comes out, it's all over with Cora.'

Nina's brow closed into a frown. 'But it's important – it might help them to catch him!'

'I know. But my marriage is important, too,' he said, realising how hypocritical that would sound. He looked away, embarrassed, and felt grateful that she didn't challenge him.

At length she said, in a measured tone, 'I suppose we could send it anonymously. With a note?'

He shook his head. 'Wouldn't work. It needs a credible witness – context – to back it up. Otherwise it's merely a drawing of a man's face, and who cares?'

'Then what was the point of doing it?'

'I don't know. The problem only occurred to me as I was drawing the thing.' She leaned back on the sofa, and blew out her cheeks. What a lot of fuss for nothing. Stephen had been gazing off, abstracted; then he turned his head towards her, his expression intent. 'Wait – I have an idea.'

She looked at him, raising her eyebrows in mute enquiry.

'You should take it to the police,' he said.

'What?'

'You present it as your own – why should they doubt it? And you *are* the one who saw him.'

Nina pointed to the sketch. 'I couldn't draw that – I'm not capable of it.'

'But who's to know? The important thing, as you said, is to let the police have it. You tell them it's the man you saw,

36

they get it to the newspapers, maybe someone will recognise him.'

Her expression remained dubious. 'I don't know. What if they rumble me?'

'They won't. They'll simply think you're a decent citizen who wants to help – which is what you are!' He sensed her teetering towards consent, and gave her a final push. 'Look, if it is him, he's done in two girls already. You could save someone else's life.'

She looked at him still. The case was unarguable, she saw that. Lying through her teeth, pretending the drawing was her own – hardly something that would test her skill as an actress. And she could lie in good conscience, she supposed, given this likeness in front of her might be instrumental in catching a killer. The end would justify the means. And yet something about the business unsettled her profoundly.

She picked up the sketch. 'Well, then,' she said, in a resigned voice, wishing once again that she had never clapped eyes on him.

# 3

Jimmy shifted in his seat and sneaked another look at his pocket watch. Half past eight. What?! He had last checked about three hours ago and it was ten past. Had his trusty timepiece given out at last? It had been with him since the summer of 1914, just before he went to France. Bought in a little shop on the Strand, he remembered. 'It'll work for sentries, that will,' the man had said. Jimmy, in uniform at the time, was offended to have been mistaken for a mere sentry – then realised that it was the fellow's sales patter. *Centuries*. It'll work for *centuries*. Well, twenty-two years so far without mishap . . .

No, he knew there was nothing wrong with his watch. It only *felt* like three hours ago. Time was proceeding as normal. It was the play – his fourth this week – that was dragging. He looked along the row (he always sat at the end, to make a quick getaway) and found every other face dutifully still, slightly uptilted, aglow in the footlights. What was it about this domestic drama – he rummaged for the title, without success – that kept them so entranced? Oh, it was averagely competent, averagely performed, averagely staged and lit. It positively *shimmered* with averageness. That seemed to be enough for them. For the critic, though, it was a killer. He, too, had a duty to entertain, on the page as opposed to the stage, and nothing choked inspiration more effectively than the play that was neither good nor bad. Give him something uproariously great, or loutishly inept, just so long as it was something he could get his teeth into!

He willed himself back into the action of the play. The character in the tweed suit who had entered the scene a few minutes ago had just revealed a noticeable lisp. Perhaps he could make something of that, a racy paragraph on the telltale signs of a – no, much too dangerous. Nine out of ten readers wouldn't even know what he was talking about . . . That tweed suit, now. It was very like one he had had made, years ago, by Huntsman, was it? – he could picture it, the long bolt of cloth on the cutter's table . . . a sort of marmalade colour with a windowpane check in purple, no, more like heather than purple . . .

A rasping, catarrhal *cggghhhuh* snapped his chin up suddenly from his chest, where it had been lolling. My God, that snore – *that was him*. The man in the next seat had turned an enquiring face. He had just fallen asleep – *narcolepsia dramatica* – and not for the first time lately. Quite an irony that he should be restless in his own bed at night only to drop off while on duty in the stalls! He found that the older he got the less well he slept, he wasn't sure why. Eating and drinking late perhaps had something to do with it; but then he had always eaten and drunk late. Somehow he had lost the knack for sleep. What did Macbeth call it? 'Sleep that knits up the ravelled sleave of care,/The death of each day's life, sore labour's bath,/ Balm of hurt minds . . .' tee-tum, tee-tum, tee-tum. He was getting old – sixty next year. Back in the long ago he could have recited that speech entire. He would quote long runs of Shakespeare to amuse his dinner companions, who listened and smiled at one another as if to say, 'Jimmy's at it again.'

His body was starting to fail, too. Corpulence had crept up on him, stealing away his once-compact figure. At night when he rolled over in bed he felt certain parts of him slower to turn than others. The manoeuvre now had to be executed, as it were, in stages. In the morning he struggled to crane himself forward to reach his feet, and had to lie in a foetal position just to put his socks on. His belt took an ever longer circuit around the rotunda of his stomach. He seemed to be going to the doctor more often, though Harley Street's finest could discover nothing very wrong with him, aside from the usual wear and tear. (The last fellow, a Scot named McAlister, had suggested he cut his daily wine consumption from two bottles to one – Jimmy had privately dismissed him as a Presbyterian.) Morbid thoughts oppressed him; his vague fear of death had metamorphosed into a black butterfly of neurotic terror. The other day he had been browsing through the week's letters from readers when he opened one from a correspondent named Philip D'Eath. He had dropped it as though he might a plague victim's handkerchief. When his secretary later picked the letter off the floor and asked him how he wished to reply, Jimmy had refused to have anything to do with it.

He peeked at his watch again. Quarter to nine. Though his attention had wandered he could sniff the interval approaching, like a gun dog picking up a scent. And here it came, a seemly diminuendo; the sense of a hiatus; the curtain's slow descent. Applause. For this relief, much thanks . . . Jimmy was out of his seat and hurrying up the aisle before the lights had come on. The prospect of a drink always quickened his step. The white-jacketed barman fixed him a large whisky and soda, which he took to a corner table and set to work. He had a little notepad in which he'd jotted down his first paragraph, always the trickiest – that, and the last paragraph. He now had the play's title in front of him: *Change of the Guard*. Even *that* was average.

A good drama is as solidly constructed as a good house. The foundations should be hewn from realism, the ground floor from character and action, the upper floor from pattern and symbol. Within, its staircases and doorways should allow smooth passage from one part to another. Laurence Markwick's *Change of the Guard* at the Duke of York's follows these precepts with a rigorous competence. The materials are first-rate, the workmanship is sound. But is it a house one wishes to inhabit for longer than ten minutes? This story of a cuckoo in the marital nest offers careful observation of human frailty but nothing that resembles spontaneous feeling. There is not a line in it that surprises, nor a gesture that intrigues. The view from its windows is perfectly transparent – and perfectly trite.

Jimmy read it through again. He loved the way his prose fell into place. He was also rather sick of it. Forty-odd years of theatre-going, at least thirty of them spent writing about it, was bound to blunt your edges. True, with experience had come a certain godlike assurance: it was impossible to avoid the feeling that his critical verdicts were consistently and remarkably *right*. What use in being a critic otherwise? The problem was in finding different ways of saying the same thing over and over again. He had played variations on the 'good house' analogy at least, oh, half a dozen times in the last ten years. Reading through the proofs of his latest collection of reviews he had been aghast at the way the same phrases – jokes – aperçus – infested his paragraphs like bothersome weeds. His secretary had spotted them too, and had entered polite notes in the margin: *Perhaps change this?* A list of repetitions was appended. Change? He would if he had the time. But he was too busy attending the plays, or reading the books, or writing half a dozen other articles at once to finesse every last word. Deadlines massed overhead each week, like ravens pecking on the roof. His memory, capacious as it was, couldn't always identify the same amusing *jeu d'esprit* he had essayed six months before.

He would tot up his aggregate of words published each year and note it in his diary. His total for the previous twelve months had come to 432,000, either written by his own hand or dictated to his secretary. Nearly half a million words . . . He sometimes had the sense of being a stoker, shovelling his words into a furnace whose white-hot maw kept consuming, demanding, consuming. As fast as he wrote them they vanished into the flames. No amount would ever satisfy it. The only escape he could conceive, his only respite from feeding the fire, was death. And he didn't want to think about that.

A shadow had fallen across his table. He looked up to find a large lady favouring him with a shy but hopeful simper. Her floral dress was straining across her voluminous bust and backside. Jimmy was already writing a *Punch* caption in his head: 'A steatopygous matron from the provinces, excited by her night out in London's fashionable West End, encounters a Renowned Theatrical Personage' . . . He sighed, and put down his pen.

'Madam, you're standing in my light,' he said, his expression unsmiling.

The lady took an apologetic step sideways. 'Ooh, I am sorry. I just wanted to ask . . . if you were enjoying the play?' *Ply*, she pronounced it. Her accent carried the unmistakable flat drone of Brum, sharpening his irritation.

He took a deep breath. 'In the theatre I never allow myself to succumb in the smallest degree to the arbitrary and unreliable sensation you are pleased to call "enjoyment". That is a word to be used strictly in relation to such pleasures as pâté de foie gras, vanilla ices or Scotch whisky – the last of which I *had* been lately enjoying.'

She blinked her bewilderment at him. 'So . . . you don't like it then?' *Loik eet*.

'For the sake of argument, let us say: it is giving me the pip.'

She nodded, brightening at the colloquialism. Somewhat emboldened, she leaned towards him again and said, sotto voce, 'Are you who I think you are?'

Jimmy capped his pen, pocketed his notebook, and stood up. 'I most certainly am not,' he said curtly, and turned on his heel. Behind him he heard her gasp, and felt exhilarated by his rudeness. What a pest, barging in on him without so much as a by-your-leave. The look on her silly face as he crushed her! That would keep him going through the second half. He strolled back into the auditorium, nodding at this or that fellow scribbler – it was press night, so they were all in. He was about to return to his seat when a hearty hand clapped him on the back.

'Erskine! How are you?'

He turned to find a tall fellow with a florid face and an unnerving dark gaze fixed upon him. His projecting voice and wide-lapelled chalkstripe suit bespoke a boisterous confidence. Jimmy had absolutely no idea who he was. But he sensed he ought to know him, and muttered a *hullo*.

'I was talking about you only the other day,' the man continued, 'with my old friend Stephen Wyley. I'm organising a dinner to raise funds for the Marquess – we hope to relaunch the place. Your presence would be a tremendous boon to us.'

Dipping his hand into a breast pocket he took out a business card and handed it to Jimmy. It was embossed with the House of Commons portcullis, beneath which was printed: GERALD CARMODY, MP. So that's who he was. Jimmy had no memory of meeting him before, though he knew his type: the varsity swagger, the entitlement, the bullying familiarity with men whose acquaintance he had never previously enjoyed.

'You're a friend of Stephen Wyley?' said Jimmy, pouncing

on the only bit of information that interested him. He owned one of his paintings, and nurtured a secret longing to have his portrait done by him.

'Ye-e-ers, we were at Oxford together. He's pledged his support. It should be a grand occasion – no trash!'

Jimmy nodded approvingly. 'Well, if it's not a press night I'm sure I could see my way to attending. Call the *Chronicle* and ask for my secretary's number – he looks after my diary.'

'Splendid!' boomed Carmody, his eyes glittering. He shot out a meaty hand, which Jimmy felt obliged to take. 'Toodle-oo.'

Jimmy had reached his seat when he noticed the man in the row behind glaring at him. What on earth was *his* gripe? His eyes slid along to the woman sitting next to him – and then he knew. It was the Brum matron he had recently put in her place. She looked merely embarrassed; he – the husband, presumably – looked furious, clearly having taken umbrage on his lady's behalf. Oh dear, just his luck to be sitting in front of them . . . He drooped in his seat, feeling the man's eyes burning into his neck. The lights went down, mercifully, and he was once more enfolded in the smothering competence of the painted people onstage.

St Martin's Lane was aswarm with the theatre crowds just emerging from their evening's entertainment, the pavements thronged with men carrying the odour of sixpenny cigars and women wearing fake pearls and implausible hats. Brilliant traffic was bunching and growling, spurting and halting in broken processions, eager for a way out. Jimmy, despairing of a cab, hurried through Seven Dials and thence into Shaftesbury Avenue. While everyone else was heading for the late-night Tube and bus, his own evening was just beginning. He lived round the corner from the British Museum in Princess Louise Mansions, whose grimy terracotta facade belied the furnishings of his own bachelor rooms within. Extravagant in most things, where his flat was concerned he was positively Babylonian. A huge art deco mirror greeted his entrance into the hallway, where his shoes clacked pleasingly on the varnished parquet. Prints and paintings covered almost every inch of the living-room wall. On the chimney piece stood a marble bust of Irving next to a Lalique vase, the expense of which put him in a cold sweat even now. On top of the drinks cabinet a gramophone's brass horn flared like a huge petalled flower. The cream-coloured carpets were lamb-soft, and the very devil to keep clean: Mrs Pargiter, his char, was often on her hands and knees scrubbing them. At his desk, where he now installed himself, certain literary treasures were laid out. An inkstand bought at an auction of Oscar Wilde's personal effects; a blotter that had once belonged to Balzac; a fountain pen presented to him at an awards lunch by Kipling. He had attended Kipling's funeral at the Abbey in January, and had surprised himself by weeping.

From the kitchen he had brought a plate of cold partridge and half a bottle of sparkling hock, his fuel for the task. He had been rehearsing the second and third paragraphs of his review during the play's interminable last act; another one would push it over halfway, then with any luck momentum would see him to the end. Sometimes he would spend an hour trying to get a sentence right; at others, he could cuff a paragraph into shape within ten minutes. He wrote as if he were composing music, testing each line over and over for harmony, phrasing, rhythm. His method entailed so much crossing out, with so many revisions and embellishments, that a page of his longhand prose would end nearly blackened. He would then make a fair copy of the text on his typewriter, and set to work on that, amending, tinkering, cutting. If his secretary was about he would give it him to read and make suggestions; he tended to curb Jimmy's more baroque flights of fancy. Come to think of it, where *was* he tonight?

The excitement of the evening ahead lent speed to his composition. By 11.15 p.m. he had it done, typed and ready to go. Eight hundred words in forty minutes: not bad. He telephoned for a taxi, and by quarter to midnight he was slouching in a chair by his editor's desk at the *Chronicle*'s office. The latter was a cove named Gideon Lambert, who smoked Woodbines and seemed to take pleasure in never praising anything. Jimmy thought the man didn't pay him quite the respect he was due, but he knew him to have influence 'upstairs' and so didn't make a fuss.

Having read through Jimmy's copy in silence, Lambert looked up. 'What's this – "his steatopygous form" . . .?'

'From the Greek,' said Jimmy, 'meaning excessive flesh on the buttocks.'

'I don't think our readers will know the word.'

'Then they need only consult a dictionary.'

Lambert was shaking his head. Jimmy sighed and said, 'Would our readers prefer "fat-arsed", d'you suppose?'

For answer the editor scored a line through it. A short telephone call followed, consisting mostly of grunted *hmm*s and *yuh*s. Lambert rang off and shot a look of amused resignation across the desk.

'That was subs. They have to cut ten lines from it,' he said, nodding at the review.

'You're joking.' Lambert tweaked his mouth in a languid way that Jimmy found rather maddening. 'Odd, isn't it, how one's deathless prose becomes in a subeditor's hands so very mortal. Can you imagine a painter bringing in his canvas and the frame-maker telling him he must cut two inches off the foreground to make it fit?'

Lambert spread his palms wide. 'Either you can do it, or they will.'

Jimmy clicked his tongue in annoyance. 'Tell them to send up a proof.'

While they waited Jimmy parked himself on the office's

horsehair couch and leafed through the paper's late edition. His eye stopped at a headline on page three: SCOTLAND YARD RELEASE SKETCH OF TIEPIN KILLER. Alongside the story was a pencil portrait of a man's face, apparently drawn by a member of the public who may have seen him at the hotel. Rather a professional job too, almost an artist's impression. The identity of the second victim had been confirmed; she had just started working at the Imperial as a chambermaid.

'My God, they're not even *tarts* he's murdering . . .'

'What's that?' said Lambert, lighting another cigarette.

'The girl who got strangled last week. Lived with her mother in Bayswater – perfectly respectable family.'

Lambert didn't bat an eyelid. 'We thought he might be another Ripper. I think everyone here's a bit disappointed.'

'Charming,' said Jimmy, quietly shocked.

He was of an age to have lived through the Ripper murders. In the autumn of 1888 he was a schoolboy in Birmingham, though news of Whitechapel prostitutes being brutally slaughtered was not slow to catch on in the provinces. Jimmy had first read of them in his father's *Daily Telegraph*, and could recall his fascinated revulsion on learning precisely what the word 'disembowelled' meant. Also the word 'prostitute', come to think of it.

'Well, at least this sketch gives them something to go on,' Lambert was saying as he studied the page. A short silence intervened, and Jimmy looked round to find Lambert staring at him through the smoke. 'That's an interesting pin you're wearing, by the way . . .'

Jimmy snorted his amusement at the implication, fingering the gold pin that speared his tie. 'I use it only for its designated purpose.'

But Lambert was enjoying himself. 'You even *look* rather like him,' he mused, squinting between Jimmy and the sketch. 'Can you account for your whereabouts on the evening in question?'

'Are the subs going to be long? I have an appointment to keep.'

'What, at this hour?'

'The night is young.' Jimmy shrugged, wary of his curiosity. Lambert was just the sort of tittle-tattler who could do him damage. Changing the subject, he fished out the business card lately entrusted to him and handed it across the desk.

'Know anything of this fellow?'

Lambert wrinkled his nose. 'Gerald Carmody. Mm, used to knock around with the Blackshirts, before he fell out with Mosley. Met him a couple of times.'

'He claimed acquaintance with me, but I didn't know him from Adam.'

'That wouldn't stop Carmody. He puts himself about. I gather he's running a theatre in Covent Garden – belonged to his wife's family.'

'Yes, the Marquess. He's trying to raise funds – asked me along to a dinner in support. I suppose I ought to lend my name.'

'But of course – a theatrical legend such as yourself . . .' Jimmy thought he detected a note of sarcasm in his voice, but Lambert's expression was impassive. 'He's not altogether trustworthy, of course,' he continued, handing back the card to Jimmy. 'He oughtn't to be giving out these things for a start – he's not an MP any more.'

At that moment a copy boy poked his head round the door, waving a proof of Jimmy's review. For the next twenty minutes Jimmy fiddled furiously, breaking up paragraphs and honing down sentences with the pained but beady eye of a master jeweller forced to cut a beautiful gem. Ten lines – lines he had lovingly composed – gone! Still, better he did the job than allow some sub to get his paws on it. When he had finished he placed it on the desk before Lambert, who was now slumped in his chair, blowing smoke rings at the ceiling.

'I'm off. Are you going to have another look at it?'

Lambert lifted his chin in vague acknowledgement. 'I'm sure it'll do.'

Jimmy bristled. This was too much. 'It will more than *do*,' he said coldly. 'Much as it might surprise you, my copy does not come by the yard, like cloth for curtains. Nor is it something to be topped and tailed like a French bean. It is a piece by James Erskine – therefore it will be the outstanding ornament of tomorrow's newspaper.'

He didn't wait for Lambert's response to this blast of magisterial hauteur, brushing past the copy boy who had been loitering at the door. He was halfway along the corridor when the response did come, belatedly: a rising three-note screech of hilarity, accompanied by another's low appreciative snigger.

Back in the cab, which he had kept waiting, Jimmy fumed uselessly over the scene he had just exited. He had forgotten how much he disliked Lambert. *I'm sure it'll do* . . . Time was when he would have had him carpeted. The Erskine of old would not have suffered such impudence from a subordinate. That time was fading. Jimmy felt himself to be a person of diminishing consequence. It was partly to do with age. Young men like Lambert didn't care tuppence that he was the great drama critic of his era; they just saw a fat old man in checks and a bowler who had to walk with a cane.

It might have been different, had luck been on his side. Or should he say *looks*? In his early twenties he had strutted the stage himself, working in a repertory company whose productions had caught the eye of the local newspaper. His Laertes at that little theatre in Edgbaston was hailed as a triumph (he still had the cutting somewhere) and for a while he had even understudied the Prince. He possessed a melodic voice and a decent athletic figure, but as time went on he noticed that the roles being offered to him were getting smaller and, strangely, older. Instead of the dashing romantics he longed to play, directors were casting him as uncles, loyal advisers, second dukes. Three years after his 'triumphant' Laertes he auditioned for another *Hamlet* and was asked to read for – the gravedigger! Frustrated, he eventually took aside Mr Becker, the manager of the company, to ask why he was being overlooked for the major roles. Jimmy listened to him blather for a while before he pressed him to give an honest answer. Becker paused, embarrassed, and then he said quietly, 'I'm sorry, James, but nobody will cast you for those parts. You simply don't have the looks.'

So there it was. He could have persevered in defiance of the man's judgement, but in his heart he knew he had heard the truth, or something like it. He quit the company, without so much as a goodbye to anyone, and worked for a time in his father's drapery business. It was a desolate period in his young life. For months he avoided the theatre altogether, sickened at the thought of his lost future. Then, during a week's holiday in London, he went to see Henry Irving play Dubosc in *The Lyons Mail*, and was transfixed. On returning to his lodgings he wrote a review of the play, rhapsodising over three paragraphs on the actor's ferocious gusto and individuality. He had written pieces for the school magazine, but nothing before had so fired his enthusiasm, or his pen. He sent it to the *Post*, with a covering letter, and the next day an editor wrote back. The paper couldn't run his Irving review, but would he care to try out as their London theatre correspondent? Four weeks later, following a brief interview, the job was his. The performer in him had not been wholly thwarted; henceforth he would create his own sort of drama from the stalls, to be enjoyed in print the next day. It was revenge of a kind. But in thirty-eight years he had never forgotten the critical verdict Mr Becker had passed, regretfully, on his physical appeal.

The cab had stopped on Charlotte Street, quiet at this hour, though he could see the lamps still agleam inside Bertorelli's. He paid off the cabbie – quite a fare after all his waiting – and found the covered alley by the side of the pub. Newman Passage: don't mind if I do, thought Jimmy. At the foot of the alley was a cobbled mews, where he counted off the numbers until he reached the door he'd been told about. A sullen-faced bantam who answered his knock gave him the once-over before stepping aside. The lounge he entered was long and dimly lit, like a Mayfair clubroom, and occupied by men in murmurous colloquy. Not knowing anyone, Jimmy was about to settle in a corner armchair when a strapping fellow with brilliantined hair and a neat moustache approached him.

'Mr . . . Quex, is it?'

'Call me Jimmy,' he replied, accepting the man's handshake.

'Sergeant Teague, sir. What'll you have to drink?' Without waiting for an answer he called to another man lounging nearby. 'Bottle of Black & White, if you will, Reg. Two glasses.'

'And a tankard,' added Jimmy. The man nodded and slunk off.

Teague looked at him in a genial way, but said nothing, so Jimmy began the story of his evening, and made a little comic anecdote of his dropping off during the play. Teague only listened, though when the Scotch arrived at the table he poured them each a good three fingers and raised his glass. 'Here's how.'

Jimmy drank and continued to talk of the London theatre and its audiences, cracking the odd joke, but Teague just sat there, nodding benignly. It seemed that whatever he said, and however amusingly he said it, he could not pierce the fellow's carapace of polite indifference. Jimmy, used to entertaining company, decided on a different tack.

'So, Sergeant,' he began, looking about the room, 'you're all from the Albany Street barracks?'

'Indeed we are, sir.'

'I've done me bit for the King, too. Captain in the Army Service Corps, '14–'18. Mostly in Le Havre and Boulogne, you know, looking after the horses. Much safer than the front, of course!' Jimmy thought he should make this modest admission in case he came across as a shirker. Teague at last responded.

'No shame in supplying a good service, sir.'

Jimmy heard the ulterior meaning in his words. 'Quite so,' he said, taking out his wallet and laying two ten-shilling notes on the table. The sergeant winked, and calmly folded them into his pocket. Jimmy looked around at the other clientele, huddled in convivial clusters. He experienced a stab of panic. 'These men are all . . . I can trust in their discretion?'

'Absolutely, sir,' said Teague, smiling. 'Allow me to conduct you upstairs. I've a couple of friends I think you'd like to meet.' He signalled to his man to carry up the Scotch and the tankard, and Jimmy followed after.

At four o'clock the two guardsmen said their 'g'nights' and pushed off, each of them ten bob to the better. Jimmy, sprawled on a divan, hauled his trousers back on and went downstairs in search of Teague. He didn't mind having to do all the talking – in truth he rather enjoyed it. But the sergeant had gone, so there was nothing else for it: home, James. Back on Charlotte Street the facades of cafes and shops gazed out, oddly hostile, the serried upper windows glimmering from the reflection of the street lamps. He headed for Bedford Square, his ears pricked for other footsteps, though there really was nobody about, not even an early milkman. His shadow seemed to gain on him as he walked, and he looked in fright over his shoulder to check he was not being followed. He hated having to walk home

– he hated having to walk *any*where – and took to muttering some verses to keep himself company.

> We aren't no thin red 'eroes, nor we aren't no blackguards too.
> But single men in barricks, most remarkable like you;
> And if sometimes our conduck isn't all your fancy paints,
> Why, single men in barricks don't grow into plaster saints.

Indeed not!

He had just reached the British Museum, nearly at his door, when he saw a lone, lean figure strolling in his direction. The helmet gave him away. He had heard stories of policemen disguised as trade, soliciting men like himself. One couldn't be too careful. A discreet exchange of looks, a descent into the public lavatory – and the surprise snap of the handcuffs. Gotcha!

'Good morning, Constable,' chirped Jimmy, with an insouciance he didn't feel.

'Sir,' he replied, with a tap to his helmet, walking on.

Jimmy wondered how respectful the bobby would have been had he witnessed his recent 'conduck' with the guardsmen. The younger of the two had been rather shy when he asked for his usual. 'What – in there?' he said, looking at the tankard on the table. Jimmy watched as the man unbuttoned his fly and flipped out his cock, giving it a quick peremptory tug; a few moments later an arc of urine drummed inside the pewter, then slowed to a dribble. The man gave himself a shake, and withdrew.

'That's the stuff,' said Jimmy, taking the remainder of the Scotch and upending it into the tankard. He sniffed a thin ammoniac odour, then put the vessel to his lips and downed it in great gulps.

He went softly down the hall, shrugged off his coat and peeked into the living room. Through the grainy dark he saw the recumbent form of Tom, his secretary, asleep on the sofa. The bed he had made for himself was, like everything he did, severely neat; he had even tucked in the blanket corners. With tender feelings of relief Jimmy crept into the room to turn down the lamp. As he did so the prone body on the sofa stirred, and a sleep-blurred voice came: 'Jim – that you?'

He gave him a little pat. 'Yes. Go back to sleep. Bring me in some tea at eight, will you?'

Tom grunted a vague affirmative.

'Good man,' whispered Jimmy, backing out of the room and closing the door.

# 4

Madeleine jumped when the waitress put down the pot of tea at her elbow. She'd been miles away. 'Sorry, dearie,' cooed the woman, who must have seen her startled expression because she patted her hand in apology. A sudden hot surge prickled at Madeleine's eyes. It was the sort of random gesture of sympathy that could set her off these days, she didn't know why. The waitress, older than the others, had just asked her something, and mechanically she replied, 'No, nothing else, thank you.'

'Right you are,' she said, and moved away. Madeleine's gaze followed her halting progress around the other tables, where she would stoop enquiringly, nodding through the orders on her notepad, sharing an inaudible moment of cheer. She treated all of her customers in the same affable way, and none of them seemed to find it unusual. If only – if only this nice old lady were her friend, the things she would tell her, all those things choked up so tight inside they felt like some terrible indigestion. But then perhaps she would only frighten her off, for who would wish to be tainted by her sordid packet of despair?

Without removing her thin scarf she put her fingertips to the skin around her throat, which still felt sore, weeks after. She looked about her to check that nobody was watching, and, of course, nobody was. Who were these people, she wondered, these blithe patrons of the tea room, jawing away to one another without a care in the world? How had they come by such unthinking gaiety? She drew the scarf around her protectively. It was one of only two souvenirs from her time at Diprose's, the smart ladies' clothing establishment off Piccadilly. She sometimes tormented herself with the notion that all might have been well if she had stuck it out there. If she had been a little more self-possessed . . . The manager, Mr Campbell, had seemed quite the gentleman, asking her how she liked working in the linen and hosiery department, often popping down from the third floor to say good morning. She soon learned why. He was old – at least forty-five, she supposed – and immaculately turned out, with a pocket square in blazing scarlet or gold to offset his dark double-breasted suits. She had once seen him in the Burlington Arcade reading a newspaper while a shoeblack worked away on his gleaming oxfords.

At first, when she was required at his office to help with the mail orders, she thought his standing rather close to her was a helpless eccentricity – she had noticed the tendency in others before. When he started to touch her she said nothing, but tried to keep her distance if they happened to be left alone together. He must have taken her silence as encouragement, because he became bolder, not just rubbing up against her but actually snaking his hand along her neck and shoulders. She didn't know what to do. She was friendly with a couple of the other assistants without their being actual friends, but she sensed that telling them about Mr Campbell's interferences would not be welcomed. They would think her a troublemaker, or the type of girl who sought attention. Her superior in the hosiery department was a middle-aged lady, Mrs Pearce, whose horn-rimmed spectacles alone were enough to repel any thought of confiding in her. Her obsequious regard for their employer left no doubt in Madeleine's mind whose side she would take if the story came out.

The next and last time it happened was one afternoon after Campbell had returned from lunch. She had been distracted by some footling paperwork and hadn't noticed him sidling into the room. Before she knew it he had twisted her around and pressed his mouth against hers; the smell of meat and alcohol warm on his breath made her recoil with nausea. She could not remember exactly what he said after she pulled away, but his tone suggested that she was being a spoilsport, and that all he was after was 'a bit of fun'. She was not entirely in command of herself as her open hand swung wildly at his face and connected with a smack that actually spun him sideways. When he righted himself his expression was one of such stupefied incomprehension that she felt suddenly inclined to laugh. Instead, she snatched the bright handkerchief from his breast pocket, wiped her mouth and threw it on the floor. 'You will not do that to me again,' she said quietly, and turned on her heel. She said nothing to anyone as she went downstairs to the staff cloakroom, retrieved her hat and coat and walked out of the shop.

It was the bravest thing she had ever done, though once the giddy sense of righteousness had evaporated she wondered if it wasn't also the stupidest. In her haste she had not even collected the previous week's money. The rent at the boarding house in Camden was cheap enough, but it still had to be paid. She would not go back to Chertsey, where she had lived on and off with her aunt since the age of twelve. It was not that Aunt Beryl had been unkind – merely unmaternal. Aside from arranging for her to attend the convent school and ensuring that she had regular meals and clean clothes, she seemed barely to know what to do with her niece. Beryl liked to go shopping, do crosswords, eat violet creams and hold bridge evenings with her WI friends. It was only in her late teens that Madeleine realised that children as a species bored her aunt into fits. So she had left

Chertsey for London two years ago, without regret on either side.

She had thought, naively, that it would be simple to get another job, but employers demanded references, and of course she had none from Diprose's. She knew not a single person she might call upon in London. She wasn't sure if her shyness was to blame, or whether circumstances had conspired in her failure to form friendships. An only child, she had a faint memory of her father, a lawyer's clerk in Dorchester who had been killed at Ypres in the autumn of 1917. She had been loved devotedly by her mother, a pale, beautiful and neurasthenic woman who was in and out of hospitals for most of Madeleine's short life. She had died of complications from pneumonia in 1926. If her aunt, living a distance from neighbours, had made little effort to bring out the gregarious instincts within her, convent school actively repressed them.

On her first or second day there she had formed a bond with the one child who looked lonelier than she did, a fourteen-year-old girl named Veronica whose skin was caramel-coloured from a childhood spent in India, where her father was a colonel in the army. Some girls laughed at the sing-song accent Veronica had acquired and called her a 'darkie'; Madeleine, however, was entranced by her extraordinarily pretty eyes and slim wrists. For weeks they were as inseparable as honeymooners, oblivious to all, until one of the nuns, Sister Ignatius, summoned the girls to her office for separate interviews. Madeleine could not imagine what she had done wrong, though Sister's tone as she spoke became metallic with admonition. Did she know that Veronica was actually a year older than her? Yes, she did, they knew each other's birthdays, it was one of the first things they had talked about. And what else did they talk about? Having never known an adult to express such interest in her, she responded with an earnest inventory of topics – dogs, music, parents, illness, food and (what was inexhaustible) the fascination of Veronica's life in India. The nun let a silence hang before she asked if there was not something odd about two girls becoming so close to one another. Madeleine didn't understand what she was being asked to admit, though she could tell from the pursing of her interrogator's mouth that she was not quite pleased. Another silence intervened, rather like the one in the confessional when the priest waited for you to list your sins. Eventually Sister Ignatius said, 'We do not encourage particular friendships among pupils at our school. They give rise to vanity and self-indulgence, and they trespass on the devotion that is more properly owing to Our Lord. Do you understand?'

She had nodded, not understanding at all. Later, she had asked Veronica about *her* interview, and the halting account she had given of Sister's counsel was no more enlightening than her own experience of it. They had not been forbidden to associate with each other – that would have been impossible – but it seemed that, once it had been noticed, the light and spontaneity began leaking out of their 'particular friendship'. Madeleine had sensed she was the keener of them to make things as they once were, hoping Veronica would settle back into being the affectionate and bewitching girl she had first known. And she had continued to hope even as Veronica drifted away, making other friends and apparently forgetting those early avowals of loyalty that remain, in some children's hearts, stronger than death. A year later she had disappeared, back to live with her family in India, and was never heard from again. It might have surprised her to know how lasting her effect had been on one particular friend from her convent days.

Madeleine's life had changed a few months ago, not long after she left Diprose's. She had been in a Corner House like this one, staring into the middle distance, pondering the very real possibility that she wouldn't be able to pay that week's rent, when a man slid softly into the bench opposite.

'Pardon me, miss, but you're breaking my heart.'

'– sorry?' she enquired, startled by the intrusion. He had taken off his hat and tilted his head in smiling sympathy.

'It's hurting me just to look at those big sad eyes of yours. It's like your sweetheart's just upped and left. I know, none of my business – you can tell me to buzz off if you like.'

His air of twinkling suavity suggested that she wouldn't. Madeleine regarded him hesitantly. He was thirtyish, well groomed, expensively dressed, and his manner, though forward, was not unpleasant. He had produced a silver cigarette case which he now held open across the table. She shook her head: years of inhaling her aunt's Pall Malls had put her off the habit. He took one himself and lit it, steering a jet of smoke sideways from his mouth. His name was Roderick Astill, and he worked as a booking agent for clubs in the West End, a line of business in which he appeared to be doing rather well.

'That's why you caught my eye,' he drawled. 'I thought – she must be a dancer.'

Madeleine frowned and looked away. 'Nothing like that. The only job I've ever done is shop assistant, and I lost that a few weeks ago.'

'Oh, shame. Left you a bit short for the rent, has it?' The precision of this shot in the dark unsettled her. She managed a little shrug. 'Too bad,' he continued. 'That's London – sort of place you could always do with a few bob more.'

Guarded at first, she gradually opened up to Mr Astill's keen-eyed charm – he was the sort her aunt used to describe as 'debonair'. Even the affected way he held a cigarette, between his middle and ring fingers, had a raffish appeal. He talked a great deal, but he listened too, when she was at last persuaded to tell him about her time in London, about

Campbell's vile behaviour and her fruitless search for a job ever since. The street lamps were casting daubs of yolky light on the cafe window before she realised it had gone seven o'clock. Mr Astill noticed her glancing at his wristwatch.

'Well, you've turned down a cup of tea, and you've turned down my cigarettes. Will it be third time lucky if I ask you to dinner?'

'Oh, no, really –'

'Come on, Madeleine. You look half starved.' He gave her a comical pleading look. 'I mean, you wouldn't want to hurt a chap's feelings, now . . .'

She replied, with a pained little smile, 'I don't want to hurt *anyone's* feelings.'

'Well, then!' he cried, giving the table a triumphant smack, as if the matter were decided. 'On with that coat, and we'll put our best foot forward.'

She could think of no reason to decline. He was probably right about her looking starved – she had been skimping on meals of late, desperate to make economies. She could do with a proper feed. And the company was far from disagreeable; he was not quite as smooth as he pretended to be, which she liked. It wasn't his cigarette case or the name-dropping that impressed her, but the endearing way he had conceded her right to tell him to 'buzz off'. Out on the street he crooked his arm in invitation, and she took it. They walked a little way up High Holborn before he stopped at a car, dark green and open-topped with a huge gleaming grille that made it look important. He was hovering about it proprietorially, and she blinked.

'Is this – *yours*?'

He laughed as he unlocked the passenger door. 'What, you think I'm a car thief?' Any lingering suspicion that he was just 'talk' fell away, and she hesitated again.

'Mr Astill, I'm not sure –'

'It's Roddy, please. Hop in, would you? – that dinner's not going to eat itself!'

He drove them into Soho and parked in a side street with the air of someone who might have owned the place. They ate at an Italian restaurant where the staff all knew him, and with the veal saltimbocca they drank a heavy plum-coloured wine, very different from the sort she used to sip after her aunt's bridge evenings. Mr Astill – Roddy – did most of the talking, which she didn't mind, though by the end of the night her head was swimming (the second bottle had come and gone) and she felt a bit of a fool as she stumbled on the way out. She worried he might try to take advantage of her when they were back in the car, but he played fair, and drove her home to Camden. Before she got out of the car he asked her if she would join him for another dinner, this Saturday.

Madeleine woke the next morning with a dry mouth, a crashing headache and a memory of having agreed to meet again. She ought to have said no, she wasn't sure why, though by the time Saturday came round she found herself excited at the thought of being taken out. When he called for her he looked pleased by the effort she had made: she was wearing her one good dress, crêpe de Chine in navy with a cream trim, her other purchase (at a staff discount) from Diprose's. It showed off her long legs, which she noticed him gazing at. This time he took her to a members' club in Mayfair where they dined in the company of Roddy's friends, most of them loud, good-looking types his own age, with a few older men he called – in a sly aside to her – 'hangers-on'. She was astounded by their capacity for alcohol, the women as well as the men, and though she couldn't keep up with that she joined them willingly enough in the dancing that followed at the next club. It was all very gay and exhilarating. Roddy, rarely straying from her side, made sure none of the younger chaps hogged her company, and once again drove her home through an unpeopled ash-grey dawn. 'You can consider yourself one of the fast set now,' he said, holding open the car door as if he were her chauffeur.

The following week they met for dinner again, only this time there was just one other with them, an older fellow named Brevett whom she recognised from the Saturday. His pudgy, sallow face expressed an air of impatience, as though he needed to be somewhere else. He took little interest in her, preferring to talk business with Roddy. Madeleine, not caring either way, acquiesced in the role of mute and drank the wine that Roddy absently poured from a carafe. When they repaired afterwards to a smart flat off Cavendish Square – it had a porter operating the lift – Brevett seemed to remember his manners, and pointed out to her a few land-marks visible through the huge picture window overlooking the city. He poured them all brandy in huge balloon glasses and played a lot of parping jazz records on his gramophone. Both men lit cigars the size of dynamite sticks. At some point a bottle of champagne was opened, and she downed a couple of glasses very quickly. By now the blood was drumming in her ears, and she resolved to give herself a good talking-to in the morning about alcohol; she liked it, but it plainly didn't like her.

She was examining a large abstract oil painting on the wall, mesmerised by its thick careless whorls of paint, when she sensed a shadow at her back. She looked round to find Brevett, his face flushed from drink and a light in his eye. Roddy, who'd been there five, maybe ten minutes ago, had disappeared.

'Come over here and let's finish this pop,' he said, steering her towards a couch and clunking down the champagne bottle on a low mirrored coffee table. Through the unsteadying grip of the drink she felt a shiver of anxiety, and her smile tightened as he allowed himself to cosy up against her.

'Roddy was right, you're a bonny wee lass,' he mused, then frowned as his hand encircled her pale wrist. 'Though you need some meat on you. Perhaps one should say a *bony* wee lass, ha ha!'

When he twisted himself round to kiss her neck she tensed, though she didn't pull away. 'Would you mind – not doing that?' she said, trying to sound friendly but firm. It was as though he hadn't heard, for instead of desisting he broadened his field of fire by caressing her knee.

'Mr Brevett, please,' she said, pushing the hand as it crept northwards up her thigh. 'I'm not . . .' she began, trying to keep her voice steady, 'I'm not what you think I am.'

He did stop then, and drew himself back to look at her. 'I see . . . Then, pray tell – what do *you* think you are?'

Madeleine blinked at him, hearing the amusement in his words. She might have told him she was a friend of Roddy's, but in the light of what was happening that could no longer be true. She was silent. Eventually she lifted her eyes to Brevett, who was glowering at her. 'Nothing? Let me put it another way. What exactly are you doing in a private residence, at this hour of the night, in the company of a man who has just paid for your supper?'

'I didn't – I thought it was – Roddy was –' she stuttered, the drink scrambling her tongue. It was true: she had presumed on a stranger's hospitality, had let someone else pick up the bill in exchange for – what? Her charming company? The company, it turned out, was a basic requirement, and her charm was neither here nor there. It was humiliating that she could be so naive, so unknowing. She had actually believed Roddy was *fond* of her . . . Her eyes had begun to glisten, but she bit back tears, sensing how much they would irritate him. Brevett stood up, and with an exasperated *harrumph* stalked off to the adjoining room. She heard him on the telephone, muttering angrily to someone she presumed was Roddy, for the only words she made out distinctly were '. . . for the sake of a silly tart who won't drop her drawers'. So that's what she was – not 'fast set' after all. His voice grumbled on for a few minutes more. When he emerged he was holding her coat.

'Here,' he said, throwing it on the couch next to her. 'Looks like our Mr Astill sold me a pup. Well . . . you live and learn.'

She sat there for some moments, not daring to raise her head. Brevett had planted himself squarely in front of the picture window, absorbed in its panoramic view west. She heard him light his cigar again. When he turned back to the room he looked surprised to find her still there.

'Go on, then,' he said wearily. 'Buzz off.'

Two days after this Roddy had called on her. This time he didn't even bother taking her to a cafe. They just sat in the car, his unsmiling gaze fixed on the windscreen as he recounted his terrible disappointment in her. There was a glint in his eyes that she hadn't seen before, and even his voice sounded different. It was still a businessman's voice, only now she understood what business he was in.

'I'm sorry,' she said. 'I just can't . . .'

He let a silence stretch out, then said, with slow deliberation, 'Madeleine, it's time to be honest. Aside from a pretty face, you have nothing of interest to anyone. I mean, *nothing* – no professional skills, no connections, no friends, no money. You are behind with your rent. You can barely afford to eat. You're not the type to go begging. So how do you propose to live?'

She swallowed hard. 'I – I could work in a shop, somewhere.'

'You've tried that one. Wouldn't call it a roaring success, would you?'

The salt sting threatened behind her eyes, and again she blocked it. The shame of it. The shame of it would kill her.

But then, who would know? Her parents were long gone. She had no friends – he was right about that – and nobody at her boarding house had a clue about her. She could return to Chertsey, to her aunt, but what promise of a life did that hold? It would crush her to go back there.

'So what's it to be?' said Roddy presently. He craned his head round to look at her. 'Shall we say eight thirty, tomorrow night?'

She stared dead ahead, and nodded.

'Good,' he said, and took out his wallet. He peeled off two five-pound notes and handed them to her. 'Buy a dress, a low-cut thing. Get two, one in black, one in red. Also stockings, and a bottle of perfume – something expensive. You can use what's left over for the rent.' He leaned across her suddenly, and for a moment she thought he was going to strike her, but he caught the handle and pushed the passenger door open. 'Off you go. Oh, and do something with your hair, for God's sake. It looks like a bloody sheep-dog's.'

That was in May. She had learned the routine in the months since – Roddy had provided an efficient and unsentimental education. She had learned what to say, and what not to say; when to stay, when not to stay. It surprised her how quickly she got used to it. She had imagined it would be disgusting, and it was, but not often, and not to the degree that she couldn't face it again. Roddy didn't treat her badly, and he paid enough for her to afford better digs, on Bayham Street. Most of the time she barely impinged on his notice; he had other girls – a whole stable, it seemed – to look after.

But she felt more alone than ever. During the day she would sit by the window in her bedroom and watch the people passing below, or else she would wander up Camden High Street and have tea in a cafe, mooching until her evening appointment. 'Maddy the moocher', Roddy called her. She was doing so right now, watching the old waitress on her rounds about the room. It was tempting to catch her eye and ask for a bun or a slice of cake, just so that she might chat with her for a few moments. But the woman was run off her feet – she didn't have time to idle away with customers. Madeleine touched her hand to her neck again; beneath the scarf she wore a necklace of bruises. So far she had managed to hide them from Roddy. If he saw them he would want the story right away, and she wasn't sure she could fool him.

It had happened about three weeks ago. She had been in Russell Square and, it being a warm day, she had bought a penny ice from the little stall and settled on one of the public benches. An armada of ragged white clouds was heaving across the sky. She hadn't noticed him approach, but nodded when the man asked her if he might sit down. He had a long-jawed sort of handsomeness, with eyes of a peculiar dark intensity. His hair had a youthful lustre – she wondered if he dyed it. They got talking, and she gathered that he was a commercial traveller down from the Midlands. He was rather well spoken. He asked some questions of her, intimating that he knew what line of work she was in. It seemed that he was staying at the hotel just over the way. Would she care to meet him up there in fifteen minutes? Madeleine had never done business with a client except through Roddy, and wondered if it was quite safe. But she had never been offered such money before. How would it be to earn something 'off the books'? She watched the man walk away across the square's garden and disappear beyond the perimeter railings.

Twenty minutes had gone before she made up her mind. She stole through the crowded foyer of the Imperial without catching anyone's eye and made for the lift. She got out at the fourth floor, unnerved by the sinister emptiness of the long corridor ahead, quite different from the teeming activity downstairs. Willing herself onwards, she gravitated past high arched windows and fire doors until she reached room 408. She knocked and entered, as he had instructed. The bedroom was empty, but he called to her from the bathroom that she should make herself comfortable. She looked about the room, drab and anonymous, with a nostril-twitching staleness from all the tobacco smoked by its previous occupants. The double bed's quilted headboard offered a forlorn touch of homeliness.

The first thing which struck her as odd was the absence of any luggage. Would a commercial traveller not have a suitcase lying about? She quickly peered into the living room, also empty. A minute or so passed before he emerged, jacketless, from the bathroom, drying his face on a towel. The second odd thing was that he closed the bathroom door with his hand sheathed by the towel, as though he feared contamination from the doorknob. The sleeves of his shirt had been rolled up to reveal meaty forearms, and he had removed his tie, which he was absently winding about his hands, trying different knots.

'Take off your coat,' he said in a voice that had lost the coaxing tone of earlier. He moved behind her, and she thought for a moment he was going to help her off with it. Instead he slipped his tie around her throat and spun her round to face him. 'This suits your colour,' he said, as he made a knot in the silk and fixed it about her throat. The colour of the tie was purple and black, which made her wonder why he thought it suited her. He was staring intently at her, his head very still like a snake's, and she felt a tiny spasm of fear. He grasped the tail of the tie in his hand and jerked it up very suddenly, his arm a gibbet with her head caught in the noose. She gasped in surprise, and he laughed, letting his arm drop. He told her to lie on the bed. As she did so she began to loosen the tie from her throat.

'Leave that alone,' he said in a toneless command. He

68

climbed onto the bed, straddling her. He bent his head over her, his eyes narrowing in enquiry. She noticed he had started to sweat – there were damp patches on his shirt and fine beads of moisture along his hairline. There was something unsettled, something 'off', about his expression, and she realised that her impulsive decision had been a mistake. She was beginning to see why he had not touched his hand to the doorknob – he would leave no trace of himself here.

'I'm sorry,' she said, trying to rise, 'I really think I ought to go.'

'What?' he said distantly.

'Please, I'd like to go. Please.'

He gave her a mock frown of disappointment. 'Go? I'm just getting started.' His weight pinned her to the bed. He had taken the tie in both hands and was tightening it again around her neck. She made a panicked grab at him and caught hold of his hair before he shook her off. His sinewy frame was far too strong for her. She heard herself pleading with him, but he wasn't listening, only watching, his eyes twin black holes of ruthless compulsion. As she choked and struggled, she prayed to be spared, though no words could form in her throat. She hadn't prayed in some time, since those nights she thought about her father, who was dead, and her mother, who was soon to be. Going, going . . . but suddenly the agonising pressure on her windpipe lifted. The man had raised himself up, his body tensed like a dog. It was a knock at the door. He clamped his hand fiercely over her mouth and whispered through clenched teeth, *Not a sound*.

There was a pause, and then a voice came, a woman's, clear and finely spoken: 'Is everything all right?' Madeleine felt her life trembling in the balance: if whoever was at the door decided to walk away, she would die in this room. A drop of sweat from the man's forehead ploshed on her cheek. The voice came again, more urgently: the woman was going to call reception and ask the manager to come up. A furious twitch had started beneath his eye as he seemed to consider the situation, then he rolled off her. Madeleine, sobbing for air, clambered off the bed, dizzy from the lack of oxygen. She staggered a few steps, picked her coat off the floor, and looked round at him. He was rolling down his shirtsleeves, his dark eyes glistening and malignant, like a predatory animal driven off its kill. Yet all he did was raise a finger to his lips, as if it were understood that the price of her escape was silence: he seemed to know that she wasn't the sort who would tell.

She bolted out of the room, startling the woman outside the door, who jumped back to let her pass. Her heart was a wild cat pounding inside her chest as she ran down the corridor, eyes blinded by tears. She reached the lift and stabbed a frantic hand against the bell: she didn't wait for it, too terrified to linger, and blatted through a nearby fire door instead. Not until she was outside on Russell Square did she slow down, keeping her head low: the shock of the experience thrummed in her blood, had set her limbs to trembling. She knew how lucky she had been, but every time she pictured his face – the face of a man who had wished her dead – she felt another helpless convulsion shake her body. Her throat ached. Halfway down Guilford Street she saw an old public drinking fountain, and she stopped, suddenly weary. Turning the little brass tap she splashed water on her face, and felt around her neck, tender, and throbbing in agony. The taste of bile in her mouth was bitter. The trembling wouldn't stop, but she didn't care: it meant she was alive.

"Scuse me, dear, someone's waving at you.' Madeleine looked up. It was the nice waitress, nodding towards the cafe window, outside of which Roddy now stood. He was pointing with theatrical impatience at his watch. She was on the clock.

'Thank you,' she said to the waitress, who smiled and moved away – she was on the clock too. Madeleine stood and shrugged on her coat. She counted out some loose change for the two pots of tea, and a tip. On her way out she didn't notice the newspaper discarded at the next table, folded to a page featuring the story of a recent murder, inset with a reproduced sketch of a man's face. So she remained quite unaware of herself as perhaps the only other person in London who could say whether that face belonged to the 'Tiepin Killer'.

# 5

Nina had never been inside the Nines, though she knew men other than Stephen who were members. It was a tall Regency terrace on Dover Street, its dark brick facade projecting an air of such unillusioned authority that no comment upon itself seemed necessary. As she made her way across the black-and-white-tiled floor she wondered at those men who passed the stations of their life – public school, university, club, boardroom – exclusively within wood-panelled interiors such as this. Hard to imagine what they would make of her landlady's wallpaper.

The wizened porter who took her coat and hat directed her up the balustraded staircase. She passed the critical gaze of grandees trapped in portraits from the previous century. 'The Nine's Club' had been founded in the 1860s by a cabal of men prominent in literary and artistic circles, the most renowned of the eponymous nine being Dickens and Thackeray. One of the two had resigned (Nina couldn't recall which) following a spat over a close friend who had been humiliatingly black-balled. The Nines had had its ups and downs since then – as well as Dickens (or Thackeray) it had also lost the apostrophe from its name – but was presently enjoying a period of fash-ionable loucheness. There was even a waiting list to join. Entering the bar, she spotted Stephen deep in conversation with a man of about his own age, whom she half recognised.

'And here she is,' said Stephen, rising from the table and dipping his head graciously to her proffered hand. He introduced his companion as Ludovic Talman, a smiling, slick-haired man with a pinkish complexion. He gave a little bow of acknowledgement, then glanced back at Stephen. Nina had the feeling that she had interrupted a conversation which they would prefer to keep private. At Stephen's prompting – both men were drinking gin and it – she ordered a slightly reckless Martini.

'Stephen said you're having a great success at the Strand. *The Second Arrangement*?'

'Yes, we've been lucky, it's enjoying quite a run,' she replied, still trying to place him.

'Nina's wonderful in it,' said Stephen, gazing at her.

'I'm sure she is,' said Talman with an appraising gleam in his eye. 'I hardly get to the theatre these days.'

'You know that Ludo's running things at Marlborough Studios now?'

Nina experienced a tiny frisson of excitement, though she didn't bat an eyelid. *Of course*. Talman was a film producer who turned out comedies and melodramas on a shoestring and then invested a fierce energy in promoting them. Nina, who took a lofty view of screen acting, was nevertheless alert to the vista of opportunities an introduction might throw open. She resolved right there to put on a sparkle for him.

Talman noticed her gazing about the high-ceilinged room. 'Your first time here, Miss Land?'

'It's Nina, please . . . Yes, it is. I've a feeling this place hasn't changed much since Victoria's day.'

'Quite right,' said Talman, with a sidelong glance at two elderly gents murmuring over their drinks at the next table. He dropped his voice. 'One might say the same of our members. I've just been talking on that very matter with Stephen. I'm trying to secure his help.'

73

Nina looked quizzically at Stephen, who gave a characteristic shrug to indicate that Talman should explain.

'I'm on the club committee,' he continued, 'and we've recently come to an agreement that the Nines needs a bit of a spring clean – a dab of colour here and there.'

Nina thought of the saturnine portraits she had passed on the stairs. 'I can see why, but . . .' Her eyes darted to the adjacent pair of old boys.

Talman understood her look. 'Oh, it wouldn't be anything to frighten the fogeys, of course. My main idea is for a mural – along that wall – a group portrait of the club's great and good.'

'That might be rather spiffy.'

'I know! We're aiming for a British version of that Fantin-Latour painting, *Un Coin de Table*, d'you know it? Unfortunately we've had quite a job persuading our designated portraitist.' He nodded across the table at Stephen, who was at last obliged to speak.

'I'm honoured to be asked, of course, but – I fear the amount of work it'll involve. I've a fair few things to be getting on with.'

Nina modulated her tone to a husky appeal. 'Oh but you must!' she said to Stephen. 'Only imagine your work displayed in this setting. And, let's be honest, nobody else will do it so well as you.'

Stephen gave her a shrewd look, conscious of being soft-soaped. 'I'll have to think about it . . .'

Talman seemed to twig a weakening in his reluctance. 'D'you know, that's most remarkable. Miss Land – Nina – may I congratulate you? I've been pleading with him this last hour and got nowhere. But the minute you show up he begins to yield –'

'I've not yielded to anything,' said Stephen quickly, but it was clear Talman had scented victory, for he resorted to a line few artists had ever been able to resist.

'The fee would make it worth your while, of course.'

Stephen offered a distracted smile, and said that his agent would need to be consulted – which he knew was tantamount to a surrender. Talman gave Nina a surreptitious wink, as though acknowledging a successful alliance. She sensed that this might be her moment.

'I suppose you're preparing a new film,' she said airily.

'Oh, I've always got something in the works,' Talman said with a pleasant grin. 'I'd read an outline for a murder mystery, but recent events seem to be outrunning whatever our scriptwriters could invent.'

Nina, with a tingle of foreboding, said, 'What events would they be?'

'Why, the "Tiepin Murders" of course. A crazed killer on the loose – his signature a grisly violation – a city in terror! Now hasn't that all the elements of a box-office smash?'

'It needs an ending,' said Stephen quietly, catching Nina's eye. She couldn't tell if he was warning or encouraging her.

'True. But quite a stroke of luck about the witness, and the sketch. Of course the man could be anyone – the police made three arrests on the strength of it and had to let them all go. I joked with one of our people at a production meeting that it looked a bit like him, and he came back, quick as a flash, that I was the only man at the table wearing a tiepin! Just like Wyley here . . .'

Stephen had already heard it. Tiepins had quickly become a subject of macabre drollery in club rooms and saloon bars – to wear one at the moment was practically to invite chaffing. He had an inkling that Nina was about to let the cat out of the bag, and attempted a diversion.

'Shall we order some lunch?'

Talman, who had not been a scheduled guest, began to make his excuses when Nina stopped him with a conspiratorial touch on his sleeve. 'I might be able to help you with that story.'

75

Talman looked bemused. 'Really?'

She saw Stephen shake his head in admonition but plunged on with an account of the afternoon at the hotel, her unwitting interruption of the woman's ordeal in room 408, and her fleeting glimpse of the man who was now, beyond question, the chief suspect in the police's investigation. She was careful in this to omit any reference to Stephen's involvement. When she had told the same story to the man at Marylebone police station she had twice come close to letting his name slip. Her inquisitor, Detective Inspector Cullis, had conducted the occasion with an air of scrupulous courtesy, notwithstanding the suspicion on his thin face that Nina was not playing straight. Convinced that her evidence would be welcomed as a gesture of responsible citizenship, she had not bothered to rehearse her story and, under questioning, had come up short. Why had she left it five days before coming forward? What was she doing on the fourth floor of the hotel anyway? Did she not think of reporting the incident immediately to the hotel manager? Sounding like a liar to her own ears, she was stumbling through the interrogation when Cullis examined the sketch – 'her' sketch – of the man she had seen.

'It's an accomplished piece of work,' he mused. 'Did you study art?'

'No, I didn't. I studied drama.'

'Ah, of course. Very professional, anyway.'

'Thank you,' she replied warily.

Cullis then opened his desk drawer and took out a pencil. 'I noticed you haven't signed it,' he said, pushing the pencil across to her.

'Well, it's not that sort of – I don't intend to *exhibit* it.' Her laugh sounded uneasy.

'But if you wouldn't mind, anyway, just so's we know it's yours.'

For a moment she thought he was pulling her leg, but his expression was blank. She picked up the pencil and, with a little shrug, signed her name beneath the drawing. The detective took back the sketch, and fixed a curious, narrow-eyed look on her.

'"Nina Land",' he read. 'That's interesting . . .'

'That's my name,' Nina said, wondering where this was going.

'No, I mean, it's interesting because – well, if you examine the angle at which the charcoal is stroked over the paper, it looks as though the artist is left-handed. But you signed it, I see, with your right hand.'

Nina felt prickles of sweat beneath her arms, but she strove to keep her voice light. 'I didn't realise you were an art critic as well, Inspector.'

Cullis gave a sardonic chuckle. 'Not as such, miss. I was just speculating . . . but if you say it's your work, why should I doubt it?'

'Why indeed?' she said, unsettled by his ambiguous tone. 'Will there be anything else?'

There was nothing else, for the moment. Nina sensed, however, that her act of public-spirited decency had back-fired, and that Cullis had smelt a rat. He had already seen how nervous she was; that last exchange, about the sketch, had nearly undone her altogether. Something in his pale eyes, or in his voice, suggested he was on to her imposture. As soon as she was allowed to leave the station she hurried across Marylebone Road and into a public house, where she bolted down a large brandy.

Nina also omitted this interview in her account to Talman, who blew out his cheeks. 'Well! Face to face with the Tiepin Killer! You showed a rare pluck confronting him like that. The police must be grateful to you.'

'I suppose so,' she said, blinking out a sudden image of Cullis's face.

'What do you think of this one?' he said to Stephen admiringly.

Stephen gave a tight smile and looked at Nina. 'She's got some nerve.'

'And what of the girl he almost – did she go to the police too?'

Nina shook her head. 'They think she was just someone he picked up. But she'll know better than anyone what he looks like.'

Stephen, who had twigged Nina's bid for Talman's interest, decided to take a direct approach. 'Are you still casting, Ludo? Nina has talents other than crime-fighting.'

Talman, apparently unaware he had been played, now became flustered. 'Oh, but of course – your agent must – please, send my office a publicity photograph, and we can – there's another casting arranged . . .'

Nina, pretending surprise at this offer, said, 'I'd be very pleased to.'

'The pleasure is mine, dear lady,' said Talman, who had risen and was offering them both his hand. 'And thank you for that marvellous story.'

Stephen, suddenly alarmed, said, 'Ludo, please don't spread it about. Nina's a witness in a murder case – it's strictly hush-hush.'

Talman marked his solemn nod of agreement with a finger to his lips, which did nothing to reassure him: he knew the producer to be a waggle-tongue. The moment he had gone Nina gave Stephen a wide-eyed look of girlish excitement.

'Darling, you're so clever to introduce me! D'you think he was serious about an audition?'

'He certainly took a shine to you,' he replied. 'Though I'm not sure that was the best way to secure his patronage.'

'What d'you mean?'

Stephen paused, lit a cigarette and blew a pensive jet of smoke. 'I mean, it's not safe to go blabbing about your involvement in this thing to Ludo – to *anyone*. The police won't like it, either. They're obliged to protect your identity.'

Nina shook her head. 'Don't be silly. I'm perfectly safe, and I don't intend to go *blabbing* in any case. I'm just thrilled at the idea – a film for Marlborough! I didn't realise you even knew him.'

'You'd be surprised at the people I know,' said Stephen wryly. 'I half wonder if Talman has asked me to do that mural just for the sort I can bring in.'

'Oh – such as?'

He suppressed a weary sigh. 'Clients of mine – members of the nobility, society types. I can think of someone straight away that Ludo will beg me to approach.'

'Who?'

'Well . . . try the most famous man in England.'

Nina gave a little giggle. 'Um, the King?'

By way of reply Stephen held her gaze. Nina's mouth fell open. '*No . . .*'

He nodded faintly. 'Few years ago, at a weekend shoot. We weren't even properly introduced. David – as he was then – started chatting to me, I think, because we were the only men there not wearing hats.'

'Heavens,' breathed Nina, more impressed than she wished to be. 'What was he like?'

'Friendly, in a distant sort of way. He had no idea who I was, because the next time we encountered one another he asked me how the work was going on my *symphony*.'

Nina laughed. 'A royal connection, all the same – and he's a member of this place?'

'No, but he's been in a few times, and I think his grand-father was an honorary president back in the long ago.'

'So you may end up painting the King?'

'Very unlikely. He's got other things occupying him at present – affairs of the heart, you know.'

'You mean, the American woman?'

Stephen nodded. 'According to those in the know, he's quite besotted with her – won't give her up for anything.'

'How romantic. Makes me think rather better of him . . .' She turned a narrow look on Stephen. 'What would you do in his place?'

He heard her meaning in the question. 'I hope I'd – do the right thing. Now,' he said, hailing a waiter, 'how about that lunch?'

On his way to the Ivy Jimmy saw two young men being dragged into a scuffle with a group of drinkers outside a pub. The latter were tough working men, older, who cupped their cigarettes inside brawny hands and stared hard into their pints. They had stopped them with an abrupt call, and were now using their weight and number to push them around. Jimmy would have felt sorry for the victims but for the fact they were both dressed in a uniform of black shirts and trousers. He despised this idiotic business of playing at Mussolini, though you didn't see so many of them on the streets nowadays, and the *Mail* had gone very quiet since its rallying 'Hurrah for the Blackshirts' a couple of years back. One of the youths, having taken a punch to the head, had collapsed on the pavement. Passers-by were dodging their way around the brawl. Jimmy would have done too, had he not been watching the scene through the window of his idling cab.

In the lobby the Ivy doorman, Abel, helped him out of his coat.

'How are ye keepin', Mr Erskine?'

'Oh, tolerably well, thanks. Anyone in last night?'

Abel gave a brisk shake of his head. 'No, sair. Only riff-raff.'

In the restaurant the hubbub of the lunch crowd was warming to a fine crescendo, just before the second bottle turned them rowdy. The decorous waltz of the white-jacketed waiters around the tables and the stained glass of the mullioned windows always conjured for him the image of a first-class dining room on a luxury liner – only nicer, because you weren't trapped at sea. Lunch was Jimmy's favourite time, and today's was a proper occasion, the launch of his new book. He always celebrated at the Ivy, though when his publishers had baulked at the expense he had whittled down the invitees from twenty-five to twelve, not without some whingeing on his part. As he approached the long corner banquette it pleased him to see that he had been seated at the head, between László and his agent Claude, his bald head almost glossy in the light. 'O vision entrancing!' cried László, his sweet gargoyle features crinkling into a baby-toothed smile. 'James, you've some catching up to do,' at which he grabbed for the bottle of champagne and began filling a coupe.

'Greetings, all,' Jimmy called down the table, feeling an agreeable surge of bonhomie. How delightful to preside over a gathering of his familiars – his peers, if not quite his equals – knowing they were there to celebrate *him*. Well, that, and of course to eat and drink, buckshee. From the other end of the table Edie Greenlaw, his actress friend, waved and blew him a flamboyant kiss. They had met one night shortly after he had given a stinking review to a play in which she starred, though he had singled out her performance for praise. On being introduced she had said to him: 'I suppose that, unloved as you must be, you are the least loathsome of your species.' 'I will cherish that compliment, madam,' he replied. They had both laughed, and ended up having dinner together.

Edie was the only woman invited. On either side of her were Gilbert and Barry from the *Chronicle*, then the impresario Felix Croker, who already looked a bit tight, fellow drama critics Rufus Forbuoys and Dickie Mellinger, his publisher Jack Voysey, and his dear friend Peter Liddell, who was of the same vintage as László. But then his eye stopped on a vacant space.

'We are only eleven. Where's Tom?' he said to no one in particular.

László shrugged. 'Probably typing up your copy. Or fobbing off the tax inspector. Or tidying your flat. The slave's lot.'

'Tom isn't a *slave*,' he said, resenting László's shrewdness.

'He's your loyal factotum,' said Claude, which was meant to be supportive but didn't sound quite right either.

'Well,' he said, feigning nonchalance, 'we'd better get on and order.'

László and Claude resumed an argument they were having about Wagner, to which Jimmy made distracted contribution. He was still preoccupied with Tom, and the possible reasons for his absence. They had not been getting on of late, and Jimmy could only just admit to himself that it was his fault. It was more or less by chance that Tom had become his secretary – and factotum – nine years ago, and he had pretty much run Jimmy's life for him ever since. For most of that time they had rubbed along in bickering companionship. But their most recent row had been terrible. It had blown up over a typewriter, of all things: Tom had been on at him to replace the ancient one, and Jimmy had kept refusing, on the grounds of needless expense. They had argued about it on and off for months. When, finally, the machine had packed up for good, his hand was forced; a stationer he knew in Holborn did him a deal on a 1932 flat-top Smith-Corona in green. It was a beauty, they agreed, and peace was restored *chez* Erskine once more.

It had lasted until the moment Tom received the following week's pay packet and found it twenty shillings light. Jimmy explained that he'd taken out his share of the typewriter's cost, since they both used it. Tom had hit the roof, launching a tirade of wild abuse and shaking with such a fury that

Jimmy worried he might have a turn. Instead he disappeared for three days. When he returned to the flat neither made any mention of the row, so it had hung in the air ever since. For the last few weeks they had exchanged a minimum of tight-lipped civilities. He had felt a quiver of guilt, though not enough to apologise, or to return the money he had docked. The worst of it was that Tom's outburst seemed born of grievances held long before the provocation of the typewriter. But still he had said nothing. 'Do unto others as you would have them do unto you' was, he thought, an excellent principle – for others.

'James. *James?*' Someone was hauling him back to the present. The head of a grilled trout eyed him morosely from his plate. He had scarcely noticed himself eating. László was staring at him in puzzlement. 'Are you all right, my dear fellow?'

'Yes . . . of course I am,' he said defensively.

'You looked like a tart in a trance,' said Felix Croker.

'Was it a vision, or a waking dream?' asked Peter with his mild doctorly concern.

'Oh, I was just thinking of some unpleasantness I saw on the way here. Two of Mosley's idiots getting seven bells knocked out of 'em.'

'Serves them right,' said Claude. 'You know he's marching through the East End next week?'

'Someone'd better pull up the drawbridge,' said Croker with a snigger. 'They'll be out for the Hebrew's blood.'

László, the only Jew present, was used to such chaffing. 'The Englishman's home being his castle – yes, I see your meaning, my dear Croker, ha ha. Alas, my boarding house has not been equipped with such an amenity. The drawbridge is not much favoured anywhere in Shoreditch, I believe. But perhaps I may importune my landlady to prepare a cauldron of boiling oil for the occasion?'

Jimmy felt his heart ache as he listened to László's

courteous English, still inflected with traces of his Hungarian forefathers. They had come to London in the last century seeking a refuge from the wildfires of local anti-Semitism. The young László had been a prodigy at the violin, and the pride of his family. At nine years old he was playing solo at the Queen's Hall; at twelve he had written an opera. Alas, as he matured into nervous youth, his public recitals became faltering and error-strewn, so much so that he eventually admitted defeat and stopped performing. Now in middle age he scraped by as a music teacher and lived in what was practically a hovel off Commercial Road. He was Jimmy's closest friend; sometimes, he thought, his only friend.

'You must come and stay with me, László, out of harm's way,' he said.

'That is most kind of you, James, but it would be simply *crazy* to hand those Fascist fellows the victory by scurrying hither and thither.' Crazy, which he pronounced 'chray-zee', was László's favourite word.

'I'm afraid there's going to be an awful lot of scurrying if Herr Hitler continues unchecked,' said Peter.

'Depends how far they're prepared to let him go,' said Claude. 'Austria will be next.'

Barry said with a journalist's decisiveness, 'It's war, sure as eggs is eggs.'

Croker shook his head. 'You're wrong about that. We fought Germany in a British quarrel. We aren't going to fight them in a Jewish one.'

'That, may I say, is spoken like a true Mosleyite,' said Peter. 'In any case it's not just Hitler. Look at what the Italians did in Abyssinia. Gassed the poor blighters.'

'Abyssinia is a long way from Charing Cross.'

'Not for an air force it isn't.'

More Cassandra-like forecasts and counter-forecasts flew back and forth as Germany's expansionist ambitions were debated. Jimmy, impatient at not being the centre of attention, looked down the table at Jack Voysey, who seemed to read the appeal in his eyes, for a few moments later he tapped on his wine glass and stood up.

'Gentlemen – oh, and Miss Greenlaw, I beg your pardon – I'm so pleased we are gathered to celebrate the connoisseurship of a very singular man. Jimmy, as he has written somewhere, has a great taste for old books, old manners, old wine, old music –'

'And young men,' snickered Croker, just audibly.

'– but it is his marvellous instinct for identifying what's new in drama which has been his special gift to readers. This collection of his latest reviews and essays, *Withering Slights*, shows the full measure of the man' – there was more stifled tittering at that – 'in his wit, his erudition, his incomparable discernment. It is a book we are very proud to publish. So kindly raise your glass – to Jimmy.'

Voices rang in enthusiastic echo of the toast. Somebody called out 'Speech!' and Jimmy, needing no encouragement, rose to his feet.

'Thank you, Jack, for that ebullition of unmitigated generosity. A newspaper man once wrote of me that "you could learn more from Erskine when he's wrong than from most other critics when they're right". I suppose he meant that as a compliment. What I would say to him, in all humility, is that I haven't been wrong about a play since 1924, and on *that* night I happened to be afflicted with a head cold.' This provoked a gratifying ripple of laughter, though Claude's murmur of 'Very true' somehow flattened it as a comic sally. Having warmed them up with a few of his shorter anecdotes, he took a deep breath. 'There is another I would like to thank today, someone who has read the proofs of my last six books, corrected them – even, I might say, improved them. He has been a punctilious editor, a faithful understudy, and a cheering companion of more first nights than I care to remember. He also gave me the title of this latest tome. I only wish he was at table with us now, but I shall toast him all the same – to my secretary, Tom Tunner.'

As the toasts dwindled in chorus, László, who alone of them knew the truth of Jimmy's debt to Tom, said, 'Where *has* the dear fellow got to? James, you did remember to invite him –'

'For God's sake, man, who d'you think organised this damned lunch?' Jimmy snapped, unable to keep the irritation out of his voice, and László shrank back in surprise. Peter, quick to mollify, looked about him.

'While we wait for pudding, shall we have a round of Five Greatest?'

A mixture of groans and cheers met this suggestion. Jimmy loved to make lists of his favourite things, and 'Five Greatest' was a parlour game that allowed him wide indulgence. That he was the authority on theatre nobody at the table would dare to question: he had seen more plays, and more of the great stage performers, than all of them put together. Yet he also prized his discrimination in many other fields of interest, including horses, wine, painting, American film and French literature. It didn't much matter what was at issue: Jimmy was confident that in any dispute over taste he would always carry the day. He looked along the table in search of challengers.

Rufus Forbuoys, an elderly theatre critic with a face like a jaundiced owl, spoke up. 'I wonder, Jimmy, how you are on cricket . . .'

'Pretty good,' said Jimmy, which counted as modesty from him.

'Right, then. The five greatest batsmen?'

Jimmy protruded his lip thoughtfully. 'Well, you'd start with W.G., of course. Then the three aitches – Hobbs, Hammond, Hendren. And Bradman, on behalf of the colonies.'

There ensued some debate over whether Sandham and Hayward should be in the running. Edie Greenlaw looked around, bemused. 'Can you explain what sort of game this is?'

'Hard to say,' said Jack.

'But – how does one *win*?'

Dickie Mellinger shook his head. 'Not that kind of game, poppet. It's really just a chance to show off.'

'You pick a subject, and Jimmy will give you the five best examples off the top of his head – or you challenge him with a better one.'

'And then he tells you that you're wrong.'

Edie frowned lightly. 'What d'you mean by "wrong"? It's just an opinion.'

Nobody deemed this worthy of a reply. Peter said, 'How about . . . five greatest names in Dickens?'

Jimmy nodded in approval. 'Splendid, Peter. Let's see . . . Poll Sweedlepipe, Jerry Cruncher, Podsnap, Wackford Squeers . . . Mrs Todger!'

Hoots of laughter and mock-affronted 'oohs' greeted this last. 'How about Dick Swiveller?' called Croker.

'Are you talking about a character or an occupation?' said Jimmy, catching the ribald mood.

'I always liked the sound of Tulkinghorn,' said Claude, not catching the mood at all, 'but I won't challenge the master.'

Jimmy replied with a gracious nod, then glanced at László, who had fallen silent since his snappish rebuke. Seeking forgiveness, Jimmy decided on a subject to bring his friend back. 'Let's have a music round, what d'you say?'

'I'd say let's have a different game,' said Edie, and was immediately shouted down. Greatest operas was considered too boring. Greatest symphonies was too easy. Then Dickie Mellinger suggested string quartets, and Jimmy was off and running.

'Haydn's Emperor, Mozart's K. 575, "Rasumovsky", "Death and the Maiden". And Chopin Op. 9, number 2. How about that?'

'Sound, very sound,' said Peter.

'What do you say, László?' asked Jimmy.

László, seeming to hear the apology in Jimmy's tone, nodded his head. 'All good. Perhaps great. But not the *greatest*. With respect to my friend, I would list them so: Purcell's G major fantasia, my beloved Brahms in C minor. Charles Ives's second. Ravel's one and only. And Beethoven's Op. 131, which the man himself called the greatest of his late quartets. *C'est tout!*'

Jimmy listened in a kind of wonder. Where friends were concerned, his expectations of intellectual replenishment were low. You kept bringing a bucket to the well, and found it nearly dry – it did not take long to discover the shallowness of their conversational range. So he associated with them out of mere habit and affection. László was the exception. You dropped the bucket, and when you hauled it up there was always something surprising from him, something that slightly altered your view of things. He had known László for nearly twenty-five years, yet to his knowledge they had never once discussed Purcell, or Charles Ives. He sensed the table awaiting his response, the critic's verdict on the amateur.

'Bravo, my dear. I couldn't have chosen better myself – and didn't.'

László, warming to this benediction, revealed a toothy smile like two octaves of a miniature piano. He had the sudden pleased look of a twelve-year-old boy. Peter gave him a little pat on the back. The arrival of the pudding trolley put an end to the competitive jollity, and while the others were umming and aahing over the *tarte aux pommes* Jimmy ordered a bottle of Sauternes to see them through.

Felix Croker, a cigar in blast, narrowed his eyes at the

host. 'Heard you've signed up for Carmody's charity thing, Jimmy.'

Had he? Jimmy couldn't remember. Perhaps Tom had replied on his behalf. Unwilling to be thought dozy, or senile, he nodded.

'Gerald Carmody?' said Peter, incredulous. 'Why on earth would you be knocking about with him?'

Jimmy shook his head. 'I don't – I'm not. He ambushed me at a press night claiming to know me –'

'It's for a good cause, mind,' interposed Croker. 'To save the old Marquess from going bankrupt. I've put my name down.'

'But you know the fellow's a blackshirt,' said Peter, and turned to László, 'and a Jew-baiter.'

'Actually he's parted from Mosley,' said Barry, through a mouthful of pastry. 'A mutual dislike. Carmody's now running an outfit called the British People's Brigade. Sad, really – do you remember when they used to call him Labour's coming man?'

'I can think of other things to call him,' said Peter. 'Honestly, Jim, do you want to be seen keeping company with a – a Fascist bully?'

'But it's got nothing to do with politics,' said Jimmy, suddenly alarmed. 'The fellow is trying to save his theatre. We can't have it go dark, can we?'

'Indeed not,' said Croker. 'Carmody's politics are his own business. We are simple theatre folk pledging our support for a great old stager.'

And our money, thought Jimmy, wondering how his finances stood at present. He'd been avoiding an interview with the Inland Revenue for months. Peter meanwhile was muttering darkly to László and shooting looks in his direction – for heaven's sake! – as if Jimmy had just arranged supper with Mussolini himself. He rummaged for an emergency excuse.

'Really, Peter, it's just a charity dinner. And I only signed up as a favour to a friend.'

'Oh – who?'

That tore it. 'Stephen Wyley.' The fib was out before he could stop himself.

'The painter? I didn't know you knew him.'

'One moves in different circles . . .' But now a few of them were staring at him interestedly: the dropped name had made a louder splash than he'd intended. He would have to bluff it. Croker's ears seemed to twitch like antennae.

'Aren't you the dark horse? Why have you been keeping him from us?'

'Well, we're not close . . .'

Peter gave him a knowing look. 'Is he – from our end of the ballroom?'

'No, no, he's married,' said Jimmy, hoping not to be tested on his acquaintanceship any further.

'Oh well, mustn't touch him if he's *married*,' said Croker.

'Pity, that,' mused Dickie Mellinger. 'He looks such a nice boy.'

Jack Voysey, looking uncomfortable, said, 'Now, now, gentlemen. Jimmy, I'd be most interested to meet your friend Wyley – there's been talk in the office about doing a book on him. So far he's resisted, but if we could approach him informally . . .'

Jimmy smiled wanly. 'Well, I could ask.'

Jack tapped his nose, as if the deal was done. Jimmy brooded for a moment; he realised that his ambition to be painted by Wyley had seduced him into the falsehood. And at the heart of that ambition was – what? Vanity, for sure, but something else, something deeper. To be memorialised by one of the leading portraitists of the day was a validation of his life's work. They might not dedicate a statue to a critic, but who would deny James Erskine a painting? Warmed by this thought, he called for more wine.

At ten past three, just after Barry and Gilbert had headed back to Fleet Street and a mood of leave-taking descended on the table, the missing guest finally arrived. Edie was the first to see him approaching.

'Darling! Whatever's happened to you?'

'It's Banquo's ghost,' said Jack.

Tom, naturally pale-skinned, was indeed wraithlike, and a raw purplish bruise glistened on his cheek. He looked groggy, and Peter rose solicitously to help the latecomer fold himself into the seat next to Edie. All eyes were on him.

'I do apologise to you all. I'm afraid I was' – he gave a forlorn little chuckle – 'unavoidably detained.'

Jimmy, incredulous horror in his gaze, thought of the blackshirt fracas he had witnessed on the way. 'My dear fellow, what in heaven's name – were you involved in that affray on Shaftesbury Avenue?'

Tom shook his head, batting away the question. 'Please don't concern yourselves. It was nothing, just a silly accident. Now I wonder if I may beg a cup of coffee?'

While László squabbled with Peter over whose honour this would be, Tom said quietly to Edie, 'So – what have I missed?'

'Ooh, your ears must have been burning. Jimmy gave a speech, ever so amusing, and of course most of it about himself. Only he ends it with this big vote of thanks – to you! Didn't he, László?'

László nodded solemnly. His gaze had turned somewhat tender since Tom had sat down. 'I have not often heard James speak so very *sincerely*. He called you his greatest editor and most loyal companion – and moreover said you furnished him with the title of this book!'

Tom blinked his surprise. '*Jimmy* said that? László, either you've had too much to drink, or *he* has.'

But László shook his head, and permitted himself to clutch Tom's arm in emphatic denial of the charge. 'Not I, dear boy. Those were his words. Miss Edith will be my witness.'

Edie smiled. "Strue. Though poor László nearly got his head bitten off when he suggested Jimmy had forgotten to invite you. "Who the bloody hell d'you think organised this lunch?"' she said, in droll mimickry of Jimmy's bluster.

László giggled, as a schoolboy might at his pal's twitting of the master. Tom looked up the table at his employer, face now bleared with drink, a stray gobbet of chocolate blancmange flecking his shirt front.

'That's our Jimmy,' he said to Edie, with a thoughtful smile. 'He immatures with age.'

# 6

The late-morning sun, silvery and thin, peered through veils of cloud that faded to wisps. The elusive alternation of gloom and light was unsettling, for no one could rightly say what sort of day it was. Madeleine had been wandering in Covent Garden. With her work confined to the evening, she was at a loose end during the day, and had got into the habit of long aimless walks. She would leave her boarding house in Camden mid-morning and strike out, usually to the west, lingering in a park if it was fine or else in a cafe when she got tired. Roddy had got that right: she was a moocher. One afternoon she had gone as far as Chelsea Embankment, and had spent so long gazing at the river that a policeman had stopped to ask if anything was the matter.

She continued through the market's cawing tumult of traders and hawkers until she came to one of the cobbled byways that veered off towards Drury Lane. It was an odd thing about London, she thought, the way you could be in the hurly-burly one moment, then round the corner find yourself on an empty street, alone. Only it wasn't quite empty; she could see someone – a vagrant, a drunk – slumped on the pavement twenty yards ahead. She had already made up her mind to walk around him when she realised the crumpled body was moving, no, *jerking*, like a fish plucked from the water and gasping out its last on deck.

Closer inspection revealed him to be a youngish man, neither vagrant nor drunk, though in evident distress. He was semiconscious, his face horribly pale, the colour of old milk. Around his mouth the skin was a queer shade of blue.

Madeleine knew that one shouldn't try to constrain a person having a seizure. Quickly removing her coat she rolled it up and knelt down to cushion the man's head. He must have fallen, because he was bleeding from a cut to his cheek. The spasms that shook him were beginning to slow. As his limbs relaxed she somehow managed to turn him onto his side. She checked his pulse. His skin was clammy to the touch, and he had gone quite limp. With a silent exhalation of relief she got up off her knees and sat down on the kerb. A trickle of saliva glistened at the corner of his mouth; she took out a handkerchief and wiped it away. As her own heart settled to a steady beat she noticed for the first time his neat attire, a brown herringbone jacket and plaid tie, and light twill trousers, now with an unfortunate rip where he had gashed his knee. His hair was straight and dark, almost black. It was about a minute before he stirred. She saw his eyes twitch, flicker open, and his head lift, slowly.

'Hullo,' she said, trying to make her voice soft. People waking up after a fit would be confused and sometimes upset. You had to explain to them what had happened, and that everything was back to normal – or as normal as it could be. The man, half raised, was squinting at the rolled-up coat on which his head had been lately pillowed.

'What's – ?' He looked around, and started on seeing her.

She leaned across and lightly rested her hand on his shoulder. 'Please, don't be alarmed. You had a – you must have fallen over. Are you all right?'

He blinked, and put his hand to his bleeding cheek, wincing. 'I'm so sorry to have – is this your coat?' He was now trying to stand up, and she was quick to hold him as his legs buckled like a newborn calf's. His frame seemed to be vibrating, thinly, from his recent trauma, and the lost expression in his eyes clutched at her heart.

'Look, I think there's a hospital not far from here.'

The man, staring at her, was still dazed. 'Er . . . I don't think that's where I'm going,' he said with a frown. But he allowed her to take his arm and walk a few steps. There *was* a hospital, she had wandered past it earlier, if only she could find the street again. The man was talking to her in a desultory, slightly anxious manner, mentioning names of people – his friends? – as though she would know them. She guessed he might have a concussion.

'D'you remember *your* name?' she asked him.

Up close his eyes were a striking olive-green colour. 'Yes – it's Tom. Sorry, have we met?'

'No, no,' she said quickly. 'I happened to be passing –'

He stopped suddenly, and said, 'Was I just lying on the pavement? Is that how you found me?'

'Yes. I think you've had a – a fit?'

Tom slowly closed his hands over his face. 'Oh God. *Oh God* . . .' He stood there, his face still shielded, and seemed to be whispering to himself.

Madeleine, after a considerate pause, said, 'Um, will you let me take you to the hospital? I think it would be for the best.'

He took a moment to compose himself, then nodded, and they walked on. She tried to preoccupy him with chat, recounting how she liked to go for walks and would discover new districts of the city quite by accident – just today, for instance, she had no idea she was in Covent Garden until she saw its name over the Tube station. She sensed him brooding by her side, not speaking, though he may have been listening, because he would give a little nod from time to time. They walked along pavements green with refuse from the market, and heard the booming cries of porters and costers at their backs. On reaching Henrietta Street she was relieved to see in the distance the red-brick front of the hospital she had passed earlier.

Once inside, she found a nurse and explained what had happened. It was established that a doctor would examine him presently, but first he would have the cut on his face cleaned. Tom hadn't spoken since his despairing exclamation, but now, as the nurse took charge of him, he turned to Madeleine.

'Thank you for –' She sensed his unwillingness to recall the accident too explicitly.

'Oh, no, it was –' she was going to say 'a pleasure' but stopped herself in time. She didn't really know whether the etiquette existed for such an encounter as theirs.

The nurse, overhearing, said to her, 'Will you be waiting here? After a seizure it's advisable for the patient to be accompanied home.'

'Oh, I'm sure that's unnecessary,' Tom cut in. 'I'll be all right looking after myself. Goodbye, miss.'

Madeleine, briefly at a loss, looked at the nurse, who shrugged. Before she could think of what to say they were off down the corridor and out of sight.

By the time the doctor had run through his tests Tom had a headache and an awful metallic taste in his mouth. It seemed he had suffered a mild concussion, though the X-ray confirmed there had been no damage to his skull. As he was obliged to explain, he'd had his first seizure when he was an eighteen-year-old, in the army. The attacks became less frequent in his twenties, and in the last seven or eight years he had seldom been troubled at all. A few months ago, however, he had been ambushed by one, then another, and was alarmed to note a new intensity in their effect. He decided to ignore them, hoping they were an aberration. But his experience this morning suggested they had been lying in wait, ready to pounce. The doctor asked him if he had been under particular stress or strain – the usual trigger for an attack – and Tom had paused briefly before saying 'no'.

Nearly two hours later they allowed him to leave, on the understanding that he was to go straight home and rest. He felt frail, and debilitated, as though he had been forced through an arduous drill. He was on his way out of the entrance hall when a voice called him. He turned to see the young woman who had helped him on the street.

'Hullo again,' she said, reading his face uncertainly. 'D'you remember – I –'

'Yes, of course. I do beg your pardon, I didn't ask your name . . .'

'Oh, Madeleine – Madeleine Farewell.'

'Farewell?'

'Yes,' she said, blushing. 'It's silly, isn't it? I always seem to be saying goodbye to people, even when I've just met them.'

He smiled at that. 'It's not silly. Though perhaps rather sad. Well, thank you, Madeleine Farewell.'

It was nice, she thought, the way he said that. 'What did they do with you? Is everything . . .?'

'Oh, just some tests. I'll be right as rain.'

He needs a lie-down, she thought, worried by his fragile look but not sure it was her business to tell him.

Tom, collecting himself with an effort, said, 'It's so kind of you to wait for me.'

She gave a little shrug, and said, 'It isn't any trouble.'

'You really are a Samaritan, aren't you?' he said, looking at her wonderingly. 'Would you allow me to thank you – with a cup of tea?'

'Oh, there's no need –'

'Please,' he said. 'Just as one more favour to me.'

They found a Corner House and settled at a table by the

window. Tom, still shaken, put on a show of his best manners, and tried to block from his mind the dismal fact of his illness's return. It depressed him the more for having believed he'd got clear of the thing. It was his rotten luck that it should recur just as he was planning a significant change in his life. Or was it the anxious contemplation of such a change that had set off the old trouble? He took out a cigarette and lit it, but the first lungful of smoke made him so nauseous that he stubbed it out almost immediately.

Madeleine could see how distracted he was. 'When you first woke up – I'm not sure you'll remember – you told me about some people you were going to meet. I think one of them was called Jimmy.'

Tom let out a groan of disgust. 'Dammit. Sorry – you've just reminded me . . .'

'What is it?'

'A luncheon I was meant to attend. At the Ivy. Jimmy is my employer – it's to celebrate his new book.' He glanced at his watch. 'Oh well, too late now.' He'll think I missed it on purpose, Tom reflected gloomily.

'Isn't the Ivy quite near? It's only quarter past two,' said Madeleine.

'No, please, forget I mentioned it. I'd be no company for them anyway.'

At that moment a waitress arrived with the tea they had ordered, as though to underline Tom's non-attendance at the lunch. He gave the teapot an absent stir.

'What sort of books does he write, your employer?'

'Oh, mostly about the theatre. James Erskine – drama critic of the *Chronicle*.'

Madeleine looked blank. Tom looked incredulous.

'You've never heard of him?'

She grimaced apologetically. 'I don't read the papers much. Is he famous?'

'He'd like to think so,' he said with a laugh.

'Are you his . . .?'

'Secretary, officially – dogsbody, really. I do all sorts – editing, correspondence, some writing if he's too busy. And quite a bit of fetching and carrying.'

'It sounds rather a nice job to me,' she said.

Tom, sensing his ingratitude, began back-pedalling. 'I know, I know, I'm lucky to have it. He gave me my first start in journalism, when I was young – younger. And he taught me about the theatre – the plays we've seen! . . . I just didn't think I'd be with him for, what, nine years?'

Madeleine nodded. 'I used to like the theatre. My aunt took me now and then – just amateur productions, you know.'

'But you don't care for the West End?' he said, bemused.

'Well, it's difficult, because I work in the evening,' she said, and instantly regretted it.

'I see. What d'you do?'

'Oh . . . I work near Piccadilly, at a nightclub.' This was partly true. When she had no clients of an evening she would serve drinks at one of the underground dens from where Roddy operated. The hours were late, and the customers could be a vulgar lot, but it was better than escort work. Tom was secretly surprised. This girl looked anything but the brassy nightclub type – judging from her face and manners, he would have pegged her for a schoolteacher, or a nurse. That reminded him.

'By the way, you showed great pluck back there. Most people are petrified by someone having a fit.'

Madeleine smiled sadly. 'My mother had epilepsy. I learned what to do if – you know, not interrupting the fit, protecting the head from damage, that sort of thing. Have you had them all your life?'

He shook his head. 'The first time I was eighteen. I'd been serving in France – the trenches – for about six months. There'd been a lot of shelling, with some terrible

. . . casualties.' He broke off and swiped his hand wearily across his face. 'I can't exactly recall what started it – I was fixing a bayonet or something, and I started to shake. Everything went white and I was thrown to the ground. I don't know what happened then, but I'm told it gave the boy next to me a fright.'

'So they sent you home?'

'Eventually. At first they thought I'd got the wind up and this was just a ruse to get out of there. When it happened again they had a doctor examine me, and after that there wasn't any doubt.'

'My father was in the trenches,' said Madeleine. 'He was killed at Ypres, though they never found him.'

'I'm sorry,' Tom said, and paused. 'When they discharged me I felt, well, *relieved* of course. But guilty, too. Knowing how many of them would die . . .'

A sudden look of mortification seized her. 'Oh, no, I didn't mean – you mustn't feel guilty for surviving. That's not why I mentioned my father. I didn't really know him.'

He looked at her. The thought of offending him had caused her genuine alarm. Who was this woman? It had been a long time since he had encountered such *feeling* in someone. She had suffered, too, you could read it in her face. Madeleine said, 'Is something the matter?'

Tom, blinking away his reverie, laughed at himself. 'I beg your pardon – miles away. I wonder, you said you liked the theatre. I go all the time, for free. D'you ever get a night off?'

'Hardly ever,' she said. 'Nights are – busy.'

'Surely you could ask your boss?'

You don't know my boss, she thought. 'He'll say he can't spare me.'

That seemed to decide the matter. Tom helped her on with her coat, somewhat bedraggled from its recent adventure. Feeling rejuvenated by the tea, he thought he might show his face after all. Outside, the afternoon had come into its own; the silvery sun had elbowed through the massing clouds and wasn't going to budge. At the door of the Corner House they performed a hesitant minuet of departure.

'I'm going to walk up towards the Ivy,' he said. 'I feel I ought to call in, for some reason.'

'I'm sure they'd understand if you didn't,' she said, eyeing his bruised cheek.

He put out his hand. 'Well, thank you, miss – and farewell!'

She smiled her acknowledgement. 'Goodbye. I hope you feel better.'

Tom turned up St Martin's Lane, aware of his slightly valetudinarian pace. He was older suddenly. Now that the attacks had started again he knew he had to be on guard. Next time there might not be anyone around to help either, he could fall on the pavement, crack his head, bleed to death . . .

Behind him he heard pattering footsteps.

'Excuse me, er – ?' He turned to find Madeleine, slightly out of breath from running. 'I'm sorry to – it was awfully nice of you to invite me to the theatre, and I'm sure if I give them enough notice I could get a night off . . .' She had gabbled it out in a nervous flurry.

'Righto!' he said, smiling. 'What d'you say I give you my telephone number and you let me know when you've an evening off? Is there anything in particular you'd like to see?'

'Oh, no, not really . . . You decide. Please.'

He wrote his number on a cigarette card, and handed it to her. 'It's my employer's telephone, but I always answer it.'

She examined the card for a moment, as though she might commit the number to memory. 'Thank you,' she beamed, and waved before walking off again.

\* \* \*

By the time the company at the Ivy dispersed, Tom was feeling faint again. He knew he ought to have taken himself home, but his sense of duty had got the better of him. Jimmy, cheeks rouged from the drink, seemed to have forgotten about his late arrival, and was now too befuddled to care. The afternoon was darkening as the stragglers emerged from the restaurant – Tom, László, Edie, Felix Croker, with Jimmy swaying at the rear. Abel, the doorman, pointed at the cab across the street.

'There's yer chariot, Mr Erskine. Been there since one o'clock.'

'Since one?!' cried Edie. 'Jimmy, really – why didn't you send it off?'

'Taxis are his favourite extravagance,' explained Tom.

'I'm an invalid,' said Jimmy, pointing to his stick.

'But you only live about five minutes' walk from here.'

'Doesn't matter,' said Tom. 'I've seen him hail a cab to get from one side of the road to the other.'

Jimmy, oblivious, clambered into the taxi, raising a vague hand to them as the car pulled away. Edie glanced at her watch and said to Tom, 'If you're going east we could get a cab, too.'

Tom nodded, and turned to László. 'How about you?'

'I think I shall walk. In a moment of idiocy I gave my last shilling to some beggar on the Charing Cross Road.'

Croker made an incredulous *pfff* sound. 'You know, László, I sometimes wonder if you're actually a Jew at all. You're the only one I've met who's never got any money.'

László responded to his mocking tone with a characteristic shrug, and Tom wondered why the constant stream of jibes never seemed to upset him. Perhaps he had become immune to them.

'We're going quite near Commercial Road,' Tom said to him. 'Why don't you come with us?'

László gave him a shy smile. 'Most kind of you, Thomas,

but I shall be happy to use that estimable conveyance Shanks's pony.'

They said their goodbyes, and parted.

In the cab home Edie kept up a lively run of chat, for which Tom was grateful. He felt too depleted to be marvellous company. She was telling him about a recent holiday in Athens and an outing to the theatre with her friends one night. 'Of course none of us had *a clue* about the language – all Greek to me, darling – but Dot insisted we go – home of drama and all that. So we went. It being Athens we thought we'd go for a tragedy, Sophocles or the like. We took pot luck with something called *The Sister of the Mother of Karolos*, thought it sounded, you know, high-flown. Well, it took us a while before we realised – this was no tragedy. The audience had started giggling, for some reason. Next thing they were rolling in the aisles! We just sat there. D'you know, Tom, a whole hour went by before I realised we'd stumbled into a Greek version of *Charley's Aunt*!'

Tom laughed. '*The Sister of the Mother of Karolos* – you're right, it does sound like a tragedy. Jimmy would love that story.'

'I know! It'll probably end up in his next book.'

'I hope you didn't mind being the only woman at lunch. I did point this out to him, but . . .'

'You know Jimmy,' she said, shrugging. 'Women bore him. He only puts up with me cos I'm as rude as he is.' She looked at him. 'I gather you two haven't been getting along.'

László must have told her, thought Tom. 'Things have been . . . He's become very needy of late. Hates being alone in the flat, so if he's not got company he expects me to sleep on the couch. And of course he's the most appalling hypochondriac. I think the only conditions he hasn't complained of yet are anthrax and dry rot.'

'Well, he *is* getting on a bit,' she said.

'Doesn't he know it. At heart he's scared of dying.'

'Hmm. I'm a teeny bit afraid of that myself.'

'No, this is different, it's an obsession. The other day I was sorting through his post – you know he gets a lot from readers – and found this letter from someone, a Mr D'Eath – is that how you pronounce it? I showed it to Jimmy, and he looked at it like Macbeth at his dagger. First he accused me of playing a prank on him – said it was in "very poor taste". When I assured him it was nothing to do with me he went pale, and dropped it on the floor.'

Edie drew her brows into a puzzled look. 'What's the matter with him?'

Tom shrugged. 'I dunno. It was like he'd received a personal summons from the Grim Reaper. When I asked him how he wanted to reply he waved it away – just expected me to deal with it.'

After a pause Edie said, in a softer tone, 'He's so fond of you, though. When he thanked you in his speech he sounded like he really meant it.'

Tom shook his head, brooding. 'I can't keep doing it, Edie, this job. It's one thing to be his secretary, but I don't want to be doing his shopping, fetching his pills, minding the flat. And it's not like he pays me extra. I've been on the same screw for six years, and whenever I've –' He stopped, and looked at Edie. 'Sorry to go on . . . I think it's time he got one of his boys to look after him.'

''Sfunny, isn't it,' she said, 'how Jimmy still chases after 'em, at his age? I suppose it never leaves you.'

'That's something else he's terrified of – getting caught.'

'I'm not surprised. A friend of mine got done a couple of weeks ago. He was hanging about the arches by the Adelphi when some man approached him. Of course he thought he was a pansy – round there you would, wouldn't you? So they've found a quiet corner and my friend's just dropped his trousers, when the feller gets out the Brendas and tells him he's under arrest.'

'Brendas?'

'Brenda bracelets – handcuffs, darling.'

Tom grimaced. 'I think Jim rather enjoys the risk – like walking a tightrope. He's always on the hunt.'

Edie gave him a sly look. 'Has he ever, you know . . . with you?'

Tom smiled. 'He wouldn't dare.' This wasn't quite true. When he had first started as his secretary in 1927 he had known that Jimmy was queer but had no inkling of his promiscuity. He didn't regard what his employer got up to as any of his business. It had taken three or four weeks for the boundaries of their relationship to be established beyond doubt. Tom had been standing in the flat's galley kitchen reading a newspaper when he felt Jimmy sidling up behind him. Next thing he jumped as an exploratory hand dipped down the back of his trousers. While he couldn't recall exactly what he had said it must have been something of sufficient clarity, for Jimmy, without any change in his expression, uncupped his palm and withdrew. 'Please yourself,' he murmured equably.

The taxi had pulled up at Fashion Street in Spitalfields, where Edie lived. 'Bye, darling,' she said, stroking Tom's cheek with maternal tenderness. 'Get some rest – you look done in!'

Alone in the cab, Tom wished he had found a way to tell Edie about his seizure that morning. They didn't know each other particularly well, but he discerned in her a sympathetic confidante, and he had few of those. Yet he was anxious that the news didn't get back to Jimmy, who would be sure to gossip about it. He didn't want his prospects damaged by rumours that he wasn't altogether well.

It had taken him long enough – months – just to convince himself that he was entitled to leave Jimmy. The prospect of his defection had put him in mind of the time they first met, nine years ago. It had happened in a roundabout sort of way. Having graduated from King's College, London – the first in his family to attend university – Tom had got a job as assistant at a gallery near the British Museum. The pay was pitiful, but the work unstrenuous. Whenever he could afford it he would go to the theatre, and had taken to writing short notices on spec for a small magazine. After some pestering of the editor he managed to secure a semi-regular slot, enabling him to attend the occasional press night. Of course he knew James Erskine, doyen of the London drama critics, by sight – his photograph was often in the papers. He read him avidly in the *Chronicle*, and in every other paper and magazine he wrote for. Too much in awe to approach the great man, Tom would occupy a seat as close as he dared and eavesdrop on his chat: if Erskine did not have his usual retinue of young men about him, he could be seen jawing with his fellow critics before curtain-up.

One afternoon at the gallery while he was varnishing a frame, Tom overheard a voice from the ground floor that seemed familiar. Rising from his knees to peer over the mezzanine rail, he beheld the unmistakable figure of James Erskine in discussion with the manager, Mr Dearden. He stopped what he was doing, and stared. Here was his moment – a chance to introduce himself, to confess his sincere admiration, perhaps even to mention his own modest efforts as a theatre critic . . . He moved towards the stairs before a sudden paralysing doubt checked him. Erskine probably met young hopefuls like himself all the time, indeed a famous article of his had complained of being buttonholed by strangers from noon to nightfall. He had read elsewhere of the man's legendary brusqueness: the time a visitor had said to him, 'I mustn't outstay my welcome,' and Erskine had snapped, 'Who said anything about welcome?' Such chastening reflections caused Tom's step to falter. By the time he had reached the stairs the object of his inflamed curiosity had gone.

Later, as Tom was about to leave for the day, he stopped at Dearden's office and enquired about their famous customer. 'Erskine? He comes in now and again. He bought one of those Bevan lithographs.' Tom nodded, regretting his earlier hesitancy with renewed anguish – he could have held his own in a conversation about Bevan. 'Matter of fact,' continued the manager, unaware of the favour he was bestowing, 'he asked for it to be delivered to his flat. Tomorrow morning?'

'First thing,' said Tom, his heart dancing.

The cab had arrived at Wapping High Street, where Tom got out. He had been living in rooms above a tobacconist's whose window display seemed not to have changed since 1918. The rent was cheap, probably with good reason. He was lying in bed one night recently when he felt something cold and scratchy ghost across his face. He sat bolt upright and turned on the light: there, on his pillow, sat a grey mouse, twitching from its recent exercise. He knew that the shop downstairs was often beleaguered by mice, but they had not infiltrated his own quarters before. Clearly this one had decided to move up in the world. He had mentioned it the next morning to his elderly landlord, who gave his head a mournful shake and said, 'They get everywhere. It'll be rats next.' Tom, impressed by his fatalistic tone, had made no further complaint.

In the tiny kitchen he shared with another lodger he opened a tin of soup and tipped it into a pan, then watched it warm over the gas ring. He was still thinking about his first encounter with Jimmy. He had arrived at his Bloomsbury mansion block that morning bright and early – too early. The porter had directed him to the first floor, but Tom's respectful tap at the door had met no reply. After a louder knock also went unanswered he pressed the bell, which he could hear buzz within. Another long pause. Convinced that the owner was not at home he was about to withdraw when he heard a shuffling step followed by an irked ratcheting of a safety lock – and the door swung open. Jimmy stood there in a purple-and-green paisley dressing gown, his meagre strands of hair in disarray and his expression crumpled in sullen fatigue.

'I do not take kindly to being roused before eleven o'clock. And I am not at home to bailiffs at any –'

'Sorry. I'm just here with your, er, Bevan . . .' Tom held up the packaged print in hopeful mollification. Jimmy frowned at him, bemused.

'Ah . . . You'd better come in.'

Tom passed down a long hallway into the living room, noting the cream carpets and the inky-blue wallpaper and wondering if those colours would have been better suited the other way round. His eye was irresistibly drawn to the wind-up gramophone and its flamboyant brass horn; all it needed was a small fox terrier cocking an ear. It was difficult to see where the new acquisition might be accommodated: almost every inch of wall space was crammed with oils and prints. Even the fireplace had been requisitioned as a niche for a small painting of the Sussex coast. Tom set the package down on a coffee table and waited while Erskine removed its coat of brown paper and string. The print, composed in muted greys and charcoals, depicted a horse sale in a yard; men in cloth caps and bowlers stood about listening to the auctioneer.

Jimmy stared at it meditatively. 'I used to go to sales like this, just after the war. So many horses on the market back then.'

'You bought one, didn't you?' said Tom. 'You wrote a piece about it.'

'Good Lord, you remember that? Must have been for . . .'

'The *Tatler*,' supplied Tom.

Jimmy looked at him in surprise. 'Is this a reader I see before me?'

'Yes. A devoted one. Your theatre column in the *Chronicle* is my first port of call. As a matter of fact,' he added shyly, 'I do some reviewing myself – for a little magazine called *Autolycus*.'

'Never heard of it.'

Tom, sensing he'd taken a wrong turn, reverted to a subject the critic would find congenial. 'I've always thought your "About Town" articles should be collected.'

Jimmy puckered his mouth consideringly. 'Hmm. They are quite amusing in their way.'

They talked a little more about theatre – or rather Jimmy talked, in his brisk magisterial tone, and without so much as a pause. Tom, overwhelmed into silence by this monologue, eventually said, 'I'm awfully sorry, I have to get back to work.'

'And I have to get back to bed,' said Jimmy. 'Would you mind letting yourself out?'

Tom, abruptly dismissed, pondered this interview on his walk back to the gallery, and felt most unhappy. He had met the great critic of the age, and had failed to shine, a natural consequence of not being able to get a word in edgeways. But how could one interrupt a man such as that?

He continued to rue his lost chance for days afterwards. But fate had decided to throw him another bone, and this time he caught it neatly in his jaws. The editor of *Autolycus*, unable to attend the after-show party of a new musical, had sent Tom along in his place. On entering the venue and finding no one he knew there, he mooched around for a few minutes, intending to leave once he had drunk a sufficient quantity of the free champagne. Wandering into a little anteroom he saw a familiar portly gent with an unlit cigar clamped in his mouth, patting his pockets in search of a light.

'May I?' Tom said, a match poised against the box.

Jimmy, barely glancing at him, grunted his thanks as he

fired up the cigar. Scarcely believing his luck, Tom lit a companionable cigarette of his own, and said, 'Have you hung the Bevan yet?'

Jimmy almost cricked his neck with a spectacular double take. 'Do I – have we met – ?'

'Tom Tunner – from Dearden's? We talked about horses.'

His expression started to clear. 'So we did . . . well . . . perhaps you wouldn't mind fetching me a Scotch and soda.'

Tom, not minding at all, hurried off. On returning, however, he felt his heart sink to see Jimmy deep in conversation with another, a gangly fellow with a slight stoop. Tom handed over the Scotch and introduced himself.

'Peter Liddell,' the fellow replied genially. 'How d'you know Jimmy?'

'Oh, I don't –'

'Delivery boy from Dearden's,' Jimmy explained, crushingly. 'Also a reader of mine, you know.'

Peter smiled knowingly. 'Ah, then you'll always be welcome!'

Tom, emboldened by Peter's friendliness, glimpsed an opportunity. 'I was actually saying to Mr Erskine that he should collect his "About Town" pieces in a book.'

'Haven't the time, dear boy. Always bloody *working*.'

'Yes, I know. That's why I'd do it for you – as your secretary.'

Jimmy responded with an archly sceptical look. '*You* – my secretary? And what qualifications d'you claim for such a post?'

Tom, hardly believing his own nerve, said, 'Well, I have a degree in English from King's. I know your writing inside out . . . and I don't mind hard work.'

Peter nodded sagely. 'Sounds just the ticket to me, Jim. And you're always saying you need the help.'

Jimmy was scrutinising him; he would become accustomed

to that beady-eyed look over the years. 'Do you write? I mean, in decent prose.'

'I write theatre reviews, for a small literary magazine,' he replied. From his blank look Jimmy had evidently forgotten their conversation in his flat the other morning.

'Very well. Send me eight hundred words on a recent play – anything you like – and I'll have a look. If your industry is any match for your impudence I imagine we should get along very nicely.'

So it proved. Tom's 'test' review was duly dispatched, and Jimmy replied the next morning to say the job was his – though not without a patronising afterthought on certain 'amateurish' lapses in his submitted article. He would pay him fifty-five shillings a week, scarcely an adequate wage by the standards of the day, but Tom didn't care. He had got the job, a job finessed out of nothing but his own initiative. He was on his way.

Having finished his soup, Tom took the stairs down to the shop below. Allenby, landlord and tobacconist, was hunched over his counter reading the late edition of the *Standard*.

'Evening. Twenty Weights, please, Mr Allenby.'

Almost without looking round the shopkeeper plucked a packet of cigarettes from the shelf. 'He's done another one in, I see,' he said mysteriously.

'Beg your pardon?' said Tom.

Allenby looked up at his tenant. 'Blimey, what 'appened to you?'

Tom self-consciously touched his wounded cheek. 'Oh, I took a tumble. Nothing serious. You were saying . . .?'

Allenby nodded at his newspaper. 'Girl found strangled, in Bloomsbury. Police sez it's this "Tiepin Killer" again. I dunno, with all these marches and murders, the streets round 'ere aren't safe to walk . . . I 'ave to send the wife out for everythin'! Ha ha.'

111

Tom offered a feeble laugh in echo while trying to read the story upside down. THIRD TIEPIN MURDER: GIRL NAMED. It seemed the victim's facial injuries were so severe they had had to consult dental records in order to identify her. So much for that artist's impression of the suspected killer. Did the police really have any clue about catching him?

'Poor woman,' he muttered under his breath.

'Yeah, nasty bisniss,' agreed the old man, before adding, 'Lookin' on the bright side, though – them *Standard*s 'ave flew out today!'

# 7

As they drove around Richmond Park the tops of the trees seemed to shimmer, ablaze in their sudden motley of green and russet and gold. The sight of them thrilled and saddened Stephen; he felt it was exactly what he had been put on earth to paint, and yet it seemed he had never done them justice. His sequence of autumnal pictures, *London Pastoral I–IX*, was one of the few things he'd ever taken pride in, and of course it had fallen flat with the public. They only wanted to see his portraits. He felt a sharp stab of melancholy and blew out his cheeks, as if to shoo it away.

'Something the matter, darling?' asked Cora, glancing from the passenger seat.

He smiled and shook his head, then looked in the mirror at Freya and Rowan, muttering between themselves on the back seat. They were down from school for the weekend – Cora's parents had invited them to lunch – and he was already wondering what new and disturbing changes had been wrought in them since they were last at home. Rowan had grown into a fusspot, airing doubts and complaints in a manner more befitting an old lady than a nine-year-old boy. On stepping off the train at Waterloo that morning the first thing he'd said was, 'Perishing cold in that carriage.' Stephen had sought confirmation from Freya, who had merely raised her eyes heavenwards in an impersonation of sore-tried tolerance. She was Rowan's senior by three years, a terrifyingly serious and self-contained girl whom her brother held in a kind of baffled awe.

'Is the camera back there?' Stephen said.

Without a word Freya held up the tan leather case, as though she were his assistant. He pulled the car over and turned to his wife, who groaned.

'I'll be two ticks – we're in plenty of time,' he said quickly, slinging the case over his shoulder. He got out of the car and took a few steps up the grassy verge. Behind him he heard the car door shutting; Freya had decided to accompany him. He walked on a little further, then stopped. Taking the black-and-silver Leica out of its case – it was cold to the touch – he began lining up a shot.

'What picture are you taking?' asked Freya, just behind him.

'Hmm? Oh, you see that stand of trees on the hill . . . I just need to, you know, remember the shape of them.' So saying, he peered through the viewfinder and, after a dithering pause, he clicked. 'There. Let's go.'

As they turned back towards the car Freya said, 'Are you going to paint those trees?'

'I think I might.'

With a quizzical narrowing of her eyes she said, 'But . . . if you have a photograph of something why do a painting as well?'

'That's a very good question,' he said, with a half-laugh. 'I suppose – it's nice to have both! I mean, you're right, a photograph shows us exactly what we've seen: in this case, those trees. A painting, on the other hand' – they were back at the car, and he held open the door for her to climb in – 'well, that's a more personal view.'

'What are you talking about?' said Cora brightly.

Stephen started the engine and, with a quick glance round, steered the car back onto the road. 'Ah, Freya wants to know why we should paint when we have photographs.'

A smile dimpled Cora's cheek. 'If we didn't have painting, Daddy wouldn't have anything to do.'

'That's one way of looking at it,' said Stephen, feeling diminished. In the mirror he saw Freya's brow darken in disappointment – she wasn't being taken quite seriously. He cleared his throat. 'The thing about painting, Freya, is that it's not just about what we see – it's also about what we feel. So, if I ever get round to painting those trees, I'll be thinking of how they looked *and* about the moment I saw them. I'll remember that it was the day we drove down to Granny's with our two lovely children, home for the weekend, and how we were all in such a good mood because of the fine weather –'

'I'm not in a good mood,' said Rowan blankly.

'Oh, will you shut your bloody arsehole?' said Freya in exasperation.

Cora gave a startled gasp. 'I *beg* your pardon?'

'Mr Mulhall says "bloody" all the time,' said Freya.

'I don't care what Mr Mulhall says. It's not language I wish to hear from a young lady.'

'Is Mr Mulhall your English teacher?' asked Stephen.

'No, he teaches domestic science,' supplied Rowan.

'Oh, right. So what's the name of the carpentry fellow?'

'*Stephen*,' said Cora, in a tone that indicated he was altogether missing the point.

'Yes, um, Freya – it's not nice to tell people to shut up, no matter how much we want them to. And I think using words like – well, it isn't really on, old girl.'

'And you can apologise to Rowan,' added Cora.

A long beat followed, then Freya said, 'Sorry.'

Stephen glanced at Cora, but received no supportive look in return. Tipton Hall, a grand country house in Hampshire, had recently been converted to a 'community' school that valued practical skills over traditional learning. Under the supervision of its liberal-minded headmaster and founder,

Mr Edwin Goode, the pupils did housework, studied carpentry and tended the large vegetable garden, growing their own food; Rowan had already told them about the number of potatoes he'd picked that week. Stephen had gone along with Cora's scheme – her own mother was quite the freethinker – and was hoping that the children had taken to it.

He worried, though, that Mr Goode's radical philosophy of education might be privileging the hand at the expense of the brain. Literacy, for example. Freya was not a concern on that score: her newly acquired taste for profanity aside, she had shown herself a quick learner, and at present was cracking through *Barchester Towers*. Rowan, however, seemed to care little for reading, and even less, to judge by his ill-formed efforts, for writing. Even the way he set down his own name in a jumble of lower- and upper-case letters struck him as faintly pathetic. He feared that the boy might not be altogether intelligent. And what about that name! How on earth had he consented to Cora's branding the boy *Rowan*? Why had he not pushed for something solid and sensible, like Jack, or Fred? He couldn't remember.

'Look, there's Granny waving!' said Freya as Stephen parked the car. The Hamiltons, Cora's parents, lived in an imposing Georgian terrace on Richmond Hill, with a covetable view over the Thames. Freya and Rowan clambered out of the car and raced like hounds for the front door, Freya getting there first, as she did in most contests between them.

'My darlings!' cooed Mrs Hamilton, as she bent to greet her grandchildren. 'Brought the smashing weather with you, I see.' She embraced Cora and offered Stephen, last through, a feathery kiss – on his lips – which rather wrong-footed him. It was the sort of thing she did. Granny Hamilton belied her name, being hale and trim and girlishly good-looking, even at sixty. He suspected that she might have enjoyed a racy youth.

They made their way to the conservatory where a table for lunch had been laid and, on the far side, seated in a high-backed wicker chair, Mr Hamilton puffed on his pipe. He had been absorbed in *The Times* crossword. Older than his wife, though tall and lean like her, he met them with a slightly bemused air, as if their visit had been sprung on him at late notice. With Stephen he maintained a business-like distance, possibly on the assumption that any duty of friendliness was his wife's domain.

'Douglas,' Stephen said, with an ingratiating nod of respect. 'How are you?'

Mr Hamilton gave a little groan of disappointment. 'Keeping busy, you know. Round of golf a day . . .'

'Keeps the doctor away?'

'Hardly,' replied Mr Hamilton, frowning at this frivolity. 'No need to ask what *you've* been doing,' he added, with an oddly accusing look.

Stephen was momentarily thrown. 'Erm, I can't imagine . . .'

For answer Mr Hamilton picked up his *Times* and riffled through it, while Stephen's heart stuttered at the abyss.

'Here,' said the old man, cuffing the page as he handed it over. Stephen looked – and breathed again. It was a society paragraph about himself, and his latest commission at the Nines Club in Mayfair. He had begun on the projected mural last week while the committee was still in heated debate as to who should figure in the portrait. Ludo Talman had already indicated that the original nine sitters would now be closer to fifteen.

Stephen ran a cursory eye over the item, and looked up to find his father-in-law scrutinising him. He understood that look: it mingled a complete indifference to his painting with a puzzled irritation that it should merit a reference in the newspaper. 'I've barely started on it,' said Stephen in mild apology. 'They're still jockeying for position among the membership.'

'Is it true what it says – about the King?'

'I'm not sure he'll agree to sit for a group portrait.'

'Well, quite,' said Mr Hamilton, as though he might have advised His Majesty on the subject himself.

Cora, decanting a bottle of wine at the table, said over her shoulder, 'They're putting the bite on him all the same. Stephen's been asked to write to him.'

Mr Hamilton looked aghast. 'You mean, you . . . *know* him?'

'Very slightly. We met at a shoot some time ago – we've exchanged a few words now and then.'

Freya, egged on by her grandfather's disbelieving tone, said, 'Dad, would you have to go to Buckingham Palace?'

Stephen winked at her. 'Probably.'

'What a bleeding lark!' she cried.

A stunned pause followed. Cora put her hands on her hips and stared at her daughter. 'Freya. What did I just say in the car? About language like that?'

Freya, not at all abashed, said, 'What's wrong with that? It's not "bloody" or "arsehole".'

Granny Hamilton, who had just set down the *boeuf en daube*, let out a peacock shriek of laughter. 'I must say, that school of yours sounds a caution, darling!'

Her husband was less amused. 'Haven't heard language like that since I was in the service. Well, as the book says, as ye sow, so shall ye reap . . .'

From Mr Hamilton's sour look it was clear he considered Freya's father in some degree responsible for her verbal delinquency. Stephen felt the injustice of this, but said nothing. Protesting that the school was Cora's idea would sound weak. He seemed to spend his life nowadays toeing the line, doing things he didn't want to. That charity dinner for the Marquess Theatre, for instance. He had sensed the game was up when Cora mentioned it to him one evening.

'Do you know this fellow Carmody?'

'Hmm. From Oxford. I bumped into him a few weeks ago.'

'Well, he's being the most frightful pest. Says you agreed to attend some dinner – for a theatre fund? He rang twice yesterday and again this afternoon.'

Stephen found himself cornered one morning a few days later. He usually didn't answer the telephone at home, but both Cora and Mrs Ronson were out.

'Wyley – at last!' boomed a familiar voice.

'Gerald, hullo,' he said, and felt his shoulders slump.

'You're an elusive chap. I've rung your place a few times already – talked to your lady wife.'

'She said something about you calling.'

'Well, it's this dinner for the Marquess – just rounding up the troops, as it were.'

'To be honest, Gerald, I'm fearfully busy at present. I've just taken on a huge commission for a club in Mayfair –'

'Yes, the Nines, I heard about that. Bully for you, old chap – but surely they give you the evenings orf!' Carmody paused at this; when he spoke again his tone had changed. 'Of course, in an ideal world I'd extend the invitation to a lady – your friend Miss Land, perhaps. Or would that privilege be reserved for your wife?'

Stephen couldn't fail to hear the insinuation. Carmody was loud and abrasive, but he was no fool. He must have guessed that Nina and he were somehow involved on more than a friendly footing; or else he had seen them coming out of the hotel lift that afternoon.

'Perhaps I should ask both of them,' Stephen replied coolly, though he knew that Carmody had the upper hand. He couldn't risk making an enemy of him. 'Put me down for a couple of places. I suppose a cheque will be –'

'Oh, we can discuss that later. As a token of gratitude I'll take you for lunch.'

'Lunch?' Stephen closed his eyes and pinched the bridge

of his nose. He would much rather have paid up to Carmody's charity and be done with it; now he was saddled with not one but two undesirable engagements. Cora was right – an infernal pest. Stephen decided that the most profitable use of his time would be to host Carmody at the Nines, where at least he could get straight back to work after lunch. A date the following week was settled, and he rang off.

On the day of their meeting something odd happened. Carmody had telephoned to confirm, and on hearing that Stephen would be driving from Chelsea into the West End he had asked a favour – another one. 'I'm at my headquarters just off Eaton Square. Would you mind picking me up there and we can drive straight to lunch?' Stephen, wondering what he meant by 'headquarters', had taken down the address and agreed to call by just before one.

The Carmody HQ turned out to be in a cul-de-sac at the south end of the square. The grey peeling stucco of the building's facade and the dusty windows indicated a neglect unusual for this expensive neighbourhood. Stephen mounted the steps and tapped the brass knocker. Moments later the door opened, and a young man dressed head to toe in black stood at the threshold. Nonplussed, Stephen said, 'I'm sorry, I was given this as Gerald Carmody's address . . .'

The youth nodded and invited him inside. The hallway was crammed with bundles of newspapers, while along one wall a giant poster proclaimed MIND BRITAIN'S BUSINESS. He escorted Stephen to a room just past the central staircase. 'If you'd care to wait I'll find Mr Carmody for you,' he said, and trotted up the stairs. In the waiting room other posters adorned the wall – VOTE BRITISH PEOPLE'S BRIGADE the most prominent – and someone had framed the front page of the *Daily Mail* from January 1934, with its famous headline HURRAH FOR THE BLACKSHIRTS. On a long trestle was arranged a selection of pamplets; Stephen lit a cigarette and flicked through one entitled 'The Future of National Socialism'. His eye skated over its declamatory paragraphs – 'So many men and women are seeking leadership in a country whose government has been enfeebled . . . we live in a society ruled by alien Jewish financiers, who throttle our trade and menace the world's peace . . . British people in the East End of London have received notice to quit from the Jews, but this time we are going to give the Jews notice to quit.'

He suppressed a groan, and dropped the pamphlet back on to the pile. Minutes ticked by, and, assuming that he had been forgotten, he decided to seek out Carmody for himself. Hearing activity from the upper rooms he took the scuffed, uncarpeted stairs and wandered along a corridor. More posters blazoned the motto MIND BRITAIN'S BUSINESS and urged support for the British People's Brigade. Following the sound of voices he found an office with the door ajar, and craned his head around. Standing at a desk, absorbed in discussion, were two more young men in blackshirt uniform. Both wore armbands with a lightning flash encircled in red. Stephen gave an apologetic cough and said, 'Would you happen to know if Gerald Carmody's around?'

The older of the two, dark hair slicked back from his forehead, looked over at him. 'Enter,' he said, before resuming his conversation. Stephen sidled into the room, and plumped down on a desk chair against the wall. He took out another cigarette and lit it, at which the slick-haired one broke off from talking and approached him. Up close a pinkish scurf of acne bearded his jaw. He was perhaps no more than twenty.

'Name?' he said, hands behind his back and chest thrust forward.

'Erm . . . Stephen Wyley,' he said pleasantly.

'Stand to attention when you talk to me,' he hissed, 'and put that cigarette out.'

Stephen, smiling, rose slowly to his feet. 'I think there's some mistake . . .' The martinet's expression darkened as he took in this nonchalance.

'You find this amusing?' he shouted in Stephen's face. The other young man, with close-cropped hair and pinched features, looked in fear at his older comrade. Stephen felt it first as an involuntary giddiness in his lungs; then, unable to stop himself, he burst out laughing.

'I'm so sorry,' he said, between gasps, holding up his hands in a gesture of appeasement. He sensed the youth getting ready to take a swing at him, but before he could do so another voice cut in.

'It's all right, Franks, this chap's with me,' said Carmody, interposing himself. He was wearing a flannel suit, but with the same lightning-flash armband. Franks, lip curled in disgust, continued to glare at Stephen. 'I'm afraid you've been misdirected to our recruiting office, Wyley. Young Franks here is rather zealous in the cause!'

'So I see,' said Stephen, slightly shamed by his laughter. 'Well, I'm sorry not to oblige you and the, er, Brigade.'

Carmody nodded, and with a hand on his shoulder eased Stephen out of the room and back towards the stairs. 'My apologies,' he said in a low voice. 'These young fellows get carried away with all the clicked heels and saluting.' There was in his tone something Stephen had not expected: it sounded like embarrassment. They were through the hall and descending the front steps just as a trio of blackshirts were coming up. Carmody hailed one of them, who detached himself from the others. He was a shortish man of about thirty with a pugilist's stance and a long scar down one cheek. He greeted Carmody with a forearm salute, and they fell into a brief muttered discussion. Stephen, standing to one side, was evidently not to be introduced, though he had a vague memory of having seen the man before.

Their encounter at an end, Carmody bid him farewell and the man, with a quick glance at Stephen, disappeared into the building.

Carmody, beaming again, said, 'Shall we proceed?'

'My car's just over there,' said Stephen, who waited a moment before saying, 'I thought you'd quit Mosley's gang.'

'Indeed. Tom and I have gone our separate ways.'

'So what's this British People's Brigade? They look quite a lot like the Fascists to me.'

Carmody stopped and looked back at his offices. 'It's our little piece of Britain, old chap. We're going to create a new spirit in this country, and we won't be asking Mussolini for any more handouts.'

'By "we" you mean . . .'

'Myself and the gentleman I was just talking to.'

'Oh. The one who looked like a boxer?'

Carmody smirked back. 'He's not scared of a fight, that's for sure. But he's also a formidable mind, and the best young orator I've ever heard. Joyce is his name – William Joyce.'

They had reached the car. Stephen, who had never sought out Carmody's company, even when they were at Oxford, now felt rather ill at ease with the man – he would really have preferred not to be seen with him. Too late now. He unlocked the passenger door, but before Carmody could duck inside he said to him, 'One thing, Gerald. I don't think the club will let you in wearing *that*.'

Carmody glanced down at his side, and took in Stephen's meaning. After a moment's hesitation he removed the lightning-flash armband from his jacket.

Stephen resurfaced in the present to find most of his *boeuf en daube* still uneaten. Freya was just concluding an account of the life of Ruskin. He seemed to have missed something.

'. . . and though at first I would have chosen Nightingale, I'm quite pleased to be in Ruskin.'

'What d'you mean, "in Ruskin"?' asked Stephen, bewildered.

Freya directed a puzzled look across the table at him. 'Have you not been listening to me?'

Stephen sought help from Cora, who gave him a forbidding frown. 'Freya's been telling us about the school houses at Tipton. They're all named after – tell him, darling.'

Freya raised her eyes heavenwards and sighed at her father as a teacher might at the class dunce. 'The school's got four houses, each named after a famous person – so there's Mill, Pankhurst, Nightingale, which is Rowan's house, and Ruskin, which is mine. He was a very distinguished man who wrote about painting and architecture, and he had a very great beard.'

'Or was it just a grey beard?' asked Stephen.

'I think Mr Mulhall said it was "great".'

'Eminent Victorians,' said Mr Hamilton, with a raised eyebrow that argued they were no such thing. Freya took the remark innocently.

'Yes, you see, they all represent a different – er –'

'Aspect?' supplied Stephen.

'– *aspect* of life. Medicine, philosophy, art and, um, politics.'

Mr Hamilton stared into his wine glass. 'I would have thought Gladstone a fitter representative of British politics than the Pankhurst woman.'

'Which is why you were educated at Harrow and not Tipton, my dear,' said his wife smoothly, then turned to Cora. 'And talking of eminent Victorians, we went to see the revival of that play you recommended the other night – *The Second Arrangement*. Awfully good.'

'Isn't it!' said Cora. Stephen kept very still as he listened, wondering which facial expression of his would be the least incriminating. He observed their back-and-forth discussion of the play, a Wimbledon of psychological torture. Just when it seemed about to end Cora said, 'The woman who plays Hester I thought was marvellous.'

'Hester – oh, was that the lover?'

'Yes. Stephen actually met her a few weeks ago – what's her name, darling?'

'Nina Land. I met her at Henry's show. She bought one of his paintings, I think. Must have quite a good eye.' Why was he still talking? She had only asked for her name – just say it and shut up.

'I got into quite a state during that scene with the letter,' Cora continued. 'I couldn't help myself, could I?'

Stephen, with a lift of his chin, agreed. 'The waterworks, I'm afraid.'

'Poor Ma!' cried Freya.

'Poor Stephen,' said Cora with a giggle, 'I think I embarrassed him.'

Frantic for a diversion, Stephen looked over at Rowan's plate, the meat untouched. 'What's wrong? Are you not well?'

Rowan shook his head, and said quietly, 'You said we should always leave a little on the plate for Mr Manners.'

'Yes, a little. Not every last morsel of beef.'

Freya, with a sidelong look, said, 'He's decided to be vegetarian. Mr Mulhall says that meat isn't good for us.'

'Good heavens,' said Stephen, 'this Mr Mulhall is quite the oracle. Does he ever have an opinion that you don't instantly adopt?'

'Rowan, darling,' said Cora, 'I think it would be very rude to Granny if you left all that food. And to Mrs Arkwright who's gone to the trouble of cooking it.'

With a forlorn glance up the table, Rowan said, 'I'm sorry, Granny.'

'That's all right, poppet,' said Mrs Hamilton, cheery to a

fault. 'I don't much care for meat, either. Perhaps you'd come and help Mrs Arkwright with the pudding. It's Grandpa's favourite.'

Mr Hamilton, recovering from the unsuspected presence of a vegetarian, seemed mollified. 'Guards' pudding,' he said. 'The delight of my boyhood.'

'It sounds grand,' said Stephen, looking at Freya. 'Guards' pudding, eh? Nothing there to offend Mr Mulhall.'

'Don't bank on it,' said Mr Hamilton with a grimace. 'The man's probably a bloody pacifist as well.'

They all laughed, and Freya, sensing the rarity of her grandfather rousing the table to mirth, joined in. Stephen watched his daughter, and felt a desperate squeeze on his heart. She was somewhat mysterious to him. In her fair complexion and long limbs he could see Cora; no doubt her cheekbones would eventually follow suit. On the paternal side he wanted to believe he had passed on to her his equable temperament, and perhaps his watchful eye. But he wondered if he could claim that much credit – Freya's personality seemed cut from a quite different cloth. Who was this dark-eyed sprite they had created? He supposed there was always an element of the child playing at the role of adult, most obviously in her recent adoption of swearing, though what he found far more disconcerting was her absolute self-possession. He didn't have such poise as a twelve-year-old. He didn't have it as a thirty-five-year-old, come to think of it.

He sometimes considered what would happen if his affair with Nina were to be revealed, how Freya would react – how they all would react. Cora, he knew, would be hysterical. The irony of her sobbing at Nina's stage performance as the lover had not escaped him; what bitter tears might follow once it were known that the very same woman now occupied the role in real life, with her own husband? As for Rowan, he couldn't guess his reaction, having no idea what was going on in his head. He was an odd little boy, mopish, passive, neurotic, altogether lacking his sister's vivacious spirit. In truth Stephen already felt guilty about him; he had never imagined finding so little of interest in his own flesh and blood. He loved him, of course – how could he not? – but it seemed to him a love born of anxiety, and duty, rather than a deep genetic affinity. His sense of having failed with Rowan was counterpointed by the tender shock of Freya suddenly becoming the centre of his life. He didn't know how, or when, but there was no use denying it. Should it ever come out that he had betrayed them, he could imagine – no, he didn't have to imagine, he had already been visited in a dream about it. Somehow his secret was out, and the shame of it burnt through Freya's look of incomprehension, of disbelief, a look that said, You did this – *to us*? Nothing in the world could have pierced him as that look did.

In the first few seconds after waking he felt so disturbed by the dream's horrific unmasking that, even as relief flooded his nervous system, he vowed to himself that it must never happen – that he must end things with Nina, and quickly. Yet as the day wore on, he felt his panic subsiding, and he allowed that he may have been hasty in making resolutions. Cora had greeted him at breakfast with a face unclouded by the smallest suspicion. Freya was at school, in Hampshire, and a long way from uncovering the vault at the bottom of his heart. He was safe, still.

The goldish late-October light was receding from the Hamiltons' garden as Stephen, on a terrace deckchair, smoked a cigarette and doodled in his notebook. Its recent pages were filled with minutely different configurations of a group portrait, roughs for the one which would eventually adorn the wall of the Nines. Enjoying a few moments alone while Mr Hamilton dozed and Freya entertained the others at the piano, he started to sketch the contours of a face. How odd that his wife should mention Nina like that. It was as though she had inspected the recent turnover of his thoughts and plucked out the incriminating image almost to tease him. And yet she suspected nothing: why would she?

He was the least likely of adulterers. Thirteen years of marriage and not once had he strayed. He had friends who played away, one or two of them apparently proud of it, and he despised them. Cora had not given him any reason to look elsewhere. She was beautiful, and clever, good company, a fond wife and an excellent mother. She also had her own money, and filled their house with lovely things. He knew how lucky he was. So why had he allowed himself to start falling in love with someone else? He sighed, knowing the answer already. It was simply this: Nina was different, more self-assured, more *interesting*, a single woman who lived for late nights and fast company. With her *he* could be different too, no longer the dutiful husband and father but another, idealised self, a dashing individual who was his own man, not a creature pulled every which way by obligations and responsibilities. He wanted to recapture that thrill of being new and mysterious to someone, someone who didn't take him for granted. Was this how most men justified themselves in the business of betrayal? He didn't know, but it was what he felt. As he sketched, her face filled his mind's eye, and he felt a sudden pricking of desire.

A shadow loomed at his shoulder. 'Who's that?' said Freya, peering down. He hadn't heard her approach.

'I thought you were playing the piano?'

She shrugged, and continued to stare. Stephen, feigning a casual air, added a little cross-hatching to the sketch.

'She looks nice. Who is she?'

Stephen paused. 'She's an actress –'

'Oh, the one you met recently?'

'Yes. Her name's Nina. It was just your mother mentioning

her that made me think . . . Anyway, you're right. She is nice.'

'She's the lover. In the play. I know what a lover is, by the way.'

'I see.' He closed his sketch pad. 'So – school's all right, then?'

Freya nodded, folding her arms.

'How are you off for friends?'

'There's a girl called Cassandra. I like her. I'm not sure she likes me.'

Stephen, turning in his chair to face her, frowned. 'I bet she does. Who wouldn't like you?'

'I wonder,' she mused, 'do you ever think of us, of me, when we're at Tipton?'

'Of course. Quite often, as it happens.'

'So you miss us?'

Stephen squinted at her uncertainly. 'Yes, I do.'

She nodded appraisingly. 'It's just that, if you miss someone, why would you bother sending them away in the first place?'

He had not seen that one coming. If she had asked the question in a self-pitying or plaintive way he might have dismissed it as child's talk. But Freya spoke as she so often did, with a cool matter-of-factness; there was no apparent intention to manipulate his sympathy. He decided to meet it head-on. 'Are you unhappy there?'

'Not really. I'd just rather be at home.'

'Rowan too?'

'I think so.'

Somewhere he heard a door open and Granny Hamilton's laughter. He shook his head, not knowing how to answer. He reached over and put his arm around her shoulder. 'Will you let me have a think about this?'

Freya signalled her acquiescence.

'By the way,' he added, 'I forgot to mention. Grandpa

Wyley has some drawings you might be interested in. He inherited them from his father, who was taught at Oxford by – can you guess?'

'Who?'

'Ruskin, back in – oh – the 1870s. Your house! Anyway, George Wyley, your great-grandfather, kept some of Ruskin's drawings from those days and left them to the family. Shall I dig them out to show you next time?'

'Bloody hell – yes!' she cooed.

Stephen sighed. But what was the use in rebuking her? If it were anyone's fault it was that bloody ass Mr Mulhall.

# II

# A Face to Meet the Faces

# 8

Widening her eyes at the bulb-fringed mirror, Nina gave an involuntary shudder. Hair scraped back off her forehead, the glazed white paint on her face made an unnerving contrast with the vampish mascara around her eyes. It was a face that seemed to have swum out of an unhappy dream.

'My God, I look a frightful old witch,' she said, a damp flannel poised against her cheek.

From across the dressing room came a voice: 'I wouldn't say *old*.' Dolly, her dresser, was smirking in the reflection.

'You horrible hag!' Nina laughed, and threw a slipper that skimmed over Dolly's head. She turned back to her dressing table, a battlefield chaos of pots, paints and cratered powders, littered with the used ammo of lipsticks and blunted eyebrow pencils, glittering puddles of jewellery, corpses of cigarettes twisted in ashtrays and the bomb-site tumulus of a discarded feather boa. Her quarters had become so sluttish that she forbade entry to everyone but Dolly and the call boy. Slowly she began wiping her face clean of its mask.

'Full tonight,' she said absently.

'To the doors,' replied Dolly, as she picked up clothes and hung them over Nina's folding screen.

'Did you hear the Colonel?'

'I know. Missed his cue again.'

'Whole thing's a bit ragged at the moment.'

'He should call a rehearsal.'

'Tighten it up, yes.'

This laconic review of the show continued back and forth, as brisk as Morse code. Dolly, with her thirty-three years' experience in theatrical dressing rooms, was the least surprisable person Nina had ever met. Months of intimate proximity had forged a kind of telepathy between them. It had become almost impossible to keep secrets from her. She sometimes felt that Dolly was like a mother to her – the sort of mother you could talk to – which, in the light of how things stood with her actual mother, was a considerable comfort.

Only now did she spot the decorous bouquet of flowers behind her.

'Who brought them?'

'Call boy.'

'I mean, who sent them?'

'There's a note.'

She plucked the neat little envelope from its pin and opened it.

Dearest N,

Surprise! Wanted to hand these in personally but the boy said nobody enters the lady's dressing room on pain of death. Will you meet me at the club afterwards? I'm there till midnight, probably later. Break a leg – isn't that what they say? S.

'Oh, the dear booby,' said Nina with a pleased giggle. 'They're from him.'

'Fancy.'

'He wants to meet me later.'

Dolly lifted her chin knowingly. 'Is his wife all right with that?'

Nina half snorted in reply, and read Stephen's note again. She had supposed him to be too reserved for such spontaneity. Could it be he was really missing her? She had instructed herself not to go chasing after him. It was up to him to make the running in this affair – he was the one with the wife and children, after all. She would not plead for his company. Admittedly, it was nearly killing her. When they were together she had to stop herself blurting out that she was sick with love for him. At times she felt her restraint to be bordering on the masochistic. One evening when he told her that she was looking especially beautiful, she had batted it away with a queenly tilt of her head, while inside her heart thumped against her ribs.

'You 'aven't forgotten about milady?' enquired Dolly, breaking into this train of thought.

'No – though I wish to God I could.'

'Milady', or Nina's mother, had been in the stalls this evening with her older sister Felicity. The tickets had actually been reserved for her younger sister Bee, who had cried off the previous day for reasons unknown. Now she would have to meet them for supper when she would much rather have gone straight to Stephen. What's more, she would have to pretend pleasure at seeing her mother: a performance *after* the performance. She picked up a tangled pair of stockings from her table, gave them a wary sniff and decided they would do.

Dolly gave a philosophical pout. 'Well, you only get one mother.'

'Hmm. I find one is more than enough. What was the secret with yours?'

'Well . . . I didn't see so much of her. She was out working the whole bleedin' time, doing people's laundry, raddling the steps, off to the factory. And there was seven of us kids, of course – no time to dawdle!'

'Seven? She must have been exhausted.'

'Yeah,' sighed Dolly. 'No wonder she died young. First rest she'd ever 'ad.'

Ten minutes later Nina was dressed and out of the place. With a quick goodnight to the stage-door man she dodged through the post-show crowds milling on the Aldwych and made for the dining rooms on Catherine Street. Her vexation with familial duties had been somewhat mollified by Stephen's note. With any luck she would be on her way to him in an hour or so.

'Heavens, you look tired,' said Mrs Land by way of greeting.

Nina bent in low to kiss her, then did the same with Felicity, who said, with more tact, 'You were good – really awfully good.' Felicity was her senior by five years, taller than Nina but not as fine-featured. She was the most even-tempered of the three sisters, and the easiest to like. Her life was settled at home in Guildford: she had a husband who did something at the Treasury, three young children, and a black Labrador. She came up to town infrequently.

'Thanks, Fliss. I didn't expect to see you here.'

Mrs Land shook her head. 'It's such a shame Bee couldn't come. She was going to bring one of her colleagues.'

'Why couldn't she come?' said Nina.

'Oh, she's quite out of sorts. They work her to the bone at that school.' Nina only nodded. Her mother tended to talk of her favourite child as though she were the only person who had ever had a job.

'So we were the lucky beneficiaries,' said Felicity brightly. 'Second time for you, Mum.'

'Yes, well, I didn't mind seeing it again,' said her mother, and Nina waited for a word of praise, a pleasantry – in vain.

A waiter had arrived to take their order, and Mrs Land, coquettish in the presence of any moderately handsome man, made a little show of being taken by surprise. 'Oh, I do beg your pardon,' she said. 'Perhaps you could tell us the specials this evening?'

'Braised veal with carrots, madam.'

Nina snapped her menu shut. 'I'll just have a mushroom omelette, thanks.'

When the wine arrived Nina bolted down a glass and immediately poured another: it took the edge off her mood. Still thinking of the flowers Stephen had sent, and the accompanying note, she hardly heard what her mother and sister were talking about – a bridge evening with people she'd never heard of, and a driving holiday in the new car which John, Felicity's husband, had just bought. It was when the conversation turned to their friend and benefactor Eric Dorsch that her ears pricked up.

'The last time I saw you he was going to take you out to dinner,' said Nina.

Her mother blinked. 'Ah, we had to postpone that, I'm afraid. Eric's so busy at the moment with his Spanish aid committee – orphans from the war there, you know. Hundreds of them are being sent over.'

'But you think he's keen to marry again.'

'I have an inkling he is,' said Mrs Land, with a little smirk. 'Poor Monica's been gone three years now, and a man like Eric will need a companion in life . . . He told me only the other day how much he values me – I've done a few mornings as a volunteer in the office, finding homes for the little ones.'

'Volunteer work? You?' She must be crazy about him, Nina thought. She had never before expressed the remotest interest in helping displaced children. It wasn't stretching a point to say she could barely muster an interest in her *own* children.

Felicity was perhaps thinking along the same lines, for she now said, 'Is this what you wanted to talk to us about? Are you going to get married?'

'Well, I don't *know*,' said Mrs Land, with a look that suggested she would take a proposal in her stride. 'It's not beyond the realms of possibility. But no, that's not what I wanted to talk to you about.'

'What is it, then?'

She put on her 'thoughtful' expression, which Nina found faintly ominous. 'I had a talk with the solicitor this week, and he's advised me on certain – amendments to my will. Practical things.'

'Your will. I assumed we –'

'Yes, of course, whatever savings I have will be divided among the three of you equally. The same goes for the jewellery.'

Nina looked across to her sister, who was frowning. The 'savings', as far as she knew, were negligible, and the jewellery was mostly paste. 'So what have you changed?' Felicity said.

'Well,' she said with a decided air, 'I've been thinking of the future, and what it holds for you all. You two are set up, of course. You've got John and the children in Guildford, and Nina has her career, which I'm sure will go from strength to strength. So that's splendid. Poor Bee, on the other hand, is a junior-school teacher with scarcely a penny to her name, scraping by in that horrid boarding house in Fulham. You know how I worry about her . . .'

'So you're going to leave her some extra money?' said Nina, still in the dark.

'No,' said Mrs Land with a beatific shake of her head. 'She's going to have the house.'

Nina, not wanting to believe what she had just heard, gave a little gasp. 'What?'

'She hasn't got any security in her life, so I want to make sure she's provided for. I am her mother, after all.'

Felicity still wore a puzzled frown. 'Mum, I know Bee has had a hard time of it lately, but she's twenty-nine – there's

138

plenty of time to find a husband and get a new job. You like to think she's some poor waif, but she's not. I mean, aren't we entitled to a share as well?'

'But, darling, you have a house – and all the money you need. I'm sure you'd feel better knowing that she'll have a roof over her head.'

'*I* don't feel better,' said Nina, failing to keep the asperity from her voice. 'What kind of *security* d'you think I have? What happens when my career goes to pot and I can't even get a job in rep?'

'Don't be silly. You'll always have work. What about those film people you said you're going to meet?'

'A screen test, that's all. And the idea of "always" having work is nonsense. Do you know what I have lined up after this run? Nothing, that's what.'

Felicity, hearing her sister's aggrieved tone, attempted a more conciliatory approach. 'I'm sure Bee will appreciate the thought, but I can't imagine she'll agree to the idea of us being . . . cut off.'

'You're not "cut off",' said Mrs Land with an irked little movement of her head. 'It's very hurtful of you to suggest I would do such a thing. Anyway, I've already discussed it with Bee, and she's got no objection to the plan at all.'

*That's* why she hasn't come tonight, thought Nina. She's not out of sorts – she's just embarrassed to face us. Keeping her voice low and steady, she said, 'Of course you must dispose of the house as you wish. But I would ask you – no, I would beg you – to reconsider, and I'll tell you why. You may think you're being generous, and Bee may think so too, but in the long run this will cause nothing but ill feeling. D'you not see?'

As she listened, her mother's mouth seemed to contract into a thin hard slot. Plainly wrong-footed by her daughters' uncooperative response, she had gone on the defensive. After some moments of cold silence she spoke in a tone Nina had come to know well: resentment mingled with defiance. 'I really don't know why I bothered to tell you. I should have just amended the will and left it at that.'

'That would have been a nice surprise for us,' said Nina with a sarcastic half-laugh.

At that Mrs Land rose from her seat and, with a look of hurt dignity, said, 'I'm going to powder my nose. I hope on my return you'll have recovered your manners.'

Nina stared straight ahead as her mother stalked away from the table. She found she was in a tremble, whether from shock or indignation she didn't know. She couldn't speak. Not knowing what to do with herself she took out a cigarette, and struck the match so fiercely that it flew out of her hand and landed on the table. Felicity, calming her, took the box of matches and lit it for her. She took a great gasping lungful of smoke.

Moments passed before she looked to her sister and said, 'Sorry, I'm – I feel like I've just been . . . mugged.'

Felicity shook her head rather sadly. 'No – merely disinherited.'

'You know what's behind it? She believes Mr Dorsch is going to ask her to marry him. Then she'll go to live in his house and let Bee move into hers.'

'Isn't that rather presumptuous of her?'

'Not as far as she's concerned. She thinks she's a catch.'

Felicity looked doubtful. 'I'd better go and check on her.'

'And I'd better leave.'

'Don't you dare,' Felicity replied sharply, standing up. 'I'm not going through this on my own.' She went off in the direction of the Ladies.

The temptation was to bolt, but somehow she resisted it. By the time her mother and sister returned to the table she had managed to compose herself. By unspoken agreement the incendiary subject was not mentioned again; all was politeness and deference. How Nina got through dinner she couldn't say. She made a show of listening, though contributed barely a word herself. There was nothing wrong with the omelette she had ordered, but every mouthful disgusted her, and she gave it up half eaten. She ordered a second bottle of wine, and drank most of it. Her senses had blurred somewhat, though not to the point of oblivion that she craved.

'Darling, are you all right?' said Felicity, taking her by surprise.

She nodded, and checked her watch. 'I must go. I promised to meet a friend at his club in Dover Street.' Her words seemed to come out mechanically.

'Well, that's on our way. We could drop you.'

The thought of having to feign civility for even ten minutes longer sickened her. She stood up and, with all the actorly guile at her command, projected brightness into her manner. She thanked them for coming, and for taking her to supper, and wished them 'safe home'. Her mother accepted a kiss goodnight with not a trace of her previous ill temper. Indeed, it was as if none of the earlier conversation had actually occurred.

Hailing a cab on the Aldwych she plumped herself on the seat and felt her head swimming. She must have had at least a bottle and a half of wine, with a large cognac floated on top for good measure. The glare of the West End street lamps through the dark enclosure of the cab played games of chiaroscuro across her face. She didn't want to think about what her mother had done – and she couldn't think of anything else. The bitch. The *rotten bitch*. How could she, really? It was one thing for her to have made Bee her favourite. She could bear that. But to advertise the preference to the point of changing her will, no, that was too much. It was unmaternal: it was unforgivable. She replayed the conversation, and gave a bitter laugh at her mother's describing Bee's 'horrid little boarding house' in Fulham.

So what about her own horrid boarding house in Marylebone? Did her mother think she could simply up sticks and move wherever she pleased?

And what havoc would follow. Nina had meant it when she told her of the ill feeling it would create. My God, it was like *Lear*, with Felicity and herself as Goneril and Regan. 'Striving to better, oft we mar what's well . . .' It was a legacy that could warp them all for years. Perhaps Felicity would be all right about it, having a more equable character, not to mention the *security* of a husband and a large house. She would probably have to play the peacemaker, once Nina got round to telling Bee exactly what she thought of her accepting their mother's poisoned bequest. *She's got no objection to the plan at all*. No wonder! Inheriting the house would allow her to escape her miserable accommodation; she might even take in a lodger or two, making the house pay and freeing her of the job she professed to hate. How could their mother not foresee this as a source of strife? Possibly because she had so little imagination. It had enabled her to behave without guilt her whole life.

The cab had arrived. She could see shadowy figures ambling through the porticoed entrance of the Nines, the light from its upper windows hushed and discreet. She had just made her way into the entrance hall when she heard her name called from above, and there was Stephen trotting down the stairs, looking as eager as a new prefect. That, and his cheery 'halloa', coming so quickly on top of the high turbulence she had been fielding all night, caused an unforeseen reaction. A hot prickling welled behind her eyes, and suddenly she was watching him approach through a helpless blur of tears.

Madeleine hurried along the Strand, dodging around the window gazers and pavement pounders and office workers streaming home. The night carried a little chill in the air.

Buses rumbled past, their dim interiors and expressionless passengers reminding her of old saloon bars, with the conductor on his platform like a welcoming publican. Roddy had pulled a face when she told him why she wanted the night off. 'The theatre? What d'you wanna go there for?' She began to explain how she and her aunt used to enjoy the local am-dram, but he didn't seem in the least bit interested. 'Should find better things to waste your money on,' he called over his shoulder. She had decided not to tell him she was someone's guest for the evening.

She had assumed the Strand Theatre would actually be *on* the Strand, but it wasn't, and she had to stop and ask a newspaper vendor for directions. As she followed the curve of the Aldwych she realised she had no distinct memory of what Tom looked like. When they had spoken on the telephone the previous week, the voice was familiar but she couldn't put a face to it. In her mind's eye she saw a thirtyish man of medium build, dark straight hair, and a face that was, well, average-looking. It was odd to have spent intense moments in another's company and still be unable to describe them.

People were swarming through the theatre's doors as she arrived. Her mood was somewhat tense about the night ahead of her.

'Madeleine,' called a voice.

He was standing under a lit sign that announced TONIGHT AT 7.30. She returned his uncertain wave as she threaded her way among the crowd.

'Hullo! I wasn't sure I could remember' – she began, and saved herself at the last moment – 'where this place was.'

'The name's a bit confusing, I suppose, not being on the Strand . . . Well, we've just got time for a drink.'

He led her through the jostling foyer and up the stairs to the circle bar. She asked for a gin fizz, a drink Roddy had introduced her to. Tom, amused, had the same. She kept stealing quick glances at him, weighing up her imperfect recollection against the man she saw in front of her. He was perhaps a bit older than she had initially estimated, there were flecks of silver in the floppy hair that fell across his brow, and his manner was more at ease; that wasn't surprising, really, given the disconcerting nature of their first encounter. He caught her looking at him, and seemed to read her thoughts.

'Don't worry, you're absolved of Samaritan duties this evening. The play would have to be quite atrocious for me to have another turn like that.'

'You look very well,' she said with a laugh, relieved that he could make light of his illness.

'I've been feeling much better,' he admitted. 'And I've been looking forward to seeing – erm – this again.' Tom, too, had swerved away from forwardness at the last moment.

Madeleine blinked her surprise. 'You mean, you've seen the play already?'

'Yes! I reviewed it when it opened. I was deputising for my boss.'

'So you don't mind seeing it again?'

'Oh no. There's a terribly good actress in it – and of course I thought it'd be something you might enjoy.'

The bell rang, calling the loiterers in the bar to take their seats. They had barely managed to sip their drinks. Tom, clinking his glass against hers, shot her a look of mock alarm.

'We'd better gulp these down. Here's how!'

She watched him drain his glass in one, and followed suit. As the sharp juniper coldness bolted down her insides she regretted not having a strong head for drink, though the subsequent lightness in her chest was really quite pleasant. Tom led her into the chattering gloom of the circle, and she admired the nimble way he edged along the row to their seats. She felt glad to have dressed up for the occasion.

The lights were just dimming when she turned to him and said, in an undertone, 'I'm sorry, I've already forgotten the name of this play.'

Tom leaned in at a respectful distance to whisper, 'It's called *The Second Arrangement*.'

The play was a melodrama, set in the 1890s, concerning a well-regarded politician, the coming man of his party, who's about to marry a young heiress. Everything seems set fair when, out of the blue, he meets an old flame of his at a London gathering. This lady, who has been abroad, is no longer quite respectable, and has no fortune. But it's plain she is more the politician's sort of woman than his young intended will ever be. At first he's not sure he recognises her, but once he does the effect on him proves momentous: he realises that his passion for her, far from being extinguished, burns more fiercely than ever. The second act ends with the politician arranging an assignation with the woman in a seaside hotel: is he going to jeopardise his forthcoming marriage and political career?

As the curtain was rung down for the interval, Tom looked hopefully to Madeleine for her reaction. She had been absorbed in the drama, as far as he could tell; though now, with the house lights up, he detected in her a troubled abstraction. On the way back to the bar he tried to jolly her along.

'It's not quite so assured as the first time I saw it. What about the old boy – missed his cue completely!'

'Yes, I noticed that,' she said, still preoccupied.

'You're not finding it a bore?'

She looked at him in confusion. 'Not at all. I was enjoying it very much. It's just –'

'Yes?'

'The actress playing Hester – is that the one you thought was terribly good?'

'Indeed. You disagree?'

'No, no, she's wonderful . . . I just have a feeling I've seen her before.'

'She's quite well known – Nina Land.' The name triggered no recognition in Madeleine. 'Perhaps you saw her photograph in one of the illustrated newspapers,' suggested Tom.

She nodded, still wondering; she was not in the habit of reading newspapers. Tom had reached the counter, and was trying to catch the barman's eye when he heard his name called. He looked round to see Jimmy's old pal Peter Liddell, offering a little salute from the other end of the bar and pointing to a bottle of champagne he had on the go. Tom turned back to Madeleine.

'There's a friend I've just spotted over there. D'you mind if we join him?'

Madeleine signalled her willingness, and they wriggled their way through the press of bodies. Peter, who had the stooped posture of one conscious of his lankiness, greeted them with a benign smile.

'Peter, hullo. This is, um, Madeleine Farewell.'

'Miss Farewell – very pleased to meet you!' he said, offering her his hand. After László, Tom liked Peter the best of all Jimmy's friends, who tended to be rather strong meat. He had been grateful to Peter from the first time they met, nearly ten years ago, when he had openly encouraged Jimmy to give him, a perfect stranger, a job as his secretary.

Peter nodded at a little coterie of men chatting away in the corner. 'We've got a bottle of pop open,' he said. 'Will you have a glass?' He began pouring.

'Are you a theatre person, too?' she asked.

Peter laughed. 'Don't be deceived by these matinee-idol looks. I'm actually a doctor.'

Madeleine smiled. 'I suppose you get people coming to you with all sorts of imaginary complaints.'

'Of course!' he replied. 'Though I'd say about eighty per cent of them were from our friend Jimmy – I'm sure Tom's told you about him.'

'Are you his doctor, then?'

'Used to be,' Peter said. 'His ailments were so many and various it became practically a full-time job. If I hadn't stopped being his doctor I think it would have killed me – or else I would have killed *him*.' He nodded at Tom. 'I don't know how this fellow has managed to stick with him all these years. He's too saintly.'

Tom made a grimace. 'Not really. And it might not be for that much longer.' Even as he spoke he regretted it. Peter's confiding manner had tempted him to candour, and now his widened eyes couldn't have looked more intrigued.

'So you're going to leave him?'

'For God's sake don't say anything – please. I've been thinking about it for a while, you know, and . . . now might be the time.'

'Have you been arguing?'

Tom made a sound that was half-sigh, half-snort. 'We're always arguing. I don't know, it's like . . . being stuck in a bad marriage.'

He felt Madeleine's eyes upon him as he spoke, and wondered how that admission would sound to her.

'Well, it's difficult,' said Peter, 'but it could be for the best . . . Jim'll be upset, of course – he's come to depend on you.'

Tom, trying to reassure himself, said, 'I'll just have to find the right moment.'

Peter gave a slow sympathetic nod, and Tom changed the subject.

'How d'you like the play?'

'Not bad, the odd Victorian creak notwithstanding. Nina Land is superb, I think.'

'Isn't she! Madeleine here thought she might know her.'

Madeleine blushed. 'Oh, I'm probably mistaken . . .'

Peter, seeing her awkwardness, said kindly, 'She's got one of those faces, hasn't she? I remember Jim raving about her in something a few years ago.'

'He's always been quick to spot talent,' said Tom, mindful of giving Jimmy his due.

'We're meant to be meeting him later,' said Peter. 'Why don't you join us?'

Tom looked to Madeleine. 'A drink after the show?'

Wanting to be agreeable, she smiled. 'That would be nice.'

The interval bell had just rung. Peter downed his glass and said, 'Righto. I have to look after this lot' – he gestured at his contingent behind him – 'but I'll see you at my club. You know the Nines on Dover Street?'

Tom nodded, and they dispersed in the direction of their seats. Madeleine, having observed Peter's manner and the company he kept, now wondered if Tom was queer too. Devotion to the theatre wasn't necessarily a sign, though the business did attract a certain type. He dressed with care, and he seemed on very familiar terms with Peter. Perhaps what most inclined her to think so was his behaviour towards her. He was friendly, and had nice manners; he didn't try to peek down her dress, as other men did, or stand too close. She had become used to men giving her the eye, the ravenous gleam that meant they wanted to possess you or, if the mood went the other way, do you in.

The play had resumed, and again her attention was held by the actress playing the lover: Nina something. *She's got one of those faces*, Peter had said. Had she met her at Roddy's club? An ever-changing traffic of women flowed through the place, dancers, waitresses, street girls, it was hard to keep up with them all. She felt sure she hadn't spoken to her, yet she recognised her voice, slightly husky, quiet at first, then raised . . . she had been on her way out . . . her way out. She leaned forward in her seat, staring hard. Oh God, it was *her*. That afternoon in the Imperial. It was the woman who had knocked on the door. The voice that had saved her life. She had nearly run the woman down in her rush to get out of there. Now Madeleine remembered the face, and the startled expression as she careered past her.

She found her breathing had become shallow as the panic returned. The bruises on her neck had faded, but how she had come by them remained vividly present. The insect-blackness of his eyes, the hands bunched about her throat, the droplet of his sweat feathering her cheek . . . She felt her stomach lurch, and the dizzying approach of nausea. Grasping Tom's arm for leverage she rose, amid bemused murmurings, managed to whisper that she had to get some air and stumbled across him towards the aisle, hardly seeing, but moving headlong.

Absorbed in the drama, Tom had not noticed Madeleine's turmoil, and was taken aback by her sudden barging exit. What on earth was the matter? He had sensed an uneasiness in her just before the interval, but she seemed to recover herself once they got to the bar. He experienced a moment's indecision. The play was gravitating to its climax, and he was loath to miss it; on the other hand, she might be in real distress, in which case –

He found her outside, sitting on a fire-door step, head bowed, her shoulders rising with her deep breaths. He called her name, softly, and she looked up. The colour had fled from her face.

'Are you all right?'

She closed her eyes, and nodded. 'I'm sorry . . . I thought I was going to be sick.'

'It wasn't the excitement of the play, was it?'

She gave a pained half-smile. 'I don't know what it was – I just had a moment of – panic.'

'Panic?'

She had not meant to say that, because it invited a question. She gave her head a little shake, as though to dismiss the word. 'I sometimes have these . . . turns, when I'm in public.' She was making it up on the spot, but his grave expression indicated he believed her completely.

'Oh dear – that sounds like what I've got!'

She felt awful about lying to him, the more so for knowing his own illness to be the real thing. But she had been forced to bluff. If she told him the truth about her encounter with the actress, he would naturally wonder what she was doing at a hotel in the middle of the afternoon. And it was important to her that he didn't know how she earned a living. She wanted to be just an ordinary girl to him. They continued sitting on the step for a few moments, looking down whenever the footsteps of a passer-by below sounded in their ears. Tom gave his watch a furtive glance.

'D'you think you might like to go back in?' he said.

The shake of her head was decisive. 'But please – don't let me stop you,' she added, catching his eye.

'Oh, I wouldn't dream of it,' he said, smothering a surge of disappointment. 'Perhaps we should stroll for a while – some fresh air might restore you.'

He helped her to stand, and as she rose she had to keep down a dangerous lurch in her gullet: unbearable to be sick in front of him. She felt his eyes nervously upon her as they began to walk, her hand light in the crook of his elbow. Tom wondered if Madeleine's discomposure had something to do with her recognising Nina Land, but he sensed how little she would welcome his prying. So he paid her the courtesy of silence instead. They had reached the Strand when he looked at her again.

'We could take up Peter's invitation and pole over to the Nines . . .'

'I don't think I can face it,' she replied, and felt another stab of guilt on seeing his crestfallen expression. 'But I wouldn't mind a quick drink before I go home.'

A bus had just halted, and Tom said, 'Come on then.' Before she could reply he had hopped onto the platform and was holding forth his hand. He seemed to her suddenly boyish, standing there against the pole, and the bus was already pulling away when she darted up to join him.

# 9

Jimmy, whose stride was imperious before he had to use a stick, now found himself *skulking*, there was no other word for it, like one of those men who hung about disreputable bookshops in Soho. He was in the *Chronicle* building, just off Fleet Street, and had somehow got lost on his way to the arts department. His plan to slip in and out unnoticed had collapsed straight away. The chap at the desk had given him a very peculiar look, possibly because the slouch hat he wore was so obviously an attempt at disguise.

He stopped a copy boy hurrying down the stairs and learned that Lambert's office had been relocated to the fourth floor. Dammit – so much for his ruse to avoid the lift. By the time he got up there he was wheezing like an old horse. It was the asthma, exacerbated no doubt by the weight he kept putting on. He found the office at last, and knocked on the open door.

Lambert, glancing up, called out a greeting, then frowned as he examined his visitor's shadowed face. 'Christ, is that a black eye?'

Jimmy, entering the room, didn't immediately reply. He parked himself on the horsehair sofa, removed his hat, and folded his hands over the head of his cane. 'Domestic accident,' he said curtly.

'I wondered what was up,' said Lambert, with the faint approach of a smile in his eyes. 'Not like you to miss a deadline – two of 'em, in fact.'

'I was operating out of one eye. As a critic I generally prefer to use both.'

Lambert had stepped around his desk for a closer appraisal of the damage. '*Phoo* . . . that's a proper shiner, isn't it?' He paused, and smirked. 'Bit old for brawling, aren't you?'

Jimmy looked away in disdain. 'As I said, it was an accident. At home.' His tone was coldly dignified, though to his own ears it still lacked conviction.

'Right, yeah,' Lambert said, in the sceptical way that infuriated Jimmy. He had been holed up in his flat for days, shielding himself from the public gaze. Necessity had at last forced him out. The bailiffs were threatening another visit, and he needed to raise money quickly. In the usual run of things he would have sent Tom, but securing an advance from the paper required documents to be signed – or countersigned, or whatever it was – in person. It was humiliating, of course, to come cap in hand to one's employers, particularly for someone as well remunerated as he was, and he had made a private resolution that his accountant's letters must no longer be ignored.

A secretary had arranged the paperwork, to which Jimmy now appended his signature. He was conscious all the while of Lambert's insinuating presence as he stooped over the desk.

'Looks like someone's in Queer Street.'

'What?' said Jimmy, mishearing.

'You. Hard up.'

Jimmy felt himself breathe again. 'I've one or two creditors to pay off,' he replied, *not that it's any of your damned business.*

Lambert, lighting a Woodbine, stared into the distance.

'How does it go? "Annual income twenty pounds, annual expenditure nineteen nineteen and six –"'

'"Result happiness" – yes, thank you, Mr Micawber. May I?'

Lambert picked up the buff envelope from his desk and handed it over. 'Are you going to count it?'

Jimmy's instinct as a gambler was always to count it, but he didn't want to give him the satisfaction. 'I'm sure it's all there,' he said, sliding it into his breast pocket. He was nearly out the door when Lambert said, 'By the way, Barry asked you to call by. He's on the third floor.'

Jimmy scuttled off, irritated by this unforeseen diversion. Barry Rusk was one of his oldest friends, a man of like age who had started out as a hack before rising through the ranks of the paper. His was a classic newspaperman's face – lined – and from the distracted expression on it today Jimmy surmised he had not been called in for a pat on the back.

'What happened?' asked Barry on seeing Jimmy's swollen eye.

'Oh, you know . . .' He sighed, though Barry's raised eyebrow suggested a fuller answer was required. 'I had one of my little adventures.'

Barry, who understood the code, shook his head. He rose from his desk and closed the door of his office against the hubbub outside. 'Honestly, Jim – I don't think you quite understand the danger you're in.'

Jimmy tried to make his chuckle sound devil-may-care. 'Wouldn't you say I'm wearing the evidence?'

'I'm not talking about that, though God knows why you'd want to hang around people who'd spit in your eye as soon as look at you.'

'Ah. What "danger" do you mean, then?'

'There was a luncheon on the top floor last week, hosted by our dear proprietor Lord Swaim. The usual thing – high

154

matters of church and state discussed over smoked haddock and Meursault.'

'Oh. Shame I wasn't invited,' said Jimmy lightly.

Barry gave him a level stare. 'Your name came up, actually. You know Swaim likes to regard his newspaper as a bulwark of moral values, British probity and all that. Well . . . rumours have reached His Lordship's ears of a prominent writer in his employ who's been keeping some low company. He's concerned that if the man's behaviour became public knowledge it could damage the paper's good name.'

Jimmy felt a claw squeezing the inside of his chest. Swallowing, he said, 'How much does he know?'

'Enough that you should worry. He knows that you bat for the other side.'

'*What?* How on earth – ?'

Barry's frown was pitying. 'People talk, Jim. You know that. It's not like you've been a model of discretion. I dare say there's a nice story behind that shiner you've got there . . .'

Mention of it caused Jimmy to raise a protecting hand over his brow. He thought he should hear the worst. 'So he wants me out?'

'Well, he got very exercised – quoted our old King, as a matter of fact – "I thought men like that shot themselves." Fortunately the editor managed to calm him down – spoke in your defence, described your column as one of the most prestigious in Fleet Street, beloved of our readers, et cetera. You ought to be grateful to him. He got you a royal pardon.'

'Good old Bostock. He always liked me.'

Barry shook his head. 'You're not off the tumbril yet. If Swaim gets wind of any more of your antics, your feet won't touch – I mean it. Bostock defended you because you're a big name on the paper, but he won't risk his own neck to save you. If I were you I should lie low – and for God's sake keep it in your trousers.'

'Yes, of course, you're quite right,' muttered Jimmy, feeling chastened. Barry had never told him off like this before, it really wasn't his style. That was a warning in itself. They talked for a few minutes longer before Jimmy sensed that Barry was waiting for him to leave – perhaps to embark straight away on his regimen of prudent behaviour.

He emerged from the building in a state of low-level panic. He had become so used to walking the high wire of his sexual proclivities that he had almost forgotten how suddenly the line might snap and pitch him into the abyss. Despite what Barry said, he *had* been discreet, relatively speaking. If there were whispers about his errant ways nobody had yet pinned anything on him. Unlike other inverts with a reputation to protect, he had never been arrested, or blackmailed, or – until last week – roughed up. Well, now he knew there was a first time for everything . . .

His adventure had been entirely on the spur of the moment. Having dashed off an amusing little squib ('Who Reads Film Criticism?') for the weekend paper he called in at the Criterion for an early-evening plate of oysters. It would tide him over until his late supper with Peter at the Nines. In observance of his new austerity drive he ordered a half-bottle of the Muscadet. That went down quicker than a homesick mole, so he had another. Rolling out into the crowds around Piccadilly, he caught an autumnal whiff of petrol and roasting chestnuts in the air, with a layer of something else beneath: possibility. He crossed the road and called in at the blazing Long Bar in the Trocadero, a favourite hunting ground, but this evening so raucous he could barely hear himself think. He made for Soho instead, his step growing purposeful as the streets narrowed and darkened around him. As soon as he glimpsed the iron railings on Broadwick Street and its beckoning sign, GENTLEMEN, he felt the old thrumming in his blood, a sensation of delight that was inseparable from fear. Does a mouse resist the cheese even when it sees the trap? He walked past, then stopped and waited.

The late-October night had drawn down its blinds. A dreary street lamp threw a cone of light by which one could survey the anonymous visitors filing in and out of the public lavatory. It took Jimmy's trained eye to distinguish between the ones who called in for a piss and those furtive few who had other things in mind. That pale-faced youth, for example, the one with the sliding eyes who had disappeared below a few minutes ago, he'd had a proper air of mischief . . . Jimmy glanced left and right before quitting his lookout post and descending smartly down the steps. The stench of ammonia mingled with detergent started a throb in his trousers. A dingy bulb lit the long room and its reeking enfilade of urinals along one wall, where a single figure was occupied, eyes straight ahead, a slight tilt to his back. A fierce stream of urine could be heard hissing against the porcelain. Jimmy went to stand at the next one along; the man, indifferent, shook his peg and buttoned up. Without so much as a glance he departed, his steps receding upwards to the street. It seemed he was alone, though he felt certain that his quarry had not exited the place.

Behind him were three cubicles, two of them with the door ajar. The last one stood seductively closed. Jimmy liked a touch of coyness, it lent the illusion of having to earn his fun. He sidled over, and with a cough as his introduction he pushed at the door, which was unlocked. The youth, straddling the toilet bowl, gave him the once-over.

'Thought it might be you,' he said with a snicker. 'Seen ya outside. I thought, 'e's a dirty dog. Am I right?'

Jimmy wondered what sort of reply was expected. 'Well, I'm –'

'*Yeah*, a right dirty dog,' he continued, rising to his feet as he appraised Jimmy. He was a shortish, wiry youth of about nineteen or twenty in a brown wool suit. Jimmy had liked his shifty, vulpine gaze, though he hadn't noticed the discoloured scar down the side of his jaw. In one quick movement the boy grabbed him by his coat front and shoved him down onto the seat he had lately occupied. The force of this little manoeuvre caused Jimmy to bang his head against the thick iron pipe running up to the cistern.

'Ouch! My dear fellow –' Jimmy began laughingly, and stopped on catching a glint of something steely in the boy's hand. This was not what he'd had in mind. The boy casually brushed his cheek with the knife's tip. He leaned forward and patted down Jimmy's breast pockets, then fished out his wallet. He opened it, and pulled a face at its meagre contents. Pocketing the money, he began examining the rest. Jimmy's hand tightened around his walking stick.

The boy drew out a card and read: '"Press pass . . . Mr James Erskine . . . the *Chronicle*." Ha, a journalist, eh? Maybe you could write about *me*.' He threw the card away, and picked out another. Emboldened by his distracted look, Jimmy sprang forward, whirling his stick through the air and catching his opponent a sharp blow on the forearm. The knife clattered on the floor. He was nearly past him when the youth recovered his balance and swung a fist that connected explosively with his eye. Jimmy felt a white starburst of pain shoot through him as he crumpled onto the toilet floor, and thence into unconsciousness.

In the days following this incident Tom had telephoned Princess Louise Mansions repeatedly and received no reply.

It was so unlike Jimmy to withdraw from company that he went round in person one afternoon, only to be told by the porter that Mr Erskine was 'indisposed', and had given instructions that he wasn't to be disturbed.

'What's wrong with him?' asked Tom, knowing how much Jimmy feared to be left alone.

The porter shrugged. 'Ain't seen hide nor hair of 'im, sir. Though he must be around,' he added, 'cos I took delivery of his wand this morning.'

Tom was puzzled, until the man pointed to the back wall of his office, where a new walking stick was propped.

In the meantime he had resolved to hand in his notice to Jimmy. The decision was long overdue. They had been together nine years, and he knew it would be better to quit while they were still on speaking terms. When he had started, his duties had been clearly defined: editing, proofreading, liaising between his editors and publishers, deputising for him when he went on holiday. Perhaps he had been too efficient in the job, because Jimmy eventually had him running his diary, his finances, his housekeeping, his travel arrangements. His life. Nor had he been remunerated for this ancillary work. He had squeezed one meagre pay rise out of him four years ago – or was it five? That business over the typewriter was really the last straw . . . He acknowledged his own share of the blame in allowing him to get away with it.

The mysterious silence ended one Friday morning when he received a note from Jimmy asking him to call at the flat. On his way there Tom carefully rehearsed what he would say, a few sincere, straightforward phrases outlining his decision to leave, his gratitude for nine years' employment, and his modest hope that he had been of service. There would be no mention of Jimmy's meanness, his ill tempers, his selfish and graceless behaviour, any of it – they would part as friends. If Jimmy wished to provide him with references . . . no, he would not even ask for that, he would simply shake hands and be on his way. He found that he was whistling as he stepped off the bus. *I should have done this years ago*, he thought as the porter admitted him.

Upstairs Mrs Pargiter, the char, answered the door. 'I've just brought 'im his tea,' she said, nodding towards the living room. This was odd in itself: usually by eleven Jimmy would be blazing away in his office, meeting a deadline.

He gave a brief tap at the door and walked in. Jimmy was sitting in one of the winged armchairs with a tray across his lap, spooning out a breakfast egg. His eyes were shielded by a pair of dark glasses, which gave Tom an abrupt lurch of fright.

'Oh my God – what's happened?'

Jimmy put down his spoon and, with the grave dignity of a dowager removing her lorgnettes, presented his face. Tom stepped closer to examine his black eye, which was now a livid blue with yellow striations.

'You look almost relieved,' said Jimmy, with indignant surprise.

'I am. When I saw those dark glasses I thought you'd gone *blind*.'

'For a few days I practically was – couldn't see out of this one.'

On the coffee table steam was drifting from a china teapot. He bent down and poured them each a cup, adding Jimmy's milk and sugar. The invalid took the proffered tea with a mournful air.

'I presume the traditional concomitant *sympathy* is on the way,' he muttered.

Tom made an apologetic motion with his head and sank into a chair opposite. 'Who did this to you?'

Jimmy looked away, and sighed. 'A wanton boy. I could

bear the bruising, but he took my pocket watch, too. Had it since I went to France . . . twenty-two years.'

'I'm sorry, Jim, that's rotten luck. What did the police say?'

Jimmy stared back. 'You think I went to the police.'

'Why not? You've been –' He read a mixture of embarrassment and defiance playing over Jimmy's features, and understood. 'Oh . . . I see.' So it was like that.

As though able to read his thoughts, Jimmy murmured, '"I grow old, I grow old" . . . Beastly little thing, assaulting a fellow like me. Thirty years ago I would have boxed his ears.'

Tom heard a note of self-pity. 'To be honest, Jim, you're lucky it *wasn't* the police, what with their tricks. You might be in Pentonville by now.'

'I fancy that's where my employers would like to see me. I had a rather disagreeable chat with Barry at the *Chronicle* this week – told me Swaim was on the warpath. Apparently my private life has become a liability to the paper's so-called reputation.'

'They wouldn't dare drop you,' Tom said.

'I'm not so sure. They say he hates queers like Mosley hates Jews.'

As Jimmy's gaze dropped a shaft of compassion pierced Tom's heart. It wasn't the damaged eye that did it so much as the air of defeat; he'd never seen him look so frail and dispirited. The valedictory phrases that had been on his tongue were beginning to sound untimely, and he knew he would have to steel himself to utter them. It would have been so much easier if he'd done it two weeks ago. Or two years ago.

Jimmy was gazing in silence at the debris of his breakfast, and out of instinct Tom stood and removed the tray from his lap, brushing off the crumbs with a napkin. He then poured a fresh cup of tea and placed it in his hands.

'There – the cup that cheers,' he said.

Jimmy took a sip, then gave Tom a level look. 'You know, even in my darkest moods, the one thing that's kept my pecker up – if you'll pardon the phrase – is the knowledge I could depend on you.' His eyes had gone moist as he spoke. 'Thank you, Tom, from the bottom of my heart.'

*Oh hell*, thought Tom, who now felt quite the blackguard for the knife he was about to plunge. 'Well, I just do my job,' he said quietly. 'Actually, I've been meaning to have a word with you . . .'

He looked at Jimmy, whose expression had softened into beatific indulgence as he said, 'I think I know what it's about.' Tom blinked wonderingly. Was it that obvious? 'I've been taking you for granted,' Jimmy continued, 'and I want to make amends. So I'm going to pay you an extra five bob a week, and I'll throw in your half for the cost of the typewriter.'

Tom would have laughed if he hadn't been so appalled. Here was a misunderstanding of comic, no, *tragi*comic, proportions. He could almost believe it was a sly bit of gamesmanship on Jimmy's part, but from his tone he clearly thought he was dispensing true largesse. He had recast himself as the Generous Employer. 'Your half' for the typewriter . . . What a nerve. As for the five-shilling raise, it was neither large enough to make any difference nor so small as to free him from a show of gratitude.

Jimmy sensed an uncertainty in Tom's silence. 'Was there something else?'

Tom shook his head, and managed a weak smile. 'No. Thank you.'

'Good man!' he said, evidently feeling better for the conversation. 'Now – to business. There's a big dinner in aid of the Marquess I gather I'm supposed to attend. Know anything of it?'

Tom, slightly dazed, said, 'I replied on your behalf. It's next week.'

'Evening dress?'

'I expect so.'

'Hmm. I'm not sure I can still get into my dinner suit . . . I suppose I should hie me to Moss Bros. A lot of bother. Perhaps if I gave you my measurements you could call in and get one for me . . . Tom?'

Tom, miles away, forced himself back to attention. 'Sorry?'

'Hiring a dinner suit – from Moss Bros.'

Tom stared at him for a moment, wondering if Jimmy saw the irony in this resumption of the old routine – the routine of master and servant – and the way it followed hard on the heels of his admission that he'd taken Tom for granted. But his expectant look seemed quite oblivious.

'Moss Bros, right,' he said. 'I'll see to it.'

Edie Greenlaw had asked Tom if he cared to bring a friend to the party. It was her fortieth, and she had hired rooms at a hotel in Half Moon Street. When he arrived, the main room was already in a roar with a lot of people he didn't know. Edie's friends were mostly from the theatre, but she was also honorary queen bee to Jimmy's coterie of fast young men. She had them gathered about her now as she hailed Tom from a crescent-shaped plush banquette. They were all drinking a raspberry-coloured cocktail called an Albemarle Fizz. As he approached a couple of the youths stared appraisingly at him. Next to Edie sat Peter Liddell, busy trying to comfort a young fellow named Jolyon who had drunk too much at a recent 'do'.

'I'm so terribly embarrassed . . .'

'Well, we'd all had a few,' Peter conceded.

'Oh, but to fall asleep and just *lie* there.'

'My dear boy, don't fret about it. You were the still life of the party.'

Jolyon, not quite understanding, gave a worried nod. Edie then screeched with laughter, and ordered more drinks.

'Where's that nice girl you brought, Tom?' she asked.

'Oh, she's just gone to the powder room.'

After their night at the theatre, he had waited a while before he called on Madeleine again. He had enjoyed her company, though he wasn't quite sure she had enjoyed his so much. She was a strange one, girlishly eager to please but rather distant when he asked about her life. She had told him a little of her early years; he knew about her being orphaned, and the convent school, and the aunt she once lived with – in Chertsey, was it? About her present circumstances, though, she was damnably mysterious. He gathered she had digs in Camden, and earned enough to afford good clothes and taxis. But she was vague about her job, saying only that she worked most evenings at a nightclub.

He had decided to surprise her by showing up there unannounced, though from the fright that seized her face on seeing him he wondered if it was such a good idea after all.

'Tom . . . what are you doing here?'

'Oh, just passing by. Thought I'd pop in!'

She was looking furtively about her. Roddy wasn't in the place this evening, fortunately, but there were others there who knew her.

'How – how did you know I worked here?'

'Oh, Peter – you remember meeting him at the theatre? – he told me he spotted you coming in here the other night, and I took a chance that this might be . . .'

He could tell already that she didn't much like surprises. Still glancing about her, she led him out of the club by a side entrance. They stood in a service yard that stank of old beer and urine.

'Sorry, I shouldn't have burst in like that,' said Tom. 'It was a spur-of-the-moment thing, you know.'

'Oh, well . . . it's just the boss here – he doesn't like us mingling with customers unless –' She shrugged, leaving the sentence uncompleted. Then a light came into her eye, and her tone brightened. 'Thank you, again, for the other night. I did so love being at the theatre.'

*Not enough to stay to the end*, thought Tom, who nevertheless gave a little bow in acknowledgement. 'I was wondering – er, an actress friend of mine is having a birthday party tomorrow night, not far from here. Would you like to come?'

Just then the door opened and one of the barmen came out, carrying a crate of empties. His interruption flustered her again, and she made as if to go back inside. 'I'll probably be working late tomorrow,' she said.

Tom gave her the address of the hotel anyway, not really expecting her to come, then quickly went on his way: she was too nervous to be around.

Madeleine, to her own surprise, did come to Edie's party. She was rather touched by Tom's continued interest. It seemed more than form's sake that had prompted this second invitation. Yet she couldn't fool herself that the attraction was romantic. She now felt sure that Tom was what Roddy would call a nancy boy, or, in more hostile mood, a 'poof'. Most of his friends, to judge from this evening, were male, and in the way he spoke about his employer, Jimmy, she sensed their relationship had once occupied more than a professional footing.

Peter, the only other person there she knew, had been charming to her, but she didn't want to exhaust his company. With Tom momentarily distracted, she excused herself to go to the Ladies. Inside the cloakroom she presented herself before the row of mirrors; at the far end a woman was leaning against the sink, head bowed in thoughtful absorption. Madeleine first fixed her hair, which had come loose from its pins, and then got to work with her lipstick.

In her lateral vision she sensed that the woman was scrutinising her. It wasn't just men, you see, women too were on the hunt nowadays. She was in clubland, after all, where anything goes. A tune she half knew came into her head, and dissolved just as quickly. She kept her eyes straight to the mirror, pretending not to have noticed she was an object of interest. She took out her compact and made a show of examining her nose. The woman had just dabbed her neck with perfume – it was Jicky, the same one she used – and was now edging closer. Madeleine readied herself – and on seeing her face recoiled in fright.

'I'm sorry, I didn't mean to frighten you,' said the woman. 'I'm – we've seen each other before. Haven't we?'

It was a face she had recently fled, the actress, materialised as if from a sinister masque or hallucination. But how, *how* . . .? Madeleine felt her hand gripping the cold porcelain of the sink. She needed it to keep herself upright. The actress was talking to her again, and she forced herself to listen.

'It *is* you, isn't it? At the Imperial. You came out of the bedroom. I was standing there. Please say you remember me.'

Madeleine found her voice from somewhere. 'I do – I do remember. As a matter of fact I saw you onstage. I recognised you.'

'You mean – at the Strand?'

'Yes. You were playing Hester.'

Now Nina looked shocked. 'Golly, what an odd coincidence . . . Perhaps we were fated to meet!'

She said this in a lightly musing way, though Madeleine saw from her smudged eyes that the woman had been crying. They continued to stare at one another for a few moments, not sure of how to proceed.

'I'm Nina, by the way,' she said, holding out her hand. 'Edie and I are old friends.'

Madeleine offered her name, and hand, in return. Nina sensed the unavoidable subject hovering between them, blocking the light.

'That afternoon – what was he – had you met him before?'

Madeleine shook her head, and swallowed. 'We met in the square. He – he asked me to come to his room. The money was more than I'd ever been offered. I knew it was a risk, but – it's always a risk.'

'I saw the marks on your throat. He was going to kill you, wasn't he?'

Madeleine's affirmative was the merest twitch of her chin. She swallowed again, her voice barely audible. 'He had a tie around my neck, choking me. I remember thinking, I'm going to take my last breath in this room, and there's not a thing I can do.' She stopped, and looked intently at Nina. 'Then I heard a voice – your voice. If you hadn't knocked . . .'

To Nina it still seemed remarkable that they were having this conversation at all. 'When you saw his sketch, in the paper, did you not think of going to the police?'

'What sketch?' asked Madeleine.

Nina stared at her. 'Of *him*. It's been in the papers, surely you've . . .'

Madeleine shrugged. 'I haven't seen it.'

'But it's been all over the place – the Tiepin Killer?'

A glimmer of recognition dawned in her eye. 'I've heard people talking about that . . . You mean – ?'

'It's him. The man who attacked you. He's strangled three other women.'

Madeleine's hand jerked to her mouth, so that Nina saw only her eyes, wild with horror. It was one thing to have encountered a random woman-hater. It was quite another to know that you had escaped, by mere good fortune, a psychopathic murderer. A creature of the headlines. She felt a bolus of something lurch upwards through her gut. At a crouched run Madeleine burst into the adjacent stall and clutched the bowl, gagging. All that came up was a mouthful of foul yellow bile. Her eyes watered with the strain as she coughed again, painfully. The tiles were hard and cold against her knees, but she stayed there, shivering, gasping, not certain of what her gorge might do next. Some moments passed before she caught a fluttering movement at the corner of her eye; Nina was holding out a handkerchief, which she took with a faint gasp of thanks.

When she at last picked herself up and emerged from the stall, Nina was leaning against the wall, arms folded, a cigarette in her hand. She was considering Madeleine with a narrow-eyed look that mingled sympathy and fascination.

'Better?' she said, to which Madeleine replied with a nod, though her face still wore a lugubrious pallor. She examined her reflection in the mirror, briefly dabbed her eyes with the handkerchief, then looked away in disgust. When Nina next spoke her tone had become businesslike. 'You do realise that you and I are the only people who can actually identify him?'

'You saw him too?'

Nina nodded. 'Briefly. And in poor light. You could give a far better picture of him than I could.'

'Maybe,' she said, in a non-committal way.

'There's no "maybe" about it, dear. You were with him for – what, twenty minutes?'

'I'm not going to the police, if that's what you mean.'

Nina expelled a thin plume of smoke from the corner of her mouth. 'Look, he's killed three already, and they're no nearer to catching him. You could help save a girl's life.'

Madeleine heard the implication in her words: *like I*

168

*saved yours.* 'Easy for you to say,' she replied, hearing her voice harden. 'D'you suppose I want to tell the police how I make a living?'

'I think they'd welcome any information.'

She looked away. 'Not from a tart they wouldn't.'

That silenced them both for a while. Tart she may be, thought Nina, but she wasn't in the usual run; her voice, her manner betrayed hints of a life once used to better things. She didn't have that gleam of pert calculation you met so often in Soho working girls. When she had raised her head from the toilet bowl a moment ago Nina had noticed a tiny gold cross at the hollow of her throat.

'Are you a Roman?' she asked casually.

Madeleine blinked at her, and nodded. 'I've not . . . in a while. Are you?'

Nina shrugged. 'My father was. He used to take us to Mass with him now and then. Does that qualify me?'

'I think so,' Madeleine said doubtfully, and they both giggled.

After a moment Nina's expression changed, became serious again. 'Look, I've got a friend I think you should meet – he works near here.'

'He's not the police?'

'No, no. He's –' She hesitated, then plunged on. 'He drew the face of the man you . . . met. It's a five-minute walk, that's all. I just have to make a telephone call to check he's there.'

Madeleine, though unwilling, saw the obligation she was under. This woman had saved her neck. A five-minute walk. 'I'm here with a friend. D'you mind if we just slip out?'

Once they had retrieved their coats, Nina led her out of the hotel and thence took a left into Piccadilly. They didn't say much to one another as they walked, sensing the strangeness of their coming together. Arriving at the Nines, they proceeded to an upper room that was undergoing redecoration or some other job: the smell of paint and turps curtained the air. Pale dust sheets hung on the furniture, and drugget covered the floor. The dim gaslights revealed a work-in-progress, a mural of a group portrait, though the seated figures whose outlines had been limned were all without faces.

'Hullo – Stephen?' Nina called into the gloom. From behind a screened door a man emerged, wiping his spattered hands on a rag. He smiled uncertainly on seeing that she was not alone.

'Hullo, I was just finishing up,' he said, turning on a table lamp.

'Stephen, this is Madeleine.'

He stepped forward and extended his hand, which Madeleine took. 'May I offer you a drink?'

Madeleine glanced at Nina, who said, 'I think we could both do with one, actually.'

While he poured Scotch into tumblers, Nina tried to maintain a reassuring face for Madeleine's sake; she felt the anxiety in her silence.

'Down the hatch,' said Stephen as he distributed their drinks with unsuspecting cheeriness. Madeleine took a sip and felt the alcohol burn in her throat, but it tasted better than what she had just disgorged in the toilet bowl. Nina was now talking in a low voice to Stephen, whose expression turned sombre as he listened. He muttered something in reply, then disappeared behind the door. When he returned he was holding another rough of the sketch, which he handed to Madeleine.

She felt a shock of recoil as she examined the pencil drawing. It seemed to be his face, in outline at least. But it would be of no use to the police. She looked at Stephen.

'You drew this?'

Stephen nodded. 'From Nina's description. Is it him?'

'I thought at first it might be –' She turned in puzzlement to Nina, who said, in almost a panicked way, 'What? What is it?'

'The hair . . .' She thought she had recognised the eyes, the mouth, but she realised that couldn't be the case. 'I don't think it can be the same man. He wasn't bald.'

# 10

The clock on the mantelpiece had chimed half past midnight, and still they remained in the upper bar of the Nines, smoking, talking. Madeleine had left a little while ago. In front of them were ranged the half-painted figures of the mural, mute and faceless, yet somehow conveying the impression of watchers; Nina found them too sinister to look at for long.

Stephen, pacing up and down, stopped for a moment. 'Can she be trusted? After all, I mean –'

'Why would she lie?' said Nina. 'He tried to strangle her! She's got more reason than most to want him caught.'

That much he had to concede. 'But how can you both have seen this man and still not agree on what he looks like?'

She shrugged. At first she had thought Madeleine was mistaken, and asked her to look more closely. It *had* to be him, surely? No – she had examined the portrait again – the man who had attacked her in room 408 had dark hair.

Nina ticked her nails against the glass tumbler, thinking. 'Unless' – she began, looking up of a sudden – 'is it possible there were two men there, one in the bathroom . . .?'

'How long was it between the girl – Madeleine – running past you and your entering the room?'

'I don't know – ten seconds, maybe, allowing for the little half-corridor that connects the door to the room.'

He thought about this for a moment, then wrinkled his nose. 'Unlikely. Wouldn't she have noticed if another man had been there?' Another silence intervened before he spoke again. 'It leaves one other possibility to consider.'

'Which is . . .?'

'Which is that the man you saw wasn't the Tiepin Killer. I know the circumstantial evidence is strong that he was in the hotel that afternoon – but it's not a cast-iron certainty. The man in 408 may just have been a random lunatic. After all, no one has identified him yet from that drawing.'

'But it must be him – he was that close to killing her –'

Stephen shook his head. 'But he *didn't*, which at the very least raises a doubt. This man doesn't make mistakes – he's killed three women so far and the police haven't a clue. The one person who may have encountered him has categorically stated that the sketch released to the newspapers is not the fellow who assaulted her. You see what this means?'

'That we may have been in error –'

'More than that, my darling. Our small contribution to the case may be seen to have misled the police. We could be accused of hampering their investigation.'

'Not intentionally,' she said.

'It amounts to the same thing. Because of us they may have been looking for the wrong man.'

Nina stared at him. The charge looked a difficult one to deny. It was as she had feared; they had invited catastrophe through the front door.

'So what do we do? Tell the police I made a mistake?'

Stephen steepled his fingers, considering. 'Best not, don't you think? Sleeping dogs, and all that.'

And, tired of pacing, he flopped down into an armchair. It was an unsatisfactory note on which to end the conversation, but Nina could think of nothing else to say. Her gaze drifted across the faceless figures on the wall. 'When are you going to put faces on them? They rather give me the creeps.'

'Ludo's still thrashing out names with the committee. Apparently there's quite a brouhaha about who's to be in it. Threats of resignation and all sorts.'

'Really?'

'I know. You'd think it was the Last Supper I was painting – instead of members of a club nobody cares a button about.'

Nina pouted slightly. 'Well, *they* care, I suppose. They think if Stephen Wyley paints them they'll be securing their little bit of posterity.'

'They're fools if they do. Nobody'll remember them – us – at all. Tell me, those portraits on the staircase you passed on the way up – d'you think anybody looks at them and thinks fondly, "Ah yes – old so-and-so"? They're gone, *and* forgotten.'

'Darling, you're awfully morbid tonight. What's the matter?'

His mouth made a noise that was somewhere between a laugh and a sigh. 'I'm sorry – things on my mind. My twelve-year-old daughter's written to me asking to be removed from her school. I'm terribly behind on my work. And I have that infernal dinner of Carmody's to attend this Tuesday.' He looked at her. 'I can't persuade you to come with me, can I?'

She gave him a pitying look. 'You know you can't. I'm working. What about Mrs Wyley?'

'Bridge night. And Cora hates that sort of thing anyway. Can't say I blame her.'

Nina, with a half-smile, decided not to make a fuss of this unintended slight. She realised how seldom either of them mentioned his wife, though her invisibility had become in itself a kind of presence to her. One of the few things she knew about 'Cora' was that she had cried at her performance in *The Second Arrangement*, giving a reluctant dab of interest

174

to the mostly unfavourable picture she had formed. The only photograph of her she had seen, at Stephen's studio, showed a willowy fair-haired woman, unsmiling, slightly prim in the English way, and so different from her own looks as to deepen her confusion. Was it merely a need for variety that had prompted Stephen to stray? She had wondered about that from the moment of their first tryst at the Imperial – and still did.

Tom had been receiving ominous signals from within. He had come to regard his body as a city state locked in a volatile conflict between sickness and health, the one under continuous siege from the other. His seizures, those internal earthquakes, had not troubled him for years, to the point where he had imagined them to be a thing of the past, a finished chapter of his life. Alas, they had been merely biding their time, waiting for his defences to drop. The spies and informers of the interior had stayed vigilant, though, and warned him when trouble was on its way: a slight tremor in his limbs, a keening headache, a sudden disabling nausea. Sometimes, if the alarms came early enough, he could make provision, could gather himself to neutralise the threatened assault. He would lie on his bed, a cool flannel pressed to his brow, the curtains a saving shield against the light. There he would stay, as still as an effigy on a tomb, waiting, willing the frenzy that loomed at the corner of his vision to pass by.

The blame, in a way, was his own. Having decided on a clean break from Jimmy he had felt a satisfaction in taking the initiative. That he had endured nine years in the job had become a cause of wonder. Was it pity that had kept him loyal to a miserly and manipulative employer? Or was there a natural indecision that had baulked his instinct to quit? Some amalgam of the two must have been in play that morning he had intended to hand in his notice. Somehow at the vital moment his nerve had failed him, and instead of shaking off Jimmy for good he had allowed himself to be enslaved once more, this time his tenure sealed with a wage increase so paltry as to be humiliating. Consciousness of this failure had first made him wretched; now it was making him ill.

It so happened he had been reading *Macbeth* again, and was struck anew by the spiritual and psychological emergencies of the tragic hero. Driven to murder his way to the throne, Macbeth can't help revealing his fragile mental state as the play proceeds. First, about to dispatch the sleeping Duncan, he stands irresolute, hallucinating the dagger in his own hand; then, having fled the dead man's bedchamber, he becomes almost hysterical in the company of Lady Macbeth, worrying away at the fact that he could not say the word 'Amen' back at the scene of the crime. 'I had most need of blessing, and "Amen" / Stuck in my throat.' (How quickly his guilt follows on his deed.) His Lady, aghast that he has not disposed of the bloody daggers, tells him to take them back to the chamber. Macbeth, though, will not, afraid 'to think what I have done'. How has this warrior, a recent colossus of the battlefield, become so squeamish about a single murder – a murder that was no *crime passionel* but something premeditated at least since the day he encountered the Three Witches?

Even more intriguing to Tom was the Thane's reaction to later events. When he is informed by his two assassins that Banquo has been murdered, but that Fleance, his son, has escaped, Macbeth says, 'Then comes my fit again.' My *fit*? There is the first hint. In the banquet scene that follows he is gripped with horror on seeing – so he imagines – the murdered Banquo, shaking his gory locks. Again, his Lady tries to excuse his outward distress ('The fit is momentary') and gives her husband a stern talking-to in private. Turning to his startled guests, he tries to explain away his outward fright: 'I have a strange infirmity, which is nothing / To those that know me.' The more Tom thought about it, the more he believed Macbeth's 'strange infirmity' was epilepsy, which in Shakespeare's day was thought to be a form of diabolic possession – the sufferer would be either shunned or chained to the wall of a lunatic asylum. This was not the fate Tom feared. What he dreaded was having a seizure in public, in front of people he knew, people he should have told of his condition but hadn't. He could not pretend, as Macbeth did, that such a fit was 'nothing to those that know me'. He had been close to telling one friend or another, but in the end had kept quiet: he couldn't bear the pity that would pour down. Only Madeleine had witnessed him in that state, and something about her recessive manner suggested she wouldn't be one to gossip.

Madeleine: she was a puzzler. He couldn't honestly say if his company was a pleasure to her or not. When he had made his surprise call at the Elysian, the club where she worked, he'd felt about as welcome as a leper. She was awkward and nervous with him, could barely catch his eye, and as he left – she'd dismissed him, really – he was more or less convinced their brief acquaintance was over. But he was wrong, for there she was at Edie's birthday party last weekend, as diffident as ever but friendly again, perhaps even pleased to see him. He had introduced her to people, and though she wasn't naturally a gregarious type he sensed her making the effort to be agreeable. It all seemed to be going well until she disappeared to the Ladies. As the party's hubbub rose he began to wonder where she'd got to, and, feeling somewhat responsible, he eventually set off in search of her. He was edging through a press of people when he saw her and another woman emerge from the basement and head for the exit. They hadn't noticed him, but he got a good look at the other woman and shrank back in surprise. Could it have been – ?

They were out the door and gone. Baffled, Tom retraced his steps to Edie and dipped his head towards her.

'Do you know Nina Land, by any chance?'

'Yes, she's here,' replied Edie, looking around her. 'Known her for donkey's. Why – got your eye on her?'

'No, no . . . I've just seen her leave the room – with Madeleine.'

Edie pulled a quizzical face. 'How curious. Do they know each other?'

I doubt it, thought Tom. But seeing the two of them together – their tense expressions, the purpose in their step – had made him wonder. That night at the theatre, Madeleine seemed to have recognised Nina Land; it had preoccupied her through the interval. Then she'd had that funny turn afterwards . . .

His curiosity was left unsatisfied, in any case, because Madeleine never returned to the party. Tom gave an involuntary groan. He was lying on his bed still, the flannel like a blindfold across his eyes. The city state, his body, was in commotion, and his mind was emptying of Madeleine, of *Macbeth*, of everything. He had to reduce himself to perfect immobility, and hope the convulsive forces within would spare him another outbreak of violence.

Stephen had arrived at the Marquess fund-raiser in a mood of creeping dread. He had loitered outside the venue, the huge old Carlton on the corner of Pall Mall, to have a condemned-man's smoke and delay his entrance for as long as decency allowed. Shadowed by a recessed doorway at the foot of Haymarket he watched as cars and taxis stopped to disgorge yet more tailcoated men at the hotel entrance, their shirt fronts brilliant against the bluish-black autumnal evening. The odd bray of laughter pierced the air, and caused his heart to drop a notch further. Once inside the place he did the same thing as always on such an occasion, knocked back the first drink very quickly, and took another for company. Skirting the packed reception he could hear Gerald Carmody's voice, bullying its way to the noise's crest. He looked about for theatre people, the sort he had met through Nina, but saw no face he recognised. There wasn't much glamour about this lot – or even a whiff of money. So much for Carmody's boasting that 'Larry' had pledged his support.

It was only after they had sat down at dinner, and the wine waiters were ghosting unobtrusively along the tables, that Stephen felt the evening suddenly take an upturn. He had introduced himself to the fellow on his right, whose dwarfish stature and faintly comical aspect reminded him of something carved in stone and leering from a church tower. Yet the man himself seemed quite oblivious to the oddity of his appearance. His old-world courtesy was somehow of a piece with his accented English, which became excitable once he learned that Stephen was an artist.

'Oh, I mostly do portraits these days,' he said, on further enquiry.

The man squinted, his face clearing. 'Ah, Wyley – so you are *Stephen* Wyley?'

Stephen admitted that he was, at which his interlocutor drew back in an exaggerated gesture of respect. 'You are too modest, sir, to imply such a limit to your talent. I know your landscape paintings, and regard them with the greatest admiration.'

Stephen felt himself blush with pleasure. It had been a while since he had heard someone – anyone – enthuse about the work dearest to his heart. As the man talked it became clear that his praise was no idle flattery either, he could describe what he had seen – the early paintings of the Suffolk borders and the clouded Norfolk coastline ('something of Boudin there'), his rain-misted Scottish moors, even his cherished series of park studies, *London Pastoral I–IX*.

'My God, you liked them? *Nobody* liked them, Mr – er – Tunner,' he said, glancing at the typed place card in front of him.

The man gave an apologetic smile. 'Ah, I should explain – my friend Thomas – Mr Tunner – was indisposed this evening. I took his place at short notice. My name is Balázsovits, László Balázsovits,' he said, with a shy little dip of his head.

'Delighted,' Stephen replied, meaning it. 'I must say, it's very gratifying to talk to someone who actually knows my work. I suppose you are in the business yourself?'

Again came the slightly injured smile. 'I regret to say I am not. Whatever small powers of discrimination I have I owe to my parents – they instilled in me, from an early age, an appreciation of music, of literature, of art. Our house, when we lived in Regent Square, was always full of it.' He paused for a moment at this, and his gaze turned reminiscent. 'I remember them taking me once on a visit to Vienna. We went to all the great museums, we dined at the large restaurants, we attended several concerts, and of course it was very, uh, overwhelming to a young boy. Well, when we returned home my father set me an exercise (I was educated at home, you see) to write about all the things I had seen in Vienna. Which was crazy! I thought "too much" – how could I begin to describe such variety? So: I decided to write my essay about just one thing.' He held up a single digit in illustration. 'Can you guess what it was?'

Stephen thought he could. 'A painting?'

'Very good! Yes, a painting, which I saw at the Kunsthistorisches Museum one afternoon. It was called *Self-Portrait in a Convex Mirror* by a young Italian named Parmigianino – perhaps you know it? It is a remarkable thing, small, circular, like a barber's mirror – indeed, the painter had a carpenter lathe a hemisphere of wood to produce the mirror's identical proportions. Now, at first the portrait seemed to me simply a clever and amusing trick, its imitations of convexity finessed *just so* – the window and the walls behind the face bowing and arching up to the ceiling, the pale hand of this pretty young fellow (no more than a boy!) looming forwards, like a player shielding his cards. But then as I stared I began to see it in a different light. I realised that Parmigianino was painting in a way both literal and metaphorical, a double conceit, and for the early sixteenth century a very original one. It was literal in showing us only what he could see in the mirror, but also metaphorical in exploring the deep human unease of confronting one's own image. That elongated hand, which distortion has made larger than the painter's head, was there to remind us of illusion, nature's illusion in the glass, and our inherent failure to grasp the truth of ourselves. Do you see?'

'I think so,' said Stephen, after a pause. In fact he had become rather mesmerised by the tiny fluctuations that had been enlivening László's face as he spoke, a face he had initially thought like a gargoyle's but which now seemed to him something marvellous, and rather affecting. Of course he could not explain this to its owner. 'And you wrote all this in your essay?'

'Oh yes. My father I recall was a little . . . bemused. He had asked me to write about Vienna and I had presented a piece of art criticism. But as I explained to him – is it not more useful to study one thing well than to cover a dozen things superficially?'

'Did that satisfy him?'

'I suppose it must have done. The next time I saw the piece was in the pages of a local newspaper. Although,' he added, narrowing his eyes, 'I do not recall being *paid* for it.'

Stephen laughed, and said, 'So you're a writer?'

'No, no. In my younger days I was a musician –'

The conversation was interrupted at this moment by a

shout of mingled greeting and relief from a rotund, wheezing gent, who took the vacant seat next to László and immediately enjoined the wine waiter to fill his glass. He drained it quickly, and, after a fleeting grimace at its taste, called for another.

'James, good evening,' said László, then turned to the guest on his other side. 'I think perhaps you know Mr Stephen Wyley –'

'We've never met,' said Jimmy, forgetting his bogus claim of acquaintance a few weeks before and leaning across László to shake Stephen's hand. 'James Erskine.'

'Mr Balázsovits has just been telling me about Parmigianino. For a musician he knows a great deal about art.'

'*Musician*,' said Jimmy, with a sidelong look. 'Is that what he called himself? I suppose he's also told you he knew Brahms – in fact he once held the door open for him.'

László frowned at him. 'As I explained to Mr Wyley I was a musician in my youth –'

'And now you're a piano teacher,' he declared, for Stephen's benefit. Jimmy's meanness was born of irritation: he had specifically requested a seat next to Wyley and somehow it had been misassigned to László, who wouldn't even have been invited had Tom not cried off the day before. (A severe headache, he had claimed over the telephone.) He looked around at the other diners, expecting to recognise a few faces, and failing. The starter had just preceded his own arrival – fried sprats – and he forked in a mouthful.

'Ugh, greasy,' he muttered.

László, who had already cleared a plate of these dainties, offered to take Jimmy's from him, and was soon making light work of them. He ate as one who feared this meal might be his last, which, given his precarious finances, was not an unreasonable anxiety. Stephen watched in barely concealed surprise. László, catching his expression, looked abashed and said, 'They're very good – better than what

I'm accustomed to. I often take my supper at a fried-fish shop in Cable Street, near my lodgings, where the quantity is known to be –'

'I'm sorry – Cable Street, you say?' The name had clanged on the air like a warning bell. Stephen leaned forward inquisitively. 'Were you caught up in that business the other week?'

It took László a moment to realise what 'business' Stephen had meant. 'Oh! No, indeed, I was not.'

'But with the blackshirts and the police and whatnot, you must have *heard* it at least?'

László shook his head. 'Alas, not even that! My neighbours kindly allow me the use of their piano on a Sunday, and while the hand of history was close by I myself was practising Chopin in their back parlour.'

'Good Lord,' said Stephen.

'Yes, it came as quite a surprise the next day. I am reminded of the story of Louis XVI on the day the Bastille fell. He returned from a day's hunting and wrote in his diary, *Rien!*'

'Which Chopin?' asked Jimmy.

'Oh, Ballade Number 1.'

'No wonder you couldn't hear anything. All that *presto con fuoco*.'

Stephen had noticed that the man seated opposite him was attending to their conversation quite closely. He had a long scar down one cheek, and sat ramrod-straight in his chair. After a moment he recognised him as the man he had seen Carmody saluting on the steps of the British People's Brigade HQ. He couldn't remember his name. When their eyes briefly met Stephen gave him a provisional half-smile – the sociable minimum – and was ignored. It didn't bother him, for he sensed around the man a force field of brooding aggression he had no wish to engage. He also appeared to be drinking a great deal.

183

Jimmy, out of Stephen's earshot, was in heated whispering remonstration with László, who had dug in his heels over something. It continued, off and on, through the serving of braised pheasant with chestnut purée. The evening, which had begun at a hearty volume, was approaching a roar; even Carmody's boom had been drowned out. Only when László saw that their argument had left Stephen isolated did he rise from his chair and, with a little bow that blended apology with grievance, went off to the Gents – allowing Jimmy to pounce on the vacated seat. He had the air of a man who had just got his way.

'Hope my friend wasn't boring you,' said Jimmy airily. 'He means well, but he drones like a bagpipe.'

'He wasn't boring me at all. In fact I was greatly enjoying his company.'

Jimmy, hearing a thin note of reproof, changed tack. 'A friend told me that you're doing some work at the Nines.'

'Yes, I've been hard at it. A mural. Are you a member there?'

'No. The friend I mentioned once invited me to join, only to discover that there was a considerable amount of resistance to my election. Same thing happened with the Garrick. And I imagine I am eligible for blackballing at several other clubs around London.'

'I'm sorry to hear it,' said Stephen leniently.

'The critic's fate,' said Jimmy, trying a cavalier shrug. 'It's probably to do with some idiot actor I once offended, extracting his little revenge.'

Stephen, realising only at that moment who Jimmy was, couldn't resist saying, 'Perhaps you've come across a friend of mine. Nina Land?'

'Of course. I've followed her with great interest, ever since *Fire in the Hole*.'

'She'll be pleased to hear it.'

'But let me ask you something,' said Jimmy, changing gears with a clank. 'I dare say you're much in demand?'

'I have a fair bit on, with one thing or another.'

'Well, here's the thing. I turn sixty next year, and have been minded to mark it in some way. I now know what it should be. By an unforeseen stroke of good fortune I find myself this evening seated next to the very man I should choose for the job – if I may, the Van Dyck *de nos jours*!'

'A portrait of yourself . . . I see.'

'Well, they say nobody ever raised a statue to a critic, but I don't see why there shouldn't be an oil painting of one.'

Stephen looked steadily at him, wondering if his conceit was a kind of joke, a balloon to be popped with some self-deprecating remark. But Jimmy's expression was untouched by any humorous intent. Before he could reply he felt someone clap his shoulder, and turning he found Carmody beaming down at him.

'Wyley! Been meaning to collar you – I wanted to thank you for that very generous cheque.'

Stephen would have preferred to keep his charity a private matter, but he supposed Carmody's loud expression of thanks was intended *pour encourager les autres*. A sudden loud crump made him flinch, and the flash of a camera bulb whited the air; the photographer had timed it to catch him in a handshake with Carmody. 'When do you plan for the Marquess to reopen?' he asked.

'Oh, all in good time,' said Carmody in a more confiding tone. 'We've got a fine tailwind of support.' Surveying the vicinity of the table, he now gave a brief wave to the scar-faced man who had been watching Stephen. 'Have you two gentlemen met? Stephen Wyley – William Joyce.'

Focusing somewhat blearily on this introduction, Joyce lifted his chin in acknowledgement. His well-spoken voice was at odds with his pugilistic aspect. 'So you're a contributor, Mr Wyley?'

Stephen nodded. 'Gerald here has been very, uh, persuasive. And the cause seems a good one.'

'The best – the best,' replied Joyce in correction. 'We must defend our great institutions. It is the British way.'

Stephen thought this rather grandiose language to use about the theatre, though drink had clearly stoked up his mood. At this moment László resumed his seat at the table next to Jimmy. His return had been noticed by Joyce, whose brow creased into an amused frown. 'This fellow has been an object of curiosity to me all evening,' he said, as if László were some exotically plumed creature. 'I would surmise from your accent that you are – Austrian?'

László gave a little shake of his head. 'A close neighbour, sir – Hungarian. Though I was raised in this country.'

'And your name?'

'László Balázsovits.'

'Balázsovits,' Joyce repeated, with an emphasis on the final consonants. 'A Jew, then.'

'Again, raised in this country,' said László with perfect civility.

Carmody, who had witnessed these last exchanges in agitation, now spoke up. 'Joyce, may I have a moment? – there are some others I'd like you to meet.'

A nasty daggered silence followed, then Joyce rose from the table. 'Gentlemen,' he said, by way of excusing himself, and allowed Carmody to lead the way. Jimmy turned to László.

'That was rather like watching the Gorgon turn on Perseus.'

'A very drunken Gorgon at that,' said Stephen.

László, pleased by the attention, gasped out a laugh. 'But Perseus cut off the head of Medusa, did he not? Our Gorgon remains unslain.'

'I think it might be safer just to avoid his gaze,' said Jimmy, 'else we might all be turned to stone.'

Stephen had followed Joyce's progress to a distant table, where several men had stood up to be introduced. Carmody was making no bones about presenting him as the guest of honour. With pudding served, diners were now stetching their legs about the room and firing up cigars.

Jimmy noticed Stephen glance at his watch, and thought he should seize his moment. 'To return to our earlier conversation, Mr Wyley, I hope we can come to an arrangement regarding . . .'

Stephen nodded, understanding, and said, 'I'm booked up for at least the next four months. Perhaps you should consult my gallery –'

'I'd be delighted,' said Jimmy. He was not to be put off, and Stephen, in a sudden mood of weariness, said, 'Did you know Millais once said that the only thing he enjoyed about portrait painting was putting the highlights on polished boots?'

'Oh, I quite understand that,' said Jimmy. 'The only thing I enjoy about writing is putting in the punctuation.'

The tables were being cleared, and the bar, located at the end of the long ballroom, was already thronged with men. Stephen thought it strange that the dinner, aside from Carmody's brief introduction, had ended without a single speech in support of the Marquess. He suggested a last drink, to which Jimmy and László both made eager agreement.

'So Carmody tapped you for a contribution,' Jimmy said as they waited at the bar.

'He has a way of making it impossible to refuse,' admitted Stephen, who noticed that László was still skulking around the table they had just left. 'What's he doing?'

Jimmy let out a sigh of exasperation. 'Oh, for heaven's – He's gathering up those discarded bread rolls to take home.'

Stephen flinched slightly. 'Is he that – hard up?'

'Afraid so. Hasn't a farthing to his name.'

'But he was telling me of holidays abroad, and a house in, where was it, Regent Square?'

'Years ago. His father lost all their money in some swindle. László has gone from being a pampered princeling to a virtual indigent within a generation. And yet' – his laugh was fond – 'I don't know a more cheerful man.'

The object of their discussion was approaching, having cleared the bread basket. The pug-like face, stirred to delight by his recent haul, caused Stephen's heart to turn over. 'Well then, that should be our toast – to cheerfulness.'

László, the paper bag bulging under his arm, was about to respond when, from a knot of men standing behind him, a hissing noise started up. It was led by a man whose company they had already entertained that evening. Stephen had heard the single muttered word bandied back and forth among them, and had tried to ignore it. The word, of course, was 'Jew'.

Joyce had stepped forward, his face ablaze. He plucked László's bag of rolls from his hand and tipped out the contents. 'This is the Jew from Hungary,' he announced to his party, 'or rather, the hungry Jew, eating his way through the bread like a weevil.'

László, startled by this mocking disdain, explained, 'Sir, the bread was left over on the table. Nobody was –'

'The Lord giveth,' Joyce continued, not listening, 'and the Jew taketh away. And still the lesson goes unheeded. Is it any wonder that the economy is in crisis when the country allows Jews to plunder its resources?'

A braying chorus of support had risen behind him. The mood in the room had become volatile and anticipatory, in a way that reminded Stephen of those moments before the foxhounds are let loose. Interposing himself between László and his persecutor, he said quietly, 'You've had rather a lot to drink. I think you should offer this gentleman an apology, and then get out.'

At that, Joyce thrust his face close to Stephen's, so close he could see the long discoloured crease in the skin that some thug's knife had carved down his cheek. His reply came in a sour updraught of alcoholic heat. 'I'd sooner hang than back down to a stinking Jew.'

Before he quite had command of himself Stephen reached for Joyce's collar and was pulling him within range of a butt to his face. But Joyce tore himself away and landed a flailing fist to the side of his opponent's head. This set-to might have escalated had not several diners jumped into the fray and, amid many fierce obscenities, contrived to separate them. It took some moments for the blood singing in Stephen's ears to cease; the coaxing, conciliatory voice that he eventually heard belonged to Carmody, who had led him out of the room and into the foyer.

A couple of bruisers from the hotel's security staff hurried past them towards the ballroom, from where shouts and imprecations still carried.

'Might be for the best if I call you a taxi,' said Carmody, clapping a hand on Stephen's shoulder. Stephen brushed him off.

'What is this, Carmody? I thought you were raising money for a theatre –'

'So we are, my dear fellow.'

'I didn't see much charity back in there. And I didn't realise that Jews weren't welcome.'

Carmody returned a look from under his brow. 'We should save this discussion for another time,' he said coldly, and nodded over Stephen's shoulder to where Jimmy and László were collecting their coats. 'In the meantime, you ought to be careful about those you pick a fight with. They won't all be gentlemen like our Mr Joyce.'

'If he's your definition of a gentleman then God help us.'

Carmody's jaw tightened, and he was shaping to make some hostile retort when he stopped himself. He only said, 'Thank you, again, for your support. Goodnight.' He turned on his heel and left Stephen there.

Jimmy and László were hovering by the door, waiting for him. Their looks of concern were so solemn he felt himself begin to laugh. 'I believe we were about to have a nightcap before that little . . . interruption. If you're both still game I know just the place. Shall we?'

# II

Madeleine, who thought herself too dull to have many friends, was fortunate in being able to attract friendliness in others. People felt protective towards her, and would go out of their way to help her. Why this should be she had no firm idea; whenever she stopped to think about it she supposed it was because they felt sorry for her. It couldn't have been because she told jokes, or said witty things, because she hardly ever did. Even certain punters seemed to have a tenderness for her. She sometimes caught a glance from one of them – across a dinner table, or in a taxi, or while he was putting his trousers back on – that seemed, pityingly, to ask, *How on earth did you end up doing this?* It was a question she still asked herself.

She didn't care about the punters. But she was glad to have the affection, and perhaps the trust, of some of the girls. Working at the Elysian, she had got to know a handful of them quite well. Some had been on the game for years and rented their own rooms, down squalid little alleys, or tucked away on the upper floors of a pub or a shop. There were no names under the bell to indicate who lived there: you just had to know which door to knock. She still remembered her surprise the first time Rita, one of the older girls, invited her 'home' for a cup of tea, and they had entered a grimy terraced building on Berwick Street she had thought long abandoned; in fact, beyond the reeking doorway was a honeycomb of rooms covering five floors, reached via a narrow staircase that dog-legged on each landing.

Rita was sitting opposite her now, absently filing her nails. She was an amply proportioned woman in her early thirties, full-lipped and auburn-haired, with a laugh that tended towards the raucous. Tonight she was on duty, which meant wearing what she called 'full battledress', a rabbit-fur coat over a tight silk dress, sheer stockings and shoes with large witchy buckles. Her powdered face was offset by dark, thickly lashed eyes that roved busily around the room. They were in the front bar of the Blue Posts on Rupert Street, round the corner from the club. A lot of the girls drank there, as did their ponces; sometimes Roddy would call in, usually to check that nobody from the club was skiving. Rita had put away the nail file and was inspecting her face in a compact.

'God, I've got lovely eyes. Reckon they're me best feature, don't you?'

Madeleine smiled her agreement. It was true, she thought, they were lovely, almond-shaped and coloured a sort of underwater green. They had slid from the mirror and narrowed on her. 'You got nice eyes, too,' said Rita, a little resentfully, as though she had just noticed the competition. 'They're so clear! J'ever put drops in 'em?'

'No . . . that's just the way they are,' she replied, then added, 'I like the way you've done your hair.' She knew Rita liked to be complimented on her hair.

'One of Doreen's girls did it for me,' she cooed, giving the back of it a little primp. 'Arthur's always sayin' how much he likes my hair.' Arthur was her ponce, and for the last couple of years also her 'feller'. Madeleine gathered it was quite common for the personal and professional to merge in the life of a working girl.

'How is Arthur?' she said, calling to mind a dumpy,

twinkling man of about forty-five who displayed a hound-like devotion to Rita.

'Oh, you know . . .' A smirk played on her lips as she pondered her next words. 'Did I tell you what happened last week? Had me laughin' fit to bust.' Rita loved to tell a story, and Madeleine made an attentive audience. 'I'd had one of them days, you know – got through about thirty punters in an afternoon, one in, one out. Best take in ages. By the time I got home I was nearly dead on me feet! So I get into bed next to Arthur and tell him the day's take – and he was ever so pleased. *More* than pleased. It gets him all frisky, hands runnin' all over me, sayin' *ooh you're a clever gel*, and this, that and the other . . . 'nuff to make you blush. I told him to give over and let me get some kip. D'you know what the twit said?'

Madeleine tipped her head slightly, not daring to guess.

'He props hisself on his elbow and switches on the bedside light. Then he stares at me, all solemn like, and says, "What's the matter? Are you seein' another feller, then?"' At this she threw her head back and let loose a throaty cackle. Madeleine couldn't help joining in, though it wasn't the story that tickled her so much as Rita's exuberant delight in telling it.

'So 'ow's things at the Elysian?' said Rita, recovering herself.

'Oh, you know,' said Madeleine, picking up Rita's own shorthand.

'Roddy keepin' you busy, I s'pose. How long you been an escort now?'

'Um, a little while. Since April.'

Rita looked searchingly at her. 'You mind my askin', Maddy – j'ever do one of 'em at home? A punter, I mean.'

Madeleine shook her head. 'No. I wouldn't want to.'

'Roddy don't mention it, then? Could make y'self a lot more bunce if you did.'

Madeleine thought carefully before replying. The thought

of punters at her own place appalled her, but she didn't want to say as much for fear of giving offence to her friend. If Rita wanted to do thirty men in an evening that was her business – but it wasn't something she could do herself, and she didn't want Roddy or anyone else telling her that she should.

'I don't have your energy, Rita,' she said, which was at least true.

Rita responded with a sardonic chuckle, and took a sip of her port and lemon. Madeleine was on gin. Some moments passed in silence, then Rita said, 'You know Alice, don'tcha?'

'Alice . . . you mean the girl with the odd – ?'

Rita nodded at Madeleine's uncertain look. 'Yeah, that one.'

'D'you know what's wrong with her?'

'Apart from bein' half crazed on drugs, nothin' a miracle wouldn't cure.'

'Drugs?'

'Wakey-wakey pills. Amphetamines, they're called. You think I've got energy – that one can do forty, fifty, in a night!'

Madeleine pictured Alice now, a rake-thin blonde about her own age whose jokey, high-pitched chatter, amusing for a few minutes, would then wear the listener down. It was like having to deal with a clever but restless child; a little of her company went a long way.

'Anyway, she wanted to talk to you,' Rita added.

'To me? Why?'

'I could hardly tell – you know what she's like. Gabbled through some story about a punter she was out with. Seems this feller was askin' after a girl called *Madeleine* . . .'

Her immediate thought was: Tom. She'd been feeling guilty about him ever since she left the party that night with Nina. She ought to have offered an apology at least, even if she couldn't explain to him why she had to go. He was a nice fellow, gentle, possibly a bit lonely – one of those queers who didn't really get on with other queers and preferred female friendship. In the end she had rung his office number, but instead of him answering it was another man – the famous 'Jimmy', she presumed – whose tone was loud and brusque, and she rang off without leaving a message.

Rita was looking over her shoulder at someone, and muttered, 'Talk of the devil . . .' Madeleine turned, expecting to see Alice, but it was only Roddy, who plumped himself down at their table.

'Ladies,' he said by way of greeting.

'What do you want?' said Rita, with a slight curl to her lip.

'Just keeping an eye out,' he said. He was always keeping an eye out. With his cowlick oiled back and a paisley tie that didn't match his shirt, Roddy looked very much the spiv this evening. He gave Madeleine a little pat on the knee. She had noticed him making a greater effort at friendliness towards her recently – a look, a wink of complicity – which she found rather unnerving. He was now holding his cigarette case out to her.

'I don't, thanks,' she said.

'I will,' said Rita, plucking one from under the metal band. She then turned pointedly back to Madeleine. 'Anyway, as I was sayin' – *before* we were interrupted – it's prob'ly some wild story Alice has got into her head. It may not even be you he was askin' after . . .'

'Who was asking after?' said Roddy, frowning his suspicion.

'Seems as Maddy's got an admirer. Popular girl, see.'

Roddy gave Madeleine a smirking look. 'I know that. They all love Maddy the moocher. She's a sweetheart.'

Rita, with her nose for an opportunity, added, 'Then you ought to treat her nice, else some punter's gonna steal her away.'

Roddy returned an unillusioned stare. 'She knows what side her bread's buttered – don't you? By the way, I've got one for you later.' He took out a card and handed it across the table to Madeleine.

'The Mirabelle – what's that?'

'New place, not far from here. I'll drive you there.' Again, a note of solicitude chimed in his tone. It was unlike him to drive her to a job. He rose from the table, glancing at his watch. 'I'll be back here at ten.'

With him gone she felt able to relax once more, and Rita's lively company would beguile the time until she was back on the clock. The pub filled up with Soho's restless flotsam, the air drowning in smoke and perfume. They had just been served more drinks when Rita's gaze was distracted.

'There she is,' she muttered, and gave a little beckoning gesture with her eyes. Madeleine looked round to see Alice shouldering through the crowd. Even from this distance you could see her gaze unsteady with chemicals. She gave Rita a swooning kiss in greeting, then to Madeleine, whom she didn't know well, a girlish wave. As soon as she sat down her foot started to beat out a jerky pattering rhythm.

'My, you wouldn't believe what I've been through today –' and for the next few minutes she embarked on a detailed and uninterruptible account of her most recent job, rehearsing not only what she had said, but what the punter had said in reply, to the point where she was almost acting out a two-hander for the stage. With no end in sight Madeleine slipped off to the lavatory, returning in time to hear Alice finally winding up the story, whose point all of them had by now forgotten.

Rita let a polite pause settle before she changed the subject. 'Here, Alice, I was just telling Maddy 'bout that punter you mentioned the other night – you remember?'

Alice's face went blank, momentarily stunned by the effort of recall, and then of a sudden cleared. 'Yeah, yeah . . .' She narrowed her eyes, as if she were lining up a pistol shot. 'Oh, he was a strange one, all right.'

Rita glanced at Madeleine, who read in her eyes the same thing she was thinking. But they kept quiet, encouraging Alice to go on. It transpired this man had picked her up in the lobby of a hotel in Piccadilly; smart, dark-haired, nicely spoken, plenty of money – she thought he was a salesman or something – expensive clobber and whatnot. But there was definitely something odd about him . . .

'What d'you mean, "odd"?' said Rita.

'Well, we'd gone up to his room – a suite he had! – and he just sat there, not taking off his clothes.' She paused at that. 'Well, he did, he took off his tie, and sort of, I dunno, played around making knots with it. An' all the time he's talking about the sort of girls he likes, which I thought was a bit rude, with me sitting right there in front of him. I mean, what sort of feller does that – ?'

'Yes, yes,' Rita cut in, trying to keep Alice's story on course. 'But what did he say about Maddy?'

'I was *coming* to that,' said Alice, with a petulant jerk of her neck. She composed herself for a moment, refusing to be hurried. 'So I start to undress, but he's still not moved from his chair – just staring, miles away, like he's in a world of his own. And then, out of the blue, he asks me do I know a girl called Madeleine, 'bout so tall, dark hair? – he obviously knew you from somewhere.'

Madeleine's throat had gone dry. She swallowed hard and said, 'How did he know me?'

Alice looked vague. 'Said he met you once, that's all. And that he's been looking for you since.'

Rita, staring at Madeleine, said, 'Are you all right, love? Maddy?'

Yes, they had met, beyond question. The description fitted, as did the detail of his playing with the tie, the one he had tried to strangle her with. And she had told him her name.

Stupid, stupid. She remembered now – when he had first approached her in Russell Square, before she had realised the danger, he had asked her . . . His face, the dark pupils sliding like mercury in his eyes, the eerie purr of his voice, the meaty hands pinning her down . . .

She forced herself to speak. 'You didn't tell him – I mean, anything – where I lived. You didn't –'

Alice, flinching at the distress in her voice, said, 'Course I didn't tell him. Not that I could anyway! I just said I knew you, 'at's all.'

'Who is he, this feller?' said Rita.

'Just someone I met a while ago. He was – he tried to hurt me.' It was like a bad dream coming back to her, only this man wasn't part of any dream, he was as real to her as her own hands. *He's been looking for you since*. How long would it be before he found her? Her eyes made a sweep of the bar, the anonymous faces around her suddenly unknowable, menacing. She felt her hand shake as she raised the glass to her mouth. Where could she be safe from him now? Every street corner, every pub, every tramcar she rode, he would be somewhere close, watching. Rita was pressing Alice for more information.

'His name? Well, they usually make it up, don't they?'

'But d'you remember it, or not?'

Alice squinted into the middle distance, trying to retrieve it from her addled brain. After a few moments she gave a sighing shrug. Rita, who saw how the news had upset Madeleine, tried a tone of consolation.

'Don't worry about it, love. That sort are like a bad smell, honestly – they just go after a while.'

'Yeah, she's right,' said Alice, chipping in. 'I've known some right pests in my time, waiting outside cafes, on the lookout. Why, this one feller kept following me home – like a dog!'

'Who was that, then?' said Rita.

'Oh, I must've told you 'bout him,' she said, launching into another of her garrulous stories, with Rita supplying interested *ooh*s and *really*s in between the few pauses. As she listened Madeleine felt a gloom enfolding her. She couldn't bring herself to tell them – that the man who had been asking about her wasn't some fool, some run-of-the-mill 'pest' you could brush off. Perhaps if Rita had been on her own she might have told her the whole thing, but with Alice – well, she suspected that once Alice got hold of something it didn't stay secret for very long. And the more people who knew, the greater was the danger to her. She had heard the stories of girls who'd been attacked by punters, some quite badly, it was a risk you had to take, but so long as a ponce or some other protector was around you generally didn't have to worry. There was Roddy, of course, but she didn't dare tell him that she'd gone 'off the books' with a man; he'd think she was doing it all the time.

'Wait,' said Alice, tapping Madeleine's arm, 'I *do* remember – Rusk. The punter's name was Mr Rusk.'

'That ring a bell?' asked Rita.

Madeleine slowly shook her head. Did it? She thought she'd seen that name recently, but couldn't recall where. Alice, reluctant to see her feat of memory go to waste, said, 'What if I see him again? They usually come back for more, even ones like him.'

'Don't go anywhere near him,' said Madeleine, in a voice edged with panic. 'Please, Alice, I mean it. If you do see him again, call the police.'

Alice pulled a face of mock alarm. 'All right, all right!'

'Promise me you will.'

Alice glanced at Rita, as though to share a joke, but Rita wasn't smiling. 'All right. I promise – cross my heart and hope to die.' She gave a nervous giggle.

Rita was scrutinising her. 'What's this about, Maddy – I mean, "call the police"?! Who *is* this punter?'

'I told you . . . he tried to hurt me. I just know he's – dangerous.'

She couldn't tell them any more. If she became known as the woman who had escaped the 'infamous' Tiepin Killer, the more people would talk – and the more likely the trail would lead him to her. It was better to lie low and keep quiet. If by some mischance Alice encountered him again, she would know what to do.

A few minutes after ten Roddy returned to collect her. He couldn't be persuaded to buy them another round of drinks, though he chatted with them for a while. As she was leaving with him, Rita muttered to her, 'Be careful,' and Madeleine heard in her tone something more than ordinary solicitude; it sounded like she'd given Rita a fright.

Roddy had stopped the car for a moment to buy cigarettes. While he was gone Madeleine took out her purse and removed a folded clipping of newsprint she had secreted there. It was the story in the *Chronicle* which Nina had first brought to her attention, headlined THIRD 'TIEPIN' MURDER VICTIM NAMED, with the pencil sketch of the alleged killer alongside. She stared intently at the face, wondering at the eyes and why they seemed familiar.

She heard Roddy opening the driver's door, and she put away the cutting in her purse. He appraised her with one of his up-and-down looks, a lightning-fast inventory of her person that would precede some tart remark about her hair, or her dress. This evening he just nodded, which was as close to approval as he ever came. They set off again through the streets, dark and glistening from a recent downpour. She could feel Roddy's sidelong glances at her; eventually she looked round at him.

'Is there something the matter?' she asked.

'Hmm? Oh, no . . . Just wondering how you were getting along with – things.'

'Fine,' she shrugged. 'Things are fine.'

'Only I don't want you to think you're alone out here. I mean, I'm not just your boss, I'm also keeping an eye out for you, like – well, like a friend would.' He paused, waiting for a reaction. When none came he continued. 'So if you're ever in need of someone to, you know – because things can get rough – it's important to have a feller who knows what's what . . . out there . . . D'you understand?'

Madeleine looked at him for a moment, then nodded at something over his shoulder. 'I think we're here.'

The Mirabelle's sign was picked out in hot-pink lights. Roddy, clicking his tongue in distraction, parked the car. Without looking at her he took out his wallet and peeled off a five-pound note, which he held forth between his middle and index finger. Madeleine waited, not saying anything.

'What's wrong?' he said. 'Aren't you going to take it?'

'What's it for?' she asked quietly.

'A bonus – just a little something for your . . . you know.'

Madeleine didn't know – she hadn't done anything to earn a 'bonus'. But she was not so well off that she could refuse it, and trying to act high-minded would be lost on Roddy in any case. She reached out to take the note from his fingers, expecting him to pull it away, as he did for a joke, but this time he just let it go. 'Thanks,' she said, catching his eye briefly; she sensed his satisfaction at dispensing this bounty.

He jerked his head towards the restaurant as if to say, *Off you go*, but then seemed to remember his new-found gallantry. 'Wait,' he said to her, climbing out of the car. He walked round to her side and opened the passenger door, something he hadn't done since the very first week they'd met. She got out and straightened her clothes while he stood there, hesitating. He seemed about to add something, but the thunk of the car door as she closed it checked him.

'Night, then,' she said, keeping her voice as neutral as she could.

'Yeah, night,' he said, in the tone of someone who hadn't quite had his say.

The evening might have passed like any other. The punter's name was Turnbull, a director of a commercial paints firm from Walton-on-Thames. He'd been married for twenty-three years, had a son and two daughters (all at boarding school), and spent most of his weekends sailing off Bournemouth. They had a holiday home down there. The conversation was friendly in its limited way, tolerably tedious, and mercifully free of self-justification. Madeleine found it hard to listen to them complaining about their marriage, the shortcomings of the wife, the lack of under-standing. It seemed to double the disloyalty. She always expected them to be different, these men, but the longer she continued as an escort the more they resembled one another – whether they came to her out of frustration, or loneliness, or lust, they all ended up sounding the same.

The dinner at the Mirabelle was disappointing, though they both drank quite a lot. The horrified way in which Mr Turnbull stared at the bill made Madeleine think there might have been a death threat scrawled on it. But he didn't cause a fuss, thank goodness, and paid up. A taxi took them to a hotel near Charing Cross, where she found herself addressed as 'Mrs Turnbull'. She noticed the reception manager dis-creetly peer over the desk to check if they had any luggage, then nod to himself: it was to be a short stay. The room, on the top floor, offered a view down towards the river; she could see it glint in the dark. The lace curtains were dusty, and the ancient radiator stone cold, but she didn't mind. She sensed that Turnbull was in a slight hurry, careful not to miss the last train home.

It proved to be even swifter than she'd hoped. The bedside

light had been off for no more than two minutes when she heard a groan, and he rolled away from her, muttering an apology. She remembered Rita's phrase for it – 'he got off a stop too early'. Once he had crept away to the bathroom she switched the light on again. She shifted her weight away from the middle of the bed and pulled back the blanket to examine the sheet, where the usual memento had been left: a map of Ireland, just drying. The sheath, which he hadn't managed to get on, lay next to it like a shrivelled party balloon.

She was still getting dressed when he emerged from the bathroom, drying his face with a towel. It needed only a glance for her to notice something amiss. His hair had taken on a strange lopsided look, as though a gust of wind had blown it sideways – and then she realised.

'What's wrong?' he said, catching her frown.

'I think it's –' She found herself unable to tell him that his wig had slipped, so she merely gestured with her eyes. He gave another groan – a bad night had suddenly got worse – and he turned back to the bathroom. She felt rather sorry for him, though she was also thinking of the funny story it would make when she next saw Rita. (Keep your hair on!) And then she was thinking of something not funny at all, something horrible, in fact. It was him again, with the dark mercury eyes and the tie around her throat, whose face had reared up in memory just that evening – *He's been looking for you since*. That was it, *that* was the thing she had forgotten – her hand had grabbed at his hair when he was forcing her down on the bed, she had got hold of it for a second. A half-second. She was reliving it in her head. Now it made sense. How had she forgotten that?

# 12

'I really don't see what difference it makes.'

Nina paused at this remark and stared hard at her younger sister. If she didn't know better she might have assumed that satire was in play – except that Bee didn't really 'do' jokes. They were having tea in the Lyons Corner House at the foot of Tottenham Court Road, which was just as well: the polite chatter from other tables would prevent her from doing as instinct demanded, namely to scream in her sister's face. God knows she had enough provocation. But she also knew how to behave, having spent most of her life tiptoeing around her mother's moods. Mentally she started counting to ten, admiring in the meantime the sculptural quality of Bee's head, set off by her dark bobbed hair; it was something she had first noticed when she was a girl, that perfectly shaped skull, and it became a puzzlement over the years that so little of merit had emerged from inside it. She was petulant, tactless and spoilt – her mother's child, if ever there was.

'You "don't see what difference it makes",' Nina said slowly, in echo. 'I wonder if you'd say that if the house were bequeathed to me, or to Fliss, and you got left with nothing –'

'But you won't be left with nothing! Mummy is going to divide the rest of her things between us – her jewellery and . . . whatever money there is.'

'In other words, practically nothing. The only thing of value she owns is the house. Can you not understand how it might make us feel *excluded*?'

'Well, you shouldn't,' said Bee, spooning sugar into her tea. 'I'm not going to stop you from coming to the house, or even *living* in the house. You can have your own room – there!'

She looked rather pleased by this thought, as if it reflected a nature of pure generosity. Nina stared at her again, trying to decide whether her sister was being manipulative or merely obtuse. She suspected the latter, which gave her no comfort. 'Where there's a will there's affray,' Stephen had quipped when she told him about it. That had been no comfort either.

'Thank you for the offer,' she said with heavy irony, which Bee missed, because she immediately jumped in with an afterthought.

'Not your old bedroom, though. I'm afraid I've taken that.'

Nina took a moment to construe this. 'D'you mean to say – have you already moved in?'

'Well, Mummy said there was no point in paying rent at Fulham, and with Mr Dorsch living in that big house –'

'Wait – *wait*. You're both assuming an awful lot. How can you be certain that Mr Dorsch will ask Mum to marry him?'

Bee shrugged. 'She seems to think he will. And they looked very cosy together at the dinner.'

The dinner. This was an occasion Mrs Land had hosted for her three daughters and Mr Dorsch last week, ostensibly a casual affair but to Nina's eye a scheme to encourage the widower to regard himself as 'one of the family'. It had been quite a convivial evening, true – her mother was a good cook, and Mr Dorsch had brought round some fine Austrian muscat to drink – but Nina nevertheless sensed a misreading of the situation. While Mr Dorsch's manner was cheerful and attentive, she detected no special warmth emanating from him towards his hostess, for all her vivacity. If he did have passion it was devoted to the pursuit of his charity work for the Spanish orphans still coming over in boatloads from the civil war. The toast he raised to Mrs Land in the middle of dinner was sincere but explicitly one of gratitude for her continuing good offices as a volunteer. Nina, making silent study of the moment, caught the tiniest glint of disappointment in her mother's hitherto bright gaze. She felt almost sorry for her.

'You don't think she's deluding herself? I'm not sure Mr Dorsch is really the romantic type . . .'

'He doesn't have to be romantic – he just has to marry her,' said Bee, with a cold practicality that took Nina by surprise. 'It'll all work out in the end.'

Nina was very far from being persuaded on the matter. It had also become clear to her that Bee wasn't going to budge about the house, being unable, or unwilling, to see the injustice of it. And further argument would cause the plaintiff more anguish than it would the defendant.

She took out a cigarette, offered one to Bee, and lit them up.

'That's a nice lighter,' Bee remarked. 'Is it actual gold?'

Nina nodded, feeling an absurd thrill of pleasure that it had been noticed. 'A friend gave it to me.'

'Must be some friend.'

She allowed herself a pause before answering. 'I suppose he is. Well, when you meet someone as irresistible as me . . .'

Bee's expression wavered, doubtful, until she realised that her sister was being droll, and merely raised her eyes to heaven in humourless reproof. Nina had a slight hope that Bee would enquire further, not that she would dream of naming Stephen but because she would enjoy being mysterious about him. The hope was disappointed: something had caught Bee's eye, eclipsing any curiosity about the friend.

'This business with the American woman,' she said, gazing at an illustrated paper being read at the next table. 'Is the King allowed to marry her?'

'No. She's twice divorced. Unless they make it a morganatic marriage.'

'A what?'

'It means he could marry her but she wouldn't be Queen, and his direct heirs would be excluded from the throne. The Crown would pass on his death to the Duke of York's eldest daughter instead. Elizabeth. But the government will fight him tooth and nail over it.' She had got all this, including 'morganatic', from Stephen a few days ago, and amused herself by sounding so authoritative on the matter. Bee was staring at her in undisguised wonder – she looked almost stunned by her tone of assurance.

'So, do you think – what if they tell him he can't? Marry her, I mean.'

'There'll be the most awful row,' said Nina, choosing her words pointedly. 'Among the family as well.'

'Really?' said Bee, wide-eyed now.

'Of course – if he abdicates. Poor old Albert. You don't expect your nearest and dearest to leave you in the lurch. What sort of behaviour is that?'

She watched her sister carefully as she said this, wondering if it was a little heavy-handed. Bee puckered her mouth in disapproval. 'Shameful, I'd call it.'

Interesting, thought Nina. Her sister had moral discrimination after all. A pity it should require the story of people known to her only through the headlines to exercise it. She thought she might have one more try, to see if she could awaken Bee to a parallel case. 'It'll cause bad blood. How would you resolve it?'

Bee gave this her most pettish frown, and for a moment

Nina thought the penny had dropped. But what she said was, 'I think the King should set an example – one must *do one's duty.*'

Nina tapped the ash off her cigarette, and looked away. 'Oh, one must,' she murmured. 'One must.'

The following night before curtain-up she found Dolly smirking at her queerly. She sidled over to Nina's dressing screen and, with the proud flourish of a mayoress unveiling a plaque, plucked down a shimmering scarlet kimono.

'Look what I found,' Dolly crowed. It was a favourite item Nina believed had been lost, or stolen, weeks ago.

'Where on earth – ?'

'Only down the back of that bleedin' sofa! If you weren't such a slattern I wouldn't 'ave lost an eye lookin' for it.'

Nina, cooing her delight, had taken the garment in her hands and pressed it to her nose. 'Behind the sofa?'

And saying the words she now recalled when she had last taken it off. She had been late finishing up one night – Dolly had gone home – when Stephen dropped by un-expectedly. 'I've only got an hour,' he'd said, and in the frantic fumble of clothes being shed she had tossed the kimono across the shoulder of a sofa already doing duty as a chaotic open wardrobe. As those hurried horizontal minutes came back to her she blushed, and turned away lest Dolly should read the guilty pleasure in her face.

'You're so clever to have found it,' she cried, quickly stripping down to her underwear and wrapping the kimono about her neat figure. 'Ooh, this silk is like, it's like . . . cool water rippling over your skin!'

'Fancy,' said Dolly, deadpan. At which Nina crossed her hands, grabbed a handful of silk in each and flashed a pose at her.

'How d'you like that for a poster at the Gaumont?'

Dolly gave her a once-over. 'Oh. Went well, then?'

'Pretty well,' said Nina, who had done a screen test that afternoon for Ludo Talman at the Marlborough Studios. The reaction had been encouraging, though Ludo said he would first have to show the reels to 'the men with the money' – his producers. So it wasn't cut and dried quite yet.

She was imagining her first close-up when a knock sounded at the door. It was the call boy, whose muttered message Dolly relayed. 'Somebody for you.'

Nina, who never allowed anyone in her dressing room before curtain-up, waved him away. 'I can't possibly –'

'He sez she wasn't stage-doorin'. A young lady – knows you.'

She paused, irritated yet curious. With a lift of her chin she indicated her acquiescence, and the call boy hurried off. A minute or so later she heard footsteps come to a halt, and a quiet tap on the door. The caller's was not a face she had expected to see again.

'Hullo,' said Madeleine. 'You remember we – ?'

'Yes, yes, of course. Come in,' she said. 'This is Dolly, my dresser – it's, um, Madeleine, isn't it?'

Madeleine felt the fuggy warmth from the two-bar electric fire as she edged her way in; the place looked like a laundry room after a small tornado had whipped through it. Armchairs and sofa were heaped with clothes. Rainbow swipes of soft fabrics hung off every available upright. The bulb-fringed mirror overlooking the dressing table duplicated a wild landscape of pots and creams and brushes. Nina slyly took in her guest's polite survey of her quarters, and laughed.

'Pardon the mess – here –' She picked up a bentwood chair on which a mound of scripts rested, tipped the contents onto the sofa and set it companionably next to her own. 'I'd never make a secretary,' she said with a shrug.

Madeleine smiled and took the proffered seat, as Nina plumped herself down on her own chair. Ludo's screen test had put her in a cheerful mood, banishing the tension of yesterday's encounter with Bee. And perhaps it was also the thought of Stephen that night with his hands all over her, in this very room. She wondered now, as she often did, if he was thinking of her.

'So . . .' she began, surveying her guest, attired for the evening in a black alpaca coat with a contrasting fur trim, and a felt cloche pulled low over her brow. She looked – what was the word? – *fetching*, which wasn't how you generally thought of tarts.

'I wanted to – what we talked about the other night –' she said, halting, and her eyes flicked across to Dolly, who had seated herself at the ancient black Singer where she did running repairs on Nina's clothes. She didn't bother making a pretence of not listening.

Nina, understanding at once, put on her sweetest smile as she said, 'Dolly, would you be a darling and make us a pot of tea?'

Dolly gave a fleeting twitch to her mouth. 'All part of the service, I'm sure.' She abandoned her sewing machine and, with a thwarted air, traipsed out of the room. When the door closed Nina tipped her head in invitation: they could now speak confidentially.

'That drawing your friend did, the one you showed me the other night, of – him.' Madeleine paused, forcing herself to recall his face. 'I think I made a mistake.'

'A mistake? What d'you mean?'

'When I looked at it, you remember I said – I thought it wasn't him.'

'Yes, you said it couldn't have been the man you were with, because he wasn't bald. You seemed quite sure of it.'

'I know. That's what I thought. But something happened, recently – something that reminded me of that day, and I realised . . .' She gave her head a brief shake, as though in self-rebuke, '. . . that he probably *is* bald.'

Nina tucked in her chin, disbelieving. 'Probably? The man – you were *there* with him – surely it's a straightforward thing if he's bald or not.'

'Yes, but – I couldn't tell, because he was wearing a wig. When he was on top of me . . . at one point I managed to free my hand and grab his hair. And I felt it slip. I'd forgotten that – it was over in a moment, and all through I was panicking, trying to fight him off. By the time *you* entered the room he must have taken the thing off.'

'Hmm. No wonder we couldn't agree . . . But his face, I mean in the sketch. D'you think it was his face?'

Madeleine gave a rueful grimace. 'I do now.'

Nina nodded. This put a new perspective on the matter. She thought again of the drawing she had presented to the police. It was hardly surprising that they hadn't caught the man, given the unreliable picture they had of him. Even this woman who had been in his company couldn't tell if he had hair or not. Oh, that she had ever got herself involved . . .

A silence intervened before Madeleine spoke again. 'There's another thing. Someone I know – from the club – met a man recently who was – she said he was asking about me. I'm pretty sure it was him.'

'Oh God. How could you tell?'

'Just from her description. He kept making knots with his tie – which is what he did when he was with me.'

'Did she say anything else?'

'Only one thing – he told her his name was Rusk.'

'Rusk?' The name unaccountably rang a bell in her consciousness. She stood and began to rummage through a heap of discarded *Chronicle*s on her dresser. Somehow, through her own idiosyncratic filing system, she located the one she wanted, and riffled its pages.

'Here!' She spread out the paper for Madeleine to look at. It was a news story on the Tiepin Killer from a week ago, when the police first released a photograph of his face as sketched by 'a member of the public'. Nina pointed to the reporter's byline: *Barry Rusk, crime correspondent*.

Alice was right, thought Madeleine – they never gave their own name. 'So he just took it from a reporter,' she said.

But now a gleam had come into Nina's eye. 'Yes, but not just any reporter. He took the name of the one who'd written this story, as if it were a kind of joke. D'you not see what that means? Before we weren't sure, but now we know the man has seen his own face in the newspaper – so the man we saw must be the killer!'

Madeleine, staring at the newsprint, slowly nodded her head. She was thinking about Alice, about why 'Mr Rusk' had not done her in like the others. And now it seemed obvious; *he will use her to get to me*. Of course. 'They usually come back for more,' Alice had said, and she would know. Madeleine had got her to promise to go to the police if she met him again, but what with her being half crazed on drugs, as Rita said, it was more than likely she'd forget, or wouldn't bother.

Just then they heard Dolly's shuffling steps, returning with the tea, and Nina quickly took Madeleine's hand in hers. 'Don't worry,' she said in a conspirator's undertone, 'I think I know what to do.'

'There you are!'

Stephen looked up from his luncheon omelette to find Ludo Talman bearing down on him. He had been working on the mural since eight in the morning, and hoped to snatch a quiet moment in the smaller of the Nines' dining rooms. But there was to be no peace here. Ludo was accompanied by a tall, well-dressed man whom he introduced with a hushed respect.

'Stephen, this is Everett Druce, one of our sainted patrons at the Marlborough.'

Stephen made to rise, but Druce suavely held up his hands to stop him. 'Please – we've interrupted your lunch. Talman said you were on the premises, and I was curious to meet you.'

'Well, you'll get to know one another soon enough. Druce is one of those to be immortalised on the mural. We've just been upstairs to have a look at it – you're making good progress.'

Stephen nodded, wondering where he had seen the man before. 'We should arrange a time for you to sit.'

Druce made an apologetic grimace. 'I'm sorry to say my time is at a premium. If I don't manage to see you here, perhaps you'd call at the house one afternoon – I've a few nice paintings you might care to look at.'

'I'm sure I would,' said Stephen, catching Ludo's enthusiastic mumming in the background.

'Excellent.' He glanced at his watch. 'And now I must away. Talman, a pleasure, as always. Mr Wyley,' he said, dipping his head in farewell.

When he had gone, Ludo slid into the chair facing Stephen. He took out a cigar, dark and stubby as a turd, and lit it.

'You're looking rather pleased with yourself,' said Stephen, blowing the smoke away from his omelette.

'So would you be if you'd just renewed a contract with our Mr Druce. He's a kind of sleeping partner at the Marlborough. Attends the occasional meeting, watches the odd screen test, never interferes – and invests a fortune in the company.'

'What's in it for him?'

'A small return on his money. But mostly prestige. He loves movies, of course.'

'And he's rich, by the sound of it.'

'Oh, rich as stink, as my mother used to say. Lives in one of those huge old Georgian houses down by the Embankment. When he mentioned those "nice" paintings he was being modest. He's a serious collector – Cézanne, Monet, early Braque, you name it, and that's just the moderns. There's a Poussin in his drawing room that's worth a visit all by itself.'

Stephen was still trying to recall his face. 'I've a feeling we've met before. Did he study at the Royal Academy?'

'I wouldn't have thought so. He's spent most of his life making money – some City brokerage, I gather. That's why he's never got any time to spare.'

'Talking of which, I had a letter from the Palace the other day. You-know-who's private secretary regrets to inform me that HM hasn't time to sit for a portrait at present. I just wanted you to know that I tried.'

Ludo gave an irritated little jerk of his head. 'Damn. Probably too busy tupping the gay divorcee . . .'

Stephen offered no comment on this prurient specula-tion. Rain, pattering on, blurred the tall window. Outside, the autumn sky was as murky as an old fish tank. He gave up on his omelette, wreathed as it was in cigar smoke, and asked the waiter for a cognac. Ludo, recov-ering his good mood, decided to join him. Stephen wondered if this might be the moment to broach another delicate subject.

'I happened to see my friend Nina last night. She said you were very charming to her at the studio . . .'

'Ah, yes, Nina Land.' His producer's tone was thoughtful rather than enthusiastic. 'We auditioned her for a picture we're making called *Fortune's Cap*. She was very – spirited.'

Stephen didn't like the sound of this. 'Isn't that a good thing?'

Ludo blew out a pensive jet of smoke. 'It rather depends. She's an excellent stage actress, there's no doubt. But film-acting demands something different, a kind of restraint. "Less is more", if you will. Miss Land' – his mouth made a little click of regret – 'she's still projecting to the stalls.

Row T would have no complaints, but it won't look right onscreen. It might even look ridiculous.'

'Surely a director could instruct her to, I don't know, tone it down?'

Ludo gave a slow shake to his head. 'The truth is, she's not really what we're after. If it were Strindberg I'd cast her in a shot – ha ha! – but this is a contemporary story about deception and murder. I just don't see her in it. And strictly *entre nous*, some of the chaps thought she was a little *old*.'

'She's thirty-two!'

At which Ludo said, with a shrug, 'The case rests.'

*Hellfire*, thought Stephen. And she'd told him straight out last night how pleased she'd been! Either Ludo's charm had misled her or else she had properly deceived herself. It would be hard to bear, he knew, especially coming after her mother's despicable behaviour over the will. He felt a tug of pity as he imagined her face on hearing the news.

Ludo, seeming to read Stephen's disappointment, said in belated compensation, 'We may show the reel to a few others, I don't know, it's not final. But I wouldn't get her hopes up.'

'No, I see that . . .' He watched the rain purling down the window, and fell to brooding again. When he looked up, Ludo had fixed him with a shrewd gaze.

'Am I missing something here?' said the producer. 'If I didn't know you better I'd say that your interest in Miss Land extends somewhat beyond her career.'

'What makes you say that?'

'Call it a sordid intuition. It struck me the first time I saw you together, when she was telling that story about her moment with the Tiepin Killer. You seemed very jumpy.'

Stephen paused, holding his gaze. 'She's a very dear friend, and I'm concerned for her. She ought to have kept that story to herself. It could get her into trouble if someone put it about.'

Ludo's eyebrows arched. 'Which would imply . . .?

'I'm counting on your discretion, Ludo.'

'That's rich,' he said with a disbelieving laugh. 'To judge from the company *you've* been keeping I don't think it's my discretion we have to worry about.'

'What do you mean?'

'Gerald Carmody. Not the sort you should be seen with, old boy.'

Stephen shook his head. 'Carmody is no friend of mine, I assure you. He inveigled me into attending a charity dinner the other night – otherwise I barely see him.'

Ludo, with a dubious look, said, 'I've a notion you've not read today's *Times*.' He stood and walked over to the rack of newspapers, plucking one by its wooden rod. Riffling through it he found the page, and spread it on the table in front of Stephen. It was a news story about the activities of the British People's Brigade, a breakaway Fascist party led by 'ex-MP Gerald Carmody, a one-time comrade of Oswald Mosley and his British Union of Fascists'. Stephen's eye flitted to the accompanying photographs. One was of the new party's aristocratic sponsor, Lady Trevelyan, greeting the German ambassador to London, Ribbentrop, with Carmody dancing attendance. Another was Carmody presiding over a rally, his arm held aloft in a Nazi salute.

Still at his shoulder, Ludo read from the story: '"Having left the BUF Carmody made an alliance with fellow anti-Semite William Joyce. Together they have formed the British People's Brigade, a party devoted to keeping Britain out of a war and to fighting international Jewish finance, a ruthless conspiracy, according to Carmody, which 'stretches its hands from the shelter of England to throttle trade and menace the peace of the world'."' Ludo chuckled, adding, 'I could take that rather personally.'

Stephen shook his head. 'I don't understand what this has to do with me.'

'Try the next page,' he replied with a thin smile.

Stephen did so, and found there his own face looming out of a photograph, his expression uncertain and at odds with a manically grinning Carmody next to him. They were shaking hands. Someone had taken it at the Carlton that night of the Marquess dinner. A caption helpfully supplied: *Gerald Carmody with (right) society portraitist Stephen Wyley*. He had thought little of it at the time, of course, recalling only the camera bulb's explosive flash. If he were being honest about it, Stephen had suspected the danger of associating with Carmody all along – and yet he had deluded himself that no one would notice, or care. He'd got that wrong. At his side he felt Ludo's unspoken appraisal.

'I could hardly refuse his hand. He was our host for the evening.'

Ludo shrugged in a conciliating gesture. 'You don't have to defend yourself to me. I don't imagine for a moment you go Sieg-Heiling about the place or demanding the expulsion of the Jews, or whatever else it is they do –'

'Ludo, for God's sake –'

'– I am merely iterating your point about *discretion*, dear boy.' He looked about the half-full dining room. 'They're a liberal lot here, as you know, but they won't stand for a member being involved with – well – the Fascist fringe.'

Stephen lowered his head, rubbing his eyelids with thumb and middle finger. 'You want to know the irony? It so happened that fellow Joyce was at the same dinner, the one Carmody invited me to, drunk and spouting the most ludicrous rot about Jews – I actually took a swing at him! But of course that didn't make the story.'

Ludo puffed on his cigar. 'It sounds as though you were just in the wrong place. But guilt by association is the devil to shake off. I think your best bet is to lie low and avoid places that Carmody goes. He hasn't got anything on you, has he?'

'What? No, no. Like I said, he's not a friend.' He glanced back over the page at the photograph of Lady Trevelyan and Ribbentrop. It would not be the moment to admit he'd been a guest at the former's house. He had been tweaking his portrait of her for months. Now he came to think of it, she had mentioned her admiration of Mosley – 'Tom', as she called him. Stephen, utterly bored by politics, had ignored it. The claim of ignorance no longer felt convincing. Somehow he had managed to sleepwalk into a coven of Nazi sympathisers.

'The thing may just blow over,' said Ludo presently. 'After all, it's not as though there's a shortage of right-wing crackpots to keep the press occupied. Carmody's pretty small beer.'

Stephen nodded, not feeling reassured. It was a joke – a farce, really – but he didn't like the idea of being its punchline.

Later, too distracted to work, he put his brushes away and pinned back the dust sheet to protect the mural. Five of the members' faces had been completed, with another ten to go. No, eleven – he had forgotten the late addition of Talman's affluent friend. He made a mental note to dig out his old college record and look for Everett Druce in it; he felt certain they had met before.

He was crossing the hall on his way out of the club when a porter hailed him. He followed the man into the panelled vestibule where the staff loitered in their waistcoats and striped trews. The porter plucked a letter from one of the narrow pigeonholes and handed it to him.

'Gentleman left it for you, sir,' the man said quietly, and withdrew.

His name was written on the envelope in an untidy, boyish hand. Stephen, in a momentary spasm of paranoia, thought of Oscar Wilde and the fateful calling card left at his club by the Marquess of Queensberry, insulting him as a 'posing somdomite'. Was the news of his social blemish already out? 'Stephen Wyley: crypto-Fascist'. He looked around, to see if he was being watched. There was no one; it was a somnolent late afternoon at the Nines. With fluttering heart he cut open the envelope, whose folded contents turned out to be a photographic plate excised from a book, and a short note in the same untidy hand:

My dear Mr Wyley,

It was most kind of you to host James and myself for drinks at your club the other evening. I have enclosed a reproduction of the Parmigianino *Self-Portrait in a Convex Mirror* which you may recall being lectured upon at the Carlton Hotel dinner – forgive me, I am too apt to be 'carried away' by my enthusiasms. I fear the curse of loquaciousness has been refined through generations of my family! But I venture to hope you will not be unstimulated by the painting. As I said, it seems to me the most perfect conceit – the artist's beautiful hand, hovering, unable to grasp the truth of his own self.

Of your noble behaviour on the night in question I will say only this – it shall not be forgotten. Believe me, sir.

Very respectfully yours,
László Balázsovits

Stephen stared at the reflected face of the young painter, pale, delicate, epicene – perhaps more girl than boy. Even in this small reproduction he could tell it was a remarkable thing, like a magical apparition in a crystal ball. It was that hand at the front you couldn't help staring at, distorted by the mirror and suggesting something hidden from the viewer's gaze. He turned back to the letter and read the bit about his 'noble behaviour' again. With a rueful twist to his mouth he folded it away in his pocket, put up the collar of his coat and left the building. The bloated sky was still leaking rain as he hurried towards his bus stop.

# 13

Madeleine waited for the operator's click, then slipped the coin into the slot. The voice came on the line.

'Museum 3581 . . . Hullo?'

*Drat*, she thought, it's him. 'Oh, I'm sorry,' she said, 'it's me again, I'm –'

'Kindly identify "me", madam.'

'Madeleine – Madeleine Farewell.'

'Madeleine *Farewell*? Sounds like someone from a Restoration comedy.'

At a loss for a reply, she pressed on. 'I wonder if Tom is there. He gave me this number, you see . . .'

'I'll see if he's available,' said Jimmy, with an audible sigh. He had become used to answering the phone during Tom's absence, and now couldn't stop himself. Madeleine heard a heavy clunk as the receiver was set down and muffled voices echoed tinnily at the other end. The louder of them was the man who had answered her, and he didn't sound best pleased to be 'trotting about' with messages for his secretary. Half a minute later the receiver scraped back into life and she heard, to her relief, Tom.

'Madeleine?'

'Hullo! I think your boss must be fed up with my calling this number. I hadn't heard from you, so I – well, I was a little anxious.'

Tom felt a jolt, pleased to hear that he'd been missed. It was not a sensation he was familiar with. He explained that he had been kept to his flat by 'illness', without specifying its nature.

'I wanted to apologise,' she said. 'I left your friend's birthday party without – I should have said goodnight, but . . .'

'Never mind!' He was madly curious about that night of the party, having seen her leave with Nina Land, but he sensed it wasn't the moment to start investigating. She was rather a private person, like himself; perhaps that was why they had been drawn to one another. As he was talking Jimmy scribbled a note for him to read. With Madeleine now silent at the other end of the line, Tom began, falteringly, 'I wonder, um – that is, my employer wanted to know – if you'd like to have lunch with us one day this week. I suppose you're busy –'

'No, I'm not busy,' she replied artlessly.

Looking over at Jimmy, he indicated with only his eyebrows her acceptance: their code of facial expressions had become almost marital. Jimmy mouthed a word, and Tom relayed it out loud: 'Would Friday suit you?'

Having rung off, Madeleine returned through the slow lunchtime fug of the Blue Posts to where Rita was sitting. The latter had just applied a fresh swipe of pillar-box-red lipstick and was puckering her mouth in a compact mirror, tilting her head this way and that.

'There's me warpaint,' she said, snapping the compact shut. She turned a curious look on Madeleine. 'So – how was it last night? With him.'

'Him' was Roddy, who had intensified his campaign of charm by inviting her to dinner. It had put her in a quandary. Roddy had laid the ground during the last few weeks, driving her home at night, paying small compliments, supplying her with a perfume he knew she liked. He showed every sign of being besotted with her. To refuse his offer outright would be tantamount to an insult. But to yield might be hazardous, too, for she suspected her acceptance might be interpreted as a 'green light'. In the end she decided that it would be better to risk it and hope that an amiable distance could be preserved between them.

Somehow she got through it. Roddy had booked a table at an expensive fish restaurant off St James's Square, and seemed no more at ease there than she was. They were seated awkwardly alongside each other on an olive-green banquette, and Madeleine sensed they were intruding on a room of regulars. When they were handed the tasselled menus, heavy as photograph albums, Roddy had squinted at it in alarmed distaste ('It's all in French,' he muttered). Madeleine, with a loose grasp of the language from convent school, attempted to translate, but when it came to ordering the food he insisted on doing the job by himself. She noticed the aproned waiter smirking at his clumsy efforts (he pronounced *langoustine* to rhyme with 'Frankenstein') and was surprised to find herself feeling sorry for him. He drank at pace, and kept telling the waiter 'to top 'em up', which drew haughty glances from the maître d'.

The odd thing was that Roddy could not leave a silence alone, and yet seemed unable to talk about the reason they were having dinner in the first place. Any time the conversation veered towards the personal he would bluster through with some jokey complaint about the Elysian, or about the other girls. In a way she was glad; she must have misread his intentions, or else he had been planning to make a move and then lost his nerve. By the time they got to pudding – vanilla ice with a hot cherry sauce – her relief at this non-event was so acute that she almost persuaded herself she was having a nice time. Roddy had relaxed, too, his face reddening from the concerted effect of the wine and the Martinis he kept tipping down.

'So,' he began, lighting a stubby cigar, 'heard anything more from that feller?'

'What feller?'

'Your admirer – Mr Rusk, is it?'

Madeleine paused, her innards turning cold. 'I don't know what you're talking about,' she said quietly.

'Yes, you do. I asked your pal – y'know, Amphetamine Alice – she told me he's been looking for you.'

'And you believed her – Alice? She hardly knows what day of the week it is.'

Roddy's eyebrows were hoisted sceptically, and Madeleine realised she had to tell him something or else he'd never give her peace. She feigned a professional sigh. 'She mentioned someone to me, a punter – I'd never heard of him. You know how many I see in a week, a month.'

Roddy continued to stare at her. 'So you don't know this Mr Rusk?'

'No, I don't.'

'And you're not seeing anyone else?'

'No. I swear it.' And she looked him in the eye as she spoke, knowing it was the truth. From an involuntary twitch to his mouth she saw that he was reassured by this information. He raised his arm to the waiter and twirled his hand in a circle to signal another round.

'I can't drink any more, really I can't.'

'Oh, you can manage a nightcap. Just one before bed.'

As he drove her home she sank low in the passenger seat, eyes fixed on the corner of the windscreen, so that she was listening to London, not seeing it. The plaintive moan of buses on Marylebone Road, the clang of the trams as they turned into Hampstead Road, the distant clackety-clack of trains pulling out of Euston. On it all flowed, unceasing, oblivious. She felt her own inconsequential smallness in the larger pattern. You could live – and die – in London without anyone caring a rap. You wouldn't even be forgotten when you were gone, since no one actually noticed you when you were alive. That didn't seem so bad. What *had* disturbed her recently was a dream, horrifically vivid, about an enormous conflagration. She found herself on the streets of a city, which may have been London, she wasn't sure; it was night in the dream, yet every house was lit up – on fire – and every person she saw wore an aureole of fire, just the top of their heads in blaze. They appeared to be sleep-walking, there was no sign of panic or hurrying. The fire was coming down like rain, long, liquid curtains of it drowning the roofs, the walls, the pavements; inescapable. Windows were bursting from the heat. Someone told her to look down, and she saw that her own hands were wreathed in flames. She couldn't remember anything after that.

'All up in smoke,' she murmured into the darkness of the car.

'Eh?' said Roddy, glancing across. She had not meant to speak out loud.

'Oh . . . I was just wondering how the world's going to end.' She gave a defensive little laugh to indicate this wasn't to be taken seriously.

Roddy's stare was incredulous. 'What's with you?' He took on an authoritative tone. 'All this talk about a war, they're dead wrong. Too much to lose, on all sides. Even Hitler won't risk upsetting the apple cart.'

Madeleine watched as the lights from outside skimmed in fleeting bands across his profile. She never really talked about serious things with Roddy. Or with anyone else, now she thought about it. She supposed Tom would be a good person for that, he seemed to know quite a lot about things, but not in a superior way. He wouldn't laugh at you for not knowing much. For someone so bright and nervous he was also quite gentle – that was the nice thing about him.

They had arrived at her lodgings in Bayham Street. Roddy pulled the car over, letting the engine idle for a few moments before switching off. She had started to thank him for a nice evening when he leaned across her and, before she could defend herself, his mouth was smothering hers. It was hot and eager and stank of alcohol and cigars. As soon as decency allowed she pulled away from him. He kept his head close, then said, 'Are you thinking what I'm thinking?'

Her eyes briefly caught his gleam. 'Probably not.'

From his chuckle she could tell he wasn't remotely discouraged. He shifted his weight against her and snaked an exploratory hand inside her coat. She tensed, wondering what she had done that he could possibly have interpreted as a come-on. And there was nothing. She had been polite, and attentive; she had smiled at his bad jokes, and expressed sympathy when he was moaning about work – as though his was more burdensome than hers.

His hand was now pawing, hound-like, at the silk of her blouse, and she knew there was nothing to be gained from being ambiguous. Grasping his wrist she hauled the hand from inside her coat and matter-of-factly placed it on the car's steering wheel. Before he could protest she said, without looking at him, 'I'm off the clock, Roddy, and I'm tired.'

She made to open the passenger door, but he stayed her arm. 'I don't understand,' he said in an irked tone. 'You just said you weren't seeing anyone, but you're giving me the brush-off.'

He offered this as a piece of logic, and she reviewed the prospect of explaining why not seeing anyone had no connection at all with how she felt about him. Or she could make it simple and tell the truth outright – that Roddy was perhaps the last man on earth she would willingly offer herself to. But those words were not to be uttered, not if she wanted to maintain a spirit of civility between them. From the set of his jaw she could tell he was still turning it over in his mind, the resentment just starting to brew, and she realised then what she had to say.

'You know how much it costs – and you've got my number.'

Roddy, absorbing this cool reminder, stared hard at her. She had given him a way out. He gave a mirthless little laugh. 'I shoulda known. You can take the girl out of Soho, but you can't take Soho out the girl.'

She would have liked to slap his face for that remark, but she only nodded, as though he had just hit the nail on the head. 'Thanks for dinner,' she said in her business voice. She was no sooner out of the car than Roddy started the engine, revved it and tore off down the dark street.

Jimmy had been having talks with his accountant, Mr Wootton, who told him that he needed to start making 'significant economies'. Jimmy hated these talks, because he didn't understand anything about money other than how to spend it. His idea of saving was to order the *non*-vintage champagne and to tip the waiter one shilling instead of two. Of particular concern to Mr Wootton was his client's astonishing expenditure on taxis, sometimes three or four in a day. He was curious to know how the short distances covered by the taxi could possibly justify such enormous fares. 'Mostly I just keep 'em waiting,' said Jimmy. The accountant raised his eyebrows to a professional minimum and returned to the list of expenses.

'The man Wootton said that my earnings were – what was his phrase? – "not commensurate with my outgoings". Ha!' Jimmy was recounting his latest crisis meeting to Tom as they sat in his study one morning.

Tom looked up from the typewriter at which he'd been clattering out his employer's latest column. 'It mightn't be such a bad idea to tighten your belt, you know. I mean, if the *Chronicle* does dispense with you –'

'*What?!* Who said anything about that?'

'You did, a couple of weeks ago. Barry Rusk tipped you the wink, remember?'

'No. All Barry said was I should mind my behaviour in the light of Lord Swaim's moral crackdown. There was no talk of *dispense* . . .' He gave the *Daily Mail* he'd been scouring an irritated snap and feigned absorption in it.

'Oh, I see,' murmured Tom, hands hovering on the typewriter. He kept quiet while Jimmy brooded behind the paper. After a few moments Jimmy spoke again.

'I do take Wootton's point on the taxis, however. The expense is ruinous, and a change is required.'

Tom looked up. 'You're going to take the Underground?'

'Don't be absurd,' said Jimmy, frowning. 'That sulphurous labyrinth of noise and filth? No thank you.'

'Some of us have no choice, Jim. It's the way you get about.'

Jimmy ignored this. 'The solution is quite simple. There will be no more need for taxis if I buy a car instead.'

Tom stifled a laugh when he realised Jimmy wasn't joking. 'What?'

'You've no idea how cheap they are! The classified pages of this morning's *Mail* has hundreds of 'em for sale. A modest outlay will secure a perfectly decent second-hand motor.'

'For crying out loud. Wootton has advised you to start making economies, so your next move is to go out and buy *a car*. How is that helping? And how can you possibly afford it?'

'Well, I've got a bit of money squirrelled away – for an emergency, you know.'

'I dare say the Inland Revenue would be interested to hear that. Look, be sensible. A car is an expensive thing to run – there's a lot of maintenance involved, taxes, petrol. Keep the money for a real emergency.'

'Here,' Jimmy continued, reading down the column. 'An Austin 7, nearly new – ninety pounds! You see? If I borrowed a little extra I could purchase something stylish.'

Tom looked at him, aghast. It was as though Jimmy's extravagance was a provocation, a way of setting himself apart. No sooner had he got himself clear of one bunch of creditors than he immediately acquired another. The Revenue people didn't worry him, it seemed, though if they ever got wind of his buying a car he certainly *would* set himself apart – in prison. Then something very obvious occurred to him.

'Sorry to poop the party, Jim, but you can't drive.'

Jimmy's look turned sly. 'No, I can't. But you can.'

This was, unhappily, the case. Before being invalided out of the army Tom had learned to drive – in a field ambulance, of all things – though he'd scarcely been behind a steering wheel in the years since. He would never have been able to afford a car on his salary, and even if he had it was not something he much coveted. He wasn't even sure he could remember how to drive. And then there was the danger of his condition: would an epileptic be allowed to fill in as a part-time chauffeur? Imagine having a fit while you were tootling along . . . That could be a handy way of excusing himself. But it would also mean revealing his illness to Jimmy, and he wasn't prepared to do that. The best thing for it would be to change the subject and hope Jimmy would have second thoughts.

'You haven't forgotten who's coming to lunch?'

Jimmy lifted his gaze from the newspaper. 'Of course not. I've been mulling over what to cook.'

'Well, whatever it is,' Tom said, 'I think it would be nice to greet our guest in appropriate attire.'

Jimmy, used to lolling in pyjamas and dressing gown late into the morning, clicked his tongue in reproof. 'You're just worried I'm going to embarrass you.'

Tom felt unsettled by the precision of this remark: he *was* worried. Jimmy's inclination to tease and provoke was well known, and he could hurt people sometimes without even meaning to. He was the sort of man whose sensitivity to his own feelings didn't encompass the same courtesy to others'. Women, unless they were flamboyant, actorish types, generally bored him, and Tom feared that Madeleine might not have quite the sparkle the host demanded of his guests. And why had Jimmy invited her anyway? Tom would have been content to keep his friendship with Madeleine private; instead he was being obliged to play piggy in the middle between two mismatched strangers.

To take the edge off his anxiety he put on his coat and nipped out to the shop to buy some wine. On returning he found Jimmy already dressed and in the kitchen, a copy of *Lady Syonsby's Cook Book* propped on the counter. He had poured himself a glass of sherry and was merrily humming away. Jimmy cooked in the same way he wrote, at speed and with gusto. He was always on alert, testing strengths and flavours, quite capable of abandoning his first or even second attempt at a dish and starting again. The difference was that, with writing, his aborted efforts involved only crossings-out and an occasional balled-up sheet launched in the direction of the waste-paper basket. With cooking, his modus operandi entailed using nearly every pan, pot and bowl in the kitchen, which in its multiplying clutter began to resemble a school science experiment. There was never any question, of course, about who would do the washing-up, and Tom resigned himself to long interludes of scrubbing and stacking while Jimmy entertained in the dining room.

'If you want to make yourself useful you can start chopping that parsley,' said Jimmy, busy whisking a white sauce. 'For the starter I'm making one of my specials – egg croquettes *à la* Erskine. I hope your young friend has a good appetite.'

Tom's immediate priority was to drink a large glass of the Chablis. He wondered about that appetite: she was awfully thin, his 'young friend', now he came to think of it. He had actually never seen her eat anything. He experienced a flash of panic as he imagined them sitting down together, the oddness of it, as if he were introducing a girl to his parents. What on earth would she make of Jimmy? From the little he knew of her she was all of the things Jimmy wasn't – quiet, modest, unassertive, somewhat remote and inscrutable. *Oh God*. He had just opened the wine and was about to dispose of the cork when he decided to take a Gamble With Fate. If I can land this cork in the bin, he thought, lunch will be a success. Tom had a decent eye (he was good at darts) and lined up his throw with a practised squint. But should he try a darter's jerk from the shoulder, or was an underarm lob the safer option? Holding his breath, on the count of three he propelled the cork from his fingers in a long arc. It looped promisingly towards its target, bounced insolently on the rim of the bin – and dropped on the floor.

He turned to find Jimmy staring at the space between him and the unchopped parsley on the board. With a little *huh* he took up the knife and muttered, 'Typical. Need a job done prop'ly, do it yourself.'

Too stunned to argue, Tom filled a glass and quaffed it down in gulps.

Madeleine had never seen so many paintings and drawings in a single room. She knew that Tom's employer ('call me Jimmy') was a theatre critic, but to look at his walls you would have supposed him to be an art collector. From the outside his residence looked like any other mansion block in Bloomsbury, soot-scarred, cloudy-windowed, a little shabby. Inside, though, all was vivid and luxurious. Cream-coloured carpets, dark blue walls, plush sofas, an extravagant gramophone cocking its ear trumpet, every surface strewn with knick-knacks. On the mantelpiece stood a silver-lustre jug with peonies, flanked on either side by framed photographs of the master of the house: Jimmy as a boy, Jimmy in uniform, Jimmy shaking hands with an important somebody, Jimmy on horseback, and here was one of Jimmy and Tom at a dinner together, laughing to the camera.

Tom had looked white-faced with worry on answering the door, but he seemed to relax once he realised that Jimmy was in a good mood. The latter had emerged from the steaming kitchen wearing an apron and an expectant smile. He took Madeleine's hand and raised it, in gentlemanly fashion, to his lips.

'Welcome, Miss Farewell!' he said, candidly appraising her. 'What a lovely coat that is – I remember Sarah wearing one just like it. Tom, would you kindly fetch our guest a drink?'

Jimmy chunnered on for a while, casually answering her curiosity about the provenance of this or that painting, before disappearing back to the kitchen. Tom had brought in a tray of tall glasses in which he had mixed gin and pep. They clinked glasses. 'Here's how,' he said. Madeleine looked searchingly at him and said, in a low voice, 'I'm sorry to have kept phoning – were you very ill?'

Tom waved her apology away. 'Just a mild attack of – you know. I'm fine now.'

He too had kept his voice discreet, and she understood his illness was still a matter of secrecy. She saw from his clothes that he had made an effort to look smart, and it touched her. She took a sip of the gin – goodness, he'd mixed it strong – and pointed to the photograph of him and Jimmy on the mantelpiece.

'You both look so happy there,' she said with a little lift of her eyes.

Tom, who hadn't really looked at it in ages, smiled back.

232

'It's from years ago, a Critics' Circle dinner. I think Jimmy had just won something – that's why *he's* looking happy.'

'You must have been very proud, with him being your . . .' She realised she was fishing, but Tom evidently didn't see the bait.

'I suppose I was . . . Those were the days! He won a few awards back then.' He glanced cautiously towards the kitchen doorway as he spoke.

Madeleine's expression was puzzled of a sudden. 'Who's Sarah, by the way?'

'Oh, he meant Sarah Bernhardt. She was Jimmy's idol.' He looked at her for signs of recognition, and found none. 'French actress, last century – died about ten years ago?' She gave a helpless shake of her head. That was possibly something else Jimmy oughtn't to hear about.

'How's your friend, the doctor – Peter?'

'Pretty well, I think. He was very taken with you that night we met at the theatre.'

Madeleine looked wistful for a moment. 'How lovely it must be to have such old friends.'

'Well, it's he and Jim who are the old friends, really, I came in –'

'Who are you calling "old?"' said Jimmy, back on the threshold.

Tom raised his eyes heavenwards. 'I didn't mean "old" like that. I meant *long-standing* – Madeleine was just saying how nice it is having old friends.'

Jimmy grunted, warily appeased. He hated people thinking he was old – not yet sixty, for heaven's sake! 'Well then. Luncheon is served. Tom, would you show Miss Farewell –'

'Oh, it's Madeleine, please.'

'– would you show *Madeleine* to the dining room?'

Madeleine had not tried egg croquettes *à la* Erskine, or indeed *à la* anybody, before. They were delicious, and Jimmy nodded complacently when she said so. He had learned to cook in France during the war, he explained, and once he had rooms with a kitchen of his own he became more adventurous. The first cookery book he bought was Boulestin's *Simple French Cooking for English Homes*. It still had pride of place on a bulging shelf with the other broken-spined, well-thumbed, food-flecked volumes he had stored there since.

'He reads recipe books in bed, you know,' said Tom.

'The better to dream of food,' Jimmy admitted, and Madeleine laughed. She was rather enjoying herself, in spite of Jimmy's scrutinising her as though he had never seen a woman before. She was also intrigued to see how Tom behaved in the company of a man with whom he had professed such a disaffection – from the first time they'd met she had heard him complain of Jimmy as morose, selfish, penny-pinching, absurdly conceited and monstrously rude. He had told her he couldn't wait to leave his employment. And yet here they were, if not a picture of perfect companionship then at least one of domestic familiarity, like – well, like a loud uncle and his patient nephew. She sensed how prickly Jimmy might be, and it reflected only credit on Tom that he behaved with such forbearance around him. While Jimmy did the cooking, Tom did everything else, the answering of the telephone, the serving, the wine, the clearing, even the fixing of the old man's napkin about his throat – he was a messy eater. If there had ever been something more between them, and she was not sure that there had, it was over long ago.

Jimmy for his part was delighted by their guest. He had felt disposed to like her from the off – really, how could one resist a girl called 'Miss Farewell'? He could see what Tom admired in her too, the vague air of unworldliness, the beautiful sad eyes, the little hesitation before she spoke. My God she was skinny, though – she could have played a Dickensian waif with bones like that. Still, she had made short work of the egg croquettes, he noticed, and she'd been putting away the drink without much trouble, either. Only when the main course was served did he detect a doubt.

'Is something the matter, my dear?'

'Oh . . . no, I was just wondering . . .'

'It's called Sea Pie, basically a steak pudding with the crust on top.'

Madeleine nodded. 'It's very good. I'm just not used to eating meat – on a Friday, I mean.'

'Ah, so you're a Roman?' Jimmy's eyes gleamed with renewed interest: he had an unaccountable respect for the Catholic Church. 'I bet you haven't changed since you were at the convent.'

'The nuns would think I've changed,' she said, and her gaze dropped. 'And you?'

'Never at a convent! My parents were Unitarian. We went to chapel on a Sunday – much good it did me.'

Tom said, 'So d'you still practise?'

She shook her head. 'Not really. I sometimes call in at a church to light a candle, say a prayer.'

'Really?' said Jimmy, leaning forward. 'For what? I mean, what sort of things do you pray for?'

*For my life to be spared*, she thought, remembering the man in room 408, and the murder in his eyes. His hands pressing on her windpipe. She had prayed then – and she had been answered. But that incident was never to be spoken of. She didn't want Tom knowing she had been in a hotel room with a stranger.

Tom, construing her silence as embarrassment, said, 'It's personal, Jim. Perhaps Madeleine would rather not talk about it.'

She looked at him gratefully. 'No, it's not that. I did pray, quite recently, about something . . .' She told them about the dream she had had, of the city on fire, of how it came down in great sheeting torrents, and her terror on seeing

235

people's heads wreathed in flame. It was an apocalypse, she supposed, recalling the word from her religious doctrine classes. She had prayed that it would never happen in their lifetime.

'How absolutely frightful,' said Jimmy, with feeling. 'And what do you suppose it meant? Another war?'

Madeleine shrugged. 'I was talking to somebody the other night who said there was no chance of a war. There's too much to lose.'

'Yes, that's probably right,' said Jimmy, trying to reassure himself. She asked Tom what he thought.

'I wish I could be so optimistic,' he said, clearing the plates. 'But there seems an appetite for it. Just look at what the German air force have done in Spain. They could bomb us into oblivion if they wanted to.'

Jimmy shuddered visibly. '*Thank* you, Thomas. Would you kindly go and fetch the apple tart, it's cooling on the stove.'

While he was out of the room, Jimmy took the opportunity to have another long gaze at Madeleine. She brought to mind girls he had admired in his youth, back in the nineties, when he was still uncertain of his own predilections. It was the paleness of her skin heightened by the dark shadows beneath her eyes, like those poor creatures who slaved all the hours in match factories. And now he had made her blush with his staring.

'I beg your pardon, my dear, but you have the most remarkable physiognomy.'

It took her a moment to realise that he was talking about her face. 'Oh . . .'

'I have a theory that all women's faces belong in one of three categories. Bird, bun or horse. Bird is small and pointy. Bun, of course, is round. And horse is long, perhaps a bit chinny. D'you see?'

Madeleine wasn't sure she did. 'Which one am I?'

'Well, that's just it. Usually it's quite obvious – glance at a lady's phiz and one can tell straight away. But you . . . yours is something else. From the side your cheekbones would shade it towards "horse", yet head-on there's a delicacy of feature that suggests "bird". It's almost as though you have two different faces.'

Madeleine covered her confusion with a laugh, which Jimmy echoed. Tom, returning with the pudding, enquired as to their amusement.

'Jimmy says I've got a face like a horse, or maybe a bird.'

Tom groaned. 'Not bird-bun-horse, Jim, it's hardly polite . . .'

'No, no, as I ex*plained* to our young friend, her own face transcends the categories. It is *sui generis*!'

Now she was really lost. 'Suey what?'

'One of a kind,' said Tom with a sudden earnest look. 'Which is true.'

'Good, then we're agreed,' said Jimmy, stirring a jug of cream. 'Now, Madeleine, may I interest you in some tart?'

After she had gone, Tom began clearing up while he reflected, with relief, on the afternoon's success. Madeleine had seemed to enjoy it, had eaten everything set in front of her, and, best of all, had given his hand a squeeze as they said goodbye. That gesture, probably insignificant to her, had triggered a dizzying little skip of joy within him. She was glad to be his friend! And Jimmy had behaved himself – no, better than that, he had gone out of his way to charm her, stumbling only once with that bird-bun-horse sortie. She hadn't really understood he was offering her a compliment. Not many women would have done.

Having restored the kitchen to some semblance of order, he made a cup of coffee for Jimmy and carried it into the drawing room. Jimmy, slumped on a sofa, had a cigar in blast. He himself was rather wistful about their recent guest and the memories she had prompted of his not-yet-errant youth. Lucky the man who won her heart, he thought, watching Tom's approach.

'So. Miss Farewell . . .' he began, accepting the cup.

'I got the impression you liked her,' said Tom hopefully.

'Liked her? My dear fellow, she's the cat's miaow. The monkey's maracas! Where did you find her again?'

'Oh . . . someone introduced us. A party –'

'Well, you should grapple her to you with hoops of steel. She's a rare bird.'

'Or horse, in your taxonomy.'

Jimmy sighed. 'Ah. If I were thirty years younger, and five stone lighter . . .'

And didn't prefer boys, Tom silently supplied. Then he wondered if Jimmy might have been attracted to women in his younger years. It was not impossible. 'Thanks for being so nice to her,' he said, meaning it.

Jimmy waved this away and took a sip of the coffee. 'You might try warming the milk, Tom,' he said, wrinkling his nose. 'And pass me that *Mail* again, would you? There's a car I think we should have a look at.'

# 14

At the police station on Marylebone Road they kept her waiting longer than they had the first time. The wooden bench was hardly comfortable, so Nina stood and smoked, monitoring the door behind the staff sergeant's desk as it opened and closed. Impassive constables would stroll through the waiting hall, her presence seemingly invisible to them. To pass the time she gazed at notices of missing persons, describing what this or that one was wearing at the time they disappeared. The more she read about these people, the more convinced she was they weren't coming back. They didn't really sound like requests for information. They sounded like obituaries.

Nearly an hour had gone by when she saw him appear round the door, the gaunt-faced police officer who had interviewed her that morning, weeks ago. He had the grey pallor of a man who spent a lot of time in cramped, smoke-kippered rooms.

He reintroduced himself as Detective Inspector Cullis. 'Please come through.' It was just as well she hadn't been expecting an apology.

They settled in a narrow room of institutional grey-green brick. The door clanged shut behind them. A weak light spilled through the high window, striped with three bars.

'Are we in a cell?' Nina asked, not quite joking.

Cullis's mouth twitched with the ghost of a smile. 'Interview room. The heating's packed up, I'm afraid,' he said, glancing at the dusty ancient radiator. On the table between them he had put down a packet of Player's and a buff-coloured file. A pewter ashtray squatted at the edge. 'Smoke?' he said, offering her one, with a light.

'I suppose you're curious to know why I've come back,' she began.

There was nothing in Cullis's expression to suggest he had been harbouring any curiosity about her at all. She took his silence as an invitation to continue. 'I was wondering – about the Tiepin Killer – are you any closer to, um, cracking the case?' The slang phrase didn't sound quite right to her ears, or to Cullis's, to judge from the little pause he left before speaking.

'The investigation is continuing. We're pursuing various lines of inquiry.'

'I see,' said Nina, giving her best grave nod. 'You still have my sketch of the man's face?'

The detective inspector looked at her. Then he opened the file and removed Stephen's drawing, placing it between them on the table. The way he turned the picture around to face her felt unsettling, as though it were somehow a piece of evidence that incriminated her. Nina glanced at it, then took a deep breath.

'Inspector, there's something I should tell you, something I didn't know about when I gave my original statement. The man I saw in the hotel room – this man – I think I've given a mistaken impression of him.'

Cullis narrowed his eyes. 'Mistaken – in what way?'

She had his interest now at least. 'I think the man wears a wig.'

'You *think* he wears one . . . So you saw a wig in the room?'

'No, I didn't. But I know someone who did – the woman he was there with, that afternoon. It so happened our paths crossed again. Of course we talked about –'

'Wait a minute. By "the woman he was there with", you mean the woman he tried to strangle?'

'Yes. And she said that the whole time they were together he was wearing the wig. It must have slipped while they were struggling, because by the time I came in he'd taken it off.'

'Who is this woman? Why has she not come forward?'

'Well, for one thing, she hadn't seen the sketch of his face in the paper. And for another, she doesn't like dealing with the police. She's . . . on the streets.'

Cullis lifted his chin, unsurprised. 'So when you happened to meet again . . .'

'I showed her this sketch. And she said that he'd – that I'd got it wrong. By drawing a bald-headed man.'

The policeman's expression suddenly changed, and Nina held her breath. She'd slipped up, and hoped he hadn't noticed.

'Why did you just say "he'd"? Just then, when you mentioned the sketch, you were going to say "*he'd* got it wrong". Why?'

Nina tried to look nonchalant. 'A slip of the tongue. I meant to say "I'd got it wrong". A mistake.'

But Cullis was on the scent. 'It *was* a mistake. You meant to hide something but ended up telling – or nearly telling – the truth.'

'I don't know what you're talking about.'

'Ah but you do, Miss Land. The moment I saw you holding that pencil in your right hand I knew the sketch wasn't yours. The artist – *he* – is evidently left-handed. Now why don't you tell me who he is.'

Nina, inwardly panicking, shook her head. 'You're barking up the wrong tree, Inspector. The sketch is mine. Why should I pretend otherwise?'

'Because you want to protect his identity.'

'You're quite wrong.'

Cullis's expression had become almost pitying. 'Very well. I didn't want to embarrass you, but you force me to prove a point.' He opened the file again and took out a fresh sheet of paper. From his pocket he produced a pencil, and pushed them both across the desk to Nina. 'There are your materials. Let's see what you can do.'

Nina felt a hollowing in her stomach. 'What's this?'

He splayed his palms. 'You claim to be able to draw. Sketch *my* face.'

'You're not serious?'

'On the contrary. I need to verify the authenticity of this drawing, as part of a murder investigation. So I could hardly be more serious.'

Nina stared at him. She picked up the pencil and tapped it on the piece of paper, as blank and formidable as Everest. Why prolong the charade? He had rumbled her, and she must face a horrible humiliation. After a long pause she set it down again, without comment, her gaze averted.

Cullis allowed a moment for her mute admission to settle. Then he said, 'Just to be clear – did you see this man's face at all?'

'Yes, I did.'

'So who made this sketch?'

'A friend. He doesn't want to be named.'

'He was there with you?'

'Yes, but he didn't see the man. It was later, two days later, when my – my friend – suggested I describe the man's face to him, and he drew it.' She nodded at the sketch of the Tiepin Killer. 'We were trying to be helpful.'

'By that you mean giving the police an unreliable picture of a man you thought might be a killer – drawn by someone who wasn't even there.'

'It didn't seem –'

'And now you've decided that your portrait was mistaken, that the man in question may be wearing a wig.' His coldly sceptical tone made her wince.

'I'm sorry,' she said quietly. She couldn't meet his eye.

'We need to bring the girl in, the prostitute. Who is she?'

'I don't know. I've met her twice.'

'You have a name – an address?'

Nina swallowed hard. 'Madeleine. That's all I know of her. I've no idea where she lives.'

'Miss Land. If you're withholding information you could be in trouble. You've heard of obstructing the course of justice?'

Now she did look at him. 'I'd tell you if I knew. But I don't.'

An eternity seemed to pass before Cullis turned his gaze from her. Cigarette smoke hung like a pall between them. With a dissatisfied air he replaced the sketch in the file. 'I hope for your sake this hasn't backfired. If flawed evidence has allowed a killer to remain at large, well, you would have it on your conscience.'

He stood up and went to open the door. The interview was over.

Stephen loved the view from the upper window of Simpson's-in-the-Strand. You were so near to the street you could see right into the top decks of buses heaving along towards Trafalgar Square. He had just been watching, as in a silent comedy, a man on the number 9 sneeze into his handkerchief and then examine the contents with a satisfied air. Charming! He had not been in the restaurant for many a year, and was amused to discover that it hadn't changed a jot. They still wheeled in huge sides of mutton and beef on a gleaming silver trolley, and they still didn't admit women to the panelled dining room downstairs. He felt pretty sure that even the wizened waiter who had brought him his Martini was the same fellow he had tipped back in 1921, or whenever it was. *Change and decay in all around I see . . .* – all except at Simpson's.

Of course he wouldn't have been here in normal circumstances, he would have had lunch at the Nines, as he did most days. But circumstances were very far from normal. Ever since Ludo had warned him about his association with Gerald Carmody he had conceived an aura of guilt around himself. The photograph of him shaking hands with Carmody was like a leper's bell, warning people of his contagion. He couldn't be certain, but he sensed himself being talked about at the club; voices suddenly lowered, glances averted. He had worried over it last night with Nina, who insisted he was imagining things. 'And anyway, it's not like you're a paid-up member of the blackshirts,' she said. 'You happened to get caught with him in a photograph, that's all – it'll be forgotten by next week.'

Stephen appeared to have finished his Martini. He was about to order another when he spotted his guest looking about the room for him. Holding up his napkin he waved it in greeting.

'Hullo, Dad,' he said, impressed and somewhat mystified by the old man's sprightly bearing. His father, at sixty-eight, showed every sign of intending to live forever.

'Is that a flag of surrender?' said Mr Wyley drily, with a glance at Stephen's napkin. His tone was deep and uncracked.

Stephen smiled, returning the linen to his lap, and considered his father as he settled into his chair. He was dressed in one of the plain worsted suits he used to wear during his time as a chartered surveyor in the City, and anyone looking at him might have assumed he had just trotted along from the office. His air of beady detachment had been refined through army service, first in South Africa, later as a decorated officer in Belgium, where 'Old Fox' had become his inevitable epithet. Stephen's respect for him was intensified by an awareness of his own paltry record in comparison – two years in the Cadets. Closer in temperament and sympathy to his artistic mother, he had for many years felt remote from a man already in middle age when he was a boy. More recently he had made an effort to know his father a little better, wondering if he might absorb a strain of natural shrewdness from the Old Fox.

Mr Wyley was surveying the room with a bemused tolerance. 'Haven't been in this place for years. That waiter looks old enough to have fought at Rorke's Drift.'

'He was prompt with my drink, all the same.'

'Good man . . . What was wrong with the club, by the way?'

'Mm, I've – I'm in there all the time. Fancied a change.'

'Still pegging away at the mural, I gather.'

Stephen nodded, wondering. 'Who told you?'

'Oh. Prob'ly someone at the Turf, I forget . . .' His voice trailed off in apology, and Stephen breathed silent relief. So his recent brush with notoriety was still contained. Not everyone read *The Times*. 'But I haven't forgotten this,' continued Mr Wyley, producing from his breast pocket a folded piece of paper and handing it to Stephen. 'Happy birthday, old chap.'

It was a cheque for £50, the same thing he gave him every year.

'Oh, Dad,' said Stephen, in the half-grateful, half-reproving tone he adopted on being given anything. It was his mother who used to organise proper gifts – his gregarious, dark-eyed, life-loving mother. One year they had given him an antique easel, his first. It was still doing duty at the studio. She had died when he was in his final year at university, a time he would always recall as an incessant toing and froing on trains from Oxford to Paddington, thence by bus to his parents' home in Holland Park, each time his mother paler

245

against the pillow, and thinner from the ravages within. By the end she looked like she was dying of starvation. He had met his father on the stairs one day carrying up to her a sandwich so dainty and meagre he must have looked stunned. 'It's all she wants,' his father had explained, and Stephen had to hurry on lest he broke down right there. Even now he found himself saying things out-loud to her, as though she might be in the room with him.

'It just occurs to me,' he said, 'that Mum would have been sixty this year.'

His father nodded sadly. 'I know. She should have died hereafter.'

It haunted Stephen to think that memory of her might vanish altogether. Like him, Ella Wyley was an only child, and her parents had died before Stephen was born. Once his father was gone he would be her last surviving relative. It was a terrible regret to him that he had never drawn her, or even photographed her. Apart from a picture taken on their wedding day, his father had barely anything to remind him of her face. And there was nothing at all from her childhood.

A waiter came to take their order, cutting short his melancholy rumination.

'How's Cora?' asked his father.

'Well. Very well. She sends love.'

'And the children . . . Getting on at the *school*?'

It amused Stephen to hear Tipton referred to as if it were some notorious asylum. 'I think Rowan is fine – he likes working with his hands. Freya wrote to me again the other week asking if she could be taken away.'

'Ah.'

'She sounded quite reasonable about it. Apparently it's not because she hates school but because she misses home.'

'You should take it as a compliment. Maybe she thrives in your company.'

Stephen smiled gloomily. 'I wouldn't mind, but Cora won't hear of it. She thinks that Tipton is going to draw out their creative genius.'

'That's an optimistic idea of schooling.'

'I know. Particularly in Rowan's case.' He paused, and fishing in his wallet took out a letter composed in a blotched and tiny script. He handed it to his father. 'My son and heir's most recent communication.'

Mr Wyley put on his reading spectacles and cleared his throat. *'Dear Mummy and Daddy – I hope you are well I am well. Timmins scored twelve. Yours, Rowan S. Wyley.* Well . . . shows a certain succinctness of expression. And he's numerate.'

Stephen laughed, folding it away. 'I like the way he signed his full name, as though he were our solicitor or something.'

They were both having the Dover sole. Stephen had just speared a boiled potato from the dish when his father said, 'By the way, talking of your mother reminded me, I've just started on a bit of a clear-out. There are various things of hers to be disposed of, correspondence, books, jewellery – I thought perhaps you and Cora might like to have some of it.'

Stephen looked in puzzlement at him. 'A clear-out. You're not thinking of – *moving*?'

The old man shrugged. *'Pace* Dr Johnson, but I've had it with London. It's not for old boys like me any more. The traffic, the noise . . . I've made enquiries and it seems I'll get a fair price for Addison Road.'

Stephen felt himself winded. The house he had grown up in – for sale! It was inconceivable to him. How like his father to introduce such a bombshell with 'by the way' . . . The boiled potato was still on his fork, his hand for the present immobilised.

'Are you – I mean – is this really a good idea?'

'Yes, while I'm still able to move, it is. I've been thinking about Sussex – a little place near Arundel. Walking on the Downs, bit of golf, sea air and all that.' Into the silence left by his son he added, 'You can always visit, of course! It's beautiful countryside around there.'

Stephen was shaking his head. 'I can't believe you want to . . . The house must mean –' But what *did* the house mean, beyond his own reverence of its memories, and of a vigil kept while his mother faded away? His father had lived in Addison Road for over forty years, and if he was as reconciled to abandoning the place as he seemed why should it be such a wrench for him? He didn't know why, but he felt a shiver in his bones that might have been a forewarning of age, or of death itself.

Mr Wyley, seeing the mournful attitude into which Stephen had sunk, took on a consoling tone. 'Don't be glum about it, old chap. You know it was never the same place after she was gone.'

On that point he couldn't disagree, and eventually they talked of something else.

The address was a cobbled mews off Berwick Street. Warehouses of blackened brick hedged it about on three sides, blocking most of the grey November light. Spotting a suite of garages at the end, Tom puffed out his cheeks. This would be the fifth they had seen since Monday.

He turned to Jimmy. 'So he said he'd be here?'

They ambled up to the row of garages, wooden half-doors indicating their former use as stables. There was nobody about. Tom called out a tentative *Hullo?* and knocked on one of the windows. With any luck the vendor had forgotten all about it and they could go home instead.

Behind them a door opened; and from one of the mews flats they had walked past a man emerged. He was shrugging on a jacket over his violet-coloured shirt and patterned tie.

'Gents,' he said, with a lift of his chin, 'come to see the motor?'

Jimmy agreed that they had, and following a brief introduction, the man unlocked one of the garage doors and invited them within. A heady stench of petrol and burnt dust assailed their nostrils. He snapped on a light, and they beheld a car, or rather the shape of a car, modestly shrouded in a dust sheet. Sliding it away he revealed the long-winged body of a drophead Bentley, its sober dark green coachwork a foil to the impudent brightness of the red leather trim. For a moment no one said anything. To Tom it looked like the sort of car you could only drive at Le Mans, preferably wearing goggles and a white scarf.

'Good Lord,' said Jimmy.

'A beauty, isn't she?' said the man, with a smirk. 'A 1928 Bentley Vanden Plas, six-and-a-half litre. Four-speed manual gearbox, six-cylinder engine. Runs like a dream.'

'It's enormous,' said Tom. 'Are the brakes all right?'

The man stared at him as if he were simple. 'Course they are. Why wouldn't they be?'

Tom didn't care for his tone, but said nothing. He walked around the vehicle, pretending an air of one who knew what was what, while Jimmy amused himself with an anecdote about the first time he had ridden in a Bentley (a jaunt on the Côte d'Azur, as he recalled) and the close shave his party had had on a narrow mountain road. By the end of it Tom could see that the man was perfectly indifferent to Jimmy and his story; he didn't look a type susceptible to charm. His only object was to sell them the motor.

'This model costs £2,800 when new,' he drawled. 'The one you're lookin' at's done a few miles but it's still bright as a new tack. I don't see it going for less than £425.'

Jimmy squinted at him. 'We have to take the lady out before we start haggling over the bill, Mr – erm . . .'

'Astill. Call me Roddy.' He fished in his pocket and plucked out the keys, dangling them in front of Jimmy like a hypnotist with a watch. 'Take her for a spin, why don'tcha?'

'My, um, associate will take care of them,' said Jimmy, who had just managed to stop himself calling Tom his 'chauffeur'. Roddy, glancing at the designated driver, lobbed the keys across the bonnet to him. The offhandedness of this did not impress the catcher. Tom decided he would treat the fellow with the aloofness he deserved, and got into the driver's seat without comment. Jimmy climbed in next to him, and after some puzzled hesitation over the dashboard, they were off.

It was getting on for five o'clock as they turned onto Regent Street. It was the hour the West End took on a glistening look, the street lamps and the shop windows all lit up against the mauve dusk. People were flocking home and the pubs were about to open, and newsvendors cawed the late editions at Piccadilly Circus. They crossed into Mayfair, and steered twice around Berkeley Square just for the fun of it. The sleek length of the vehicle and its open top made Tom feel he was piloting a boat rather than a car; the streets flowed serenely on like a river, the pavement its banks. Despite himself he was enjoying the ride, not just the irresistible thrum beneath but the awareness of the car as a cynosure – he could see pedestrians watch them as they cruised past like royalty. On Park Lane they stopped at a traffic light alongside a bus, and Tom saw faces gawping through the windows at the magnificent beast with its growling engine.

Jimmy, seeing them too, turned to Tom and gave a lordly laugh.

They probably think we're a couple of swells, thought Tom. He put his foot down and they roared off again. They had got into the quieter roads north of Oxford Street when

Jimmy, looking straight ahead, said, 'He doesn't know I used to horse-trade. Bet you I could get him down to £350.'

Tom shook his head. 'Even that's too much. You said £250 was your absolute limit.'

'Well, that was before we clapped eyes on this. Admit it, have you ever driven a finer jalopy?'

'That's beside the point. You're already spending money you don't have. Remember what Wootton said about the Revenue.'

'Oh fie on Wootton and his counting house. For the sake of another hundred we could live like millionaires! Leave the scrimping and scraping to others.'

Tom kept the silence of disapproval, prompting Jimmy to cast around for a different angle of attack. It didn't take him long to find one. As they happened to pass a smartly dressed young woman walking a dog, Jimmy remarked airily, 'I dare say your Miss Farewell would enjoy a trip out in the country for a day. I can just imagine her sitting here, face tilted towards yours, her scarf striping the air behind —'

'Belt up,' said Tom with a half-laugh.

But now he came to think of it he *could* picture Madeleine next to him, quite easily. Indeed her face, her voice, had been in his head since the lunch at Jimmy's, he couldn't have rid himself of her even if he'd wanted to. Tom had had his share of love affairs over the years – there was even a short-lived engagement with a girl back home in Deal – but there'd been no one for a while. Most of the last nine years had been devoted to Jimmy, and he was not alone in feeling their relationship in that time was something closer to domestic than secretarial. He would probably never have introduced her if Jimmy himself hadn't insisted on it. He was right about her face, it *was* remarkable, and it jolted him now to think that he might be in love with its owner.

His mind was playing a trick of indirection as he said, 'Do you really think you can knock him down to £350?'

Jimmy's look was sly. 'Putty in my hands, dear boy.'

'I don't know – he looked a bit of a chiseller to me.'

'Ha! I've been my whole life around crooks, and that feller looks no worse than the ones I've dealt with on newspapers.'

'Hmm.'

Jimmy heard the note of scepticism. 'Very well. Let's make it interesting. Dinner on you at the Café Royal if I beat him down to £350.'

'And if you don't?'

'Breakfast, lunch *and* dinner at a place of your choosing.'

They were back in Soho, turning into Wardour Street. Tom was confounded to think he was now egging him on to get a price for the motor. He knew he ought to be the responsible one. Jimmy was a pathological case: it was tantamount to betting an alcoholic that he could drink *x* number of Scotches without falling over. And yet . . . He steered the Bentley into the narrow mews, and there was Roddy, cocksure and beaming at the prospect of a deal. It was surprising how quickly you could take against someone. He sensed Jimmy's face at an enquiring angle.

'£350,' Tom muttered, and they shook surreptitious hands.

Jimmy didn't beat Roddy down to £350. He beat him down to £325. Tom found it rather like watching an old prize-fighter move a keener but less experienced opponent around the ring; the tricks and feints were remarkable to behold. Roddy had taken instant and angry offence at the lowness of Jimmy's first offer ('That's just insulting'), and made to walk off. Jimmy coaxed him back, claiming that he was only 'testing the water', though his next offer was scarcely an improvement on the first. Somehow he had intuited that Roddy's hopes of selling the car were tinged with desperation: he wanted rid of the thing, and Jimmy was quick to scent his advantage. It became essentially a contest between patience and aggression, with all the guile belonging to the former. Twice more the owner threatened to walk away, and each time he was lured back into haggling. By degrees he was worn down. Once the price had inched towards £325, Roddy seemed almost bored with arguing, and he gave in.

Feeling magnanimous, Jimmy paid his victim a little compliment. 'I suppose you must be quite prosperous to keep yourself in such style.'

'I do all right,' Roddy shrugged. 'I'm in the entertainment business.'

'Is that so?' said Jimmy with a glint in his eye. For answer Roddy took out his wallet and handed him a business card. 'The Elysian Nightclub?' said Jimmy. 'That name seems familiar,' he mused, looking at Tom, who in turn stared at Roddy.

'A friend of mine works there. Madeleine Farewell . . .'

Roddy's eyes narrowed. 'You know Maddy? How?'

Tom was pleased to match his terseness. 'We were introduced.'

'*Quel petit monde!*' cried Jimmy, delighted by the coincidence. 'We had Miss Farewell to lunch only last week. And a lass unparalleled she is.'

Tom watched Roddy frowning at this flamboyant turn of phrase. He could read his thoughts as if they were a cartoon bubble over his head: *This one's a poof.* The dislike he had conceived of the man was turning slightly toxic. Tom cleared his throat in a pronounced way.

'Are we done then?' He was already backing towards the entrance of the mews.

Jimmy, buttoning his coat, said, 'I dare say you'll want cash . . .'

'Always,' said Roddy, who was still gazing after Tom, now well out of earshot. His expression had turned narrow.

'Your friend,' he said, in a curious voice, 'knows Maddy pretty well, does he?'

'Not that well,' Jimmy said, adding with a low chuckle, 'though I've never seen him so smitten.'

Roddy gave a slow nod, then turned to Jimmy. 'Get the cash to me Tuesday evening. I'll be here around seven.' He paused for a beat. 'Tell your friend to bring it.'

'Of course,' said Jimmy, who had had no intention of doing the job himself. 'Tuesday, seven sharp it is.'

As they walked back through the evening streets towards Bloomsbury Jimmy was exultant. He couldn't have been more tickled about his new purchase, or prouder of the cunning that had enabled it. He replayed his favourite moments of the recent negotiation, permitting himself a chuckle on catching Roddy's tone of petulant gruffness. (The thwarted actor had become a good mimic.) On passing a gents' outfitters he urged Tom to consider buying a pair of driving gloves – they would be useful for their 'jaunts' out of London.

'Perhaps I should get a peaked cap, too,' said Tom.

'Oh, I don't think that's necessary,' replied Jimmy, momentarily deaf to the sarcasm. A new thought occurred to him. 'We could run down to Deal for the day – visit your parents.'

This was a trip Jimmy threatened from time to time. Tom could only imagine what his dad, landlord of the Black Cow in Deal, would make of his employer. It was not an encounter he would relish in the smallest degree. To change the subject he said, 'Fancy that spiv being owner of the Elysian. I can't recall Madeleine ever mentioning him.'

'Hmm. That probably tells you something. By the way, he wanted cash – and he was quite particular that you should deliver it.'

'Why me?'

Jimmy pulled a *who knows* face. 'Maybe he took a shine

to you. In any case, just think – once he gets his money you can drive us to the Café Royal for dinner!'

He looked to Tom in the expectation of a dry response, but his companion was staring into the dark distances ahead, brooding.

# 15

Stephen was on his way to Tite Street when the headline leapt out from a news-stand at him. TIEPIN KILLER CLAIMS FOURTH VICTIM. He hurried up the stairs to his studio, a copy of the *Chronicle* in his hand, sick to his stomach with curiosity.

Another prostitute, this time found strangled in an alleyway off the Strand. Like the girl before, she had also been badly beaten. He was still reading the report when the telephone rang, making him jump. It was Ludo Talman.

'Have you seen the newspaper?'

'I'm just reading it now,' said Stephen. 'Shocking, isn't it?'

Ludo paused before he spoke. 'Yes . . . I suppose it is.'

'It's obvious the police don't have a clue.'

There was another pause, then Ludo said in a hesitant voice, 'I'm not sure we're talking about the same thing.'

'Oh . . . I'm reading about the latest Tiepin murder.'

'Er, no. Not that. You may want to sit down for this.'

Stephen felt a sudden lurch within. 'Tell me.'

'I've got *The Times*, but it's also in the *Telegraph* and the *Mail*. Carmody has been leading you a dance. That dinner you attended – the fund-raiser – it wasn't for the Marquess Theatre at all. It appears to have been a front for something called the British People's Brigade.'

Stephen had anticipated those last three words before Ludo had spoken them. He swallowed hard. 'I see.'

'Some reporter has been investigating him. He's got it in black and white, bank records, payments diverted from one account to another. The worst of it is they've published a list of Carmody's backers. I'm afraid you're on it, Stephen.'

'What?'

'You wrote him a cheque?'

*Oh Christ*, thought Stephen. The cheque. He hadn't even remembered that. 'Yes, but on the understanding that it was for –'

'The question is, did you make it out to the fund, or to Carmody himself?'

Stephen's silence acknowledged the mistake. How could he have been so naive? When Ludo next spoke it seemed to come from a long distance.

'I presume you have a lawyer.'

Stephen heard himself say his name.

'He's good,' said Ludo. 'He can probably make a case for fraud.'

'I thought I was supporting a theatre . . .'

'Of course. But you've made it difficult by writing a personal cheque. Your name is linked to his.'

Another long pause intervened as Stephen glimpsed a blighted future. Whatever help he might get from the law, the court of public opinion was swift to condemn. He realised Ludo was thinking precisely the same thing.

'It looks bad, doesn't it?'

Ludo gave a sighing exhalation. 'People will think "no smoke . . .", what with this *and* the photograph of the handshake. The club will make a stink about it. I have to tell you, the committee has just called me in for a meeting.'

'Already?' This was more precipitate than Stephen had imagined.

'Stephen, listen to me. I know you're not to blame for this, and I will offer a proper defence on your behalf. But these things gain their own momentum. It takes just one member to voice his disapproval, then they all join in.'

'Even if I'm innocent?'

'Yes. Even then.'

They talked for a while longer, though Stephen took little of it in. He felt himself being harried towards a cliff edge, with disgrace lying at the bottom. What on earth could he do? Put an advertisement in the paper denying involvement in Carmody's chicanery? Too late for that. He traced back his error in stages. He had written the cheque just before the Carlton Hotel dinner. He had been at the dinner only because Carmody had hinted at the possibility of blackmail, having spotted him with Nina that afternoon. And he had been with Nina because – well, on that score he *was* guilty. Retribution had simply taken its time coming round.

He tormented himself with the thought of friends and colleagues hearing the story. The people who knew him would dismiss it as libellous nonsense. They knew his lofty indifference to politics. Others would shake their heads and deplore his careless choice of friends. And might there be those tempted (heaven forbid) to take him for a Fascist and gloat over his exposure? The shame of it. If he were to be damned for anything it was for self-delusion, his unthinking disregard of all the dangers that came in associating with a man like Carmody. But he could also lament his bad luck in being caught in company with Nina. And then what of his father finding out? This the man who had fought in two wars defending the freedom of his country, a freedom that the British People's Brigade and their like strove to curtail.

A few minutes after Ludo rang off the telephone went again, and he answered in the certainty it would be a gentleman of the press wanting a quote. To his relief it was Nina. She had just finished rehearsals.

'I suppose you've seen the paper?'

'Yes, I have,' he replied.

'Isn't it frightful?'

Stephen, miserably aware of the ambiguity, said, 'Best you should be specific.'

'Why, the murder of course. He's killed another one.'

'Ah – that.'

Nina gave a little splutter. 'Oh, I'm sorry. Are you bored with it already?'

He winced; the corrective was deserved. He only stood on the brink of disgrace. He hadn't been beaten and strangled to death in an alleyway. 'No. I'm sorry, darling, I had other – I've just been reading about it. Ghastly.'

'I know – and I can't help feeling responsible. For not giving them an accurate description of him –'

'You mustn't think that. You tried. *We* tried. Others might not have bothered at all . . . My God! I wish I'd never set foot in that hotel.'

This was said with too much feeling for Nina to let it pass. Stephen was not one to give vent to distress. 'Darling, what's the matter?'

He told her, and Nina listened with incredulous outrage. As he related the story even he found his own part in it somewhat unbelievable.

'You're not to blame,' she said with firmness. 'You've been duped by a – by a *scoundrel*.'

'– who has a cheque with my signature on it. It's his word against mine as to what it was for.' He paused. 'And meanwhile my reputation – what's left of it – gets worked over in the papers.'

Nina had never heard him sound so low. I must be a friend to him, she thought. 'Look, how about I come over and take you to lunch?'

259

'I'd be very dull company –'

'Which is why I must cheer you up! No, don't argue. I'll just change and be with you in an hour.'

Nina was at the theatre door and heading off to Stephen's studio when Dolly came hurrying after her.

'Oi. It's milady on the phone.'

'God! What does *she* want?'

Dolly pulled a face meant to suggest the eternal and inscrutable demands of womankind. With an irritated toss of her head Nina retraced her steps back down to the telephone. She picked up the receiver with a long-suffering air.

'Mother.' At the end of the line she heard a stifled sob. 'Mum? What's the matter?'

'I am – I am –' she stuttered, sniffling, 'I am the unhappiest woman alive.'

*I very much doubt that*, thought Nina, who nevertheless softened her voice. 'Oh dear. Is this about Mr Dorsch?'

Now there came a long whimper of pity, or self-pity, which in Mrs Land's case amounted to the same thing. Whatever it was she had intended to say was choked off by an attack of sobbing that no consoling words of Nina's could staunch.

'Is Felicity with you? Or Bee?'

The gluey voice at the other end indicated that neither of her other daughters had been located. Nina, helpless, offered to come over to the house, and on hearing no objection from the distraught caller she realised, with a prickle of annoyance, that she would have to go. Damn. Stephen would wonder where she'd got to. What a morning for revelations, though!

She took a cab to King's Cross, then got the Tube to Westbourne Park. It was the first time she had visited the family home since her mother had announced it as the exclusive inheritance of her younger sister. By the time she arrived Felicity was there, with a face like the chief mourner, and Nina felt the shine had been rather taken off her mission of mercy. Her mother was propped on the sofa, dabbing her eyes; emanating a strong aura of misery, she had at least calmed down since the phone call. Felicity hovered in the background, and gave Nina a warning look with her eyes as she approached their stricken parent.

'Hullo, Mum,' she said, settling on a gentle note of sympathy. This was a time for kid gloves. 'Just tell us what happened.'

Mrs Land closed her eyes with a look of martyred anguish. In broken sentences the story came out. Mr Dorsch – 'Eric' – had taken her out to dinner, just the two of them, by which point she had become convinced he was about to propose. He did indeed have a proposal for her – 'Annabel' – something he had been pondering 'for a while', he explained. Their long friendship, of more than twenty years' standing, had been one of the most important in his life. And it had become doubly so after his dear wife Monica had departed this earth. The challenges of living alone had been mollified by Annabel's companionship; moreover, he had realised in the years since his bereavement that she was blessed not only with a tender nature (Nina heard this without a change of expression) but a capable and forthright one. Such a talent for succour could not be ignored. Which was why he hoped she would accept an offer he believed would bring out the very best in her: the post of chief administrator to his Spanish orphans' charity.

Nina glanced up at Felicity, wondering if she might discern on her face the tiniest twitch of amusement at this unforeseen climax. But whatever her sister felt was unreadable beneath her mask of concern.

'I just don't understand it,' whimpered Mrs Land, tears still glistening in her eyes. 'How . . . could he?'

'Oh, Mum, *there*,' said Felicity. 'I'm sure Mr Dorsch didn't mean to mislead you. He's too kind-hearted for that. He just wants to do right by the orphans –'

'Damn and blast those orphans!' cried her mother, a snarl in her voice. 'What about doing right by me? Has he not heard of charity beginning at home?'

The sisters were too startled by the vehemence of this to know how to respond. After a pause Nina said, 'I'll go and make us all a cup of tea,' indicating that Felicity should accompany her. Once they were in the kitchen together they gave one another a 'you first' look, and Nina obliged.

'Goodness. I wasn't expecting *that*,' she said, dropping her voice low.

'Well, nor was Mum, evidently,' replied Felicity, matching her volume.

'No, I mean that little outburst just then. Orphans! How very thoughtless of them to lose their parents and upset her marriage plans.'

Felicity pursed her lips, demurring. 'She's lonely, Nina. I know she can be rather selfish, but perhaps she didn't entirely imagine Mr Dorsch's interest in her.'

'Didn't she? All I saw at that dinner was him behaving with perfect good manners towards an old friend. If she thought it was anything more then –' Nina decided to bite back her sarcasm.

'We see what we want to see,' conceded her sister leniently. 'What she needs now is our love and support.'

Nina stared at her. 'I'm sorry? What do we owe her of love and support after the way she's behaved to us? I think it's pretty bloody amazing we're still on speaking terms.'

Felicity busied herself with the tea things, which allowed her time to consider a reply. When it came her tone was more critical. 'You sound awfully bitter, you know.'

Nina choked out a disbelieving gasp. 'Bitter? Let me remind you, it was entirely based on her deluded expectation of a proposal that she willed this house to Bee and cut us off. So yes, I *am* bitter, if you must know.'

'Shh, lower your voice. I wonder whether you'd feel so aggrieved about this if there was someone in your life. I think you blame Mum for what happened with Pa, and you're upset that any man should show an interest in her.'

Nina was for a moment too stunned to speak. It was not merely the accusatory thrust of the words that pierced her, but that it had come from Felicity, whose tolerant good nature had always helped keep the peace. She stared more closely at her, hoping to see a softening in her gaze, but there was none.

She tried to hold her voice steady. 'I knew this would happen. I knew the minute Mum told us about the will it would cause an argument, sooner or later. Only I thought it would be with Bee, not with you. Fliss, please, don't be angry. I thought you were on my side.'

Felicity clicked her tongue in irritation. 'I'm not on anyone's "side". I'd just like this family to get along with one another. You think Mum fooled herself and has now got her comeuppance – well, maybe she has. But instead of gloating you should feel sorry for her.'

The teacups and spoons rattled on the tray as Felicity picked it up, their brittle chimes underscoring her disapproval. Nina, stung by this exchange, had one last stab at defending herself. 'By the way, you may find it hard to believe, but I *do* have someone in my life.'

Felicity stopped, glanced at her. 'I see. Will we be invited to meet him?'

'I don't know,' said Nina, hesitating. 'There are – difficulties.'

Felicity's expression had turned thoughtful, and Nina knew her to be astute enough to guess what they were. But she only gave a little nod, and said, 'Well, the path of true love, and so on. I hope it'll make you happy. Happier than . . .' A meaning look accompanied this uncompleted phrase. Happier than their mother? Or happier than the usual run of Nina's affairs? She would have liked her to continue, but

Felicity was already on her way out of the kitchen, armed with the tray. Some moments later she heard her voice in the next room, solicitous again, calming their mother.

Nina remained standing where she was, her thoughts in a stir of remorse and resentment. On the one hand, she now felt shamed by that secret bat-squeak of amusement on hearing her mother's tale of dashed hopes. On the other, she sensed in her blood the slow-acting poison of genetic inheritance. She had dreaded becoming like her mother, and had striven, perhaps at a cost, to ensure she did not. She would not throw in her lot with a feckless man, would not shackle herself to domestic drudgery, would not sacrifice a career to her children and then resent them for stifling her. At the age of thirty-two, with a job, a little money and no dependants, it seemed she had succeeded. It had not mattered to her before that her most serious liaison had lasted ten months. Now she wondered if her flightiness was actually a deep-rooted fear of committing herself to a man.

Something else was bothering her. Why had she felt it necessary to tell Felicity there was 'someone' in her life? Her hackles had been up, true, but she had no need to score a point in argument, or to eke a little mystery out of the unidentified suitor. The subject of her romantic life rarely came up between them. This time it was different. She had *wanted* to tell her about Stephen, wanted to say how mad she was about him, and so what if he was unavailable? He loved her, Nina, enough to admit his mistake – that he should never have got married, they were too young, and if he could turn back the clock . . . No, she mustn't torment herself with that. She would not whine or wheedle; she would simply be what she had always been to him – adorable.

When she returned to the living room she found the emotional temperature had cooled down. Felicity had poured them some tea, and her mother's trembling lip had returned to the stiffness of old. The mood had taken a philosophical turn, and the character of Mr Dorsch, so recently a fiend in human form, was now adjudged to be merely a pitiable wretch. Nina, in a sudden uprush of generous feeling, took her mother's hand and gave it a kiss.

Mrs Land acknowledged it in a queenly lift of her head, then said, with deliberation, 'Of course, I realise the mistake I made. I should not have allowed myself to keep on giving. It made him think *I* didn't need anything.'

Nina absorbed the remark in silence, and calculated the moment it would be permissible to make her excuses and withdraw.

Madeleine had spent the afternoon at a picture house on the Charing Cross Road. The second feature, a sliver of romantic foolery whose title she had already forgotten, had nevertheless performed a vital service. It had banished her low spirits. She knew nothing like the pictures for taking her out of herself. The tatty circumstances of the place – the stale smoke, the threadbare velvet seating, the motes of dust teeming down the projector's wand of light – these seemed to enhance the truant nature of film-going. What *was* it called? It didn't matter; gaze uptilted, she was entranced by the silvered aquarium of light containing the two love-birds, the marvellous clothes and the silly friends, the swooning music, the muddling of motives that threatens the couple's happiness, the interlude of repining, and the reconciliation clinched with a kiss. A fantasy, of course, though she wondered all the same if there might be people out there who did inhabit such a bubble of charm, with their gay parties and jaunts – people whose principal concern was how they should enjoy their life, rather than (more common, alas) how they should keep body and soul together.

She emerged into the roaring dark of London traffic, but her mood had been lifted by the film. She thought she might have a drink before clocking on, and started on a diagonal course through Soho. Roddy had been offish with her since the night of their dinner, informing her of this or that punter with a side-of-the-mouth brusqueness. There were no more offers of a lift. She didn't care, so long as he didn't put her through all that business again. In spite of the job, and a natural tendency to depreciate herself, Madeleine could not help being aware that to some men she was a romantic object, as opposed to a merely physical one. Roddy was the last she would have suspected of going spoony on her – the last, and the least welcome. But recently it seemed she had detected a certain softness in Tom's eye. It was at that lunch, when Jimmy had been descanting on the attractiveness of her 'phizog', as he called it, and Tom had echoed his praise in a rather sincere way. It was confusing, their admiration, since they were both queer – only, now she thought about it, might Tom be one of those who also fancied women, like Oscar Wilde?

It had just gone five thirty when she arrived at the Blue Posts, its doors thrown back to admit the first customers of the evening. She sat at the bar and ordered a gin and pep. She was still working on her thoughts about Tom, and whether he had any inkling about what she did. He had seen her that one time at the Elysian, and had probably assumed she was some sort of showgirl or waitress. She had encouraged this assumption by declining any opportunity for discussing it. But what would happen if – well, if he actually fell for her? How long would it be before she was obliged to tell him? A common bond united them: they were both in their way outcasts, hiding in plain sight. In the eyes of the law they were criminals. Perhaps Tom, long used to concealing his sexual proclivities, would look on her as a kindred spirit, but she was not inclined to believe it. There were few men who would regard a woman of the streets in a spirit of equality, and fewer still who would choose to befriend her.

At the other end of the counter there had been a good deal of head-shaking and frowning among the habitués. The barman finally dragged himself away and brought her drink. He knew Madeleine by sight, and plied her with some inconsequential chat about the cold weather. She could sense, almost from the way he was drying a glass, that he was still preoccupied with the conversation he had recently abandoned, and to which he was keen to return. Or was he in fact trying to refresh that conversation's novelty by including her, a newcomer? Either way, he seemed to have something on his mind of greater moment than the weather.

'S'pose you've 'eard the latest?' he said, lifting his gaze from the pint glass he had been wiping.

Madeleine, pausing over the gin and pep, shook her head.

'Vicious,' he muttered, with a grimace that could hardly conceal his eagerness to continue. 'That feller, the one who strangled them women – he's done another one in.'

Numbed with shock she half listened as he elaborated on the story. The killer had gone quiet in the last few weeks, prompting speculation from some that the police, always 'questioning' suspects, had finally got their man. Others, like the barman, called it wishful thinking. Now there was no room for doubt – the Tiepin Killer was still at large.

'S'like the Ripper all over again, I'm tellin' you,' said the barman.

She looked narrowly at him, wondering how he could remember that far back, and said, mechanically, 'Where did they find her?'

He gestured with a vague tilt of his head. 'Strand. Always 'ereabouts, see.'

'But the Ripper – weren't his all in the East End?'

The man stopped cleaning his glass for a moment, and considered. 'Right enough. Mebbe that's why he leaves a tiepin on 'em. Bit of West End flash, hur hur.'

Without thinking Madeleine finished her gin in one go.

Feeling slightly dizzy as she stood, she put on her hat and headed for the door. More customers were coming in; she was preparing to brush past them when of a sudden her name sounded. She jumped, looking about her in alarm. It was Rita, her face drawn and strangely older. They sidled over to an unoccupied corner of the bar.

'You've heard,' was all that Rita said.

Madeleine nodded. 'The barman just told me.'

For some moments they gazed at one another, as if forlorn expressions might unlock some meaning from this new calamity. Then Rita shook her head.

'That poor kid.'

'What have they said about it?'

'Only that' – she put a hand to her mouth, and dropped her voice – 'they say he knocked her about before he . . .' The sentence trailed off into the unspeakable. 'To think we was just sittin' here, the three of us.'

Madeleine was so sick and distracted with apprehension that it took her a moment to digest these last words. 'What do you mean – the three of us?'

Rita stared at her, appalled. 'Oh God, you mean you don't know?' Madeleine's uncomprehending look was enough to confirm it. 'Maddy, the girl he – it was *Alice*.'

Nina had managed to get away from her mother's at last. She had caught a bus to the King's Road and was hurrying down Tite Street. Having told Stephen she would be there within the hour she was now so late that he had probably given up on her and gone out. But at the door she was answered by his housekeeper and directed up the stairs. Stephen presented himself at her knock, and the first syllable of her endearment ('Dar –') was out of her mouth when she spotted over his shoulder that he already had company. The look of apology on his face warned her. On entering the large light-flooded studio she thought it was one of his

268

fawn-like models curled up there on an armchair in front of the fire. But that wasn't the case.

She heard a strained note in his introduction. 'This is Freya, my daughter. Freya, meet my friend Nina.'

'Hullo. You're the actress, aren't you?' said Freya, unfolding her long legs and rising to greet their guest. She had been taught manners, it seemed.

'That's right,' Nina said, trying to compose herself in the face of this surprise. She took in the girl's inquisitive dark eyes, catching a trace of Stephen in her long-limbed poise. She recalled him telling her that his children boarded at a 'progressive' school somewhere, though the girl wore no uniform. 'Have you got the afternoon off school?'

'She has indeed,' Stephen cut in. 'Her mother's out of town, so she's come to see her old dad!' Again, there was a ripple of tension in his good cheer.

Freya alone seemed unfazed by this unscheduled encounter, and flopped back into the armchair. She kept her gaze on Nina, who felt as though she had been thrust onstage without adequate rehearsal. 'Sorry I'm late,' she said, turning to Stephen, 'there was an emergency of my mother's I had to sort out. Um, I suppose you've already had lunch . . .'

'Not at all,' said Stephen, who was also improvising. 'I was thinking we might pop out for a bite. How about it, Freya?'

'Can we go to a Corner House?' said the girl.

Stephen and Nina, with a quick glance at each other, agreed that a Corner House was a good idea. Out on the street they took a taxi, which eventually deposited them at Coventry Street. Nina sensed the peculiar nature of their outing, two adults constrained by the watchfulness of a young chaperone, but she did her best to appear relaxed. Once installed at a table they ordered tea and a sandwich, and Freya was allowed to have ice cream. The bustle of the cafe around them had for the moment diverted the girl's attention.

'Have you talked to the lawyer yet?' Nina said in an undertone.

Stephen nodded. 'He thinks he could get Carmody on embezzlement. I'd have to give evidence, of course.'

She shot him a sympathetic look. 'He won't get away with it.'

'Maybe not. But I'll still pay for it. I already am – you remember my telling you about that publisher, Voysey, who wanted to commission a monograph on me? Well, his office telephoned this morning. It's all off.'

Nina frowned. 'What did they say?'

'Oh, they pretended not to know – made some excuse about production costs. But I know it's this thing that's scared them off.'

'What are you talking about?' said Freya, alert of a sudden.

'Business,' said her father crisply. The waitress arrived at that moment with the tea and the ice cream, which Freya proceeded to spoon meditatively from its glass bowl. She gave Nina a sidelong glance before saying calmly, 'Did you know that you made my mother cry?'

Nina, struck dumb, looked in panicked supplication to Stephen, who himself needed a moment to construe the question. 'She means the play,' he said with a covering laugh. 'As you know, Cora was moved – to tears! – by your performance onstage.'

'Yes. I remember you saying,' said Nina, almost faint with relief. She added, for Freya's benefit, 'There's a rather emotional scene, in the third act, when I – when my character – reads out a letter.'

Freya gave her 'grown-up' nod, then said in the same even way, 'You're the lover, aren't you?'

Nina gave a small gasp, but she wasn't to be wrong-footed a second time. 'Yes, I play a lady named Hester Bonteen. She's a – You do seem to know rather a lot about this play.'

'Only what I'm told,' replied Freya pertly. 'You must be a bloody good actress.'

'Freya,' said Stephen, 'what have I told you? That is *not* polite language.'

'Sorr-eee. I meant to say, you must be a very good actress.'

Nina smiled, then said, 'Perhaps one day you'll come and judge for yourself. When you're older.'

'I'm old *now*,' she replied. 'Dad says you're going to be in films.'

'Heavens! We'll have to see about that.' She glanced at Stephen, who was holding up a half-crown he had just fished out of his pocket.

'Darling, the man we saw selling newspapers outside – be a good girl and get me a *Standard*, would you?'

Having secured a promise that she could keep the change, Freya departed. Nina, puffing out her cheeks, said, 'My, she's a caution, isn't she? I can feel myself shaking still.'

'Sorry about that. She just descended on me.'

'I know it's a progressive school, but do they allow them to swan off to London?'

Stephen shook his head. 'Of course not. It probably won't surprise you to hear she just – took off. She's AWOL.'

'Why would she do that?'

'Doesn't like the place,' he said, shrugging. 'I don't blame her. It's all about growing vegetables and putting on theatricals. I'm not sure she's read a book since she's been there.'

'Though she's learned some rather colourful language,' said Nina with a laugh.

'Apparently the teachers think it's fine for the pupils to swear. Seems a rum sort of education to me . . . Freya's a cute one, though. She knew her mother was in the country this week visiting friends, and that I'd be holding the fort. A soft touch, you see.'

'Your wife approves of the school, then?'

271

'Oh, Cora thinks it's marvellous. Freya's going back whether she likes it or not, I'm afraid.'

Nina's expression turned curious. 'Does Cora always get the last word?'

He heard the challenge in her tone. 'Mostly. She runs things. Her personality is quite, um, forceful.'

She'll never let him go, thought Nina, with a sinking heart. If she gets wind of what's been going on, she'll give him hell, for sure. She'll make him pay. But she'll not let him go. Self-confident, stern, 'forceful'. Freya, she supposed, was going to turn out just like her.

'By the way, you should probably hold off with talk about my being in films. It may never happen.'

Stephen's pained expression admitted the fault. 'Sorry. I don't remember even telling her that. Have you heard from Ludo yet?'

She shook her head. 'Not a dicky bird.'

'Well, you know film people – they take such an age to decide anything.'

Nina gave a sad little shrug. 'I don't know. Ludo will have plenty of young hopefuls begging for a part. I may be holding on for nothing.'

Stephen sensed her air of despondency had an ulterior cause. He put his hand on hers. 'The fellow who turns you down would have to be mad.'

She looked up at him sharply, and said, with an uncertain smile, 'Why would you say that?'

He noticed through the forest of tables Freya returning. The time for intimacy was narrowing fast. 'Why? Because you have an amazing talent. And because you're the smartest, funniest, loveliest woman I've ever met.'

He held her gaze for a moment before he straightened and smiled over her shoulder to greet his returning daughter. Nina was stunned. She had never heard him speak with such decision. She was the loveliest woman he had ever met. *Loveliest. Ever.* She smiled dumbly at Freya, who shot her a quizzical glance as she handed over the late edition to Stephen.

'Dad,' she said with an amused curiosity, 'did you *know* there'd be a story about you in the paper?'

# 16

It was a surprise to Tom when Jimmy pulled out a strongbox he had never seen from a bottom drawer in his desk, itself guarded by a stout Bramah lock. He slipped the catches and with the quick expertise of a teller counted out the cash note by note. Tom was then invited to recount it.

'. . . £300, £310, £320, £325.' The banknotes crackled as Tom squared them up and eased them into a slim envelope.

Jimmy nodded, and furtively rearranged the contents of the box. A telltale clink sounded, and Tom caught a flash of jewellery.

'What else have you got in there?'

'Never you mind,' said Jimmy, clapping it shut. 'The man Astill – "Roddy" – told me seven this evening, same place. Said that there'll be someone to let you in.'

'I don't understand why he didn't get his man to pick up the cash when he brought the car. Wouldn't that have been easier?'

Jimmy chuckled. 'You didn't see the feller he sent. Wouldn't have trusted him with your tram fare, let alone a wodge like this.'

Tom gave an irritated *tsk* and tucked the envelope in his breast pocket. 'How nice for you to have a trustworthy employee,' he grumbled.

'Talking of which, I shall also require your services as

driver next week – for that.' He pointed to an elaborate invitation card resting on the chimney piece. Tom got up to peruse it. The event it announced was a Green Carnation Ball at a smart address in Highgate.

'What on earth is this?' he asked.

'Note the date – thirtieth of November. The anniversary of poor old Oscar. Some, ah, like-minded friends are throwing a bash in his honour.'

'"Dress: Theatrical . . ."'

'That means it'll be full to the door with poofs and drag queens.'

Tom continued to stare at the card. 'And what am I supposed to do once we're there?'

Jimmy pursed his mouth thoughtfully. 'They won't mind if you come in for a drink. Just so long as you don't start making eyes at anyone.'

After a prolonged coldness in his manner towards her Roddy telephoned Madeleine at her lodgings. He had a job, a punter from out of town. No reference was made to the night he had taken her out to dinner, or to her politely emphatic rejection of his advances. But a certain levity in his tone seemed to imply she was forgiven, and when he suggested that she wear 'something saucy' for the occasion it was clear they had reverted to their old ways. Roddy was quite transparent, really; given how she despised him it was odd that this thaw in their relations should be so welcome.

In acknowledgement of the truce she decided to make an effort, and wore a black velvet cocktail dress with a provocative neckline. She knew he would appreciate a show of flesh. She also went heavy on the warpaint, even though she disliked it: the rouge and mascara lent her the faintly sinister look of a shop mannequin. A sable coat completed her outfit. When she presented herself to the inlaid mirror of her wardrobe she almost took a step back in surprise.

She had never looked so much the part of a Soho working girl. On the bus into town she could not help noticing the way some gazes lingered on her, mingling desire and disgust.

At the Elysian Rita, spying her across the room, did a small double take. They had not seen each other since the night at the Blue Posts when she had first heard about Alice. Rita and a few of the other girls had gone to the funeral. The murder had plunged them all into a miasma of gloom and foreboding. After a long absence it was thought – it was hoped – that the killer had somehow vaporised, gone off like an evil phantom to torment some different netherworld. But he had not departed after all, he was still out there, stalking them.

'My, look at you,' said Rita, sliding in next to her. 'Your ship just come in?'

Madeleine returned a smile. 'Roddy's got some punter he wants to impress. I thought I'd better show willing.'

'Did you two fall out or something? He's had a face trippin' him these last weeks.'

Madeleine gave a brisk shake of her head. 'Just a misunderstanding. You know what he's like.'

Rita took out a cigarette and lit it. She gave Madeleine a sidelong look, and hesitated a moment before speaking. 'I can't stop thinkin' about Alice. I mean, you told her that feller Rusk –'

'That's not his real name. It's just the one he gave her.'

'Well, whatever he's called, you told her to steer clear of him. And she would have done, too . . . J'ever wonder if this "Tiepin Killer" is the same feller who was lookin' for you?'

'I've thought it might be,' she said quietly. 'But I couldn't be certain.'

'You told her he was dangerous, remember? – the three of us were in the Blue Posts that night.'

Madeleine felt suddenly faint. *He's been looking for you.*

She found her voice from somewhere. 'I told her – I told her not to go near him.'

'I know you did. Strikes me that, if it is him, he went back to Alice cos he was prob'ly out to find *you*. And the reason is, you've seen his face.'

She had thought the same thing, the killer forcing Alice to tell him, and her not knowing where Madeleine lived. And then making her pay for not knowing . . . 'There's no telling if it's the same one I met. Could be there's more than one madman out there.'

Rita, eyes still bright with enquiry, conceded the point. In a sudden gesture of appeal she seized Madeleine's hand in hers. 'I'm worried sick, though. You have to be careful, Maddy. This punter tonight, for instance, d'you know anything about him?'

'I never ask. All Roddy told me was he's a big tipper.'

'Hmm, I'll bet,' Rita said sardonically. 'Just make sure Roddy's there when you meet him. Then at least you've got protection.' The idea of Roddy as her protector was so ridiculous she began to shake her head, but Rita was adamant. 'Look, I know he's a swine, but he has an interest in keepin' you safe. You're one of his earners. Remind him of it.'

Madeleine said she would, mostly as a way of getting Rita off the subject.

Tom had never carried a large sum of cash on his person before, and thought that Soho at night was perhaps not the best time to prove himself as courier. The envelope in his pocket felt awkward and seemed to bulge beneath his coat. He walked down narrow streets where kitchen staff loafed outside restaurants on their break, past working girls in doorways, past men on street corners watching and waiting. He had a fanciful notion that an experienced mugger could divine the presence of money on someone, in the way that certain desert tribesmen were able to locate water.

Something else was on his mind. Having agreed to drive Jimmy to Highgate next Monday, he could have kicked himself on realising that it was the same night he had arranged to go to the pictures with Madeleine. After some consideration he reluctantly decided that the dress ball, or whatever it was, had to take priority: Jimmy had no other driver, for one thing, and he would sulk for days if Tom were to let him down. Madeleine, he knew, would understand, and there was now the additional thrill of being able to collect her in the Bentley. Only think of the look on her face when he drove up!

On Berwick Street he turned into the cobbled mews, even quieter at this hour and steeped in inky shadows. He found the door of Roddy's flat and knocked. After a few moments the downstairs light went on; he heard a chain being lifted on the other side and a bolt thrown back. The door opened and a man cautiously dipped his head forward, in a way that reminded Tom of a tortoise poking from under its shell. He gave Tom a once-over.

'Are you here to pay for the car?' His voice was a flat, slightly adenoidal whine.

Tom nodded, and the man stepped back to admit him. In the weak light of the hallway he was revealed as a portly middle-aged fellow with dark hair and a feeble moustache. His unprepossessing demeanour was offset by an expensive-looking suit, though even this let him down, its too-long cuffs puddling on his wrists. The man led the way up the stairs to the living room, whose unexpected length accommodated a billiard table and even a small bar. Spread upon it was a newspaper his host had evidently been reading when he was called to answer the door.

'Roddy's late, as usual,' he muttered, folding the paper away. 'He was supposed to be here half an hour ago.'

Tom thought he might as well try a little civility. 'I'm Tom, by the way, Tom Tunner. You are – ?'

'Oh, Johns,' he said, accepting Tom's hand.

'So Roddy's a friend of yours?'

Johns tucked in his chin uncertainly, as if he might be deciding whether to claim an intimacy or not. 'We've known each other for a while. I supply his club with wine and spirits, he supplies me with . . .' His expression turned shifty. 'It's business.'

Tom sidled over to the bar and inspected the glinting line of whiskies along the shelf. He took down a bottle of Black & White. He was damned if he should be made to wait without a drink. 'Care for a sharpener?'

'Don't mind if I do,' said Johns, heaving himself onto one of the bar stools. Tom took down a couple of glasses and poured them each a hefty measure.

'Here's how,' he said cheerily, and swallowed, feeling the pleasant burn of the Scotch inside his throat. He noticed that Johns took only a small sip. 'I suppose in your line of work free Scotch isn't much of a perk.'

'You could say,' he replied. 'When I'm out for a big night I take it steady. No use in getting tight straight away.' There was something ill at ease about him; in spite of his profession he was decidedly not a habitué of Soho drinking dens.

'A big night – I see. What does Roddy have planned for you?'

Johns allowed himself a dry snigger. 'Oh, I'll probably go wherever the – er – lady wants to. I just hope she's got a bit more class about her than the last one.' He caught Tom's eye and gave a man-of-the-world shrug. 'Of course with tarts it's the luck of the draw.'

Now Tom understood. Roddy pimped girls, and this was a nervous customer. 'When you say "class", you mean . . .'

Johns wrinkled his nose. 'I can't stand to hear a common accent. The last girl was nice enough but she sounded like a bloody fishwife.'

So, a snob as well as a lecher, thought Tom. He felt sorry

for the woman who would be his escort for the evening. Yet there was something piteous about *him*, too, stroking his little moustache; he looked such a lonely sort in his oversized suit and unpolished shoes. It was pity mingled with contempt, really – but sometimes those two were hard to tell apart. He drank down his Scotch and held up the bottle for another, but Johns refused, keeping his powder dry. The desultory chat continued, without enthusiasm. Tom glanced over at the billiard table and thought about suggesting a game – then decided against it. He could imagine no pleasure in beating such an opponent.

Nearly an hour had gone when they heard the rasp of a key and the door opening. From below could be heard footfall, a man's, then the lighter steps of a woman. First through the doorway came Roddy, whose strange smirk on greeting them Tom could not quite read – until he saw who was trailing in his wake.

Madeleine stopped dead, as though she might have seen her own ghost. She forced herself to speak. 'Tom – what are you doing here?'

Tom was inclined to ask her the same question, but his voice had for the moment deserted him. In her make-up and low-cut dress she was briefly a stranger to him, and it took a few muddled seconds before he linked her appearance with Johns. Johns, the wretch he had lately been feeling sorry for. It was inconceivable that he was – that she was –

Roddy had taken upon himself the role of host, and was playing it with undisguised glee. 'Maddy, this is Mr Johns, the gentleman I was telling you about. And this is – *oh*.' He paused theatrically, between Madeleine and Tom. 'I believe you two already know each other.'

Tom's stare held in it both an appeal and a horrified dawning that Madeleine could hardly bear to meet. Johns, blind to the unfolding calamity, had stood up to greet his escort for the night – and found himself ignored. Madeleine, flushed and sick with despair, glared at Roddy. He had got his revenge. But how did he know about her and Tom? Her instinct was to slap his face; instead she turned on her heel. Roddy was quick to interpose himself.

'Now, Maddy. Mr Johns here has come all the way down from Stanmore, just for the pleasure of your company. Wouldn't be polite to let him go without a good time, would it?'

'He can take his good time and stick it,' she hissed, trying to sidestep him, but again Roddy blocked her exit.

'Why are you cutting up rough?' he asked her. He now held her by the wrist as she struggled to get past. Tom, roused at last from his stupor of disbelief, stepped forward to unhand Madeleine. This merely gave Roddy his next cue.

'Oi, what's this?' He turned a puzzled look on Tom. 'I'm trying to have a discussion with an employee. D'you mind?'

As Tom pushed him away, Madeleine broke free and made for the stairs. Roddy reared back, palms aloft in a gesture of feigned innocence. Johns had belatedly decided to join the fray, and raised his voice at Tom.

'What's the to-do about?'

Tom ignored him. He took out the packet of cash whose delivery he now realised was part of a vindictive scheme. *He was quite particular that you should deliver it*, Jimmy had said. With a contemptuous glare he tossed it to Roddy, who caught it against his chest. 'I'd better count it,' he smirked, but Tom wasn't going to wait. He clattered down the stairs in time to catch Madeleine scrabbling with the door chain.

'Wait,' he said, staying her hand. For a long moment she kept her back to him. He could see her shoulders shaking. When she turned to face him tears and mascara had smudged her eyes.

'Well? What do you want to say to me?' There was defiance beneath the misery in her voice.

Tom was still too stunned to have prepared anything. He

gazed at her, then shook his head, embarrassed. 'I – I don't know what to say.' It was the truth, but the truth can sound inadequate, too.

Madeleine stared back at him. 'Goodbye, then.' She opened the door and slipped out. He stood in the hallway, irresolute; then he thought of something he had to tell her, and hurried out into the night. It was cold, damp and cheerless. She was nearly at the end of the mews, and he called after her. She didn't stop. By the time he caught up she was halfway down Berwick Street, her long coat swinging furiously behind her.

'Madeleine, stop. Please.' He was catching his breath, and she came to a halt. The light from a nearby cafe spilled on the pavement in front of them. 'Look, you know we were supposed to go to the pictures – on Monday? I'm sorry but I've stupidly made another arrangement.'

She looked at him narrowly, not quite believing her ears. 'Is that it? Is that the way you drop someone you're ashamed of?'

Tom recoiled in surprise at her bitterness. 'I'm not trying to drop you.'

'Oh, I see. So you know a lot of other tarts, then . . .'

He flinched at that, then said quietly, 'Why didn't you tell me?'

Something was goading her to drive him off. She didn't know what it was; perhaps she couldn't bear to hear him pity her. Her voice was suddenly calm. 'I just wanted to have one person, one friend, who took me for what I am. D'you understand? Who didn't look at me like – like you're doing now.'

At a loss to tell whether her observation was just, Tom fell silent. Madeleine, brushing away a tear, seemed to nod to herself, as if coming to a private conclusion. She began to walk away, and this time he didn't stop her.

*　*　*

Stephen had been keeping a low profile since the papers had got hold of the story about his 'association' with the British People's Brigade. While Gerald Carmody's scheme to raise BPB funds under the guise of a theatre charity was now known for a fraud, Stephen's lawyer was still trying to prove his client's innocence in the matter of his alleged financial contribution. All the gossip columnists wanted to know was how one of London's most renowned society portraitists had fallen under the spell of a Fascist splinter group. More fuel was heaped on the bonfire of his reputation when it emerged that he had undertaken a commission to paint Lady Trevelyan, a prominent friend of Mosley and a frequent hostess to Ribbentrop.

Whenever Stephen saw the photograph of himself and Carmody, or the one of him at a party talking to Lady Trevelyan, he was struck by how shifty he looked. It occurred to him that a stranger chancing on his face in one of these photographs might reasonably assume he was guilty on all charges. At breakfast the day after her defection from school, Freya had looked up from a newspaper she had been studying and said, 'This one doesn't look like you.' Stephen peered over her shoulder at another photograph of him, bleary and blurred, on a night out.

'Good God, where did they find that? It must be years old.'

Freya stared more closely at it. 'Are you sure it *is* you?'

He pointed at the caption. 'It's got my name under it. They must be pretty confident. Don't let your egg go cold.'

Ignoring the egg, she began buttering some toast. 'So are you famous now?'

He gave a half-laugh. 'Having your photograph in the *Mail* isn't anything to do with being famous.'

He poured himself more coffee. They'd been getting along well since her unscheduled arrival the day before, though he wondered what she had thought of Nina making up a trio with them at the Corner House. Freya, always watchful, would probably know that there was nothing innocent about an attractive woman showing up unannounced in the middle of the afternoon. He had later negotiated a sort of deal with her: he would not report her absconding from school to her mother, and, by unspoken implication, she would not mention Nina's accompanying them to lunch. Freya would return to Tipton the next day, and Stephen would contrive to hush up the incident with her headmaster. He had also promised to reopen the discussion of her unhappy schooling once Cora was back in London. 'Don't just *agree* with her about everything,' Freya had said warningly. Stephen was amused – and chastened.

'I'm going to be out most of the day,' he informed her a little while later. 'Will you be all right here?'

Freya nodded, then narrowed her eyes. 'Is Mrs Ronson coming in?'

She had realised the snag before Stephen. 'She might be. If so, tell her you're not well. I'll sort it out with her later. Have you got anything to read?'

She shook her head. 'I finished *Barchester*.'

'Right.' He supposed it was expecting too much of Tipton to supply her with further material. He went up to the study to collect his things, then went back to the kitchen to kiss her goodbye.

'Here,' he said, dropping his pocket Oxford classic of *Jane Eyre* onto the table in front of her. 'She didn't much like her school either.'

Parking his car, Stephen crossed into Dover Street and entered the Nines. He hadn't shown his face in the club for a while, uncertain of his standing among the members since the Carmody affair. He met nobody he knew on his way up to the dining room. Taking down the dust sheet he found the mural gazing patiently back at him, patches here and there still awaiting his attention. He had neglected it these last few weeks. In the hiatus the project had lost a little momentum, and he felt a keen obligation to get it finished. For the next couple of hours he applied himself, finessing this section and that, eventually becoming so absorbed in it that he didn't even hear the door open.

A discreet cough alerted him to the incomer. Julius Anstruther, the club secretary, was a tall, episcopal figure with a great swatch of white hair that drooped across his brow like a cap. He murmured Stephen's name in greeting before he closed the door behind him, and shimmered over to examine the wall painting.

His perusal of it seemed deeply considered, and Stephen felt curious to hear his verdict. 'It's a marvellous piece of work, really,' he said eventually. His voice was so clipped as to sound nearly strangulated. He nodded at the blanks that still required painting. 'Three more to go . . .'

'That's right. I should be done within the next two weeks.'

Anstruther nodded again, this time a more ambiguous movement that seemed to withhold complete accord. Stephen knew that the secretary had been one of the earliest supporters of the mural, so he had no fear of being relieved of the job. The silence in the room had lengthened, however, and he turned about so as to give Anstruther a view of his back.

The voice came again, slower this time. 'Next two weeks,' he repeated, musing on this forecast. 'There's something we need to discuss beforehand. Something rather disagreeable, I'm afraid.'

'I see,' said Stephen, still looking at the wall.

'Would you – care to sit down while we do?'

'I'd rather not,' said Stephen, facing him nonetheless.

'Very well. It will not surprise you to hear the club has been concerned about' – he allowed himself a wince of distaste – 'the recent publicity surrounding your . . . affiliations. We value our good name, and it behoves us to keep a vigilant watch on anything that might jeopardise it. Ordinarily, political donations –'

'Sir, if I may briefly interrupt? For the record, I have not donated money to a political party in my life – ever. Now, let us speak honestly. I know the committee has met to consider my membership. Perhaps you would be good enough to tell me its decision.'

Anstruther, who evidently preferred the English manner of circumlocution, seemed taken aback for a moment by this forthrightness. He squinted at Stephen from under his brow, and after a pause continued. 'Let me say it was not unanimous. Doubts were raised as to your culpability in the matter. But – I regret to say – the majority vote was against. I'm obliged to ask you for a letter of resignation.'

Stephen nodded, gazing off into the distance, then looked directly at the secretary. 'Thank you for telling me.' He began to douse his brushes in white spirit.

Behind him Anstruther coughed again, and said, 'Wyley, one moment. The members are not yet privy to this information. I myself argued for postponing the announcement so as to enable your work here to be completed. It would be . . .'

'A stay of execution,' Stephen supplied.

Anstruther tipped his head in acknowledgement. 'As it were.'

Stephen took another long look at the mural, recalling the club's importunate plea to take the job back in September. He had only agreed to do it as a favour to Ludo. Quite ironic, he thought, to be handed his papers like this, dismissed from something he'd never really wanted in the first place. Feeling a weariness seep through his shoulders he said, 'Don't delay it on my account. Now that I've heard the sentence I'd rather not wait in the dock.'

Ten minutes later he had boxed up a few personal things and was heading out across the hall when he heard his name called. He looked up to see a man wearing an immaculate double-breasted suit in a light grey herringbone. It was Everett Druce, the financier he had met through Ludo. He offered his hand and said pleasantly, 'I've been trying to make some time to see you. For the mural, I mean – I hope I've not been holding you up.' His voice carried a reedy resonance in it, like an oboe.

'No, not at all,' said Stephen with a rueful half-laugh. 'But I'm afraid you're too late. As of today I'm no longer a member here.'

Druce frowned in puzzlement. 'Surely not?'

'The committee fears I'm a liability to the club's good name. You may have read stories in the papers . . .'

'Of course. But I didn't imagine they were true.'

'The club chooses to believe otherwise, so – I'm gone,' said Stephen, looking about the place. Druce's expression had turned thoughtful.

'That's too bad. But may I assume you would now be free to take on more private commissions?'

'I suppose so,' Stephen conceded.

'Well, then. The only reason I agreed to sit for the mural was the opportunity of being painted by you. What say you to doing the portrait anyway – as a favour to me?'

Stephen was briefly lost for words. After so much haemorrhaging here was unexpected succour to the wound. 'I really don't . . .'

Druce misread his hesitation. 'I'd pay whatever your fee is, of course.'

'I'd be very pleased to,' he said, touched by this stranger's show of support. Druce returned his smile, and handed him a card inscribed with his home address.

'As you see, I don't live very far from here. You can have a look round the house at the same time – I keep a small collection. Say, next week?'

Stephen nodded, and they shook hands on it. Then he heard Druce being hailed by another member, and he exited the Nines for the last time.

# III

# The Distinguished Thing

# 17

The Bentley bucked and hopped on its way down Charlotte Street. Tom had still not got the measure of the machine, and his passenger wasn't slow to advise or to chide. Dressed in an ochre-and-green tweed suit, Jimmy had spread a car blanket over his knees to ward off the November chill. They were exchanging thoughts on the play they had seen the previous night.

'How about that young Adamson?' he mused, referring to the pretty but gormless star of the evening. 'The accent was a put-on, surely?'

'He's a twit. Everything about him is affected, right down to the way he coughs.'

Jimmy laughed. 'Yes, even his lungs are affected!'

He took out his notebook and jotted the line down. He could use that in his review. The car made another inelegant judder as they pulled up outside L'Etoile. Jimmy scratched his head, and felt a parody coming on.

'*The car he sat in / Like a refurbished throne, / Bumped on the pavement; the chassis was beat an' old, / Rubber the tyres, and so enfumed that / The windows were dirt-thick with 'em . . .* That's as far as I've got.'

'"Enfumed"?'

'Poetic licence, dear,' Jimmy said, preening himself in the

rear-view mirror before casting the blanket off his lap. 'Are you going to pop in?'

Tom shook his head. 'Work to do. I suppose you'll want collecting.'

'The birthday boy will be sorry not to see you. Hmm. Say half past three?'

Jimmy climbed out and with a double tap of his cane against the car watched Tom drive off. He had sensed Tom's low mood all morning, and wondered if it might have to do with Miss Farewell. But something warned him off the subject. On entering the narrow front room of L'Etoile he saw László amiably engaged in discussion with a waiter, who looked at a loss, as waiters tended to be when button-holed for their opinion of *Rosenkavalier* or Siegfried's Funeral March. László behaved to all with the same high-minded but even-handed courtesy, and didn't appear to notice the odd looks he got in return.

'My good man,' said Jimmy to the waiter, 'I did telephone to reserve the corner banquette.' He indicated with a nod that the table was occupied, and the waiter hurried off with a promise to look into it. He turned his beam on László. 'My dear fellow. The happiest of happy birthdays to you!'

László's face creased into his most endearing jack-o'-lantern smile. 'James! I have taken the liberty of starting upon this intoxicating beverage.' He indicated his huge Martini glass, inside which a plump green olive was lolling.

'Do you drink from it, or merely swim in there?' asked Jimmy.

László looked at him. 'Will Thomas not be joining us?'

A line came to Jimmy as he shook his head – *The frog he would a-wooing go*. Poor László. He had nursed an unspoken *tendresse* for Tom which the years, and Tom's perfect oblivi-ousness, had done nothing to diminish. Jimmy preferred not to enquire too closely into his old friend's sexuality.

Beyond the shared joke of their being inverts, László had always seemed to him somewhat neuter, and quite probably a virgin. His deep regard and respect for women was, like everything else about him, old-fashioned. He had learned that when László was in his youth, still a piano prodigy, there was a girl he had hoped to marry. No chance of that now: who would dream of taking him on?

The restaurant's maître d' interrupted his reverie. He was explaining, sotto voce, that the four diners had been in possession of the corner banquette since midday, and were refusing to budge. Jimmy looked askance at them.

'Actors,' he sighed.

'I believe they are, sir,' replied the maître d', giving a regretful little bow as he withdrew.

He leaned towards László. 'I wouldn't mind, only you know they're *repertory* actors.'

His good mood was restored when a waiter brought him a Martini of similar dimensions to his friend's. He speared the drowning olive with a cocktail stick and popped it in his mouth. He sat back and gazed around the room, his attention briefly snagged on a woman, her back to him, wearing a hat that looked like a squashed Chinese pagoda.

'Extraordinary things people put on their heads,' he murmured. 'Now – here's *un petit cadeau* to mark your half-century.' He carefully placed the parcel he had sneaked in on the table between them. (Tom had done an excellent job with the wrapping.) The recipient gaped dumbly at it. 'Well, *go on* – open the damn thing.'

László did as he was commanded, and drew out from the box a small and worn leather case, slightly larger than a hip flask. Unfastening the clip he folded it out to disclose a dainty-looking pair of opera glasses, their black lacquer dulled with age. Lifting them from their faded velvet moulding he peered through the lens at Jimmy.

'O vision entrancing!' He giggled, looking more childlike than ever.

'I got 'em at Christie's,' Jimmy said. He allowed himself a delicious pause before adding, 'They once belonged to Brahms.'

At that László lowered the glasses, his face frozen in astonishment. Then he stared at them as if his jesting of the moment before were an impertinence. 'James . . .' he gasped, shaking his head. 'This is too much – too much.'

'I had a tenacious rival in the room. But I felt you must have them – it will lend piquancy to your story about holding the door open for him, where was it – ?'

'Vienna,' said László, in a small voice. A tear bulged at the corner of his eye.

Jimmy sighed. 'Come now, don't be a booby. It's just a silly old pair of glasses. You know, if I'd given 'em to one of my young companions he'd most likely have said, "Thanks, Jim, absolute ripper," then tossed them aside.'

László nodded, blinking through his tears. His voice trembled. 'I know such lachrymosity embarrasses you, and I apologise. But, James, this is only a wretch's way of acknowledging an extravagant kindness he can never hope to match.'

Jimmy endured a spasm of unhappiness as he heard this. László was as close to poverty as anyone he had ever known, and yet he always marked Jimmy's birthday with a gift – a second-hand book, a gramophone record – which, be it ever so modest, he could probably ill afford. Now the wild generosity of the gift he had made felt, in comparison, a little crushing; it was no rhetoric on László's part to say that he could never hope to match it. Not that Jimmy imagined he ever *would* – only that he wished it had not been explicitly articulated.

His guilt was muddled with exasperation: if only his friend weren't so poor! It even seemed to haunt his choice from the menu. Given that Jimmy was paying, why dine on onion soup when you could have oysters, and an omelette when there was half a lobster? But László was plainly enjoying himself, and he decided after a moment to do the same.

'A shame Peter couldn't join us. That's the problem with being a GP – always gets in the way of lunch.'

László glanced up from his soup. 'The dear man telephoned me this morning. He has not forgotten my birthday in twenty-six years. I gather that you are out together next week.'

'Yes, the Green Carnation Ball, for Oscar's anniversary. I expect it'll be rather louche.'

'Did you know that *The Importance of Being Earnest* was first written in four acts, and cut down by George Alexander to three? The original third act contained a scene in which Algernon Moncrieff was arrested for debt. When told that he would be taken to Holloway, Algernon says, "Never. If Society thought I was familiar with so remote a suburb it would decline to know me."'

Jimmy laughed, though he was puzzled. 'How did you find that out?'

László smiled shyly. 'You probably don't know that before the war I was the official Hungarian translator of Wilde's plays. My father was friendly with a famous theatre producer in Budapest who asked me to do it.'

Jimmy shook his head, dumbfounded by László's effortless knack for springing a revelation on him. He didn't doubt it was true, for he knew it would never occur to him to lie. 'And how does Wilde play in Hungarian, I wonder?'

'Funnier than you would think! Though of course a verb such as "to Bunbury" is not easy to construe.'

'Hmm. No doubt. Y'know, I remember that whole time around his trial and arrest. The shock of it . . . what I couldn't understand, and still don't, was why he never fled the country when he had the chance. I mean, he knew that

Queensberry had got him cold, with the blackmailers and rent boys and what have you. Prison was a near certainty. So why did he stay?'

László's expression was thoughtful. 'The human capacity for self-delusion is strong. Sometimes we refuse to see what is right in front of us. And Wilde probably did not think a man as *chraazy* as Queensberry could bring him down.'

'The newspapers didn't help him, of course. "Once they had the rack. Now they have the press." Talking of which, our man Wyley has been very ill-used.'

'A scandal,' said László with feeling. 'As a matter of fact I wrote a letter to *The Times* deploring the way he has been treated. And I also mentioned his altercation with that brute at the Carlton – nobody who was there that night would have called him a Fascist sympathiser.'

'Good for you. I didn't see the letter, I'm afraid.'

'That is because they didn't print it!'

Jimmy winced a little. 'All the same, he might have exercised a bit more caution. Fancy writing a personal cheque to a man like Carmody . . .'

'The poor fellow has been deceived,' said László, growing more heated. 'He believed he was supporting a theatre charity. Why, you yourself were taken in by the scoundrel.'

Jimmy admitted it with a shrug, and privately thanked his stars he had not been induced to contribute more than the cost of two dinners. He wondered if the damage to the painter's reputation would also scare away clients. Wyley had fobbed him off that evening by pleading other commitments. But now? He sensed an opportunity to be grasped.

He loosened another oyster from its shell, and said, 'Of course now would be the time for friends to show support. I could always, well, renew my offer of a commission.' And if business really had fallen away he might be able to negotiate on the price, too.

'That would be an honourable gesture,' agreed László,

whose expression brightened suddenly. 'We both may end up immortalised by his hand!'

'Both?'

'Ah! I forgot to tell you. I wrote to thank Wyley for his generosity that evening, hardly expecting a reply. Yet one came, and – the most extraordinary thing – he had enclosed with his letter a small pencil portrait – of me! Quite simple, possibly the work of moments, but still, a delight to behold. I must show it to you once I get it back from the framer's.'

Jimmy was aghast, though he tried to shape his features into a semblance of enthusiasm. 'Yes, you must . . .' That László – frankly, no oil painting – should have wangled a picture from one of the leading portraitists of the day, *without even having to ask*, was too galling for words. And to think of how he had fairly pestered Wyley that evening for the privilege!

'And yet I don't think we can call Wyley absolutely first class,' he continued, using his Voice of Authority. 'He's not on the level of Nicholson, or Gunn. And as for those claiming him to be this nation's Sargent – well!'

'Possibly not,' said László mildly. 'But I prefer him to all of them.'

Jimmy stared at his companion, hunched over his soup plate. It dimly occurred to him that László had secured this good fortune by virtue of being a kind and deserving person. And that he in contrast would never be thought so, despite his generosity with luncheons and parties and gifts. Unfair, but there it was. He had been in debate with himself as to whether he should invite László to the ball next Monday. It would be a friendly thing to do. But this sudden revelation of his about the sketch had nettled him, and in that moment he decided that the invitation could go hang.

László, unaware of his being passed over, had just excused himself to go to the Gents. His removal had opened a new angle of surveillance across the restaurant, and in turn left

Jimmy open to scrutiny – indeed, he could see a lady narrowing her gaze on him and whispering to her younger companion, the one in the squashed pagoda hat, who now turned her head. Her face was very familiar, though he couldn't immediately place it.

He hailed a passing waiter and said, 'Be so kind as to bring us another of those wines that maketh glad the heart of man.'

The waiter's expression was impassive. 'Muscadet, was it, sir?'

Jimmy tilted his head sideways in a gesture of agreement, and the man went off. While his attention had been diverted the squashed-pagoda lady had, with feline stealth, padded up to his table. She was dark, attractive, perhaps thirty. He must have seen her onstage, though in their mufti actors weren't always easy to recognise.

'You're Erskine, aren't you?'

'I am,' he said, hearing a combative note.

'I've got a bone to pick with you.'

'Madam, a whole skeleton, if you wish.' He invited her to sit, but she continued to stand, arms folded loosely across her chest.

'You once described me in a review as "ungainly". You also said I didn't know how to walk.'

'On the second count I was evidently mistaken. Perhaps you could – ?'

'*Fire in the Hole*, four years ago.'

Now the clouds parted, and Jimmy smiled. 'Why, Nina Land, isn't it? My dear, you're a star!'

'And *you* are a little shit,' Nina replied crisply. At that moment László was returning to the table, just in time to overhear this disobliging epithet. He slunk into his seat, glancing up nervously at the interloper. Jimmy, meanwhile, was looking around, his face a picture of injured innocence.

'My dear lady, the review to which you refer was an

*hommage*! I distinctly recall my asserting that your performance outshone all else, and that you were destined for
great things. Pray tell, how have I offended?'

'You've got some nerve, I must say. What critic in his
right mind would describe an actress as "horse-faced" and
then call it *hommage*?'

Jimmy slapped his hand on the table. 'I would! You are
assuming I use "horse-faced" as a term of insult.'

Nina returned an incredulous look. 'Likening a woman's
face to a horse's *is* generally understood as an insult.'

With portentous solemnity Jimmy held up his forefinger,
as though preparing an announcement. 'In which case I
must take recourse to my trusted companion here. László,
this lady believes I have affronted her. Would you do
me the service of propounding my theory of the female
physiognomy?'

Nina looked at the critic's fidgeting friend and sensed his
uncertainty, which made her only more curious to hear the
defence. With some fluster László began: 'I do assure you,
miss, um, that James – Mr Erskine – intended no offence.
His taxonomy is perhaps eccentric, but not without founda-
tion, I think . . .' She listened as he proceeded to explain the
rudiments of 'bird-bun-horse', to which final category her
own face apparently belonged. László's precise, accented
English, and the courtesy with which he spoke, had a
disarming effect. Nina found herself mollified, if not quite
persuaded. When he had concluded ('*C'est tout*'), she replied
with a gracious nod and turned to Jimmy.

'Hmm. I can't tell if it's twaddle or –'

'Twuth?' suggested Jimmy, and she giggled.

'I think a test is in order. I shall call on my second, as
you have,' she said, beckoning the companion she had left
at the table. A lady in her fifties, short, wiry, beady-eyed,
sidled up. She gave Jimmy and László the once-over, unim-
pressed. 'This is Dolly Langdon, my dresser. Dolly, dear,

these gentlemen have a theory I want to test. So listen, if every woman's face has one of three shapes – a horse, a bun, or a bird – which, d'you think, is mine?'

Dolly pulled a face of her own. 'I shouldn't like to say.'

Nina stooped to Dolly's height. 'Just be honest. Bird, bun, horse?'

With a reluctant air, she squinted at Nina. 'Horse.'

Jimmy clapped his hands, triumphant. 'There! Mrs Langdon, without prompting, has vindicated me.'

'The horse is indeed a noble-faced creature,' added László quietly.

'Don't push your luck,' said Nina with a half-laugh. She gave Jimmy a sidelong look. 'There may be something in it. I'm sorry for calling you a –'

'Quite forgotten,' said Jimmy, becoming expansive. 'Now, I propose we celebrate our truce by you and Mrs Langdon joining us for pudding. László, be a good fellow and pull up that chair.'

Nina glanced at Dolly, who indicated her compliance with a little moue. She supposed that Dolly's face, small and pointed, would be 'bird' according to the Erskine theory, but wisely resisted mentioning it. They settled around the table and Jimmy, needing no excuse, called for a pint of champagne with the pudding menus. Just then Nina recalled Stephen telling her about the evening of the Marquess dinner, and his being seated next to 'that Erskine fellow'. He hadn't much liked him, either, though he had found his friend strangely charming. Could it possibly be . . .? She caught László's eye across the table and smiled.

'I've an idea you know a friend of mine,' she said. 'Stephen Wyley?'

László's eyes brightened. 'Indeed! James and I were lately discussing him. It has grieved us both to see his name so besmirched. Do please tell, have you seen him since his . . . troubles?'

'Yes, last week. He's bearing up.'

'A shocking business,' said Jimmy. 'We met him the night of that ghastly dinner at the Carlton. László here even wrote a letter to *The Times* defending him.'

'Not printed, alas,' muttered László.

'I know he'll appreciate it, all the same,' said Nina kindly. 'The gallery is standing by him, thank goodness, but he's had some commissions cancelled. Even the mural he was painting at the Nines has been abandoned.'

Jimmy, unable to resist, said, 'So the club will have to hire an *extra* mural painter, as it were.'

'That's rather good,' said Nina. For all the resentment he had stirred in her as a critic she had to admit he was jolly company. Generous, too; when the champagne arrived he made a toast to his little friend, who turned out to be celebrating his fiftieth birthday. It was worth being there just to see the childishly wide grin that transformed László's countenance. 'We're celebrating, too, as a matter of fact,' she added. 'Our run ended last week. So I'd like to propose a toast to my dresser, with me through thick and thin – to Dolly!'

As her name rang in echo Dolly tried to pooh-pooh the fuss, and was shouted down. Jimmy, lighting a cigar, said to Nina, 'My God, you carried *The Second Arrangement*. I don't think anyone else could have found such wit in the thing.'

He's flattering me now, she thought, though it was not unpleasant to hear. 'I could wish some others were as appreciative,' she replied with a rueful smile. 'My agent has written to say that Marlborough Studios don't want me for their next picture after all.'

'Fie on the dolts! Cinema's loss is our gain, my dear. There will always be a welcome for you in the theatre.'

She had made light of it, but the news, coming on the day of the last performance, had deflated her just when she needed a boost. She had thought of telephoning Stephen to have a good moan, then decided not to: he had troubles enough to occupy him. And maybe it was for the best anyway. She was making a name for herself as a stage actress; to take a plunge into film might stall the momentum she had gathered.

Across the table László was enthusing over a pair of opera glasses – a birthday gift, it seemed – which he passed to Dolly for her inspection.

'Just to think these glasses once rested on the eyes of the man who composed *A German Requiem*!'

Dolly made a polite face. 'Fancy,' she said, handing them back.

László beamed at Nina. 'Who knows, in years to come perhaps something of Miss Land's will be fought over at auction.'

'Mm, anything but that hat, I imagine,' said Dolly, eyeing the squashed pagoda. Jimmy's laughter was uproarious, but Nina didn't mind. The mood had grown convivial. Anyone happening to pass their table might have supposed that the quartet of diners had all known one another for years.

They were just finishing off pudding when László sat up in his chair excitedly and cried, 'Look who's come to join us! Ladies, allow me to introduce our dear friend Thomas.'

Jimmy, who'd been in the middle of an anecdote about Sarah Bernhardt, raised his eyes heavenwards. Really! From the expression on László's face you'd have thought Brahms himself had just walked in. Tom, greeting them, accepted the chair László had eagerly wedged beside his own. It took him a moment to recognise the lady in the architectural hat.

'The last time I saw you was at the Strand for *The Second Arrangement*. Actually I went to see it twice.'

'It's true,' said Jimmy. 'He couldn't believe it the first time.'

'You were terribly good in it,' said Tom, ignoring him.

'That's very sweet of you,' smiled Nina. 'You know, this restaurant serves a better class of critic. I must come here more often.'

'Well, Jimmy's the critic,' said Tom, 'I'm just his secretary. And driver.'

Nina was astounded. 'Driver? Goodness, I didn't know newspapers paid their writers so well.'

'They don't,' said Tom. 'But he spends as if they do.' With a barely perceptible look he indicated to Jimmy that it was time to leave.

'Our carriage awaits! Ladies, consider it at your disposal. Thomas here will drive you wherever you wish.' This was less than welcome news to Tom. As he might have guessed, the car had quickly become a millstone, one more thing for which Jimmy expected him to be at his beck and call. In spite of its opulence he found he did not much enjoy driving it, and of course the vehicle was already tainted for him by its previous owner.

Charlotte Street was under lamplight as they emerged from L'Etoile. In spite of Jimmy's offer Dolly insisted that she would go home on the Tube, and László would accompany her to Tottenham Court Road station. It took no more than five minutes for Jimmy to be deposited at Princess Louise Mansions, which left Tom in charge of Nina.

'Honestly, just drop me at the bus stop,' she said.

'It's no trouble, really. Marylebone isn't far.' Tom's initial exasperation at being appointed cab driver had evaporated. There was something rather glamorous about driving an attractive young woman through town in an open-topped motor. He leaned into the back seat and grabbed Jimmy's car blanket. 'Here, that should keep the chill off.'

They turned into New Oxford Street, heading west. 'Quite a character, your Mr Erskine – entertaining,' said Nina.

'You could say,' replied Tom.

'And rather selfish?'

'Entertaining people generally are.' He paused for a moment, then said, 'I gather he treated you to "bird-bun-horse".'

'Yes. He all but threw a saddle on me.'

'I once told him off for trying out the theory on a lady he'd just met. Actually, I think you might know her. I saw you together at Edie Greenlaw's party.'

'Oh?'

'Madeleine Farewell.'

Nina heard this with a flinch of surprise, then recovered herself. 'I don't know her at all well.'

A beat passed, and he said, 'Nor do I.' She glanced at him, expecting something more, but having brought up her name he seemed reluctant to enlarge. They talked instead of Edie and what a scream she was. Nina noticed that in profile he looked more handsome than he did face-on. Unaccountable, really.

'You must be quite sociable, doing what you do,' she mused.

'In a way, yes,' said Tom, who had never felt as lonely in his life. 'I don't have Jimmy's knack for it, though. He walks into a room, starts talking and assumes people will hang on his every word. Which they usually do.'

They had reached the busy junction of Oxford Circus and Regent Street. Nina took out her cigarettes, offering him one. He reached for the packet, distracted between his hand and the wheel, and she saw the difficulty. 'Here, let me light it for you.' She did so, passing it from her mouth to his. As her hand hovered he caught a noseful of her scent, and was jolted.

'That perfume – what is it?'

'Jicky. D'you know it?'

He nodded. 'It reminds me of someone. I suppose that's what a scent is for.'

Nina felt sure then that Madeleine was on his mind. And judging by the set of his mouth he was very downcast about it. She gazed out at the shop windows of Marylebone sliding by, and wondered what to say. But Tom saved her the trouble. 'What will you do next – I mean, now the play's finished?'

'I'm not sure. As I was saying to your friends, I had hoped to get a part in a film – *Fortune's Cap* – but the studio doesn't want me.'

'*On Fortune's cap we are not the very button*,' Tom quoted. She gave a shrug. 'That would appear to be the case.'

'I'm sorry to hear it. If I were a film producer I'd sign you up in a shot.'

She laughed with self-conscious bravery. 'Then it's a pity you're not, because I need the work. Ah, here we are,' she said, indicating Chiltern Street on their right. Tom pulled the car over outside her boarding house. By unspoken agreement they would finish their cigarettes before parting.

'Awfully nice of you to drive me,' she said, trying to set a friendly tone in preparation for her next remark. Tom gave a quick smile, and after a moment she continued. 'When you mentioned Madeleine just before, I wasn't quite sure what to say. You see, I only know her by chance, really, through some odd circumstances that brought us together – it's hard to explain. From the little I do know she's a good sort, and brave, too. But I have this feeling that her life is in – disarray.' She had meant to say 'danger', and corrected herself at the last moment: it sounded melodramatic, and she didn't want to mislead him.

With palpable effort Tom said, 'The last time we spoke – I'm afraid I offended her, gravely. I was too – I hadn't realised she was . . .'

'An escort?'

He gave a slow nod, lost in thought. 'Perhaps I should have guessed. You see, she never . . .' He tailed off, unwilling to confide further. He tossed the butt of his cigarette and turned his face sadly to her. 'It was nice to meet you.'

She offered him her hand and a smile. On stepping out

she lingered on the pavement, and watched as Tom drove away up the street.

Stephen, rising late, came down to breakfast as Cora was brooding on the morning's post, scattered over the table. Something had irked her. The letter knife was poised in her long pale hand like an assassin's dagger. He decided to wait rather than provoke her with an enquiry; in the event the suspense was not drawn out.

'As I thought. No invitation to the Inchcombs' this year,' she said, pursing her mouth. She referred to the annual Christmas party thrown by their wealthiest neighbours in Chelsea.

'It might still be on its way,' he said, playing the optimist.

She shook her head. 'I know they've already gone out.'

Stephen stirred his coffee absently. 'Hmm. Dropped by the Incomes. I really have achieved notoriety.' In fact he could not have cared less about being snubbed by the Incomes – Stephen's nickname was a family joke – but he knew that it would hurt Cora.

'At least the golf club has stayed loyal,' she said, holding up the letter in her hand. 'I'm invited to renew our subscription.'

Stephen laughed gloomily. 'That may be the one place where my reputation has actually been enhanced.'

'Any news from the lawyer?'

'Only that Carmody is out on bail. They're waiting to set a date for his trial.'

'I see.'

Cora rose and began gathering the detritus of breakfast. She no longer appeared cross, merely fatigued; the worry of the last few weeks had kept them awake at night. Stephen leaned across to take her hand. 'Don't fret about the Incomes and their wretched party. We hated going anyway. Our real friends'll stick by us.'

His wife smiled tightly and continued clearing the table. After a moment she said, 'By the way, your father telephoned earlier. He's started on the house. He asked if you would go round.'

'Really?' His father, a model of self-sufficiency, rarely asked him to do anything.

'Said he has something to show you.'

Stephen could guess what it might be. Somewhere in the family home at Addison Road were the Ruskin sketches once presented to his grandfather, the ones he had told Freya about. He had been meaning to dig them out for ages: his father's house clearance would be the opportunity. He drained the last of his coffee and glanced up to find Cora, arms folded, staring worriedly into the middle distance.

'What's the matter?'

Her gaze held an appeal. 'I was just – are we going to be all right – about money, I mean? What if the commissions dry up altogether – is that possible?'

He knew he must sound confident, even if he didn't feel it. 'Of course not. I've not been wholly cast out by society. In fact I may have a new client.'

'Who?'

'Fellow named Druce, very charming, pots of money. Ludo introduced us, though I think I may have met him at Oxford – his face is familiar.'

Cora leaned towards him, an eager frown creasing her features. 'D'you think he's serious?'

Stephen nodded. 'He seemed so. He asked me to pay him a visit anyway –'

'Oh, then you must!' said Cora urgently. 'Will you confirm it with him?'

He assured her he would, pained by the edge of desperation in her tone. She clearly believed he might never work again.

Outside, the morning was brisk, with zeppelin-sized

clouds bumping across the horizon. He headed north across the Old Brompton Road and through the gracious quiet of Kensington. It was not until he reached Holland Park that it occurred to him that this might be one of the last times he would take this walk. His father had already got a buyer for the house. He passed a telephone box, and his step slowed. He would have liked to hear Nina's voice, just for a few minutes, but now that the play had ended its run she wasn't so available, and he disliked having to deal with that awful landlady. It alarmed him how much of his time was consumed in thoughts of her. He sometimes wondered if all the worrying he did – about being in the newspapers, about Freya, about his father's imminent move – was a way of displacing his one big worry over what to do about Nina. When they had last been together, on that hilariously awkward afternoon at the Corner House, he'd come as close as he ever had to confessing his love. She had looked so meltingly at him it was all he could do to stop himself. For the first time the prospect of leaving Cora had become a possibility, and he was terrified.

His father answered the door dressed, as ever, with immaculate care: regimental blazer and tie, cavalry twill trousers, shoes polished to a barrack-room gleam. In the face of such formal severity Stephen half wondered whether a salute was more appropriate than a handshake. Even the pipe he was smoking seemed a remnant of officer-class authority. But there was also something in his manner today – a kind of embarrassed solicitude – that made Stephen uneasy.

They went through the hall into the drawing room, now in the early stages of abandonment. The curtains had gone. Shelves denuded of their books looked suddenly forlorn, and paintings in heavy frames leaned in stacks against the walls. Their long occupancy had left dark rectangles on the wallpaper. The unsettled dust made his nose itch. The pair of them stood in the middle of the room, neither quite able to take in the disorder. Richard Wyley, distractedly fiddling with his pipe, broke the silence.

'Pickford's are coming round next week, but I thought I'd make a start.'

'I could help, you know, with this,' said Stephen uncertainly.

'No, no. It's all in hand.'

Another silence intervened, then: 'Cora said – on the telephone – you had something to show me.'

His father gave a thoughtful nod. 'Should I make us some tea?'

'No, I'm fine.'

'Right,' said Mr Wyley, leaving the room, as though he had just heard 'yes' to his offer of tea. Stephen bent down to look through a selection of the paintings, and found one of his own, a small Norfolk beach scene whose lines of sand, sea and sky blurred close to the point of abstraction. Its date was minutely inscribed after his initials: 1923. He stared at it, momentarily bemused at a compositional style that might have belonged to someone else altogether. It wasn't bad! – and he smiled at his own conceit. But he struggled to remember the person whose hand had painted it. Hearing his father's footsteps returning, he silently propped it back against the others.

'Come and sit by the window,' said Mr Wyley, who carried not the Ruskin sketches but a small cigarette box of ancient vintage, its edges blunted and frayed. Its gilt lettering advertised a tobacconist's on Old Bond Street that had long disappeared. They sat on the sofa, congenially knee to knee. 'I was emptying your mother's bureau –' he began, then halted, apparently at a loss. He opened the box and took out two photographs, sepia-tinged and faded. The larger was stiff, the size of a playing card, and carried the photographer's marque on its border. Three dark-haired girls, formally posed, gazed at something off-centre. The smaller photograph was a more relaxed portrait of the same trio, perhaps taken by a family member, and on the reverse someone had written, in pencil, the sitters' names: *Ella, Dorothy, Adeline*. Stephen was staring at someone he knew well but had never seen in her youth.

'So . . . that's Mum. Who are these other two?'

His father's voice was low. 'Her sisters. Ella was the middle of three.'

'Er, how can – ? Mum was an only child. You always –'

'I know.' He gently laid his hand on Stephen's shoulder. 'Her father was a Jewish watchmaker, in Edgware. The family was Orthodox – strict as they come. As soon as we met it was made clear that marrying "out" would be impossible. But we loved each other, so . . . they disowned her. Not one of them came to the wedding. As far as they were concerned she was dead.'

Stephen felt almost faint with a sensation that mingled bafflement with something darker, like betrayal. 'I don't understand . . . Why didn't you tell me?'

He heard the regret in the pause before his father spoke. 'She didn't want it known that she'd been – an outcast. You must understand how terribly painful it was for her. There were times I suggested she ought to . . . but she was adamant. I couldn't, because it wasn't my secret to give away. She felt rage, and remorse, for years – *years* – and in the end I think she couldn't bear having to explain it to you. It would have meant reliving the whole thing.' He moved a trembling finger over the girl's face. 'I thought she'd erased every trace of them. But it seems she kept these.'

Stephen stared at his mother, this dark-eyed Jewish girl he had never known, never suspected. The family photograph showed her smiling, a slender teen in a floral dress whose future was a blank – her marriage, her ostracism, her death. And her son, an unwitting innocent. There was something astonishing, something almost transcendent, in this tiny window of processed light thrown on her past. Why had he always accepted the story that she was an only child, with no living relatives? Because he had no reason to doubt it. That she should have lived with the loss of them, her own blood. The pity of it tore at his heart.

'She never saw them again – not one?'

Richard Wyley turned his head slightly. 'About five or six years after we were married – you were an infant – Dorothy, the youngest, wrote to her. They'd been close to one another growing up. They met at a cafe, somewhere in town. I don't know what was said. I think she hoped to effect some kind of rapprochement. Well, their father got wind of it – and that was the end of that. A friend told Ella that they had left London, before the war. Never heard of again.'

The photograph had blurred before his swimming eyes. All those years, and not a word, not a murmur of it. The memory of her last days came to him, her eyes sunken in their sockets, flesh withered to the bones. Had she thought of them then, her parents and her sisters, as she lay dying? Did word ever reach the family of Ella, their unforgiven? 'I wish – I wish she'd told me,' he said huskily, not sure if he meant it for his mother's sake, or for his own.

Later, as he drank the tea his father had made for them after all, Stephen picked up the photograph, the smiling one, unable to leave it alone. 'She never liked having her photograph taken, did she? It never occurred to me at the time.'

'Keep it. You should have it,' his father said, indicating the snapshot. Stephen demurred, while knowing that he would take it.

'Quite an irony, isn't it? – damned as a Fascist lackey when it turns out I'm actually Jewish, or half-Jewish.'

'I'd like to see how the newspapers respond,' said Richard Wyley. 'Those blighters should eat their words.'

Stephen shook his head. 'They won't, because they're not going to hear about it. Not from me, anyway.'

His father looked puzzled. 'My dear chap, after what they've done to you – I would have thought, well . . .'

Stephen gazed out of the window for a moment, half smiling, and realised he didn't care. Now that he had learned his mother's secret, and about his unsuspected ancestry, he knew they couldn't harm him any more. His father was staring at him in concern.

'Don't worry about it, Dad. This should teach me. You never ask for something that ought to have been given.'

# 18

It was early evening, the last day of November, as Nina stepped off the bus at the Aldwych. The Strand Theatre already appeared to have forgotten her recent triumph. All the signs advertising *The Second Arrangement* had been taken down, including the lights that had picked out her own name below the title. It was like returning to your old home to find it brutally refurbished, unrecognisable, all traces of your occupancy erased. But she realised that she had left behind, in the chaos of her dressing room, a Victorian letter knife – a gift from Stephen – and she didn't trust the management to return it.

She gave the doorman a cheery hullo and descended the stone stairs into the bowels of the theatre. The caretaker unlocked the door of her dressing room, and, switching on the light, she beheld the melancholy spectacle of change, her racks of clothes, the glittering bomb site of her dressing table, her books and bits and bobs – all gone, gone! How many hours had she lolled about on that sofa, this chair, smoking and chatting with Dolly, preparing for the curtain at seven thirty? Now it was as if she might never have been here. She waited for the caretaker to depart, then closed the door and bent down to the little drawer beneath the mirror, unlocking it with a pewter-coloured key. And there it lay, loose among the detritus of hairpins, grips, buttons, cigarette cards, cough drops, and more paste jewellery than any actress could possibly require. *Come, let me clutch thee*, she thought, holding up the blade so that it glinted in the light, its dainty pearl handle snug against her palm.

She looked again around the room, wondering if there were anything else she had missed. There was nothing. She absently picked up a cough drop from the drawer, shucked off its wrapper and put it in her mouth. Its menthol taste brought back those nights of panic when she imagined herself going hoarse, unable to speak. She tossed the little key onto the table and left the room. As she returned up the corridor she idly checked the green-felt board where notices and messages were pinned, some of them in Dolly's hand, some in the stage manager's. Her eye fell on one addressed to her, one she wouldn't have noticed at all but for the caller's name: Marlborough Studios.

A number was appended. She plucked it off the wall. It dated from last week, the day after closing night, which was why she hadn't seen it. Bafflingly, it had come some days *after* the studio had rejected her for *Fortune's Cap*. Perhaps it was a courtesy call to thank her for the screen test. But why would they bother? Or could it be that someone had had a change of heart? She walked towards the public telephone at the foot of the staircase, and paused to examine the message again. If she did reply, the potential for embarrassment was obvious; lines of communication may have got crossed, and this call had been made in error. She ought to ignore the thing. But what if it *wasn't* a mistake, what if there were plans afoot to put her on the big screen?

The operator put her through, and a moment later a man's voice answered. She gabbled out an apology, in case

314

she was wasting his time, but no, he had seen her screen test at Talman's office and had been expecting her call. It seemed that Marlborough were considering her for a different film, not *Fortune's Cap*, and would she care to have a chat about it? Her heart hurried a beat as she heard this, though she kept her voice casual. Yes, she did happen to be free the early part of this evening, and no, she didn't mind going up to Hampstead – they had an office up there. She checked her watch; if she set off now she would be back in time to meet Stephen for dinner at eight thirty. He gave her the address ('not far from the Tube') and was about to ring off when she said, 'What name should I ask for?' There was the briefest pause. 'Oh, I'm sorry, did I not say? It's Druce.'

Nina thanked him, and rang off.

Tom had got so bored with waiting that he decided to go and make himself a gin fizz in Jimmy's kitchen. He had been feeling a bit strange all day, and wondered if it was his illness gathering on the sly. A drink would calm his nerves. He poured a large slug of Tanqueray into the cocktail shaker, then added lemon juice, sugar, soda water – he didn't fancy the egg whites somehow. He tested it for strength, then carried it back into the living room. Jimmy's bedroom door was still shut. Having hired a costume for tonight's ball he had spent the last hour in there putting it on – Tom knew only that it was to be 'a surprise'.

He noticed that it had gone quiet, and called out, 'You haven't dropped dead in there, have you?'

Through the door came a muffled voice: 'Don't joke about things like that.'

'Jim, really – it's quarter to seven. We should leave here in ten minutes if we're to be on time.'

'All right, all right,' Jimmy shouted testily. There

followed some muttering and groaning from within, as if he were under a physical strain. Tom wandered over to the fireplace and, ever the diligent housekeeper, turned off the gas. He caught himself in the gilt mirror; he looked pale, and undernourished. For some reason he thought of Madeleine. This was the night they had meant to go to the pictures. What a fool he'd made of himself . . . He had thought of telling Nina Land all about it that afternoon he drove her home, but couldn't do so, despite her sympathetic manner.

The bedroom door opened, and Jimmy appeared, with a defiant expression, in a full-length Edwardian evening gown. Long white gloves came up to his elbow, and on his head sat a broad-brimmed hat decorated with a mass of black feathers. More alarming than anything he wore, however, was his face, rouged and powdered as though he might be on his way to the Folies-Bergère. The final incongruous touch was a fat cigar he had clamped between his teeth. Tom was momentarily stunned into silence. The effect was too grotesque even to make him laugh.

'Well?' said Jimmy. 'Is burgundy not my colour?'

Tom found his voice from somewhere. 'That corset looks a little tight.'

'Tight? It's like a medieval torture. It's taken me half an hour just to get it on.'

There was another pause as Tom stepped to one side, appraising him. 'I didn't realise you'd be in, erm, full fig.'

'It's a drag ball, for God's sake.'

'Yes, I know – I just wasn't expecting Lady Bracknell.'

Jimmy raised his eyes heavenwards. 'I'm not that old!' He had been holding a fan, which he now opened and wafted about. 'Lady *Windermere*, if you please.'

'Sorry,' Tom said with a stiff bow. 'Well, m'lady, your carriage awaits, so let's get a bloody move on.'

But now Jimmy was frowning pointedly at him. 'I shouldn't wear that,' he said, gesturing at his necktie. Tom gave way to a disbelieving splutter of mirth.

'You're hardly one to talk on the matter of evening wear,' he said, looking Jimmy up and down. 'What's wrong with it anyway? It's just a tie.'

'No, it's a *red* tie, dear, and where we're going that could get you into quite a bit of bother.'

'What d'you mean?' he asked uncertainly.

'It carries connotations. Just as the Masons have their secret handshake, well, a red tie signals that you belong among a certain class of men – in short, you're a poof.'

'Are you joking?' said Tom, but Jimmy only shook his head and disappeared back into the bedroom. He returned moments later holding between his fingers a clubbable navy-and-silver-striped tie, indicating that Tom should take it.

'I'm not putting that on,' he protested.

'We're not leaving until you do.' He dangled the tie in front of him. With an exasperated snort Tom snatched it from his hand and stalked over to the mirror. 'That's the fellow,' Jimmy said approvingly. 'You'll thank me for it later.'

They had got as far as the entrance hall of Princess Louise Mansions when Jimmy, peering through the glassed front door, said, 'I don't see the motor.'

Tom explained that he'd parked on Bury Place, just round the corner, but Jimmy looked incredulous. 'You think I'm going to walk anywhere in this get-up?'

'It'll take two minutes.'

'Then off you go – I'll be waiting here. And put the hood up, it's colder than Keats's owl.'

Tom shot him a weary look. Muttering, he hurried off, while Jimmy checked his handiwork in the hall mirror. He turned his face one way, then the other, caught between admiring himself and a faintly appalled suspicion that he looked like a griffin. Well, he would have to brazen it out. Just then Alf, the mansion porter, sidled out of his office, and Jimmy froze. A notebook and pencil in his hand, Alf was preoccupied with some calculation or other. Only when he looked up did he notice Jimmy standing there. A momentary flicker of uncertainty danced in his eyes, before he said, 'Ah, glad I've caught you, Mr Erskine. Milkman asked me to pass this week's bill on. Shall I put it through the door or do you want to take it now?'

Jimmy, with a dreamlike sense of incongruity, smiled wanly and took the proffered note, croaking out his thanks. Outside, the car horn parped a summons. The porter, ever helpful, pulled open the hall door and ushered Jimmy through. As he descended the steps he heard, through his muddle of surprise and embarrassment, Alf's pleasantry: 'Enjoy your evening, sir.'

Settled in the passenger seat, Jimmy mused, 'Idea for next week's column: "In praise of the British working man's sangfroid."'

He continued to chatter and chunner as they drove north through Camden and Kentish Town, the closed shops and cafes giving way to residential streets whose trees huddled against the autumnal dark. The moon was hoisted high on a canopy of clouds. Once they reached the steep climb towards Highgate Tom asked Jimmy for directions to the house. It turned out to be a Pugin mansion just off the high street, clogged with gables and turrets. A couple in long ball gowns were just approaching the wide front door. Even at a distance Tom could tell from their heavy-footed gait that they were men. Jimmy, discarding the car blanket, stepped out of the Bentley. He thought briefly about leaving his cane, he didn't want to look doddery in this crowd. But good sense prevailed. He glanced at Tom as they crossed the road.

'You look rather pale. Not nerves, is it?'

'Just feeling a bit off. Why, should I be nervous?'

Jimmy laughed at his quailing tone. 'My advice – don't catch anyone's eye and keep your hand on your ha'penny.'

A bewigged footman admitted them, and they adjusted their eyes to the candlelit gloom of a pillared atrium, already boisterous with men in varying degrees of drag. Some, like Jimmy, had gone the whole Wilde way into dowager finery; some were dressed in more epicene costumes of velvet and silk. Certain others, ignoring the anniversary theme, had come as Restoration popinjays in white stockings, frock coats and tottering perukes. Arriving guests raised their hands on spotting friends across the room – an orchard of waving palms. Tom looked around at this peacock display, wondering if he oughtn't to have made more of an effort himself. He felt a bit of a spoilsport. But wait, here came a fellow in a jacket and tie – mufti was permitted after all. As he passed, Tom gave a shy half-smile in acknowledgement of their being drag-dodgers, but the man returned only a humourless appraising look that seemed to consider and reject Tom at the same moment.

At his side Jimmy was mobbed by a bevy of young queens whom Tom vaguely recognised from nights at the Café Royal and the Long Room at the Trocadero. They were loudly amused by Jimmy's costume for the occasion, cooing and gurning as if at a monkey in his cage. 'Ooh, hasn't she got a lovely figure?' 'Is that a hat you're wearing or a lampshade?' One of them, Jolyon, gave him a squeeze. 'Dunno how you got into that corset, James. You sure all is safely gathered in?' Jimmy allowed them to giggle and goggle their fill before enjoining one of them to fetch him a drink. 'And one for my guest here while you're at it,' he said, nodding at Tom, who clearly didn't interest any of them. They continued to cluster about Jimmy in an eager jostle, claiming and excluding at once.

Deciding to leave them to it, Tom ambled towards the main hall, and was immediately accosted by an arm around his shoulder. The man, tall and stately, was attired in a cream linen suit that echoed a famous photograph of Wilde from the early 1890s. His face, heavily made up, reminded him of dear old Peter Liddell. In fact . . .

'Peter – is it you?'

'Well, of course it's me, you silly ass,' Peter cried genially. 'The question is – what are *you* doing here?'

Tom nodded across the room at Jimmy. 'He couldn't really take the bus, dressed like that.'

'Jim hasn't taken a bus since about 1922, in drag or not.' Peter's expression was kindly but rueful. 'You've made a rod for your own back with that car.'

Tom only nodded, then smiled up at Peter. 'You're looking very dapper, I must say. Where did you come by the green carnation?'

'It's not nature's doing,' said Peter with a sly glance about the place. 'A florist I know supplied me. He just dipped it in dye.'

Tom felt less of an impostor with Peter standing by, though the room with its steady whirl of painted faces and disguises was unsettling; it had the air of a slightly sinister masque. It was a wonder to him how such a world operated, how indeed it could flourish under the threatening shadow of criminal prosecution. Everybody knew the risk involved just in being here, yet there seemed not the smallest hint of secrecy about the occasion.

'I suppose this place is quite . . . safe?'

Peter frowned in amusement. 'I shouldn't worry about being molested.'

'No, I don't mean that. I mean, is it safe from the *law*?'

'Oh yes. I remember a police raid a few years ago at a ball in Holland Park Avenue, but people are much more discreet now. The rozzers wouldn't know about an event like this, and even if they did, there are lookouts posted around.'

Just then two men in raffish pale suits like Peter's presented themselves. Both sported identical straw boaters, and red ties. The older one peered closely at Tom, as if to confirm something.

'Thought so!' he said, turning to his companion, who explained: 'Seems you're the only girl here without a bit of slap on.'

Peter leaned forward enquiringly. 'And who might you gentlemen be?'

The younger flashed his eyes humorously. 'Bosie – and Bosie. Double the fun, you might say. So who's your friend?' he said, nodding at Tom.

Tom was about to speak but Peter got in ahead of him. 'This is Mr Erskine's private secretary,' he said, with a warning touch of coldness, and threaded his arm through Tom's. 'We were just on our way upstairs for the music.' And in fact the dim strains of a piano could now be heard tinkling from above. As Peter escorted him away Tom overheard one Bosie mutter to the other, 'Is he naff then?'

Ascending the staircase Tom said, 'D'you know, Jim forbade me to wear a red tie this evening?'

Peter lifted his chin in acknowledgement. 'We're just trying to protect your innocence, my sweet.'

'Well, I'm very grateful to you,' replied Tom, who nonetheless thought he was quite capable of protecting himself. 'What's "naff", by the way?'

Peter snorted out a half-laugh, and shook his head. 'Not Available For Fucking. Ah, here's another bar. Thirsty?'

At the same moment, less than a mile away, Nina was emerging from Hampstead Tube station. She had managed to freshen her make-up before leaving the theatre, but noticed as the train rattled up the Northern Line (hellfire!)

she had a ladder in her stocking. Well, nothing to be done, and in fairness Mr Druce hadn't given her much notice. She turned down the high street and into Flask Walk, quiet at this hour, though the murmurous burble from behind the frosted windows of a pub seemed to offer a provisional welcome. The address was a house on Willow Road, which sloped steeply towards the Heath. The street lamps here were so dim and far apart you almost had to feel your way along. She watched her own shadow lengthen and slide away into the enveloping dark.

It said something about her that she was ready to trot up to Hampstead at the drop of a hat, just to meet some film producer. In truth, she wanted this as much for Stephen's sake as her own; he had introduced her to Ludo, after all, and it might cheer him up if she managed to wangle a part. His voice came to her now, the afternoon they had been at the Corner House and he'd told her that she was the loveliest woman he had ever met. The words were like a little keepsake she held close, something she could take out every now and then to think upon. As long as she had his love all her worries – about her career, her mother, her disinheritance – dissolved into nothing.

She wasn't concentrating and had missed the house. Retracing her steps she saw that the anonymous wooden door set into the brick wall was actually the front gate. She clicked the handle, and pushed through onto a narrow stone path leading up to a roomy but uncongenial-looking villa. It also looked deserted – there wasn't a light on in the place. The star-mottled navy sky made a forbidding silhouette of the building's pitched roof and chimney line. She mounted the steps up to the porch and pulled on the bell, hearing it sound in the hall. No answer came. Had she got the wrong house? Pressing her face to the window she tried to make out a sign of life within. It was so dark she could barely see a yard in front of her. Standing on the porch, irresolute, she took from her coat pocket a cigarette lighter by which to check the address she had scribbled down. No sooner was the tiny flame flickering in her hand than a door creaked somewhere below. A man's voice called up, quietly, 'Miss Land, is it?'

Nina, with a breathless giggle of fright, replied that it was, and stepped down from the porch in the direction of the voice. 'Erm, would you mind putting a light on?'

He evidently didn't hear this, for no illumination came. Going back down the steps she saw a tradesman's door now ajar, though he had not bothered to wait and greet her. She had heard that film types were brusque, but really . . . 'This way,' she heard him call, and passing through she saw he had entered the house by a side door. Less certain of herself, she followed his dim outline through a back parlour, wondering if this wasn't all a bit rum. He had been expecting her, but why arrange to meet in this gloomy old backwater? Ahead, another door had been opened, and here at last a weak amber flame glimmered through the dark. Entering, she found herself in a large drawing room whose windows seemed as black as the night outside. The light was coming from a tiny oil lamp on a table. Behind her the door shut softly and her host came up alongside her in an almost feline movement.

'Miss Land, thank you for coming,' he said. His face was still in shadow as he went round the table. 'I was going to say "pleased to meet you", but in fact we've already met.'

Nina smiled blindly towards his voice. Had they? 'I'm not sure I recall . . .' – and it was too dark to tell either way. For answer he turned up the lamp, revealing his face. She couldn't immediately place him, but yes, there was something familiar about the dark eyes, the long jaw.

'We weren't actually introduced,' he said in a dry ironic tone, and in that instant she knew – heard herself cry out in fear. Oh God, God, what had she done? She took a step back, and another, before turning and bolting for the door. Which was now locked. He remained at the table, watching her. 'So you do remember. Well, as I was saying, our last encounter at the Imperial was rather unsatisfactory. I fear I may have been uncivil – but you had intruded on me and . . . my companion.'

Nina felt her knees tremble as she stood there. Through short, shallow breaths she said faintly, 'I've never seen you in my life.'

He sighed. 'We both know that's not true, Miss Land. Though it was lucky that your description of me to the police was – inaccurate? Now, come away from that door.' His tone was quietly reasonable.

Nina, her whole body shaking, took a couple of steps forward. He was staring at her, his head as still as a cobra's, measuring, evaluating. 'That's it, a little closer. I suppose you're anticipating some "extravagant" behaviour on my part, but you mustn't. You see, I just want some information – about the girl. Madeleine. I think you might be able to tell me.'

She shook her head, and felt tears blinding her eyes. How had this happened? Was her own imprudent behaviour to blame, or mere bad luck? He was talking again but she wasn't listening, she was just crying, silently, at the sudden prospect of her life being snuffed out – a life she had always imagined as so hard to let go of. *Oh, Stephen, what have I done?* She needed a handkerchief, it was difficult even to see, and she unclasped her handbag in search of it. As she looked inside she caught a glint of something unfamiliar. The letter knife. From Stephen. She must compose herself, order her thoughts. She had something he didn't know about, something to defend herself with.

He was standing by the table, behind him was a drinks trolley. Her mind raced ahead.

She took a deep breath, and said softly, 'May I have a drink?'

He stared at her a moment, following her eyeline to the grouping of bottles. He seemed faintly amused by the request, but he took up a bottle and said, 'Scotch all right?'

She nodded, and while he was half turned she soundlessly lifted the knife from her handbag and slipped it into her coat pocket. She kept her eyes on him, pouring the whisky, recapping the bottle, picking up the glass. He was coming round the table with it towards her. The handbag she had set down at her feet; the weapon she concealed against her sleeve, ready. He was five paces away from her now, four, three – he was holding out the glass in his right hand, leaving his left side unguarded. In one quicksilver move the knife was out and plunged into the hollow between his collarbone and neck. It went in deep, more than halfway down the blade, and in her fright – at that, and his savage bellow of pain – she left it there and made for the opposite door. This too was locked. She doubled back, and saw him staggering against the desk, blood spurting down his shirt front. He was trying to extract the knife, and she wished she had kept hold of it, another stab would have done for him. Too late.

There was the window, the one exit still left to her. She dashed to it and released the catch, pushing it open. She felt the cold on her face, and prepared to scream for help. But who in this black night would hear her? Her heart was drumming so fast she felt it might burst from her. Quick, quick. The windowsill was waist high, and she began to hoist herself onto it when she felt an arm strong as whipcord around her neck, dragging her down. But he had misjudged her agility, and pushing both feet against the sill she managed to topple them both onto the floor with a crash. Rolling off him she crawled across the floor towards the knife, its blade a dull gleam on the carpet. She had it in her hand, was raising herself to her knees when something heavy and square struck her hard on the head, and she fell, eyes blinking a starburst. She tried to raise herself again, but the next blow came harder still, and then there was only blackness.

Tom was on to his second gin and pep when Peter gave him a nudge. 'Guess who's here.' An extraordinary-looking person, dressed in Wildean cape and knee-britches, was sashaying towards them. A huge fedora shadowed the face, a cigarette wafting in an ivory holder.

'Hullo, boys!' a woman's voice drawled. It took him a moment to realise it was Edie Greenlaw.

'Edie, what an amazing outfit,' Tom said. 'May I touch the hem of your cape?'

Peter was gazing narrowly at her. 'My dear, you look almost like a man.'

'So do you – almost,' she fired back, and they guffawed. 'I suppose Jimmy's somewhere about?'

Tom nodded. 'You must have passed him – he's Lady Windermere to the life.'

'Actually, with that cigar he looks more Churchill's ugly sister,' said Peter.

'There's some queen really giving you the eye,' she said, looking over Tom's shoulder. It was one of the boatered Bosies they had encountered downstairs.

'Hmm, we've met,' said Peter tartly. 'He doesn't know that Tom's not TBH.'

Tom frowned. 'Pardon me?'

'To Be Had, darling,' Edie supplied. 'I don't suppose I'll be getting much in that line myself, what with the place being *abloom* with pansies.'

'Well, at least we have each other,' said Peter, and Edie, scrunching her face into a smile, rested her head on his shoulder.

'Peter's agreed to marry me if I'm still single at fifty,' she explained to Tom. 'Isn't he a dear?'

'That would be quite some wedding,' said Tom, his tone so oddly sincere that it made them both snigger.

'I'm not sure I'd wish it on him. Having to cope with Greenlaws *and* in-laws . . .' She looked at Tom. 'Talking of marriage, how are you getting on with Jimmy these days?'

'He's run off his feet,' Peter cut in. 'Literally. He's now the chauffeur as well.'

'Yes, I'd heard he'd got a car. Poor Tom! You do look a bit worn out. Is everything all right?'

Before he could reply an excited ripple of *ooh*s came from the French windows, where a lively cluster of guests had pressed onto the balcony. Sharing a puzzled look, the three of them wandered out to see what the fuss was. The view, offering a lofty perspective south over the city, was dominated by an incandescent ball of flame some miles away, as bright as a volcano on the boil. It seemed to leap and billow creamily against the dark horizon. Nobody could say for sure what it might be, though it was someone's opinion that a factory had been set on fire. Peter shook his head.

'I don't think there's any factory that would go up like that.'

The opiner came back, 'What about a munitions factory?'

'We'd hear it if there were munitions.'

Tom, transfixed by the sight, thought of Madeleine describing her dream, the one about London drowning in flames and people's heads melting like candles. It was strange, the matter-of-fact way she had told them about it, almost as if she had seen this apocalypse rather than dreamed it. A few more were crowding onto the balcony, seeking a glimpse of the fiery orb in the distance.

Feeling queasy again, Tom slipped away in search of a lavatory. Downstairs the ball was in full swing, and he had to navigate his way through a crush of men in taffeta and bombazine, in huge curled wigs or wide-brimmed hats, all chatting and chaffing in voices that strove and lifted in an oppressive roar to the ceiling. Having gained the privacy of a poky old lav, he started back on seeing his reflection in the mirror. His dark forelock hung limp over his pale, pale brow, moist with tiny pinpricks of sweat. The whites of his eyes looked sickly, as if he hadn't slept in days. He really wasn't very well, but of course he couldn't go until Jimmy was ready to.

Returning to the fray, he asked one of the barmen for another gin. As he waited a hand felt his bum, and there stood his new admirer, the younger and blonder of the two Bosies. He sniggered (Tom had jumped) and tilted his head pertly.

'You all right, girl?'

'Yes, thank you,' replied Tom, not sure if this was a greeting or a question. He was trying to remember Peter's acronym for availability – HB something?

'I've been wondering about you,' Bosie continued. 'I said to her, vada di omi-oh bona omi. You know?'

'Er, not really. What language is that?'

The youth studied him for a moment, as if trying to decide whether this profession of ignorance was sincere. Then he smiled in an indulgent way and said, 'Don't mind me. I thought you were Jimmy Erskine's catamite.'

'Just his secretary, as I think my friend told you.'

'Wanted to make sure.' His voice had come down an octave to something less camp. 'I see Jimmy around. He's got quite a taste for the Guards, hasn't he?'

Tom shrugged. 'What he does in private is none of my business.'

But Bosie went on as though he hadn't heard. 'We all know him as Barrack Room Bertha. Likes a bit of trouble, does Jimmy.' His expression had turned crafty. 'Just between us girls, d'you know where he trades? I mean, the club?'

*Trades?* thought Tom, wishing the fellow would leave him alone. 'No, I'm afraid not. That's why it's called a private life.'

'You see, I've some friends who also like a bit of rough. If you could give me a name, just on the sly, I could it make worth your while.'

It was clear that, despite Tom's stonewalling, the man would keep badgering him for information. His interest seemed to Tom more than social; in that odd change of voice and his veiled offer of money he detected something calculating – professional, almost.

He gave Bosie a tight smile of regret. 'I'm sorry, would you excuse me? I did promise to get a drink for my friend.'

He sensed the man still watching him as he walked away. Upstairs they were roaring through a music-hall song he knew well. It was one Jimmy used to play over and over on the gramophone at Princess Louise Mansions.

> By the sad sea waves, every night he took her strolling,
> By the sad sea waves, he would swear his heart was gone;
> She's the only girl he sings to, she's the girl he says nice
> things to,
> Promised lovely diamond rings to, by the sad sea waves.

The party had now spilled out onto the sloping front lawn, it being the best vantage from which to gaze on the molten spectacle glowering from the south. People stood about mesmerised, their drinking and gossiping temporarily put on hold while their eyes absorbed this indecipherable bonfire. He overheard someone saying he had not seen anything like it 'since Mafeking night'. Tom shivered as he stood among them, and remembered he had left his overcoat in the car. On his way across the lawn he heard Edie calling him.

'Have you heard? Just announced it on the wireless – that thing up in blazes is the Crystal Palace!'

'Good God,' said Tom, turning back to stare again. 'Think of all that glass. Maybe that's why it looks so bright.'

'Apparently they'd just had it renovated, too. Shame! Where are you off to?'

'To get my coat. I'm shivering like a greyhound.'

He descended the garden steps to the road, all but deserted at this hour, and broke into a little scurrying run to get to the car. He climbed in and shut the door, squirming into his coat. Good, he'd brought his gloves too. Crikey, it was chilly – he could see his breath – but the solemn stillness was calming, and he thought he might linger for a while. He heard an owl's lonely hoot, and hunkered down against the clammy cold of the leather seat.

He jumped as a figure ghosted right by his window. Bosie, again. Had he followed him outside? No, he had walked right past the car without spotting him. Tom sank lower into the seat, spying through his rear-view mirror the young man's purposeful stride. What was he up to? A few yards further down the street he saw the dull lantern glimmer of a public telephone box: Bosie had stopped, looked around a moment, and entered. Tom could see him through the glass, the receiver against his ear, then (a nod, a movement of his mouth) that he was talking to someone. Thirty seconds later, his call done, he cradled the receiver and stepped out of the box. With a quick glance at his wristwatch, he strolled back up the pavement towards the house. Tom, nearly horizontal in the front seat, held his breath as the youth came alongside the car. Had he glanced

330

to his left the jig was up, but he did not, and Tom's presence went unnoticed.

Hurrying back across the garden, Tom tried to sort out his misgivings about what he had just seen. Of course anyone could make a telephone call, it would not have been noteworthy in ordinary circumstances. But these circumstances were not ordinary, he felt, not with a houseful of men dragged up and reckless with drink. There was something furtive in the man's behaviour that had unsettled him. Re-entering the house he went upstairs in search of Jimmy. Surely a portly old gent in an evening gown wouldn't be hard to spot . . . and indeed there he was, in his element, plumped on a small sofa with a couple of young men perched on either wing. His make-up had smudged around the eyes, otherwise he looked quite in command of himself.

'Jim, may I have a word?'

Squinting through a cloud of cigar smoke, Jimmy patted the seat next to him companionably, but Tom demurred: this had to be *entre eux*. With a little sigh Jimmy heaved himself upright, cane in hand, and followed Tom into the music room. The noise there wouldn't suit a conversation either, so they found a smaller room at the front of the house, empty but for a smooching couple who ignored them. Jimmy, wheezing from the exertion, settled himself on a window seat and relit his cigar.

'D'you hear what they were playing before?'

Tom nodded. 'Hadn't heard it in a while.'

Jimmy tipped his head to one side, and sang:

*From the sad sea waves back to bus'ness in the morning,*
*From the sad sea waves to his humble 'five-a-week';*
*In a cookshop he goes dashing, who should bring his plate*
   *of hash in,*
*But the girl he had been mashin' by the sad sea waves.*

'You know I saw Vesta Tilley sing it – I must have told you. My God, the charm of the thing, Tom! Call it heresy but I'd take that over any aria at Covent Garden.' He blinked, and focused. 'So, what's this about?'

'Have you seen a couple of foppish types in straw boaters – sort of homage to Bosie?'

'They have been noted. Why?'

'I've just had a very odd encounter. One of them seemed to know a lot about you –'

'Hmm, he's probably got a play he wants me to read.'

'No, nothing like that. His interest was in your *after*-hours. Said you were known as Barrack Room Bertha.'

Jimmy sniffed. 'Hardly original.'

'He wanted a name – was ready to pay for it, too.'

'I trust you didn't . . .'

'Of course not! I'm just wondering if he's on to you – he might be a blackmailer. I mean, imagine a snapper catching you here, the photograph that would land on Lord Swaim's desk.'

Jimmy didn't care to entertain that idea. 'How can you be sure?'

'I can't. It's guesswork. But I did see him making a telephone call outside.' As he said this he went over to the window overlooking the road. A car, caught in the narrow cone of light from a street lamp, had stopped round the corner from the house. Then another car pulled up behind it, and cut its engine. They seemed to be waiting for something, perhaps to collect a guest. The door of the first car opened, and a man in uniform stepped out. But it wasn't a chauffeur's uniform –

'Tom? What's wrong?'

Jimmy, still seated, had been watching him at the window. The twitch he had first noticed in Tom's shoulders had now passed through his frame, shaking it violently, as if poked by an electric rod. Was he drunk? He called to him again, but Tom gave no sign of having heard. Then he collapsed on the floor, his limbs jerking like a clockwork toy. His eyes had rolled up into his head. Jimmy looked around to appeal for help, but the smooching couple were gone. He stared aghast at Tom's face, off-white and in spasm – it looked like an epileptic seizure. There was a procedure to alleviating a victim, he knew, he'd done a first-aid course in the service . . . The danger was in swallowing the tongue. He had bent down, awkwardly, to loosen Tom's tie when a shout came from below.

'Everyone out! The police!'

Jimmy went to the window, and saw what Tom had seen coming up the drive: a file of uniformed constables, and, at their side, the young man got up as Bosie. *Oh Jesus.* A raid! He dashed to the door and stopped, with a piteous backward glance at Tom on the carpet, then hurried off. *Save yourself, save yourself*, was his thought as he clattered down the staircase. The hall had become a scene of panicked flight, like the moment someone shouted 'Fire' in a theatre. Men encumbered by their unfamiliar garb broke into a shuffle-run of comical inelegance, though far from comical to Jimmy, already gasping with the effort of haste. In the rush for the back exit a table toppled over and glasses hit the floor with an exuberant crash.

He bolted onto the terrace and saw Peter rising languidly from his chair, as if this chaotic exodus were a regular farce.

'Peter, thank God! Tom's upstairs having a – a fit! I didn't know what to do.' Though even in his panic he knew what he shouldn't have done.

'Calm down. What sort of fit?'

'You know, what do they call it? – a seizure!'

Peter, his eyes widening, said, 'And you've left him there?'

'I can't be here,' Jimmy wailed with an imploring look. 'If I'm arrested it's the end of me.'

But Peter, shaking his head, was already on his way into the house. Jimmy, hoicking up his skirts, plunged onwards through the back garden, hearing only his quick wheezing breaths and the distant shriek of a police whistle.

# 19

'An iceberg on fire' was how one newspaper described the burning of the Crystal Palace. It transpired that heating pipes below the floorboards and years of accumulated dust had turned the place to tinder; 20,000 wooden chairs stored beneath the orchestra pit had provided extra kindling. How it had started was still a matter of doubt, though an electric short circuit was suspected. The fire had raged through the night, flames leaping as high as five hundred feet, so they said, and crowds flocked from all over to watch it. Private planes were chartered from Croydon airport for a bird's-eye view of the gigantic inferno, and the roads of south London were soon choked with cars bearing sightseers towards the spot. It took the fire services until dawn to bring the conflagration under control. All that remained of the magnificent edifice – designed by Joseph Paxton for the Great Exhibition of 1851 – was a mass of debris, fused glass and ashes, and the blackened skeleton of its steel frame. Photographs published over the following days were evocative of a bomb site.

The suddenness of its destruction stunned the public. The translucent glass palace, visible for miles around, had seemed as immovable a fixture of the landscape as the Pyramids. Despite its fragile appearance it had become a part of the national consciousness, home to countless exhibitions, concerts, meetings, performances, motor shows and flower shows, even a circus. Now, where once had stood a majestic symbol of Victorian enterprise and engineering, a terrible vacancy yawned. With it seemed to pass something of the Victorian age itself. There had been a grand scheme afoot to hold a celebration there in honour of Edward VIII's coronation.

Neither event would happen. The dust had not yet settled on the smoking ruins of the Palace when news of the royal crisis burst forth. It had been threatened for months but hitherto kept secret from most of the British public. A year that had begun with the death of one king was about to end with the abdication of another. The newspapers, pent up for so long, now flooded their pages with the tragedy of Edward and Mrs Simpson. Bishops and ministers were suddenly centre stage in the drama, enacted each day in columns of unarguable black and white. People queued at newsvendors' stalls – The King in love with an American, twice divorced! – hardly able to digest it all yet greedy for more. Some wondered whether the great institution of the monarchy would survive.

In the wake of this convulsion other news struggled to gain purchase. Interest in the case of fraudster and ex-Mosleyite Gerald Carmody vanished overnight, and nothing more was made of his unfortunate gull, the painter Stephen Wyley.

An item in the *Daily Mail* reported a raid on a house in Highgate, where men in evening gowns and make-up were engaged in 'scenes of unspeakable vice and depravity'. The police were tipped off thanks to the sacrifice of a fellow officer who, masquerading as a partygoer, had infiltrated the event. Forty-five arrests were made.

In the same edition was a brief paragraph detailing the discovery of a woman's body on Hampstead Heath. Death had been caused by traumatic blows to the head. The victim's relatives had been informed.

Madeleine, seated alone, stared at the backs of the mourners ranged along the pews. It was a Catholic service, and many of them seemed unsure when to stand or to kneel. The church was decorated for Advent, with a crib stationed at the foot of the altar, next to the coffin. From the front pew came the steady, piteous whimpering of a woman she assumed to be the mother. Her gaze fell on the printed order of service, and the barely conceivable name on its cover.

NINA JANE LAND † 1904–1936 †

The hymns – 'Dear Lord and Father of Mankind', 'Sweet Sacrament Divine', 'The King of Love My Shepherd Is' – spirited her back to the convent. As she sang the last she felt an ache in her throat, and wondered why she had come to the funeral of a woman she barely knew. It was only by chance that she had even heard of her death. She had been on a tram in Kingsway when she happened to glance at someone's open newspaper and an item headed ACTRESS FOUND SLAIN had leapt out at her. The strange thing was that, even before she began reading it, she had known with a terrible certainty it was Nina. A few seconds later the man whose paper it was had got up and alighted from the tram, and so she'd had to wait until her stop to jump down and run along the street in search of a newspaper vendor. She had frantically riffled through the pages, like a parrot diving into its feathers, until she'd found the story, and read it with a galloping heart.

Her eyes had slid rapidly, distractedly, over the salient phrases: *shock and bafflement . . . senseless and brutal murder . . . a stage actress of renown . . .* The police said there was no indication that the victim had known her killer, though they were investigating the possibility that her body had been dumped on the Heath sometime after she was murdered. There had been no mention of tiepins or strangulation, but the horrific intuition worming inside her brain had not been quelled: the man from room 408 had somehow found his way to Nina. She had felt something rise in her gorge and had to hold herself very still before it passed.

A lady, stately in hat and veil, stepped up to the pulpit and read a poem that began 'Fear no more the heat o' the sun'. At the end she explained, in a voice of quiet resignation, that this was her sister's favourite passage from Shakespeare. Madeleine saw her dab her eyes as she returned to the front pew, and felt a sudden stirring of loss. The priest in his even manner continued the obsequies, though she didn't take in any of it until the organ played, as a recessional, the adagio from the *Sonata Pathétique*. She kept her gaze averted as they slow-marched the coffin back down the aisle. The front pews emptied and people shuffled out, looking stiffly ahead, like sleepwalkers.

Outside the sky was the colour of damp flour, and the December cold pierced to the bone. The funeral cortège was waiting to set off. The mourners, she realised, fell into two distinct categories. One was the stricken gathering of Nina's relatives, at a loss, with her mewling mother at its centre. The other was a gravely flamboyant company of West End folk, trying to keep their voices to a decorous volume but now and then betraying themselves with loud exclamations of sympathy or grief. Madeleine wished she had slipped off before the end, instead of being the only person there who didn't know anyone. As the hearse pulled away she obeyed an instinct to cross herself, and she started up the drive.

She had not gone very far when she heard footsteps hurrying behind her, and turned to find a man whose face she thought familiar. He was wearing a black armband on his overcoat. His face looked drawn, and almost bruised about his eyes.

'Um, Madeleine, isn't it? I'm sorry, I don't know your – I'm Stephen Wyley. We once met.'

Now she knew him. The artist. 'Yes, I remember. How are you?' It didn't sound like the right thing to say, but she was stumped for anything else.

'Oh . . . you know,' he said, with a vague little wave back at the church. 'I'm finding it rather difficult to – it feels like some hideous dream I'm going to wake up from.' He stared off into the distance.

Madeleine sensed the tiredness in his voice, in the twitch of his eye. With some feelings it was impossible to demonstrate, or even, really, to fathom. She said haltingly, 'We hardly knew each other, and yet – for all that, I remember thinking how much I liked her. And it's awful to know that the one thing I should have said to her I never did.'

'What was that?'

She shook her head, as if she still couldn't believe it. 'I should have – *thanked* her. For what she did. For saving my life.' And she knew at that moment why it had mattered so much that she should come to this funeral.

Stephen, sunk deep in his own misery, said, 'You're right. It's always the things we mean to say . . .' He looked up, and focused. 'Are you going on to – ?'

'Oh, no. I honestly don't know a soul here.'

'Nor I . . .' He shrugged, looking lost, and by unspoken consent they fell into step up the drive. The temperature made frozen plumes of their breath. It was the right sort of day for a funeral, she thought; warmth, sunshine, birdsong would have been a wretched intrusion. Once they were on the street she prepared her expression for a parting of the ways. She had imagined that he would hurry off, their

339

mutual commiseration done, but instead he halted of a sudden and looked at her.

'Listen, I don't think I can face – *anyone* – would it be too much to ask if you'd have a cup of tea with me?'

Madeleine studied his face for a moment. He looked utterly desolate. 'Are you sure?'

His smile was almost a wince. 'I'd really appreciate the company. My car's just over here.'

They drove around the streets of Westbourne Park and thence aimlessly through Notting Hill, neither of them speaking. Madeleine didn't mind, used to being a silent passenger in the cars of strange men. She heard Stephen muttering to himself now and then, and chose not to intrude. Company was what he'd asked for, not conversation: she felt the difference to be significant.

Eventually he said, 'I thought maybe a cafe, but . . .' His voice dropped to a forlorn undertone. 'If I knew where to go, I'd go there.'

She thought for a moment, and said, 'Do you have an office?'

'I have a studio. Would that do?'

She nodded, and he drove on south towards the river. Now that a decision had been made he seemed to brighten a little, and he talked about his father, who was about to move out of London to Sussex. For the last few weeks he had been sorting through family things – albums, furniture, 'a lot of old junk' – he hadn't looked at in twenty-five years or more. His mother had kept some of the very first drawings he had done as a boy, just pictures of birds and trees and people riding bicycles. Madeleine asked him whether he had always known he was going to be an artist. Not at all, he replied, and if she had seen any of those efforts by his young hand 'you'd have been surprised how I ever became one'. She laughed at that, and for the first time in many weeks Stephen laughed too.

At Tite Street the studio was in disarray. Loaded ashtrays, smeared wine glasses, newspapers and magazines thrown in heaps, a couch with rumpled bedclothes, the grate unswept, windows so grimy you could barely see out of them. Stephen, noticing her expression, apologised for the neglect.

'The housekeeper hasn't been in for a while, so I've rather let things go.' He went into the kitchen, and returned moments later. 'It gets worse. I've neither tea nor milk. Would you mind waiting half a sec while I nip out?'

Once he had gone she went around the room collecting the dirty dishes and glasses, she shook out the bedclothes and folded them, she opened a sash to admit some fresh air. The papers she gathered up and deposited in a wicker basket next to the fireplace. She decided not to touch anything to do with his work – the half-squeezed tubes of paint, the brushes marinating in cloudy water – lest she upset some mysterious arrangement known only to him. She was washing up at the kitchen sink when Stephen returned; he looked sheepishly about at the evidence of her tidying hand.

'Here, I'll make some tea –'

'No, let me,' said Madeleine. 'I've put the kettle on – you go and sit down.'

Feeling useless, and grateful, he wandered into the main room, chilled from the open window. He knelt at the grate – at least there were coals left – and began to lay a fire. Cinders, ashes, dust. He was still unsure of how he had held himself upright during the funeral, when just to hear her name made him nearly faint with grief. The last two weeks had passed in a kind of waking nightmare, starting on the anxious Monday evening when she didn't show up for dinner. He knew no friends of hers he might call, so cautious had they been in their time together; he used to joke that they were more like secret agents than lovers. He telephoned her landlady, once, twice, and then stopped himself a third time for fear of provoking suspicion.

It was Ludo Talman who had broken the news to him. He had been at home, in his study, when the telephone rang and he had heard Ludo's voice, untypically stilted, as if he were reciting from a cue card. Nina had been found early on Tuesday morning by someone out walking on the Heath. She was fully clothed, but her coat and blouse bore traces of blood from her head wounds. The body must have been left in haste, because the police had found tokens of identification. In her coat pocket had been a business card with Ludo's name and telephone number. Stephen had heard him say 'I'm terribly sorry, old man'; the rest of the conversation he couldn't remember at all. His brain had been benumbed, and his tongue had gone silent in his head. When Ludo had rung off, Stephen had been sitting at his desk. Two hours had passed before he shook off his paralysis and managed to stand up. He'd realised that he was bleeding from a cut on his forehead, where he had been banging it slowly, continuously, against the edge of the desk.

Behind him he heard Madeleine enter the room and set down the tea tray. The fire had begun to catch, and he still knelt before it, shivering.

'I just opened this to air the place,' she said, closing the window with a bump. 'Now it's freezing!'

Stephen heard the consoling note of cheer in her voice, and felt a warning prickle behind his eyes. He wasn't sure how much kindness he could stand. 'I'm sorry to have battened on you like this. When I saw you at the church I realised you were one of the few people who had ever seen us together. I'm afraid Nina and I, we couldn't – we weren't . . .'

'I know,' she said. 'We met again, a few weeks ago, in her dressing room. I realised I'd got it wrong about your drawing of – of him. She said she would go back and explain to the police.'

Stephen nodded. 'They weren't impressed. I think by that stage it was too late. You know, from the very beginning she didn't want to get involved. She had a feeling about it. But I persuaded her.' Head bowed, he dragged himself up from the fireplace to pour the tea. In the silence that intervened they both sensed the question they had been avoiding.

Madeleine was first to grasp the nettle. 'Do you think it might have been him?'

He saw the fear in her gaze. 'It made me wonder. I don't know. It wasn't his usual method, and there was no –' He touched his tie with his fingertips. 'But I don't understand how he could have found her. Can you?'

She shook her head. 'Unless . . . unless he saw her onstage, as I did.'

'Even then he might not have recognised her. She said the room was nearly dark when she went in, and they were face to face for a matter of seconds before he ordered her out.'

'So it may not have been him at all,' she said, though she felt no assurance. This man was not the sort to let things lie – the fate of poor Alice had proven that much. If he had killed Nina, then that left her as the only one who could identify him. This would be her life, looking down darkened streets, wondering if he was out there, waiting.

No, not wondering. Knowing.

Stephen was looking around the room, bemused. 'So nice of you to tidy the place. I'm afraid Mrs Ronson doesn't get about so well any more – I need to hire someone.'

Madeleine considered this. 'Well, if you're looking, I could do it.'

He gaped at her. 'You? I thought you were –' He stopped on the brink, and reversed. 'Um, already employed.'

A ghost of a smile twitched her mouth. 'I quit the Elysian

343

a few weeks ago. I work at a pub in Camden now, do a bit of char work too.'

'Good Lord. That would be –' It wasn't clear to him if she had rehabilitated herself or not. She was a strange girl, really, rather an unworldly sort – not someone you'd peg for a habitué of the streets. 'Are you sure?'

To Madeleine's ears it sounded like a question he might have asked of himself, but she only said, 'If there's a job here, yes.'

He felt himself nodding and smiling rather stupidly. 'Well, then . . . I'm jolly glad I asked you here for tea. Shall we talk about when you can start?'

From his window Tom watched the two pigeons clucking at each other on top of the tree. They seemed to be conducting an argument via minute jerks of the head. He could see a flimsy-looking nest, over which the pair were at present standing guard. It was puzzling how they devised their timetable: did they take turns over the night shift, or did one just order the other about? Sometimes both of them disappeared at once, presumably to forage for food. But then who would be there to protect the home from – from what? A rook, perhaps; didn't rooks nest in tall trees? He wished he wasn't such an ignoramus about nature.

'Oi, you, get back into bed or I'm calling matron!'

He looked round to find Edie grinning on the threshold. Visiting hour, at last! This was his tenth day in hospital and he was almost out of his mind with boredom.

'Edie, you're a sight for sore eyes,' he said, walking into her embrace.

'How are you, darling? I mean, *really* how are you?'

'Oh, I'm fine. They're keeping me in here for tests, but I haven't had a seizure in a week. I just need to be quite careful.'

Edie cast an amused eye about his room. 'Look at this place – more flowers than Sarah Bernhardt's on a first night.'

'People have been so kind,' he admitted with an embarrassed smile.

'Well, I've brought you improving literature instead.' She dipped into her handbag and produced a book adorned with a Foyle's promotional band.

'Goodness, thank you. Not *More Poems* . . .' His expression was wry. 'Housman. One of Jimmy's favourites.'

'Didn't he go to the funeral?'

'No. Kipling's – and cried his eyes out. So how is the old reprobate?'

Edie returned a rueful look. 'I think you can imagine. Ashamed, guilty – of course – with just a hint of defiance. He insists he had no choice but to flee, never mind abandoning *you* to danger.'

Tom shrugged. 'You know Jimmy . . .'

'He said to me, "Have you noticed on my face that strange beauty which the poets tell us is the result of profound spiritual torment?" I said, "No, dear."'

They both laughed, though Tom was aware of how close a call it had been that night. Death – 'the distinguished thing', Henry James had called it. Maybe it was. But dying wasn't. Dying felt dismal. Had it not been for Peter Liddell's quick-witted intervention he would almost certainly have choked on his tongue. Lucky for him there really *was* a doctor in the house. In reward for this heroic act the police arrested Peter straight afterwards, along with forty-four other partygoers.

'I just don't understand how none of us knew – about your *thing*. Why did you keep it from everyone?'

Tom sighed. 'I don't know. I didn't want the illness to define me – you know, "Poor Tom, the epileptic." People would have treated me differently once they found out, so I decided they mustn't.' He considered for a moment. 'Well, not all people. I did know someone who was wonderful about it. And once or twice I thought of telling Peter.'

'Well, *of course*,' said Edie. They looked at each other.

'I heard about the sentence,' said Tom.

Edie shook her head. 'Another reason for Jimmy to feel guilty. He's scot-free, and Peter gets six months in Pentonville. You know he's also been suspended from practising?'

'*No*,' said Tom with a groan. 'How can they persecute someone just for wearing make-up at a party? It's iniquitous.'

'I know. And that boy you thought was trying to blackmail Jimmy turns out to be a police constable. Soliciting men so he could arrest them!'

'Peter . . . How's he bearing up?'

'I had a letter from him yesterday. Typically droll. He remarked on the strange nature of British justice – prosecuting a man on the grounds of his preference for other men, then confining him in a place where other men are his exclusive company for months on end.'

'As soon as I'm out of here I'm going to visit him,' said Tom, suddenly rather tearful. He pinched the bridge of his nose. 'He's a prince, Edie.'

'I know he is, darling . . . Now don't start or you'll have me going.'

He pulled his dressing gown tight around himself and cracked open a window. 'Here, let's have a cigarette.'

They sat by the window ledge and smoked, and Tom pointed out his near neighbours, the pair of bickering pigeons. Edie gave a half-laugh.

'Something else Peter joked about in his letter. Now that he's a jailbird he says he's willing to release me from our ten-year engagement. I wrote back and said *Not on your life*!'

Tom smiled. 'You'll have found someone before then, I'm sure of it. Some feller will sweep you off your feet.'

'I don't know,' she said, and a shadow of pain darkened

her face. 'I haven't been able to stop thinking about Nina. The police reckon there was a man in the background that none of her friends knew about – he may have been the one who did her in. An absolute sweetheart, she was. You met her, didn't you?'

Tom nodded. He could hardly comprehend the horror of it himself, and he hadn't even known her. It was only a matter of days since he had driven Nina home from L'Etoile and they had talked about Madeleine. For some reason he kept thinking about the cigarette she had casually lit for him as she sat there, passing it from her mouth to his. It was the odd intimacy of it that stuck, those lips with the breath of life on them – now emptied of it, forever.

'. . . hard to take in, isn't it?' Edie was saying. 'I mean, it's frightening the way it arrived out of nowhere. One minute this woman you've known for years is there, the next –'

Tom was still thinking of what they'd discussed in the car that day. Nina had expressed some anxiety about her next job, and whether there might even *be* a next job. And now, all the striving, the worrying, gone off in smoke. For all he knew they might have become friends. It was too sad for words.

They had another delinquent cigarette while they did *The Times* crossword together, before Edie had to go. She asked him if there was anything he needed.

'Just your constant and unwavering devotion,' said Tom. 'Oh, and some writing paper. I suppose Peter's address is –'

'HMP Pentonville. That should get to him.'

'One other thing, Edie. I really don't want Jimmy showing up here.'

Edie nodded. 'Don't worry, darling, I'll make sure. But after what's happened I don't think he would dare.'

*   *   *

Stephen was waiting in the foyer of Marlborough Studios, off York Road, when Ludo Talman came out to greet him. Ludo hadn't been at the funeral, but he had sent his bereaved friend a letter of condolence, the single one Stephen had received, for almost nobody knew how things stood between himself and Nina. And now they never would. In the letter Ludo had asked him to call at the studio so he could give him lunch.

'There's something I have to show to you first,' said Ludo, conducting him along a corridor and into a private screening room. 'Do sit down.'

Stephen sank into one of the plush cherry-red seats, wondering what to expect. One of Ludo's army of assistants brought in a pot of coffee and asked him if he required a projectionist. He shook his head and the young woman withdrew, leaving them alone. He went to the projection desk and picked up a round metal tin, which he held up for Stephen to see.

'This is a very short film one of our chaps made of Nina. It's not her screen test – that's in the vault – just a reel the cameraman shot to check the light.' He opened the tin to show him. 'Would you like to see it?'

'Yes. I think I would.' But he felt alarmed at the sudden prospect of Nina's face before him; film was a way the dead returned to us. Ludo had flicked off the lights. From behind came a click, and then the purring sprockety whirr of the reel going round. The white projection screen suddenly bloomed into life, a little stutter of numbers, abstracted shapes – and straight into a close-up of Nina, serious at first, even nervous, he could tell from the quick blinking of her eyes. A cut to another close-up, a slightly different angle, and now she was more at ease, laughing at something just off-camera. There was no sound, of course, but she was talking, animatedly, and he could read her lips repeating a phrase – 'The same thing nearly happened to me!' A smile,

348

and a vigorous nod. Another cut to her, now in mid-shot, striking a few silly poses and again convulsing in laughter. (Stephen felt an ache start up behind his throat – he would never hear that laugh again.) There was a pause; in the next shot her hair was up in a chignon, a 'stage' look, more austere than with it down. She was staring directly at the camera now, face-on, a little smile at some remark off-screen. Then, with decision, her face leaned right into the lens and she blew a kiss.

Another stutter, a white-out, and the whirring stopped. The film had lasted barely three minutes.

Ludo paused for a few moments before he walked round to turn the lights back on. His face was tense with uncertainty as he lowered himself into the seat next to Stephen.

'Are you all right?'

Stephen nodded, sombre, but dry-eyed. 'She looks so beautiful,' he said wonderingly. 'How could someone – ?' He found himself shrinking away from the question. He wanted to think she hadn't suffered, that death had come abruptly, without her knowing. The alternative was more than he could bear to contemplate. Ludo had placed the tin on the armrest between them.

'I wonder if you'd like to have it,' he said. 'It's not much, but . . .'

Stephen stared at it for a moment, his hand caressing its curved metal edge. He smiled sadly, and murmured his thanks.

As they returned down the corridor, he decided to mention something that had nagged away from the police report. 'You heard about the message she was supposed to have picked up at the theatre, on the evening she was murdered? The stage manager of the Strand said it came from this studio.'

'Hmm, I did, and it's pretty mysterious – because nobody here has any knowledge of it.'

Stephen frowned. 'There wasn't some arrangement to get her back for another look?'

Ludo shook his head. 'Not so far as I know. The letter of rejection had gone out to her agent – I dictated it myself.' He gave a rueful grimace. 'She was last seen making a phone call from the theatre, at about 6 p.m. But nobody here received a call from her. We checked.'

'Don't you have some rehearsal rooms up in Hampstead?'

'We did. But the place hasn't been used in ages – we moved all of them here instead.'

Stephen halted, considering. 'So, apart from you, who would have seen the test she did for – what was the film?'

'*Fortune's Cap*. Half a dozen of the staff, maybe a couple of producers. The police have interviewed us all, probably thinking along the same lines as you. A studio employee "crazed with desire" lures Nina out on the pretext of a film deal. They meet, she sees through the ruse, there's a violent struggle . . .' Ludo raised his shoulders in an exaggerated shrug of incredulity.

'What about the cameraman?' said Stephen, weighing the tin of film in his hand. 'I noticed she was – kind of flirting with him.'

Ludo shook his head again. 'Not a chance. That cameraman – Sidney – is about seventy years old. And half deaf. She was being nice to him.'

'Ah.'

Perhaps it was Stephen's defeated look that touched his friend, for when he next spoke something in his voice had changed. 'It must be awful, this waiting and wondering. I wish I could do something about it. But that phone message didn't come from here, Stephen.'

On returning home he could see the children through the living-room window helping Cora decorate the Christmas tree. He had collected them at Paddington the previous evening. He had not seen Freya so cock-a-hoop in months, and suspected the cause to be more than a holiday from school. On hearing him at the front door Cora had come out into the hall. There was something odd in her expression.

'What's the matter?' he said.

'I've just heard the most shocking news, and I wondered – I was having lunch with Joan Dallington today. She told me that Nina Land – the actress – was found dead last week.' She lowered her voice conspiratorially. '*Murdered*.'

Stephen's gaze dropped. 'I know,' he said. 'And it was two weeks ago.'

Cora flinched. 'Why ever didn't you tell me? I've been worrying over it all day, thinking you mightn't know.'

'I'm sorry. Ludo told me – I've just seen him.' He was aware of eliding two events to make them seem consecutive.

'Do the police have any clue about – ?'

He shook his head. 'Nothing, I'm afraid.'

'Oh, it's too awful! You met her once, didn't you?'

Stephen sensed a movement at the door of the living room, out of Cora's line of vision. Freya stood there, silent as a statue in a niche, her dark eyes trained on him. He knew then that his next words would tell her for certain what sort of father she had.

'Yes, we were introduced. She seemed very nice, for the brief time we spoke.'

Cora hurried on with her own aria of lament for the poor woman, so young and *so* talented, who could have imagined such a ghastly end to a life? Stephen heard himself mutter in agreement. When his gaze slid back to the threshold of the living room his daughter had gone.

Later that evening he sat on the couch in his study, dark but for a glimmering desk lamp. He had avoided dinner, claiming a headache, and overheard Cora telling the children not to disturb him. The fire had died in the grate, and he hadn't moved to rekindle it. He kept opening the tin and pulling out the black-and-white coil of film to examine her ghostly negative. He felt at once shocked and composed in his contemplation of her, the face ambered in translucent windows of light. There had come a reckoning he had been trying to elude these past days, and he could feel his resistance to it wane – it had been prodding at vulnerable points, finally overpowering him. It was simply this: if he had left her alone, she would still be alive.

Behind him he heard the door creak open, and a light footfall across the wooden floor. Freya sat down next to him, and waited.

Eventually, he said, 'I hope *you* have some good news, at least.'

She nodded. 'Mum says I can leave Tipton at Easter. She's going to find a school near us. St Paul's, maybe.'

'But Rowan's going to stay?'

'If he wants. He seems to like it there now.'

'Well, I'm very pleased.'

There was a pause. 'Thanks for persuading her.'

'How d'you know I did?'

Freya gave a little half-snort of dismissal: she just knew. 'What's that?' she said, looking at the metal tin on his lap.

'Something Ludo Talman gave me. A memento.'

His eyes were cast down, but he sensed Freya staring at him. Perhaps it was that word, the finality of it, that got to him. *Memento*, without its ghost companion, *mori*. Unseemly to give way in front of a child, even one as precocious as Freya, but it seemed quite beyond help. His shoulders were perfectly still; it was just the brimming at his eyes he had trouble with. As often as he brushed the tears away a fresh flow coursed down his cheeks. He didn't speak; he wasn't sure he could speak, so choked was his throat.

Only when Freya took his hand in hers did he feel a relief

from the pressure within. For some minutes they sat there, without a word to each other. But he kept hold of her hand as though it were the one thing in the world that might save him from drowning.

# 20

When sober, Jimmy consulted his conscience in the same way he might read a book on a subject that half appalled and half fascinated him. He would acquaint himself with the main argument, and then skim rapidly through pages at a time, quietly relegating information to footnotes and parentheses whenever the detail became too pertinent or accusing. He thought it foolish to enquire very deeply into matters past remedy. Concerning his recent behaviour he was aware of 'mistakes having been made', a phrase defanged of any serious power to discomfit. But he did not remain untroubled. At vulnerable moments he felt conscience's nipping bite as he recalled Tom's prone form jerking on the carpet like a fish gasping for breath. Oh God, how could he have – ?

Best not to think of it. Not his fault. Apparently he was *persona non grata* at the hospital where Tom was recovering. Edie had warned him off – the patient isn't ready to see you, she'd said. Not that he wanted to go anyway. He regarded hospitals as the waiting rooms of death. As to visiting Peter *in prison*, well, there wasn't a team of wild horses alive that would have dragged him up to Pentonville. During his frantic escape from the drag ball, with the police whistles keening in the night air and his lungs burning with exhaustion, a phrase he had read in newspapers tolled through his wearied brain: *The defendant was taken down and removed to prison.* No fate short of death was more terrifying to him, and the idea of setting foot in such a place, even as a visitor, was unthinkable.

He had been as close to despair that night as he had ever come. Having fled through at least three back gardens and scrambled over a wooden fence, he found himself on a lonely street where moonlight made horrific gnarled silhouettes of the trees. Deprived of his coat and his cane in the alarum back at the house, he was shivering with the cold and limping from the pain of his scraped knees. He looked one way along the street, then the other. Where in God's name was he? He had no money for a taxi, and in any case he couldn't see or even hear a car in the vicinity. He had nothing but the clothes he stood up in – a hired Edwardian evening gown, a string of pearls, white kid gloves and dress boots. 'Incriminating' hardly covered it. He started walking downhill – surely that was south – keeping to the shadows for fear of the police widening their net.

He turned onto another sloping street, ears pricked for the approach of a car. Halfway down he saw two ladies emerging from a side road, and he hurried to catch them up. Perhaps they would take pity on him. He took great wheezing gulps of breath as he ran, his asthma tightening in his chest.

'I say – would you – please help,' he gasped.

They turned at his voice, and he saw straight away that these ladies were in fact young gentlemen, sporting gowns beneath their overcoats. It seemed they too were fugitives from the ball, though in no apparent fright from the untimely end to the evening. They might almost have been taking a midnight stroll. One of them raised his hat in greeting as Jimmy drew near.

'Hullo, are you – oh!' The exclamation was prompted by Jimmy's collapse to his knees, in fatigue and supplication.

He heard the other one say, 'Golly, looks like she's been dragged through a hedge backwards.'

They helped him up with much clucking encouragement and propped him against a tree. His breathing was stertorous, though neither of his helpers seemed particularly alarmed. They introduced themselves as Jeremy and Vivian. After some moments Jimmy managed to gasp out his name in return. They plainly had no idea who he was, and for once in his life he didn't care. He explained, haltingly, that he had a car parked up by the house, but that his driver was indisposed.

'I don't think we can go back there, James,' said Vivian with a little grimace. 'The place will be crawling with Brendas.'

'And we've been nabbed at one of these before,' said Jeremy. 'Did you know they rub your cheeks with blotting paper to see if you're wearing slap?'

It was proposed that they resume their journey on foot, and when Jimmy groaned his new companions became solicitous. 'Don't fret, James, we'll get you home. Now, d'you like chicken?'

Jimmy frowned, mystified. 'Yes, of course –'

'Well,' said Jeremy, crooking his elbow in invitation, 'grab a wing, dear.' And they marched Jimmy, arms linked on either side, down Highgate Hill, beguiling the journey with selections from Purcell and Ireland. (As Vivian explained, they had been choral scholars together.) At Archway they found a cabman's shelter, and twenty minutes later a taxi rumbled, mercifully, into view. As they were borne through the small hours towards Holborn his companions talked with the driver about the fire down at Crystal Palace, but Jimmy merely listened in a fugue of exhausted shame.

Presently he saw from the window the reassuring outline of the British Museum, and then the cab had come to a halt outside Princess Louise Mansions. The boys helped him out onto the pavement, and he felt moved to make a short speech.

'Gentlemen. I cannot properly thank you for your kindness at this moment, but be assured that I will.' He faltered for a moment. He was still just drunk enough to force himself. 'I must – I am obliged to tell you that this evening I have been drunken, treacherous, cowardly, unfeeling, dishonest – and *lewd*.' At which his head drooped in abjection.

He sensed a moment's embarrassed silence before Jeremy, or perhaps Vivian, said quietly, 'Well, we all of us have our faults, Miss Prism – why don't you take yourself off to bed? Things will look much brighter in the morning.'

The boy was right about that. By lunchtime Jimmy had quite forgotten his doorstep confession of the night before, but he had retained, scribbled on a dress-hire ticket, the telephone numbers of his two new friends. Capital!

Having loitered among the strollers and window gazers on the Strand – his version of Christmas shopping – Stephen was still a little early for his meeting with Everett Druce on Craven Street. The house was a double-fronted Georgian terrace halfway down towards the Embankment. The brass knocker felt as solid in his hand as the clapper of a church bell. A maid answered the door and ushered him up the stairs into a drawing room of sepulchral quiet. On the walls paintings were hung and lit with a professional expertise. He could smell fresh beeswax coming off the parquet floor. Ludo had told him that Druce collected, and he was right – these were lovely pictures. He went over to examine the one which held pride of place on the far wall. It was a large oil on the classical myth of Pyramus and Thisbe, and if he wasn't much mistaken it was a work of –

'Mr Wyley.' Druce's velvety voice somehow matched the shawl-collared smoking jacket he wore. He approached

Stephen with loping strides to offer his hand. 'I see you were admiring . . .'

'It's Poussin, yes?'

Druce nodded, with an air of concession rather than pride. 'It's not among his most famous, but the subject is typical at least – love, and death.'

'Where did you find it? I didn't even know –'

'Oh, a dealer I know came by it in Amsterdam. Quite a tricky negotiation, as you can imagine.' He turned away from it to consider Stephen. 'I fear that mural of yours at the Nines is to be scrapped. No one's prepared to finish the job. Serves them right – they ought to have stuck by you.'

Stephen shrugged, because it didn't bother him any more. 'I'm sorry I had to cancel our arrangement the other week. A friend's funeral rather set me back.'

'Of course. Thank you for the note.'

At that moment a maid, different from the one who answered the door, came in bearing a coffee pot and cakes. She gave a little bob and withdrew. Druce invited his guest to be seated, and poured the coffee himself. He glanced at the black-portfolio case whose ribbon ties Stephen was unloosing.

'So – how do we proceed?'

'Well, I'll make a few sketches of you first. Once I've studied them you can come to the studio and I'll begin on the canvas. D'you mind if I pull this curtain back – catch what remains of the daylight?'

Having had his offer to help with the furniture declined, Stephen waited while Druce supervised two more of his endless staff in the repositioning of various chairs and screens. He surmised that the stuff was too valuable for him to handle. He wandered around for a closer inspection of the paintings, among them a Monet, a Caillebotte, a Sisley, two early watercolours by Braque. They seemed to glow the brighter for their domestic setting, as though they were all

358

on holiday from a national gallery. He had seen some decent private collections in his time, but this surpassed them all.

Eventually they were settled, Stephen on a bottle-green chesterfield, Druce in an armchair with the light at his back. Laying out his charcoal sticks and loose-leaf pad, he gave an abrupt laugh and shook his head.

'I must confess, I feel rather diminished in this company,' he said with a vague wave around the room. 'When did you start collecting?'

'Oh, just after the war. I was in Paris a while, for the firm. There were always bargains to be had, if one knew where to look.' As he reminisced a little on those bargain-hunting days, Stephen, half listening, made rough sketches of his sitter's face, one after the other, until he was satisfied with the contours and the shape of the head. He supposed he ought to feel flattered, really, given that the man could have afforded far more renowned portraitists than himself.

Some minutes later he felt his attention snag on something Druce had just said.

'Sorry, where did you say you studied?'

'Here in London,' Druce replied. 'Why?'

'Oh. I felt sure I knew you from Oxford . . . The first time we met at the Nines your face seemed very familiar.'

Druce tipped his head musingly. 'Can't think from where, I'm afraid.'

'I must be mistaken.' Stephen shrugged, refocusing on the charcoal as he moved it across the paper. They continued in desultory chat for another hour, until Stephen sensed a restlessness in his sitter. He suspected Druce was not much inclined to stay still when there was always money to make.

'That should be enough to go on with,' he said, and sensed Druce's relief. 'Before I go, may I – ?'

Druce gave him directions to the lavatory, and mentioned a couple of paintings that Stephen should look out for on the way down. So he was half prepared for the Modigliani at the turn of the stairs, and the Seurat at the foot. It was clear he would have to cultivate this man as a patron – perhaps he had a whole circle of friends out there eager to commission portraits of themselves. His career might not be dead after all.

On returning to the drawing room he found Druce leafing absently through the portrait sketchbook he had left on the sofa.

'Oh, d'you mind – ?'

'Please, be my guest,' said Stephen casually. He must not seem to be begging for work. 'Most of those are either friends or family.'

Druce nodded, and held up a study of a girl's head. 'Daughter, perhaps?'

Stephen smiled. 'Freya. She's twelve.'

He riffled back through the loose pages, as though in search of something. He stopped, appearing to have found it. 'That's very pretty. Who's she?'

'That is – oh – a young woman I met recently. I think she's going to be my new housekeeper. Madeleine Farewell.'

Druce's gaze glittered. 'Farewell? That's an odd name.'

Stephen nodded. 'Though not to her, I suppose. We met at – um, I have a studio in chaos, she needed the work. So we came to an arrangement.'

Druce dragged his gaze away to study him. 'She needs work? Well, I'm always looking for good staff.'

'You seem to have a full complement here,' said Stephen with a doubtful half-laugh. 'I've never seen such a well-run household.'

Druce shook his head, and said with an expansive shrug, 'I keep other properties, here and abroad. They all require looking after.'

'Of course,' said Stephen, feeling slightly dazed by the vertiginous perspectives of wealth the remark opened up. He could only stand by and hope to catch a sprinkling of it. 'Well, I'll certainly ask Madeleine if she's available for, um –'

'Hire? Please do!'

They shook hands, and with a wistful glance this way and that at the paintings he passed on the stair Stephen was shown out.

Later that evening he sat in his study, listening to carol singers on the street below. His portfolio was open on his desk, its loose leaves scattered about like a mathematical problem he was trying to solve. Something – something he had forgotten, perhaps – nagged at him, but he couldn't work out what it was. Probably Cora would be able to tell him; he heard her footsteps now outside the door.

'Why are you sitting in the dark?' she said, entering and making a beeline for one of the side lamps. She had brought in a tumbler of Scotch for him, and picked up the soda siphon from the trolley. 'Say when.'

She aimed a hissing jet into the glass, and he raised his finger. 'Thanks.'

'Who was that on the telephone?'

'Hm? Oh, it was Druce. He was asking for Madeleine Farewell's number – I'd recommended her as a char.'

'That was nice of you!'

He took a swig of the Scotch. 'Cora, I have a maddening idea of something amiss. Can you tell me what it is?'

'You mean, like a mind-reader?'

He laughed, and shook his head. She was studying his afternoon's handiwork. She picked up a finished sketch of the new client. 'So this is *Mr Druce*.' Her eyes widened in mock reverence. 'Did you ask him about Oxford?'

'I got that wrong – he wasn't there. I could have sworn I'd met him before –'

From below came a rat-tat at the door. Their looks met. 'Here's half a crown for them,' he said, as Cora made to leave. 'Perhaps you'd ask them to have a go at "*Hark, the Herald*".'

When she had gone Stephen reordered the sketches; under the dim glow of the desk lamp he examined them one by one. Druce's narrow face, the dark, deep-set eyes, the fullish lips. *This* was the thing bothering him. He squinted, dredging his brain for the elusive detail, the one that would remind him where they'd first met. Or else . . . Had he seen the man in a photograph, and then persuaded himself they'd met, when they had not? In a newspaper, possibly. The face he had drawn stared back at him, the eyes boring into his. And suddenly he knew. He had thought the face familiar without knowing whose it was – because *he had sketched it himself once before*. He reached down and opened a drawer in his desk. He felt his heart start to gallop as he pulled out an old copy of the *Chronicle* and riffled its pages till he found it.

## AN ARTIST'S IMPRESSION OF THE SUSPECT

There was his own drawing, the face of the 'Tiepin Killer', as described to him by Nina. Was he going mad? He looked at the newspaper's reproduced sketch, and then at the one he had done of Druce today. It was the same man. He knew it – knew it with a certainty that only intuition could endow. And now he thought of the glint in Druce's eye when he had identified the drawing of Madeleine – *She's available for hire*. Oh God oh God oh God. The girl he had tried to strangle in the hotel room. He had recognised her.

Stephen jumped up from his chair as if he had just been scalded. Druce's face stared back from the paper. This was the man who had telephoned him twenty minutes ago, the man he had given Madeleine's number. By now he would know where she lived.

\* \* \*

The dining room at the Strand Palace Hotel was already in a roar by the time Jimmy arrived. It was the night of Lord Swaim's annual Christmas bash for the *Chronicle* and other satellites of his news empire. The hotel's sleek and beautiful interiors usually put him in a good mood – Jimmy adored art deco – but tonight he felt ominous stirrings of unease. The day had begun badly when he was visited at Princess Louise Mansions by the police. His instant thought was that they had come to arrest him, but it transpired that the young constable, Dawes, was merely pursuing an inquiry. He wanted to know if Mr Erskine was the owner of a 1928 Bentley Vanden Plas in racing green. Yes, yes, he was indeed. So, the constable continued, was he aware that the car had been stolen?

'Stolen? Surely not.'

'Do you know a Mr Jolyon Fairweather?'

'Of course. My own driver is indisposed at present, so I've loaned the motor to Mr Fairweather while he's recovering.' Jolyon was one of his coterie of boys, and a frequent dinner guest at the flat. 'Is there something the matter?'

PC Dawes hesitated a moment, then consulted his notepad. 'We discovered Mr Fairweather at the wheel of the car in a state of extreme inebriation –'

'Well, boys will be boys,' said Jimmy with a weak laugh.

'I'm afraid that's not all, sir. There was another man in the car. He and Mr Fairweather were, um, engaged in an act of a lewd nature.'

Jimmy blinked hard. 'An act of . . . How shocking.'

'Yes, disgusting. When I interrupted them the other man was very put out – turned round and gave me a mouthful.'

Even in his anxiety Jimmy had to stop himself laughing. The policeman stared at him. 'Did you know that Mr Fairweather is a homosexual?'

'I did not,' Jimmy said, feigning puzzlement. 'What will happen to them?'

'They've been detained at Bow Street, pending charges.'

'I see. And the motor?'

'That can be collected at our depot,' said Dawes. 'In the meantime, sir, I'd be very careful about the company you keep. It's not your fault, but queers will always try and take advantage of you. It's in their nature.'

'Quite,' said Jimmy in his most responsible tone. The constable gave him a nod, and was gone.

Jolyon – the silly tart! The cheek of using the Bentley for his furtive assignations . . . Then he felt a little quiver of erotic excitement as the image of two men in the car together flickered across his mind's eye. He'd give the boy a proper ticking-off next time they met. Which might not be for a while if they sent him to prison. He would have to be more cautious – that drag-ball fiasco was the warning. They were getting too close. Pretty soon some policeman would put two and two together and realise that James Erskine was not the model of respectable bachelorhood he seemed.

He was still preoccupied with PC Dawes's visit when he took his seat between Gilbert and Barry at dinner. Most at the table were in high spirits, and under the steady replenishment of his wine glass Jimmy felt himself being coaxed in the same direction. It seemed that the King's abdication, while leaving his people in a state of shock, had given the newspaper its best circulation figures since the end of the war. Toasts were raised to this renewed prosperity during dinner, and when Jimmy saw from the menu card that pudding was to be a hot chocolate soufflé he let out a notch on his belt and lit a cigar.

Even the supercilious arts editor Lambert appeared to have entered the convivial mood, though the way he kept smiling in Jimmy's direction was far from reassuring. The man was seldom known to smile for any reason unless it involved another's personal misfortune. Dropping his voice, Jimmy leaned over to Barry.

'Have you any idea why Lambert keeps grinning at me?'

Barry protruded his lower lip. 'Could be he's sweet on you.'

'I doubt that *very* much.'

He didn't have to wait long for an explanation. Lambert, lighting another of his Woodbines, had narrowed his gaze on Jimmy.

'I was wondering if we'd recognise you tonight, James.'

Jimmy frowned his incomprehension. 'Why's that?'

'Well, I gather you're more likely to be seen around town these days in a ball gown and gloves up to here.'

He felt a warmth spring to his cheeks. 'Moss Bros suits me fine, as you can see.'

'Oh, shame. I was hoping for flounces, frills, the works,' said Lambert.

'Then I recommend you find the name of a good dress-maker.' Barry and Gilbert sniggered at that, but Lambert was not to be thrown off the scent.

'So you wouldn't know anything about a drag ball up at Highgate, few weeks back? They say half the theatre folk in London were there when the police raided the house.'

'I must belong to the other half, then,' sniffed Jimmy. 'I find very little occasion to go to Highgate.'

But the smirk wouldn't budge from Lambert's face, and Jimmy, refusing him further satisfaction, decided to take a walk. He needed a pee in any case before the speeches began. Navigating a path through the gossiping throng of diners he muttered under his breath, still somewhat nettled by Lambert's mocking insinuations. What a ghastly little shit . . . It was only on account of his being close to the throne that he was allowed such . . . such *impudence*. And then his step faltered as he considered how much of what Lambert knew got passed onto the mob upstairs – the management, the proprietor Lord Swaim. He already knew the latter couldn't stand him.

365

The hotel Gents was sparsely peopled, just a couple of punters standing at the urinals. He had to curb his instinct to join them and have a quick peek. Instead he locked himself in a stall and sat down. A minute or so later his ears pricked up at the arrival of a voice he knew; it was the *Chronicle*'s editor, Bostock, talking to someone in a vaguely appeasing manner.

'I think it would come better from you,' he was saying.

His interlocutor demurred: '. . . rather not . . . most objectionable fellow . . . He's been doing that column far too long in any case.'

'It's been said. But he deserves the courtesy at least . . .'

Jimmy, his curiosity fired, soundlessly cracked open his stall door – and froze. Side by side at the urinals with Bostock was Lord Swaim himself. And plainly the subject under discussion was Swaim's bête noire, one J. Erskine Esq. Their confidential tone indicated an awkwardness, and Jimmy had an instinctive notion what it meant.

He strained his ears to catch their receding phrases. 'Let's get it over with . . . I understand your . . . after dinner . . .' The voices drifted away, and they were gone. He emerged from his hiding place, and felt himself shaking. What dreadful serendipity, to overhear the boss and the editor lining him up for the firing squad. *Let's get it over with*. It was coming.

On returning to his table Jimmy found he had no appetite left, even for the hot chocolate soufflé. Now he understood Lambert's sardonic allusions to the drag ball; Jimmy's night of shame was out, and had handed Lord Swaim his excuse at last. He looked around the company and wondered who else had heard. Gilbert and Barry? Rumour whipped through the paper at such speed it was practically impossible they didn't know, and yet neither of them had tipped him the wink – the blighters. Or were they simply too embarrassed to mention it? Gilbert was looking rather oddly at him.

'Everything all right, Jimmy?'

'I hardly know,' Jimmy replied. 'Is it?'

Gilbert shrugged. 'You just seem a bit quiet, that's all.'

Jimmy switched his gaze to Barry. 'So much for friends . . . One of you might at least have told me.'

Barry said, 'What are you talking about?'

He looked over to make sure Lambert wasn't earwigging, and said, sotto voce, 'I'm a dead man. I just overheard Bostock and Swaim discussing it in the lav – they're getting rid of me. You didn't know?'

He could tell from their shocked faces that they did not. Barry shook his head. 'It doesn't make sense. Bostock has always defended you – for one thing he knows how many readers you bring in.'

'But it's Swaim's paper,' said Jimmy sadly. 'I'm as good as buried.'

The lights in the room dimmed of a sudden, cutting short further opportunity for speculation. The speeches were beginning. Jimmy hunkered down in his chair, feeling like some ancient Roman who'd just cut his veins in the bath and was waiting to bleed out. He had envisaged his departure from the paper quite differently: a gracious signing-off to his readers, many years hence, with some wry reference to having strutted and fretted his hour upon the page (rather good, that). His last word? 'Curtain.' This would be soon followed by a dam burst of lamentation from those very same readers, besieging the editor with letters *imploring* their beloved critic to reconsider, which in turn would prompt the paper's management to ask him to reconsider. And Jimmy, while professing his delight at this public show of support, would turn down their plea, quoting that grand old stage motto (it had the right air of regret), 'Best to leave 'em wanting more.'

But it wasn't going to happen like that, and realities had to be addressed. Cast out by the *Chronicle*, how would he get by? Vacancies for a theatre critic rarely came up, and whenever one did there would be someone keener – younger – waiting to snap it up. In any case, he had offended too many people to feel sure that another paper would want him. He could survive on bits and bobs from other outlets, but not for long, not with his extravagance. He imagined the dwindling commissions, the telephone's long silences, the slow fade into obscurity. And penury. Where would he go? He wondered if there might be some retirement home for distressed theatre folk. Even if there was, he could hardly expect a welcome there – the critic was the mongrel dog that whined and cocked its leg against the purebreds. No, he would slink away, unwanted, and lay himself down to die. My God, the pity of it –

Jimmy felt a nudge at his shoulder. Gilbert had leaned in to whisper: 'You should listen to this.'

The editor, Bostock, was at the podium, though nothing he had been saying had penetrated Jimmy's clouded consciousness. It seemed he was in the middle of some panegyric on the *Chronicle*'s veterans, 'a doughty breed of scribes who have helped make this the great paper that it is'. Through the applause and the ragged 'hear, hear's he droned on, for the evening would not be complete (he said) without his acknowledging one especially renowned member of the old guard, a servant of the *Chronicle* for twenty-seven years.

Jimmy was making a vague calculation of his own span at the paper when Bostock's next words caused him a convulsive, scalp-tingling shock: '. . . and Lord Swaim has allowed me the honour of presenting this trophy – please be upstanding for our peerless theatre critic, *Mr James Erskine*.'

Was he hallucinating?

No. All eyes had turned on him amid the purling thunder of applause. They were not giving him the sack. They were giving him an award! He thought of Kipling's line about Triumph and Disaster, and treating those two impostors just the same. Well, you had to try, you had to try . . .

Barry was laughing, his hand cupped over Jimmy's ear, trying to be heard above the noise. *'Getting rid of you, are they?'*

Madeleine stepped off the tram on Camden High Street and headed for home. She was carrying a few things she had bought in town, an aquamarine brooch and silk stockings (Christmas presents for Rita), a jar of honey and some little pastries from an Italian cookshop in Soho. She thought she might save some to take round to Rita, who was doing Christmas dinner for her and a couple of the girls she knew from the Blue Posts. She stopped off at her local to buy a bottle of wine, a red, she thought, was best on a cold night. It was a relief to her she could still afford treats. Her savings from the Elysian were meagre, but she had the pub shift three nights a week and Stephen was paying her over the odds for the two afternoons she spent cleaning his studio.

When she entered the hallway at Bayham Street the place was in darkness. She called the landlady's name, without reply. It was odd, she could have sworn she had put a shilling in the meter yesterday. Ascending the stairs she reached her door on the second-floor back and let herself in. Setting down her bag on the kitchen table she went to the cupboard where the candles were kept. But before she had opened it a sound made her jump – the rasping of a match – and turning she saw a figure behind her. He had been waiting. The wick of the oil lamp was lit, and in its flickering illumination she recognised him.

'Madeleine.'

She stood paralysed, rooted to the spot. How? And yet something in her knew that this moment had always been coming. Beneath the terrible pounding that had started in her breast she realised her fate had come to meet her, that this was the reckoning for the life she had chosen, all the men, all the hotel rooms, all the brief encounters . . . She had tried to forget them, banish them from sight. But not this one. He had never been forgotten. We meet our end on the road we take to avoid it. The stillness of his head, the dark, hooded eyes, and that voice, the way it almost purred her name.

She knew what he had come to do, but still she forced herself to ask him: 'Why me?' It came out as barely a whisper.

Druce looked at her, and almost smiled. 'Why you? I remember enjoying the fear in your eyes. And once you'd seen my face there was the problem . . .'

She swallowed, and nodded. 'Well, I'm – I'm ready. If you are.'

He cocked his head. 'You begged me last time. You begged me to stop, remember?'

She nodded again. 'Yes. But not now. I'm ready.' It was the simplest thing to say. In the near-dark of a terraced house in Camden, with the world outside hurrying on, endless in its indifference, she was ready to face her last – for she knew there was no escaping it for anyone.

He had removed his tiepin and tossed it onto the kitchen table, where it glinted. He pulled the tie loose from his neck and held it straight with both hands in front of his face. And now he did smile. 'Come here, then.'

She was still trembling, but she took a step towards him, and then another. He went to raise the tie over her head when, from below, an urgent rapping sounded at the door. Druce froze momentarily; he retreated some paces to stand at the kitchen door. It was a man's voice now, calling her name. She thought she knew it. They looked at one another, as if conspirators. Hesitating, Druce quietly opened the door and crept onto the landing. With an answering softness of foot she followed, so that when he turned back she was right behind him.

'There's nothing –' he began, but the sentence turned into an astounded roar of agony as she thrust the tiepin deep into his right eye. Madeleine released her fingers from it and darted past him. As she bolted blindly down the stairs she heard the front door being forced open, wood splintering; Stephen had made it to the first turn, they were almost in one another's arms when a shadow plummeted between the banisters, dropping fast, and the noise it made at the bottom sounded to her like a full suitcase hurled to the pavement from a high window.

When they looked down, Everett Druce's body lay sprawled, motionless, his neck at an odd angle to his shoulders.

# 21

The streets looked odd at the end of Coronation Day. They were aflutter with banners, and the pavements were strewn with discarded flags, bunting, splashes of red and white and blue. But there wasn't a single bus to be seen, and Tom trudged home amid droves of tired revellers. The busmen had gone on strike the week before, leaving the city in chaos. Tramcars had been so tightly packed that they didn't bother to stop for boarders. Every private car and taxi seemed to be out on the road, and parked anywhere they fancied. Tom hadn't gone on the Underground since he'd left the hospital at Christmas. He had been told to avoid confined spaces or potential scenes of disorder. So he walked.

In Green Park people had camped out so as to secure themselves a good view on the day. He overheard one old boy say to another, as he surveyed the rows of tents, 'Reminds me of base camp at Étaples – without the smell.'

Tom had wondered about going to the West End at all; he had no great affection for the monarchy, and nothing about the recent squabble over the American woman had endeared the institution to him. But something more than curiosity impelled him to go. He had an unfathomable intuition that this was the sort of day he would bump into her, with all of London in carnival mood, and strangers roaming about, greeting one another as if they were old familiars. He had once called in at the Elysian to ask about her. Nobody knew where she'd gone. He would even have asked Ronny, or Roddy, or whatever his name was, but he wasn't there either. He could imagine reminiscing some day in the future about the coincidence of their meeting, and being able to pinpoint it by the occasion: 'You remember, of course, it was the day of the Coronation – to think of running into one another in all those crowds!'

But he didn't run into her, or anyone. And now he was tramping back to his digs in Wapping, alone.

Since the start of the year he had picked up quite a bit of freelance work, more than he had expected. It seemed that his time in Jimmy's employ had won him a reflected prestige; one editor flatteringly called him 'Erskine's dauphin'. Tom wanted to believe the work coming in was down to his own talent, but sensed it was bestowed merely on his reputation for reliability. He felt destined to be always known as the willing secretary, the one who had 'kept Jimmy going' for the last ten years. It was not, he supposed, such a bad reputation to have.

Their sundering was never officially marked. It simply became understood that Tom would not be working for Jimmy any longer. All the same, he had expected something from his erstwhile boss, if not a full *mea culpa* then at least an acknowledgement of his unseemly (or should he call it unconscionable?) behaviour on the night of the drag ball. He had abandoned one friend in a medical emergency, and allowed another to sacrifice himself to a prison sentence. Surely that demanded some form of contrition. Tom heard from Peter when he visited him at Pentonville that Jimmy had written a letter of apology, 'or the nearest he would ever come to one'. He had boiled with rage about the whole affair while he was in hospital, but Peter's attitude of civilised drollery was a corrective. If a man incarcerated for six months could so easily forgive his treacherous friend, then shouldn't he, too?

There was of course the danger of encountering one another at the theatre. Having deputised as critic ('keeping the chair warm', as Jimmy put it) Tom was still in the habit of going to press nights, even if he wasn't reviewing. Most of the time he kept a distance, or else went on a different night. He continued to read Jimmy's reviews in the *Chronicle*, wondering if he'd detect some falling off, some diminution in the energy of the writing now that his editor-secretary had gone. He never did. The Erskine voice remained the same: exacting, adversarial, puckish. It would be the last thing of his to go. Then, back in April, he had spotted Jimmy, at the far end of the bar during an interval, characteristically surrounded by a group of his young men. Jimmy had spotted him in turn, and looked away. When the play resumed Tom noticed that the last seat on the critics' row – Jimmy's – was now empty. It saddened him, unexpectedly.

He told Edie about it over lunch a few days later. They met quite often now. In Peter's enforced absence he was understudying in the role of her best friend and confidant.

'I don't know, I thought a tip of his hat, or a wave. But nothing. He just looked away.'

Edie tilted her head in rueful sympathy. 'He was probably embarrassed. People like Jimmy don't know how to behave when they're in the wrong.' Then she suddenly frowned at him. 'You're not going back to him, are you?'

Tom shook his head, and smiled. 'Not a chance. I stayed with him for too long, and I took on too much work – another thing the doctors have warned me about. But it wasn't all bad, you know. We had fun.'

'Of course, darling. He's a caution! And if a man's to be judged by the company he keeps Jimmy comes off pretty well.'

'What, Jolyon and that lot?'

'No, they're just his boys. I mean his proper friends – you and me and Peter and László. Look how generous he's been to László.'

'I know, I know. We can rely on him for everything except loyalty.'

Edie laughed throatily. 'But we love him just the same.'

'Strange, isn't it? With certain people the normal rules don't apply. He behaves badly, lets people down, and yet we forgive him, you're right, just because he's Jimmy. When he was at his most swinish I cursed him for a monster of egotism and vanity and self-delusion, but I was wrong – I mean about the self-delusion. He knows exactly what he can get away with.'

'A "monster", darling?'

'It's a figure of speech, mostly.'

Edie nodded it away. 'Listen, I'm going to have a little dinner at Fashion Street for when Peter gets out – a welcome home. You, me, László – and Jimmy. You will come, won't you?'

'Well, I'm not sure . . .' he said with a heavy shake of his head. But when he caught Edie's hurt expression he gave up his teasing and pulled a fooled-you face. She gave him a reproving smack on the wrist in return. 'I've just had a note from László, actually,' he continued. 'He's going to some show next week, and he's very keen for me to accompany him. I don't know why.'

'Don't you, now?' said Edie, and Tom thought he heard some ironic chime in her voice. But after a moment's hesitation he dismissed it, and the talk turned to something else.


'So you didn't see *any* of it?'

'No, not a thing,' Madeleine admitted. 'After I'd finished at the bar I was so tired I went home and just got into bed. When I woke up it was all over.'

'Oh, *shame*. Maddy, you've never seen such crowds! I

mean, I can't hardly remember the last one, I was just a girl. But this . . . He looked so dignified, and the paper said he did ever so well, even with his stammer. And we sang "God Save the King" and waved our flags like mad – and then burst out cryin'!'

Madeleine was in the Blue Posts listening to Rita's awestruck account of the Coronation. She could tell that Rita found something odd about her not bothering with the occasion. She wasn't the only one. When Madeleine had been at Tite Street the day before, Stephen had asked her if she was excited about the 'big day'. She felt herself rather a party-pooper having agreed to work at the Railway Arms all day. They had taken to one another pretty well, the only wobble of alarm being the afternoon Stephen came back to find the sash windows washed and gleaming. 'Oh . . .' He'd always thought the layer of dirt created a romantic, Turneresque blur, and consequently had not disturbed them. When Madeleine saw him looking dazed by this sudden access of light she felt somehow in error. 'I'm sorry if – I just thought they needed a clean.' After a long pause Stephen gave her a pained smile. 'I know, you're right. I've become used to not seeing out of them.' She kept noticing him pause in front of the windows, as though trying to recall what had gone missing. But he lost the habit, and came to accept their new grimeless state.

Their traumatic involvement in the case of the Tiepin Murders made an unspoken bond between them. The police's questioning went on for days, and she told them the story, over and over, of meeting Everett Druce for the first time at the Imperial, and of Nina's part in unwittingly saving her life. It was soon established that Nina had in fact been the killer's fifth and final victim. Ludo Talman had confirmed that Druce, whose money backed the studio, must have seen her screen test at the Marlborough and then set about tracking her down. The house in Hampstead was found to be rented under the name Rusk, which he had taken from Barry Rusk, crime correspondent of the *Chronicle*. Madeleine gathered that Nina would probably not have known anything about her killer. To judge from the injuries to her head, death would have been instantaneous. It was cold comfort that Druce had not left his macabre signature upon her.

As to what had motivated his grisly crimes, they were no more able to explain it now than they had been at the start. The only chance of understanding would have been to question Druce himself, and that possibility had vanished at the moment he fell to his doom in a Camden boarding house. Madeleine would think of that night, and remember her strange fatalistic behaviour on being confronted by the murderer. At the time it had felt as though someone else was inhabiting her body, someone who had accepted the certainty of her own end, and was calm. She had not described this experience of transcendent equanimity to anyone, partly because it sounded so odd, and partly because she could not quite comprehend it herself. All she knew was that death – or whatever was on the other side of death – held no terror for her.

Rita, having exhausted her supply of superlatives on the Coronation, was looking at Madeleine inquisitively. 'So you're getting by, then. No regrets 'bout the Elysian?'

She shook her head. 'The money was good, better than I've ever earned. But I couldn't bear to . . . D'you ever see Roddy?'

'Hmm, I seen him skulking about now and then. What was it made you sling your hook in the end?'

Madeleine stared off into the pub's pale light. It already seemed a long time ago. 'Oh . . . There was someone – a feller. We'd been out a few times, nothing more. But I was fond of him. Roddy found out, and he made sure the feller would never look at me the same way again.'

'*Ooh*, the snake,' Rita hissed. Something else seemed to trouble her. 'You know, if you're short of money . . .'

Madeleine clasped Rita's hand in hers. 'I'm fine. Char work, the pub. And the painter I told you about has asked me if I can give his daughter piano lessons.'

Rita's eyes widened in astonishment. 'You play the piano?'

'I thought I'd forgotten how, but there's one in his studio, so . . .' Stephen had overheard her by chance, and had been so beguiled that he'd insisted she play whenever she liked. A few weeks later he'd mentioned his daughter – Freya – who might want lessons. She'd been unhappy at her school, he explained, and had recently come back to London. 'Quite a *character*,' he'd added, with a sidelong look.

'Piano lessons!' cried Rita. 'I must tell Arthur about that. He's got a piano round his place. Here, d'you think you could play this?' And she began, in a clear fluting alto, a music-hall song from the old days, something about a girl and a boy meeting by the sad sea waves. Madeleine didn't know it, but it didn't sound very difficult. She could certainly give it a try.

The morning after the Coronation Tom woke feeling rather low. He was fatigued by his footslog home from the Mall, and he knew he could have used the day more profitably than gawping at a pageant whose significance barely interested him. Now that he was cast on the open seas of freelance writing he could not afford to drift; there was no longer the safe harbour of a regular income, however meagre it had been. He had a career to keep afloat.

On emerging from his bedroom he almost tripped over the cardboard box that Allenby, his landlord, had deposited there. It was addressed to him. Inside, wrapped in newspaper, was a lady's hat box from Peter Jones, though the weight of it suggested that something other than headgear was contained therein. He felt a tender shock on lifting out the green Smith-Corona typewriter, which he hadn't touched since he was last at Jimmy's office back in November.

A typewritten letter had been wedged into the carriage.

Princess Louise Mansions, W.C.2
11th May 1937

My dear Tom,

I have been long, too long, pondering what token of manumission I should bestow upon you. The choice has preoccupied me, for I wished to communicate by it some sense of our shared endeavours over the last nine and a half years. An Erskine first edition? You would laugh. A precious *objet de luxe*? You would cry (and so would I to part with it!). A theatre programme from our first outing together? I couldn't recall it for the life of me. And then I would be haplessly borne down memory's byways thinking of all those press nights we attended together, the dinners afterwards, the parties, the jaunts, the jollities. I dare say we spent more time in one another's company than did the average married couple. Perhaps you regard our association in a less emollient spirit – something closer to Strindberg than to Wilde. But I trust in time you will remember that some of it was fun, too.

I have read your critical ebullitions these last months with great interest and, I must say, admiration. Would it be outrageous of me to suggest that you have absorbed the lessons of a master and incorporated them into your own distinctive style? You know me better than to expect modesty where none has ever been intended, but I should say you are a better writer in your mid-thirties than I was at a like age. I do not say *critic*, mind. Your judgement, measured and incisive for the most part, is still too inclined towards leniency; you are apt to hold back when you ought to go for the kill. There is another way of looking at that. You have a proper generosity of feeling, whereas the milk of human kindness has rather soured in me. Either way, I shall follow your progress with a keen eye. And since I find myself in pedagogic mood, let me remind you of advice that Johnson once gave to Boswell: 'If you are idle, be not solitary; if you are solitary, be not idle.' You may arraign my character on any number of charges, but indolence could never be one of them.

Thus we return to the subject with which I began. I had been racking my brain for the gift that should mark our professional span when lo! I saw that it was right before my eyes, indeed, beneath my very fingertips. This typewriter, once a *casus belli* between us, is surely the appropriate memento to be handed from employer to secretary – or, as I prefer to imagine, from one old friend to another. I know its owner will use it wisely, and well. It shall have no more words from me, beyond these two.

Yours,

Jimmy

Tom read the letter once, and a second time. His feelings about it were quite confused. On the one hand, there was no mention in it whatsoever of Jimmy's shameful dereliction on the night of the party. No mention of Peter being left to face the music. Nor was there any reference to Tom's illness, his time in hospital, or his convalescence. Not even a simple 'How are you?' The closest it had come to any hint of discord in their relationship was a passing allusion to Strindberg. The astonishing nerve! On the other hand, it wasn't astonishing at all. He had not really expected phrases of self-blame and remorse, because he knew Jimmy was incapable of them. Edie had him right. He didn't know how to behave when he was in the wrong. Did he even know he *was* in the wrong?

He read it again, and, with slow reluctance, he found the

best parts of the writer in it – his charm, his wit, his thoughtful praise, albeit mixed with a piercing dose of condescension. He was disreputable, incorrigible, inimitable. But it took courage, Tom supposed, to be so much his own man. He ran his fingers lightly over the metal keys. It was a beautiful thing, and as a gift – the donor was right – it couldn't have been more appropriate. He felt a surge of determination to make himself worthy of it. Leaning across his desk for a sheet of paper, he inserted it into the carriage, and scrolled down.

On the Friday of Coronation week a small gallery in St James held a private view of new paintings by Stephen Wyley. These were all of people, though the artist decided that the exhibition should be titled not 'Portraits' but 'Faces'. In the run-up to this he told Madeleine not to bother coming to Tite Street: the studio was in such disarray with paintings and dust that there was no use in cleaning the place. He did ask her, however, to come to the private view. When she enquired as to what her duties would be he looked appalled.

'I'm asking you as a guest! There's an entire staff there to serve the drinks.'

'But I don't mind serving drinks –'

He insisted that she was a guest. It was his first public showing since his brief experience of notoriety. Gerald Carmody had gone to prison for embezzling charitable funds. The British People's Brigade were struggling on in his absence; their membership, never very large, was already in decline. No mention of Stephen's alleged affiliations to it was ever made again. The matter had been laid to rest after a letter from Stephen's father appeared in *The Times*, in which he pointed out that his late wife was Jewish-born. Did this not make 'rather a nonsense' of claims that his son supported an anti-Semitic organisation?

There was already quite a crowd by the time Madeleine arrived. On the upper floor of the gallery she found a little more space to move around, though there was nobody here she knew either. It didn't matter – she was happy to look at the paintings. As she paused over one of them she felt a presence hovering near, and turning found a girl candidly gazing at her. She was fair-haired and long-limbed, with a fineness of feature that was but slightly compromised by the wilful set to her mouth.

'What d'you think of these?' she said.

'I like them. Very much. And you?'

The girl nodded, and gave a little pout of approval. Then she resumed her gaze. 'You're Madeleine, aren't you? I'm Freya. These paintings are my dad's.'

'Ah.'

'Dad says you play the piano. You give lessons.'

'Actually, I've never given a piano lesson. But I could try to teach you.'

Freya took a moment to consider this. 'My last teacher, Miss Skinner, was bloo— she was quite disagreeable.'

'Oh dear.'

'She used to pinch me whenever I made a mistake.'

Madeleine responded with a grimacing smile. 'I won't pinch you.'

'Do you think we might get on with each other awfully well?'

Madeleine looked at her, measuringly. 'I should imagine so.'

Freya smiled, too. 'That's what Dad said.'

Stephen had noticed the dark-haired man taking notes as he stooped towards each painting. He sidled over to him.

'Seen anything you liked?'

The man used his pencil as a bookmark in the catalogue. 'A good deal. I only wish I could afford it.'

'Are you press?'

'Not officially. But I want to write a piece about . . .' He waved a hand around the room in illustration. 'I especially liked the portrait of Nina Land. It gave me rather a shock.'

'Did you know her?'

'We met only once, a few weeks before she – I admired her greatly as an actress. And you?'

Stephen turned to the painting. 'We were close,' he said quietly.

'I'm very sorry. I had the impression she was – much loved.'

The current of painful sympathy between them might have been prolonged had not László just then arrived. 'Ach, I am too late! It was my particular intention to introduce you to one another.'

Stephen turned to his interlocutor. 'As a matter of fact we haven't yet been introduced.'

'Then allow me!' cried László. 'Stephen Wyley – my dear friend Tom Tunner.'

They shook hands, and Tom said, 'I gather there's a picture that my friend here is particularly keen for me to see. László, lead on.'

They shouldered their way through the scrum until they came to it. László looked at Tom expectantly. It was a small, squarish portrait of László himself, his expression an enigmatic half-smile, with his hands in the foreground of the picture appearing to shield something – a playing card, perhaps.

'*After Parmigianino,*' said Tom, frowning at the title.

Stephen nodded. 'I painted it a few weeks after I met László. He had told me about Parmigianino's *Self-Portrait in a Convex Mirror* – in fact it was more of a lecture about truth and deception in art. Well . . . it haunted me. So I did this by way of a tribute.'

Tom scrutinised the picture. Of all the people he had

known he would never have bet on László as the first to be immortalised in paint. And yet as he glanced at his friend's pug-like face, eyes alight with innocent childish pride, he could think of no one who deserved the honour more.

'That's one for your memoirs, László,' he said. Jimmy would be incandescent with jealousy, of course, having always hankered after an 'important' artist to paint him. Tom was about to make a joke of this, but then decided not to. It would only spoil László's moment to think of a friend's chagrin, even a friend as conceited and selfish as Jimmy.

The ground floor was filling up again, and other guests were congregating around Stephen. László was still in front of his portrait, holding forth to somebody. He should probably go, he had work to do. First, though, he would have another scout through the place –

'Tom?'

He jumped at the sound of her voice. 'Hullo . . . I'm – this is – erm . . .' He was finding it difficult to form a sentence, so abruptly had Madeleine appeared before him.

'How are you?' she said.

He was still staring dumbly at her. 'I'm, um, fine. How are *you*?'

She nodded encouragingly. 'I left the Elysian. I'm working for Stephen – just cleaning, you know. Oh, and it looks like I'll be teaching his daughter the piano.' What a life of surprises. He didn't even know she could play the piano.

'Strange – I was thinking of you' – he was about to say 'yesterday' and swerved away, it sounded too desperate – 'a while ago. D'you remember the night the Crystal Palace burnt down?'

'Yes, I read about it . . .' She wondered why he had thought of her on that of all nights, but from his dazed look he seemed to have lost his thread.

'Well, I had an accident that night – I nearly choked to

death. And I remember thinking I'd never be able to tell you how sorry I was for – for the night –'

Madeleine's gaze softened. She thought about letting him go on, and instead took pity. She reached out to touch his arm, and he felt in the gesture a release. He wasn't sure if she was forgiving him, or asking for forgiveness.

After some moments he spoke again, with a change in his tone. 'I didn't stop thinking about you.'

She paused, then she said, 'Really?'

'Honour bright. I couldn't even when I tried.'

They stared at one another, oblivious to all else around them.

'It's funny, I kept wondering whether you – with Jimmy and everything – I couldn't tell –'

'You thought I was queer?' His eyes were wide with surprise. Then he gave a little gasp of laughter.

'For a while. It was after that lunch at Jimmy's. I began to think maybe – maybe he's not . . .'

'You gave my hand a squeeze, just before you left,' he said, smiling and taking her hand. 'That was the moment I began to hope.'

She nodded. 'So did I. I thought, please let him be true. Please don't let him give up on me.'

He shook his head. 'I wouldn't give you up for all the jade in China.'

'Is there much jade in China?' she asked, and when she saw his face cloud with doubt she laughed. A waiter was passing by with a tray, and she plucked a couple of glasses from him. They clinked.

Tom said, 'You know, another thing about that night Crystal Palace went up in flames. I could see it from miles away, in Highgate, and I remembered the dream you told us about. Everything engulfed in fire. People's heads . . . I thought you must have second sight –'

'I don't think anyone's head was on fire.'

'No, but it was like you'd had a premonition of it. The terrible force of that conflagration – d'you see?'

Madeleine nodded, though in her heart she knew that wasn't it at all. She hadn't even seen the Crystal Palace fire. The scale of what *she* had dreamed was vast, unearthly, terrifying. A rolling tide of flame. It reduced buildings to matchsticks, it consumed cities and plains, and it incinerated people in the blink of an eye. It was a thing hovering on the edge of your vision, a black, shapeless thing. But she didn't want to think about that now.

She would concentrate on Tom, right there, talking to her. She had never seen his face so animated! Maybe it was to do with all the royal fuss, but it felt like the beginning of something. There was so much to live for.

From the *Chronicle*, October 1946:

*The Distinguished Thing*
by Thomas Tunner, Harrap, London. 8s 6d

What is good writing? What, to refine the question, sets good writing apart from the merely competent? The subject should be meat and drink to a critic, yet even for one who has eaten and quaffed his fill over forty-odd years it admits of no easy explanation. We know good writing when we see it, or rather hear it, for so much of its quality resides in a command of rhythm; it is defined not only by the choice of words, but by their musical arrangement within a sentence. 'After-comers cannot guess the beauty been' wrote Hopkins of his Binsey Poplars, a line so perfect in its melancholic lilt I shiver just to recite it. The essential purpose of writing must be to please.

These musings were brought into renewed focus on considering the novel in front of me. I should declare an

386

interest at the outset. The author, himself a critic of note, was for nearly ten years in my employ as secretary, editor and amanuensis. His keen-eyed diligence saved me from many an infelicitous phrase and clumsy repetition. He understood the pains required to make a sentence sing. One trusts, starting out, that he has observed the same exacting standards on his own prose.

The story concerns a young stage actor who comes to London from the provincial theatre at the end of the 1920s. Of course he yearns for acclaim, and endures trials and setbacks in his quest. Perhaps this smacks of triteness. But so many stories in precis *are* trite. A young lady takes against a man, then learns she has been mistaken and marries him. Yawn! A cathedral city becomes agitated over the appointment of a new bishop. Pass the smelling salts! And there you have just dismissed *Pride and Prejudice* and *Barchester Towers*. The point is that good writing transforms the commonplace into the remarkable; it sees something old in a new way. Take this little passage of Mr Tunner's in which a character's death is pondered: 'She had gone, from this place, and from every place that had once known her. Paul felt he had grown up too suddenly, faster than nature intended; now all he had was a kind of pollen that clung to his fingertips, the traces of what he had loved in her. And he knew that this would also, in time, be gone.' Here is Henry James's 'distinguished thing' – death – expressed in words of radiant concision.

Our thespian hero, Paul Wolcott, becomes understudy to Algernon Jenks, actor-manager and *monstre sacré* of the English stage. 'Algy' turns out to be the novel's other distinguished thing, a man who fears the eclipse of his legend as the years pass. He fears also being usurped by his protégé Paul, whose career he has promoted and undermined in equal measure, his base instincts at war with his natural generosity. Of course one may speculate (as others have done) on the identity of Algy's real-life model, partly from physical detail – his loud checks, his cigars, his cane – and partly from his habits and manner of speech. I myself detect some Irving in there, some Gielgud, possibly one or two others. The flaws in his character – abrasiveness, conceit, overweening self-regard – hardly narrow down the list of suspects. The man is an *actor*, for crying out loud.

Will it pain whoever the fellow is to recognise himself? As Maugham's Ashenden has remarked, 'It's very hard to be a gentleman and a writer.' I say with hand on heart that Mr Tunner has earned the right to call himself both. And let me quote the advice of a dear friend, to wit – always be reading something that will reflect well on you if by chance you were to die in the middle of it. I should be very pleased to have *The Distinguished Thing* with me at the last.

James Erskine

# Acknowledgements

I would like to thank Dan Franklin, Beth Coates, Rachel Cugnoni, Suzanne Dean, Katherine Fry, Carmen Callil. Likewise my friend and punctilious reader Doug Taylor. Thanks also to Anna Webber, my agent, and David Clasen, music maestro.

The character of Jimmy Erskine is based largely, though not exclusively, on the critic and diarist James Agate, as revealed in his superb *Ego* Vols I–IX (1935–1948). I also much enjoyed James Harding's biography *Agate* (1986).

The book that remained at my side while I wrote this novel was Juliet Gardiner's brilliant and enthralling tour d'horizon *The Thirties* (2010). I am indebted to her.

My most profound thanks go to my wife Rachel Cooke, without whose company life would be dull, cheerless and possibly insupportable.

# The Reading Guide

# About the Book

It is summer 1936 in London. Nina Land, an aspiring young stage actress, has become embroiled in an affair with the acclaimed society painter, Stephen Wyley. One sultry afternoon, following a liaison in an innocuous hotel room, Nina accidentally interrupts an attempted murder. The attacker and victim both flee, leaving Nina with only fleeting impressions of their faces.

Nina now faces a dilemma: she's not supposed to be at the hotel in the first place, and certainly not with a married man. Both of their careers could be at stake if she revealed what she has witnessed to the police. But once it becomes apparent that she may have seen the face of the man the newspapers have dubbed 'the Tiepin Killer' she realises that both her own life, and that of the escaped victim, could be at stake.

Meanwhile, Jimmy Erskine, the raffish doyen of theatre critics who fears that his star is fading, is facing his own dilemma. In an era where homosexuality is illegal, he is walking a delicate tightrope: his late-night escapades with young men and attendance at illicit drag balls threaten to expose him at every turn. He has depended for years on his loyal and long-suffering secretary Tom, but Tom in turn has a secret of his own to protect, as his childhood affliction, epilepsy, threatens to return. Tom's chance encounter with

Madeleine Farewell, the young woman who narrowly escaped the murderer's clutches in the hotel and owes her life to Nina Land, closes the circle. As the Tiepin killer continues to stalk the streets, Nina, Stephen, Jimmy, Tom and Madeleine are drawn inexorably together, but is it too late to stop the killer? And is time running out for Jimmy?

*Curtain Call* is a comedy of manners, and a tragedy of mistaken intentions. From the glittering murk of Soho's demi-monde to the grease paint and ghost-lights of theatre-land, the story plunges on through smoky clubrooms, tawdry hotels and drag balls towards a denouement as the Tiepin Killer begins to close his net around Madeleine and Nina. As bracing as a cold Martini and as bright as a new tiepin, it is a poignant and gripping story about love and death and a society dancing towards the abyss.

# Reading Group Questions

**Starting points for your discussion:**

The author offers two potential titles, which do you think is most suited to the novel: *Curtain Call* or *The Distinguished Thing*? If you were to come up with your own title for this novel, what would you call it?

It could be argued that each of the central characters in *Curtain Call* is in some way flawed. Who did you find the most sympathetic and why, out of the following:

- Jimmy Erskine
- Tom Tunner
- Madeleine Farewell
- Stephen Wyley

The novel features two women, Nina and Madeleine, who are self-supporting women in a period when this was difficult and not always viewed as a positive situation. Do you consider them feminists in any way? Do you think the novel's portrayal of women is positive, negative, or somewhere in between?

The characters on the fringe of the central narrative are particularly interesting. Consider what roles the following play in contributing to our understanding of the central characters and narrative:

- László Balázsovits
- Freya Wyley
- Peter Liddell

Consider Jimmy's final review of *The Distinguished Thing*; do you think he has grown as a character, or in any way redeemed himself?

## Questions for more in-depth discussion:

Tom suggests that Madeleine's dream of a burning London was prophetic of the Crystal Palace fire, but Madeleine disagrees. What do you think her dream symbolised, both in her personal life and in the context of the larger London society?

The naming of the central characters is almost Dickensian: what do you think is the significance of the below names?

- Nina Land
- Madeleine Farewell
- Stephen Wyley
- Tom Tunner (hint: a 'tunner' is a man in charge of a large cask of beer or wine)

Oscar Wilde is a powerful presence in the book, despite the fact that he does not feature as an 'onstage' character; he famously said 'Hear no evil, speak no evil, and you'll never be invited to a party'. Do you agree with Wilde's statement, within the parameters of this novel? What role does gossip play in *Curtain Call*?

Consider how the characters view the central themes of sexuality and politics. How have attitudes towards these changed over the intervening years?

The novel is set in 1936, on the brink of the Second World War. We as the reader know what is to come, but the characters remain largely embroiled in their own smaller dramas, and some outright deny that war will break out. Do you think they are politically naive? Do you think any of the characters could or should have acted differently with regards to the political situation? As a starting point, consider Stephen's accidental affiliation with the blackshirts.

The novel is heavily invested in the world of theatre and theatricality, and artifice plays a central role in most of the characters' lives. Which character do you think is the most guilty of 'playing a part'? And which character do you think is the least guilty of artifice?

In some ways, what happens to Nina removes a very difficult decision for Stephen. What do you think he would have done, should Nina's story have ended differently?

Not every character is redeemed, and some meet unhappy ends. What is the abiding emotion that this novel has left you with?

# Author Article: What prompted *Curtain Call*

I only know how to write stories about the past. The present is too slippery and mutable for my liking; it's ideal stuff for newspapers, diaries, blogs. It's not for novels. Nothing dates more quickly than the present. But look backwards and you have an immensity of riches waiting to be plucked. Sometimes just the numerals of a year – 1939, or 1911, or 1882 – are enough to stir me to investigate. I read Juliet Gardiner's brilliant study *The Thirties: An Intimate History* when it came out and found one year in particular sounding a note that wouldn't fade: 1936. An ominous disquiet was gathering. The year began with the death of one king and ended with the abdication of another. Deep social divisions had brought the Jarrow marchers down to London, while Mosley's Blackshirts tried to jackboot their way into the East End until they were repelled at Cable Street. A greater nervousness vibrated from Europe, where the Nazis had just remilitarised the Rhineland and looked certain to make further inroads. On November 30th the Crystal Palace burnt down, a conflagration that was visible for miles around. Its loss felt symbolic in bidding farewell to one era – the Victorian – and in its foreshadowing of another: London on fire.

The backdrop material was all there. I needed a flint to set it alight. I had in my head a single situation that came to me in a dream about ten years ago. Now dreams, as we know, are inherently boring as conversation filler, but this one had sufficient clarity and menace for me to remember. (Lucky for me I recorded it in my journal, or it would have dissolved like the rest.) A man and a woman are in a hotel bedroom together. One of them is married. At one point the man happens to see a sinister-looking person in the corridor; some hours later he reads the late edition of the newspaper and finds there's been a murder in the hotel. He has an inkling that he has seen the killer – but as a witness he's stymied, because he shouldn't have been there in the first place.

And there is the first chapter of the book: on the last day of August in 1936, Stephen Wyley, a married society portraitist, has spent an illicit afternoon in bed with Nina Land, an actress. It is she who accidentally interrupts an attempted murder in a room along the corridor. It transpires that she may have seen the face of a man the newspapers have dubbed The Tiepin Killer. The dilemma unfolds as above. This might have been the starting point of a murder mystery, but that wasn't the sort of book I wanted to write: my story was a comedy of manners and a tragedy about people forced to keep secrets, either about their health, or their sexual habits, or their livelihood. As well as my adulterous couple there was Jimmy Erskine, ageing theatre critic and bon viveur; his put-upon secretary and drudge Tom; and a young woman, Madeleine Farewell, who's been sucked into the roiling depths of Soho's demi-monde. I wanted to engineer a plot in which all five characters would meet one another – but how?

One of the things – the many things – a writer may agonise over is plot, as if getting that right will guarantee the smooth operation of everything else. I did some agonising, too, until I remembered something Hilary Mantel once wrote: don't think about plot, think about character. 'If you make your characters properly they will simply do what is within them, they'll act out the nature you have given them, and there – you'll find – you have your plot.' I had written three novels before this one, and had tended to rely on action more than character to propel the plot. Here was an opportunity to do it the other way round. I thought hard about these five characters, about the way each of them would interact, and slowly I began to make connections between them. There is a temptation to regard fictional characters as types, representing this or that emotional tendency or moral shortcoming. A novelist must never succumb to that: your characters are individuals, and they are not 'typical' of anything. Once you grasp that vital principle, the story will live – because your characters have a life of their own. Writing *Curtain Call* taught me this. A novel will go the way it wants to go, and the writer – like a director who has sent his actors onto the stage – just has to get out of the way of it.

# About the Author

Anthony Quinn was born in Liverpool in 1964. He was educated at St Francis Xavier's College, a Catholic Grammar School, and at Pembroke College, Oxford, where he read Classics. In 1986 he moved to London, working at Zwemmer's Bookshop on Charing Cross Road and renting a room in Islington so narrow he could touch both walls from the middle of it. His earliest break in journalism was to write book reviews for the recently launched *Independent*, whose literary editor was Sebastian Faulks. In the 1990s he became slightly more prosperous and moved to a bigger room, this one equipped with a kitchen and a flip-down bed. He continued to write for newspapers and magazines, and interviewed many writers, including Lorrie Moore, Alan Hollinghurst, William Boyd, Sarah Waters, Richard Ford, Jay McInerney, P.J. O'Rourke, Ian McEwan, the Amises *père et fils*. He managed to meet his heroes – John Updike, Pauline Kael, Robert Hughes – and didn't regret it. He was for fifteen years the film critic of the *Independent* (1998-2013) and also wrote a wine column for *Esquire* magazine.

Having been a judge on the 2006 Man Booker Prize he wrote his first novel the following year: the two events may have been related. *The Rescue Man* (2009) won the Authors' Club Best First Novel Award. Since then he has written three others, *Half of the Human Race* (2011), *The Streets* (2012) and *Curtain Call* (2015). He still lives in Islington, with his wife, the journalist and author Rachel Cooke.

# Author Interview

**What was the very starting point for writing *Curtain Call* – perhaps a character, or a play from the period, or the idea of the Tiepin Murderer?**

The very starting point was a dream I had about ten years ago: a man and a woman are having an illicit afternoon in a London hotel room when one of them witnesses an attempted murder. But if they report it to the police they must reveal their own adultery. The idea of the Tiepin Killer came from the Hitchcock film *Frenzy* (1972) in which Barry Foster played 'the necktie murderer', preying on young women around Covent Garden. I remember he wore this elaborate tiepin in the shape of a sword.

**Can you tell us a bit about your research process?**

It's very haphazard. I read a lot but tend not to use more than a tenth of it. My main resource for *Curtain Call* was Juliet Gardiner's smashing book *The Thirties: An Intimate History*. Apart from reading I find photographs of street scenes, shops, people, the most helpful to the imaginative process. I have one picture postcard, from around 1930, of buses circling the Aldwych that I must have stared at for hours.

**The theatre is of course at the centre of this novel – is this an area of the arts that you take particular interest in?**

I have rediscovered my love of the theatre after years of staying away: I saw an awful lot of terrible plays. Then in about 2008 friends invited us to the Donmar to see *The Chalk Garden* by Enid Bagnold. I had heard neither of it nor her, and wasn't enlivened by the prospect, yet it was superb: Penelope Wilton gave a performance of mesmerising poignancy. I can almost date my reconversion to theatre from that night. I also love musical theatre, Sondheim in particular. When they put *A Little Night Music* on a few years back I saw it three times.

**If *Curtain Call* itself were adapted for the stage, who would you want to play the central characters and where would you want to see it performed?**

Interesting question. People keep telling me that *Curtain Call* would make a great TV serial, so often in fact that I fear it will never happen. But a stage play . . . well, why not? Casting it would be half the fun. Off the top of my head, David Dawson would be good as Tom, Hayley Atwell as Nina, Simon Russell Beale as Jimmy. I'll get back to you with the rest. As to where it should be performed, could we try the National?

**You place a critic centre stage in *Curtain Call* – and moreover a critic who wrote a review four years ago that has continued to haunt Nina Land. As a writer and a reviewer, how does it feel to be both critic and criticised, and does it colour your own reviewing?**

Jimmy Erskine is actually based on a real-life critic, James Agate, who wrote on theatre for the *Sunday Times* and was immensely famous in his day. He also published a diary, *Ego*, that ran to nine volumes (1935–1948). It's one of the great records of a writer's life, and I stole from it shamelessly. For seventeen years I wrote a weekly film column, and still review books here and there. I think it's helped me now that I'm on the other side of the fence, being criticised. You become quite philosophical about bad reviews, and even learn to enjoy them – 'the usual twaddle' as Henry James called them in *The Figure in the Carpet*. Having said that, it was gratifying that *Curtain Call* got nothing but glowing reviews in the papers. Raves across the board! It will probably never happen like that again, so I'll count my blessings.

**You close with a review of Tom Tunner's new novel, which bears the same title as the secondary title of *Curtain Call* – can you expand on the implication of this?**

My original title for the novel was *The Distinguished Thing*, a phrase from Henry James, who allegedly said it as he was felled by a stroke: 'So here it is at last, the distinguished thing!' He meant his death, of course. Anyway, my publishers hated that title, and for *months* afterwards we tried out new ones, back and forth, none of them any good. Eventually, someone hit on *Curtain Call*, which both referenced the theatre and the book's preoccupation with 'final things'. It's also more euphonious, I admit. My editor said I could put *The Distinguished Thing* as an alternative on the title page, and I decided to let Tom have it as the title for his first novel – so at least someone got use out of it.

**Do you ever think about revisiting any of your characters in a new novel? If you were to, which character exerts the greatest pull on you?**

I'm very glad you ask! I've just finished a new novel, all about Freya, Stephen's precocious and sweary daughter in *Curtain Call*. For some reason she stayed with me after I finished the book, and I thought I could trace her life as a young woman, beginning on VE day, 1945. The first section is set in Oxford, where she goes after serving in the Wrens; the second (1954) and third (1962) cover her time in London as a journalist. She's been exhilarating company. The novel (called *Freya*) also reintroduces Stephen and Jimmy, who I'm pleased to say does not grow old gracefully.

**Let's end with a round of Erskine's 'Five Greatest' – can you give us your Five Greatest British Novels?**

Gosh, that's a tough one . . . I can't do 'Greatest', but I can do 'Favourite':

1) *Middlemarch* by George Eliot
2) *New Grub Street* by George Gissing
3) *Emma* by Jane Austen
4) *In A Summer Season* by Elizabeth Taylor
5) *Money* by Martin Amis